LOVE

&

MONEY

A NOVEL BY

MICHAEL M. THOMAS

LOVE

&

MONEY

A NOVEL BY

MICHAEL M. THOMAS

MELVILLEHOUSE
BROOKLYN, NEW YORK

Love & Money

© 2009 Michael M. Thomas

Melville House Publishing
145 Plymouth Street
Brooklyn, NY 11201

www.mhpbooks.com

ISBN: 978-1-933633-72-5

First Melville House Printing: April 2009

Book design: Kelly Blair

Library of Congress Cataloging-in-Publication Data

Thomas, Michael M.
Love and money : a novel / by Michael M. Thomas.
    p. cm.
ISBN 978-1-933633-72-5 (alk. paper)
1. Television actors and actresses--Fiction. 2. Fame--Economic aspects—Fiction. I. Title.
PS3570.H574L68 2009
813'.54—dc22
                                          2009009935

For Dorothy
Always loved, never forgotten

OVERTURE

September 10

Even though she's only doing 45 mph, neither too slow nor too fast to attract attention, the woman at the wheel is keyed so high she can hardly control the nondescript black Jeep. Her skin burns with an erotic anticipation so intense and possessive that it scares her: her hands are trembling, her heart feels like it's beating at twice its normal rate. The pictures inside her head, images of a kind she hasn't allowed herself to imagine in ever so long, not since high school—pornographic pictures unreeling steadily, excitingly across the screen of her awareness—are so vivid she can barely concentrate on the road. She remembers what her earliest sexual stirrings felt like and squirms at the recollection: her teenage bedroom, just like her daughter's now, all pink and pennants and stuffed animals, with her young self stretched out on her bed, hardly daring to breathe lest anyone hear, skirt rucked up at her waist, one hand working feverishly between her thighs, the other a fist pressed to her mouth to stifle any gasps of pleasure, to hold back the swelling intensity that

crowded out her vain attempt to reserve some tiny particle of awareness for the footsteps in the hall, her mother's hand on the doorknob.
Even now, she shivers at the thought of being caught, and in the next
instant wonders if her own thirteen-year-old daughter ....

Stop that! The thought is unbearable. She refocuses on her driving. It isn't easy.

The excitement that has her thrumming isn't just the prospect of
the best sex she's ever had. It's the adventure itself: the daring, the deception, the dissembling. The gamble, the risk, the bursting of boundaries. A kind of casting off of the shackles of her public existence. A
way of proving to herself that she still rules her own life, that she's
not just someone else's puppet on strings, a slave to her vast, adoring
audience, not some automaton who performs at the twist of a dial,
not a chattel split up into fat, profitable pieces for Belle and the others. She can well imagine that people in meetings say things about her
like "We don't want to mess with the brand," but she's never spoken
up, or shown a scintilla of resentment, not with all that's at stake.
But not for a second in her private heart has she surrendered the right
to be the person she knows she is. And now she's exercising that prerogative to be the real, true self who dwells within the Ms. Perfect on
the screen, the paragon of family values who lays the golden eggs.

Money has never been a concern with her. Acting, the show, the
chance to use and display her talent, that's what really matters. That
she's getting what her accountants and agents call "seriously rich"
seems beside the point. And now there's this, there's *him*. Destiny has
presented itself and she's seized it, which is her right and privilege as
a person, as a human being, even though it involves breaking through
the confining crust of career, family, responsibility, all the "oughtn'ts"
and "shouldn'ts" that go with her life and who and what she is, and
who she's supposed to be thinking about ahead of herself; to throw
off the burden of all her dependents and dependencies and contractual
obligations and just for once be able to look herself in the face and
declare, "The hell with all of you, this is for me!"

Am I crazy? She asks herself. *This is insane! What if I get caught?* It could mean the end of everything she's worked for.

For an instant, she shivers—until that wheedling, sly, now-familiar voice inside her puts a figurative finger across her lips and purrs: *But you're not going to get caught. Don't worry. You're fine.*

And of course she is. She's planned it so carefully. On Wednesdays the coast is clear at home. Now that Labor Day has come and gone, there's hardly anyone about on these back roads, not on a mid-week afternoon. She's taken the Jeep, so as not to attract attention. Worn a big slouch hat to conceal her famous face. It's cool; there's nothing to worry about.

She relaxes—until she glances in the rearview mirror. A car is closing fast. As it draws up behind her, she tries to make out what make it is, what color. Gray. It's gray! Clifford's car is gray! But it can't be Clifford. He's in the city for the day with their daughter, won't be back until late. Besides, he drives a Jaguar and this is another make. She exhales deeply and slows down. The car behind her pulls over to pass and as it goes by she sees that it's a Toyota, New York plates, nothing to worry about.

Get hold of yourself! Of course it couldn't be her husband. He's in the city, at the club. Every Wednesday like clockwork. She called him on the train just to make sure. He doesn't suspect a thing. Her heartbeat slows, her breath comes more normally, the sexual excitement returns. Almost there.

She watches carefully for the fork that leads onto Winding Crest Drive. It's only her second time driving up this way, and these roads can be tricky. This part of the countryside—being developed rapidly now with huge McMansions—is barely signposted.

She finds Winding Crest, turns off, and counts 1.3 miles on the odometer, just as she had been instructed the first time. Still, she almost misses the driveway, little more than a rutted unpaved track bearing sharply off into the woods, unmarked save for builders' and security-service signs, and a piece of cardboard with a scrawled "127" tacked on a low post. She bumps along carefully. The track, a real axle jolter, snakes a full three-quarters of a mile between a picket line of pines that she's been told have been specially trucked in from Pennsylvania. She skirts the edge of a small lake, gleaming pale orange in the late summer sunlight. She checks her watch: 5:35 p.m. exactly. Right on time—but then she always is.

A minute later, she's in the "carriage yard," a circle of dirt awaiting the Belgian paving stones stacked in two big tarpaulined piles. The trapezoidal chaos of the house looms above her. She hates this house. Hates its phony-Colonial shingle-style architecture, its scale, the state of mind it bespeaks, the vulgarity, and the ostentation. It's too big, it's completely, grossly wrong for the site. Of course, that's now completely beside the point.

The front door has been left unlocked. Inside, the main reception rooms with their hideous stuccoed ceilings are unlit. The smell of paint and wood shavings and spackle is everywhere, the air thick with plaster dust. From the back of the house comes the sound of music, music she recognizes from the last—the first—time: hot, Spanish, probably Cuban. She makes her way toward the sound, moving very quietly, wanting to surprise.

She pauses in front of the door that the music, very loud now, is coming from. She grins wickedly to herself, and stealthily pushes the door open. *"Buenas noches!"* she calls out in her lowest, sexiest voice, in the Spanish she's perfected over the years with her housekeeper.

The room is barely furnished: a daybed, a table and chair, a TV hooked to the jury-rigged satellite system, clothes strewn about, a mess of bottles and fast-food containers and painting materials. From a boom box in the corner, a singer wails, *"No le teme a la negrura."* She has no idea what the words mean, but it sounds incandescently sexy.

"Buenas noches, amor," he says. He's standing by the daybed, ready for her, stroking his cock with one hand, beckoning her over with the other. His penis looks huge, his whole attitude, pelvis thrust forward, tongue playing along his lips, eyes glittering, reminds her of

the dirty movies her husband got for them to watch toward the end of their first decade of marriage, when their life in bed, now virtually nonexistent, seemed to be slowing down. She never found those the least bit exciting, even if they did turn Clifford on, but this is different, it makes her want to reach under her skirt, touch herself. She hasn't been this excited by a man since ever so long ago, her seventeenth summer, at the lake, with the boy from Oberlin who taught sailing and kissing and finally took her virginity in the woods behind the boathouse.

She crosses the room, steps out of her skirt and panties, and kisses his neck, reaching down to touch him as she does. His erection feels huge; she can barely close her fingers around it. He puts his hands on her shoulders and pushes her to her knees. She takes him in her mouth, plays with him until, gasping, he withdraws, pulls her up, settles her on the daybed, flat on her back, knees splayed, and goes down on her until she can stand it not a second longer. "Now!" she wheezes, and he turns her neatly over, on to her hands and knees facing a tall mirror. As he enters her, she sees them in the mirror, faces contorted, and she feels him thrusting to the changing beat of the music. *"Qué me dice de un danzón, De una rumbita caliente..."*

She's just about to come when he mutters *"Momentido!"* He pauses, torturing her with long, slow strokes, reaches down beside himself and brings a small capsule to his nose. He crushes it, sniffs quickly and greedily, and then presses it to her face. She inhales the acrid vapor and her brain seems physically to expand and contract in great, shimmering waves. Now he begins to move again. *"Jesús... Señor..."* he gasps. "Oh, Jesus...!" she rasps in reply. She wriggles her behind to excite him further, hearing the breath catch in his throat as he starts to come and she does, too.

"Oh, mi Jesús....!"

"Oh Christ, oh Christ, oh Christ!"

"Ai, ai, ai! Ahora!" he cries and pulls out. Even buzzed as she is, she knows from their last time what to do. Wherever she may be in her own arc of sensation doesn't matter, can wait. She is his slave.

She—whose independent foursquare character serves as a beacon, a lodestone for millions of people who will do or buy anything—almost anything—as long as it bears her endorsement—is now reduced to nothing, a crawling creature of mindless sensation. She reverses quickly, gets him in her mouth just as he begins to ejaculate.

When he's finished, starting to soften, she pulls her head away. More—she wants more. "My turn now!" she cackles, and throws herself backwards, grabs his head and pulls his face down to her crotch. *Oh, I like this! Oh, yessss, please....*

She's just beginning to melt when there's a noise outside. She stiffens, sensation ebbs.

"What was that?" she croaks.

He pulls up, smiles at her. "Is nothing. Many animals in the woods. *Venga. Querida, venga.*" He lowers his head, resumes. A moment later she's growling and moaning with excitement.

Outside, an early night wind has risen and begins to flail the trees. The shifting, creaking branches cause the pools of deeper darkness in the eddies of the woods at the back of the house to form and reform: shadows within shadows, broken here and there by tricks of reflection, alive with whirs, squawks, snaps, crackles, grunts: a chorus to which is now added a higher voice, a desperate shivering shriek of pleasure from inside the house, full of gratification and longing—then another, then another, then another.

ACT ONE

•

Liar's Walk

I have seen also in the prophets of Jerusalem an horrible thing: they commit adultery, and walk in lies: they strengthen also the hands of evildoers, that none doth return from his wickedness: they are all of them unto me as Sodom, and the inhabitants thereof as Gomorrah.

—Jeremiah 23:14

CHAPTER ONE

September 17

The dog days of summer have lingered on uninvited and it's a dank, unfriendly day in New York, the sky pus-colored, the air tumid and overbearing, the kind of clammy, lung-clogging day that goes badly with the hell-bent uproar of the city, making everyone's nerve ends a bit more raw than usual. A sour day in a sour season—pretty much matching the mood written on the spare, frowning features of Clifford Grange as he makes his way down Lexington Avenue toward Gramercy Park. His pale gray-green eyes glance this way and that, taking in everything with a deadpan scholarly interest, his thin mouth set in a faintly downward curve of disapproval of the world around him.

He has a lively and intelligent face, if a bit too long and narrow (in this he takes after his long-dead mother) to be rated handsome. It's a very grown-up face, however, with more than a touch of age and wisdom. Clifford Grange looked forty when he turned thirty and he still looks forty now, just two years shy of fifty, and he prides himself he'll still look forty if he ever reaches threescore and ten. He carries himself proudly, as a general's son would, but in the past couple of years, his wiry frame has taken on a clenched look, like a bony, knobbed fist cocked and ready to give the frantic, noisy, crowding world around him a good, hard smack in the mouth. He's painfully, pitifully aware that he's no longer who he used to be, that he's presently merely another few cubic feet of flesh and bone competing for a fraction of personal space and recognition with throngs that don't care who he was, or is, or will end up as.

A psychologist might look at him and say, this is an angry man—and that psychologist would be correct. Clifford *is* angry. Angry at life in general, angry at his own situation—above all, angry at being angry. He was brought up by his father to believe that anger is the most pointless and wasteful of feelings and the least reliable of emotional crutches—and look how it has all played out!

He needs his father, wishes the old man were still alive to talk with, to place a hand on Clifford's fretful shoulder. How many times has Clifford told other people (for that matter, told himself): "Every man has certain stars he steers by; mine were the ones on my old man's epaulets." Clifford likes the sound of that; he considers himself a good son and a clever aphorist, even though the demand for his witty, pithy sayings isn't what it once was, back in the day when his own star was at its height in the world and in his own household, before he became what he is now: spear-carrier, house husband, and attendant lord to a brand-name megastar.

He hates feeling this way, and particularly hates the paranoia it seems to foster. Take yesterday. Late in the afternoon, as is usually the case, he'd run out of creative gas—having had not much more than vapors to begin with—and wandered up the lawn from his studio to the main house. Connie and Jenny were not yet home from work and school respectively, so he drifted into the library and tuned into TNT on the sixty-inch flat-screen—a gift from Connie's grateful producers—to watch the *Law & Order* reruns that played at this time. And guess what? The first to come on was the one where a guy kills his wife because she's a lot more successful than he is. Then, later that evening, after a perfectly pleasant early family supper, with Jenny upstairs at her homework, Connie had commandeered the remote and cruised the cable channels, and—of course—happened on *A Star Is Born* just at the bit where Norman Maine (James Mason) walks into the ocean and drowns himself. And if that wasn't enough, on top of everything else that's screwed up his life, he now has to cope with whatever the hell it is that's going on with Connie.

He reaches Twenty-first Street and the north side of Gramercy Park and stops in his tracks. A film or TV crew has set up for business on the square, with traffic cones on the cross streets and production assistants stationed at the corners. The mere sight triggers a reflux of resentment and a thirst for retribution, as if every small detail of the shoot he finds himself looking at is a sour chord plucked on the strings of his chagrin. Every element is achingly familiar. The trailers, vans, fat power cables, lights, catering spread, dollies. The throng of workers, each one responsible for an infinitesimal, regulated part of the whole. Complex, balletic, intense, organic: this is the world he understands better than any other, and—he fancies—as well or better than almost any other living person; a world in which he not only belongs but belongs at the very top of—but now a world from which he is barred simply because he made a film that had the guts to declare in word and image the things that most people still think privately even if they won't admit it to poll-takers.

He threads his way between a couple of equipment trucks, stepping gingerly over a maze of cables, and starts to cross the street. A young woman with a tag on a ribbon lanyard around her neck and a squawking walkie-talkie in her right hand intercepts him.

"I'm sorry, sir, but you can't go this way," she says politely. "Could you cross over at the end of the block, please?"

He starts to object, to say something sarcastic about holding up traffic for what will doubtless be a grade-F picture, but holds off.

Calm down! he tells himself. The kid's just doing a job—and lucky to have one, the way things are in the movie business these days. It's plain that she has no idea who he is, no idea that this tall, weedy man with the intent, direct gaze was not so long ago an artistic pillar—"artistic titan" wouldn't be pushing it—of her industry; a director whose movies would be introduced at festivals by the likes of Scorsese and Redford. It was only three years ago, while he was still editing *Crown Heights,* and the picture was generating major buzz, that *Vanity Fair* had ranked Clifford ninety-seventh on its annual raking of "the Hollywood 100!"

"What're you shooting?" he asks the young woman.

"It's *Sex & the City II.*"

"I see. Thanks." *Well, I may not be working,* he thinks as he moves down the block, *but I'm at least not working on crap like this.*

At the corner, he pauses by a trailer signposted with a name he recognizes, a woman he cast once or twice in bit parts who's now a cable series star, maybe even the next Constance Grange. Shadows move behind the lowered blinds, and he thinks about knocking. As he briefly ponders the matter, he removes his horn-rimmed eyeglasses and polishes them vigorously with the broad end of his necktie, bright red silk woven with a pattern of tiny lanterns.

He decides not to knock. Why take the risk? It galls him to feel this way, but what the hell is he supposed to feel? Here he is, a director who just a few years ago was literally on the threshold of major-studio recognition—that enchanted realm of big budgets to play with and the "suits" on his side—and now where is he? An unemployed, ostracized has-been—or "was once"—this year's Norman Maine in a *Star Is Born* marriage of his own in which one spouse rides the sky like a comet while the other thrashes on the trash heap.

Thinking this way is too depressing. Other matters concern him, something else he meant to do before leaving for the station: then he recalls that the *Prime Suspect* reruns begin on BBC tonight and he forgot to set the DVR to record it. Fortunately, one of the blessings of being married to Connie is that she knows how to operate stuff

like TV recorders and computers. Competence is her middle name—and she actually reads directions. Wednesday is Connie's day off and she's always home at this time: her assistant and the accountant will have come and gone, and she'll be working on her fan mail or going over a script before Jenny gets home from Dance Club around eight and the commotion starts.

He plucks his cellphone from his breast pocket and calls home. But there's no answer at Grangeford, which is funny. He double-checks his watch: 5:24 p.m. *Where the hell is Connie?* Well, maybe she had to run an errand—there had been some mention of Jenny needing new dance shoes—so he tries her cellphone—and gets her voicemail—which means her cell phone's either turned off—which it never is—or she's out of range—which is possible, coverage up where they live being sketchy in some areas, although he himself has never had a problem.

Clifford's a very logical thinker. Now he mentally ticks off the other possible explanations and comes up empty, which allows the *Othello*-like suspicion that has nagged at him for the past fortnight to demand satisfaction. The automatic, inescapable, general-issue male suspicion: Is she having an affair?

Reflexively, he tells himself it's out of the question. Connie's a red-blooded woman, with a normal—and by now possibly unfulfilled—sex drive, but she would never take a chance, not after the Spitzer and John Edwards revelations had shown what a public scandal could do to a career. Not after she's heard Clifford say a hundred times, beginning with the Lewinsky scandal years ago: "If there's one hard-and-fast rule in postmodern life, it's that you're gonna get caught!" No, Connie would never take the chance. The Spitzer scandal, big as it was in its time, had merely cost an unpopular politician a gover-norship, and John Edwards's screwing around had merely blackened a reputation that wasn't going anywhere anyway. Both of these were peanuts in comparison to Connie. Constance Grange is the admired, pedestaled idol of tens of millions of American women, and God knows how many gay men; she is the center of a commercial constellation already worth billions, and the people she's worked with have become her friends—and no one values friendship more highly than Connie. She's beginning to be talked about in the same breath and as being on the same level as Oprah. Oprah, for Christ's sakes! Fame, wealth, adoration, veneration: she has it all. She would never risk the smallest part of it. Not after all the work, the sacrifice, the adjusting. What about her family? Forget Clifford, she'd never do it to Jenny!

But what other explanation could there be?

Go to motive, Clifford thinks. The way his film-school mentors used to preach. Motive and character.

So: motive. Okay, *begin with the obvious. Sex. We haven't had much of a sex life—depression beats even saltpeter when it comes to suppressing a creative man's sex drive—but when we have done it, it's been okay, and certainly Connie's shown no sign of discontent in that department.*

On the other hand, in general terms, I can't have been much fun to live with these past few years. Still, Clifford has really tried hard to keep his own aching professional disappointment out of the house, and frankly he thinks that he's done a damn good job of it.

So—what then?

So—what else then! He can't imagine.

He takes out his iPhone and stares dubiously at it for a moment, then calls the Grangeford landline and leaves an answering-machine message about recording the *Prime Suspect* episode, and then calls Connie's cellphone and leaves the same message on her voicemail. One way or the other, wherever she is, she'll get the word in time.

On the far side of Gramercy Park, a patch of red and gold fluttering atop an eccentric turreted 1890s townhouse catches his eye and distracts him with pleasanter thoughts. It's the banner of the Diogenes Club, the same color with the same emblem as his necktie: a stylized lantern symbolizing the light by which the philosopher Diogenes vainly searched the ancient world for an honest man.

He's glad to be back at the Diogenes. This has been a summer he thought would never end. Every August, the month that *Here's Constance!*, her megahit TV show, goes on hiatus, the Granges have decamped to Sleeping Bear Cove, to a lakeside lodge in the northern Michigan enclave where his wife's family summered when she was a girl. Connie loves the place; she isn't a celebrity, isn't the star of the show that was number three in the season's final sweeps, and the first "outsider" in three years to break through into the top-five ratings cartel of *American Idol* and the crap "reality" shows.

At Sleeping Bear, people don't shriek, "Oh, my God, it's Constance Grange!" and break out their Webcams. Once or twice, *paparazzi* and other tabloid scum have tried to sneak in through the surrounding woods but have been promptly apprehended by Sleeping Bear Security and forcefully led back to the compound gates. At the lake, she's still Connie Grange from a town south of Des Moines where her family owned the bank and most of whatever else there was to own that wasn't farmland; Connie Grange, who first came here in a cradle, who's never forgotten who she is and where she came from.

For Clifford nowadays it's different: he may be Cliffie or Cliff or Ol' Cliff to the guys, none of whom really knows him, or understands him or has the slightest idea what he's been going through, but he isn't fooled: he knows how they really think of him: as Mr. Constance Grange.

It wasn't always this way. Until two summers ago, Clifford relished his month at the lake. While Connie and Jenny pursued an endless, seamless round of sing-alongs, gymkhanas, swimming meets, boat races, tennis tournaments, crafts sessions, and awards dinners, Clifford fitted in only when asked and the rest of the time spent the long pleasant days alternating desultory fishing and working over scripts, preparing for the New York or Deauville or Venice festivals, getting ready to pitch a new project.

Then *Crown Heights* changed everything. Last summer wasn't so bad, because Clifford could still convince (deceive?) himself that sooner or later he'd be back in the game.

But that illusion died during the intervening year, when the phone stopped ringing, the daily mail no longer brought book galleys and DVDs, and the lunch invitations dried up. So this summer was really bad. When he's home, in his studio, he can generate make-work, but at the lake he couldn't. He made a desultory pass at *Middlemarch,* and then ended up working his way through a stack of mysteries. He didn't seem able to get an interesting sentence on paper. By Labor Day, he was practically chewing the pine needles, so anxious to get out of there that he didn't even mind the trip back, which ended up taking him most of Wednesday by the time he got himself to Traverse City by taxi for a flight to Detroit—where he missed his connection to LaGuardia and ended up on standby to Newark. His womenfolk had flown home early that morning in order to get Jenny to the dock on time (she was scheduled to sail over to Fishers Island on a school friend's family's boat). Their trip had taken three hours and twenty-two minutes door-to-door for the ladies of the family. They were home by noon. But principle must be upheld, and because of what happened with *Crown Heights,* Clifford won't fly Air Barrow, the fleet of private jets and helicopters that BBN makes available to Connie, given how much she's worth to the network.

He loves getting home to Grangeford, the sprawling house two hours' drive north of New York City in tax-friendly Connecticut. He loves the place itself, the grounds, the house, the views; he loves the way they live there. Much of that happiness is a function of the way Connie's set it up. She doesn't go in for entourages or frippery. She's never shown the slightest sign of what Clifford's father used to scoff at about New Yorkers: "that inexplicable craving for the deference of headwaiters." She's a self-described "do-it-myself kind of gal," supremely confident of her ability to get things done her way on her own without putting on airs or ordering people around. In her own kitchen, on the set of her TV show, in the nearby towns where she shops, at Jenny's school, she's regarded as a model of courtesy and considerateness.

At Grangeford, the business end is pretty much kept at bay. Connie works with her personal assistant, a young woman whom the limousine picks up in Pelham before it picks Connie up at 6:30 a.m., on the drive back and forth to the Brooklyn studio. Wednesday, Connie's day off and Clifford's day in the city, is the only time she works at home.

It's an ironclad article of faith with Connie that weekends belong to her family. She's surrounded and implored all week on the set, so it's natural that she wants her weekends filled only with those people she wants to see and be with: these two and a half days are a time to purge herself of the small, irritating accretions of bother that being the center of attention brings—of dependence—for all those people at Barrow and elsewhere. Apart from the traditional Sunday night Monopoly set-to, money is never openly talked about at Grangeford. Business is for weekdays and New York City. She meets once a month at the studio with her wealth managers from First Republic Bank. Clifford isn't invited, and wouldn't attend anyway, so he has only a vague, general notion of his wife's wealth. He feels very strongly that he and Connie should keep their financial affairs separate. Of course, that was back when his was the income that set the table and secured the mortgage and kept the lawns mown at Grangeford. The house is in both their names.

The result is that Grangeford—the Grange household and domestic economy—is like one of those boats that can sail around the world with a crew of one—in this case a live-in Nicaraguan maid named Conchita who looks after the bedrooms, makes breakfast for Jenny, and goes to visit her sister in Queens on Wednesdays and weekends. Once a week, a team of bonded professional cleaners paid for by BME comes in and hoses down the decks. Twice a week, another cadre of professionals deals with lawns, trees, and greenery. Clifford, a military brat brought up to make his own bed with square corners, does for himself and acts as in-house prime contractor with respect to repairs, improvements, and groundskeeping.

Grangeford and its part of the country suit the Granges' ambitions for their daughter. They're damned if they'll let Jenny become a spoiled, gilded Manhattan hothouse flower—although they do let her watch *Gossip Girls*—or submit themselves to the dictates of some snooty private school where the parents' credit report or celebrity is more meaningful, ultimately, than the child's intelligence and personality, or the family's character and stability. Although it's under siege, there's still a lot of Old New England where they live, unlike, say, Greenwich, a mere dozen miles to the southwest, which has become a platinum-plated sewer of compulsive ostentation.

In even the recent past, just being there, in his little studio at the bottom of the lawn, shut off from the hostile world, barricaded behind his stuff, has done the trick for Clifford. But not this year. Since getting back home a fortnight ago, he's tried to work, tried to get back into some kind of rhythm, tried to resuscitate his creative enthusiasm, to sell himself on the idea that this, too, will pass—but this autumn, so far at least, no soap.

No: his situation is not going to change. He's on the permanent Hollywood shit list. Dead meat forever and hereafter. Ronnie Barrow isn't going to forgive and forget; bygones will never be bygones. Well, he has only himself to blame. Himself and his genes. His studio is full of his father's—the late Major-General Grange's—memorabilia: medals, cups, photos, framed citations, proud markers of another brilliant Grange career undone by another Grange mouth that didn't know when to stay closed. Like father, like son: General Grange had been on track for the Joint Chiefs when he blew his stack after a Senate hearing and said pretty much the same thing to the *Washington Post* and *60 Minutes* about the Armed Forces Committee and its chairman that his son would say forty years later on *The Charlie Rose Show* and elsewhere about Ronald Barrow, the CEO of Barrow Media Enterprises.

Glad to be back, he thinks. Wednesday is the day the Diogenes holds its "Twilight Talks," weekly lectures by members on their fields of special interest, followed by an early dinner. Clifford particularly enjoys these. The speakers are usually pretty interesting; the bonhomous give-and-take around the table is enjoyable—and he generally gets home by eleven. After the summer that he's had, it'll be nice to see the "guys and gals" of his regular table again, although they'll probably rag him for besmirching the table's near-perfect attendance record by missing the first talk of the new season last Wednesday the tenth.

Well, it couldn't be helped. Connie woke up that morning with what she said felt like stomach flu, which meant that Clifford had to fill in for her and accompany Jenny on what was traditionally a big mother-daughter deal: to the big city for her annual September appointments with various Manhattan doctors, including the gynecologist (Clifford insisted on waiting downstairs in the building; Connie could follow up by phone). They'd made a big day of it, and by the time they finally got home, well after midnight, they were exhausted.

The next day, Connie at first seemed her usual upbeat self. Apparently whatever it was that had laid her low had subsided sufficiently the previous day so that by early afternoon she'd felt well enough to get out of bed and attack her fan mail, even though her assistant had been given the day off.

On the curb across the street from the club entrance, Clifford pauses and tries to purge his mind of bad thoughts. He starts by trying to cancel out the list of people he's angry at, which is never easy, since by now it's really quite a long list. He's angry, for openers, with the agents of darkness responsible for his present woes, starting with that pint-sized SOB Ronald Barrow and all who sail in the little bastard, the ass-kissers and idiots and suck-ups and hypocrites and favor seekers and place-holders in "the industry" who haunt the halls of BME and the restaurants, like Michael's and the Four Seasons, that Barrow favors. For these, a Barrow-raised eyebrow amounts to an order to man the battlements and open fire.

He's angry also with the do-gooders and bleeding hearts and knee-jerks who turned *Crown Heights* into a *cause célèbre*, picketing the few theaters that were playing the picture and bombarding the blogosphere with allegations of racism and bias and a threat to boycott Barrow Media Enterprises's entire smorgasbord of productions—including Connie's show, which was just beginning find its sea legs. It was this threat that persuaded Ronald Barrow to personally order the film taken off exhibition. What some saw as a logical commercial decision—*Crown Heights* was a mere $25 million "indie" flyer by BME Lighthouse Studios; *Here's Constance!* was starting to show signs of becoming a major network hit—Clifford of course publicly and loudly attributed (on *60 Minutes*) to the BME CEO's "instinctive moral cowardice." Then he made things worse by taking out his ire on his wife, charging her with betrayal. For a month or so, the atmosphere at Grangeford was distinctly frosty, even as Clifford cooled off and admitted to himself that whatever might be laid at Ronald Barrow's feet could hardly be blamed on Connie. What the hell else could he reasonably expect her to do? Was she supposed to put her own incipient, big-time stardom on the line? For what? For her husband's delicate ego? Even then, *Here's Constance!* was drawing an audience of five million a week and the golden writing was on the wall. She'd always been supportive—but given what was on the line for her, what could she reasonably have done?

Maybe if Clifford's old man had been alive, things would have gone differently. It was very thoughtless of General Grange to drop dead on a Florida putting green just when Clifford was finally satisfied he had a *Crown Heights* script he could go with, a script he had persuaded BME Films's independent production arm that *it* could go with. If anyone could have foreseen the shit storm that *Crown Heights* was likely to stir up, it would have been the general. He made a paternal specialty of saving his son from himself. He got Clifford to tone down the lesbian angle in *Hearts of the City,* and to sanitize the language in *Brothers and Keepers,* the two films that had finally opened the way to studio-level financing. For all of Clifford's life, his father had been his "go-to guy," his "count-to-ten, take-two-deep breaths guy"—and then, just when those abilities were needed most crucially, the old man had shuffled off the mortal coil, leaving Clifford to rely on the one person whose judgment he had every reason not to trust at such a juncture: himself.

But most of all, ultimately and finally and in the last resort, when he thinks it all through and comes back to the place where it begins, Clifford knows that he needs to shut down his anger gene. It's simply not doing him any good. It wastes precious energy and ingenuity, distorts, distracts, and misdirects his creative impulses. Creativity is where he needs to put his energy and ingenuity—not in finding new ways of cursing out Ronald Barrow and "the system." Facts are facts; Clifford is where he is and he more than anyone else put himself there. He should have shut up and taken his beating and let *Crown Heights* die and gotten on with his career. But of course he couldn't. Not and still be Clifford. When deputation after deputation of blacks and Jews and Catholics and feminists and gay-rightsers and any number of combinations thereof kicked up their noisy fuss, Clifford should have hauled up the white flag, should have signaled to the dark-suited men upstairs in the BME Tower on Central Park South that it was their call and however they made it, that would be okay with him. He should have just shrugged and shut up—not referred to Ronald Barrow as "a moral midget" on *Charlie Rose*—and told himself what real grown-ups tell themselves, what he's certain his father would have counseled: okay, you win some, you lose some, but the one thing you do: you get on with your life. You move on.

Easier said than done, however. And now what daily makes it worse is Clifford's awareness that the critics of *Crown Heights* may have had a point. He watched it on DVD for the first time in two years the other day and he lasted only twenty-five minutes before losing patience. Making the film had somehow blinded him to how overwrought his script was. He had gotten carried away and let narrative turn into propaganda. Instead of telling a story, he was preaching a sermon. It's clear now that he did push everything too far, that some of his characterizations did verge on ethnic and racial stereotypes, the way the talking heads claimed. He sees now that he had to do it differently if he was going to sell his ideas, put over the point he was trying to make: that the city, the country, the world had become a stink hole, with corruption running like filth in the gutters; that we had come to live, gasping, in a miasma of political and financial exploitation and a desperate craving for celebrity and money; that life had degenerated into a state of things in which there was no god but Mammon and the only truth seemed to be real estate.

If given a second chance, a fresh start, he won't make the same mistake again. But how likely is that? It's coming up on three years next spring since the market for Clifford Grange's particular genius effectively shut down. *This is what cancer must feel like,* he thinks as he crosses the street. It's exactly as his professor of playwriting at Northwestern used to say: "In an artist, the creative juices are like fresh water feeding and flushing a pond. Dam 'em up and it'll turn brackish and kill everything that lives in it."

And now this...this whatever it is that's going on with his wife.

He realizes that his suspicion may just be an adjunct to his general paranoia. It's not that he has any *proof* that something's going on with Connie, but there's no getting around the fact that practically from the day they got back from Michigan, Connie's been on a tear, she's been a real pain in the ass.

Well, first things first—and the club is the right place to start to regain some handhold on a normal kind of life, a normal *civilized* kind of life.

The Diogenes Club occupies a wide six-story building that faces north over Gramercy Park. One architectural guidebook describes the clubhouse as "the most fanciful, not to say peculiar example of 'Robber Baron Beaux-Arts style' in Manhattan." The club itself, founded in 1895 by a group of Manhattan artists and dilettantes as an institutional rebuke to the pushy and philistine "400" society of the day, was intended to be as odd as its premises. It took its name and its original style from the fictional club created only three years earlier by Conan Doyle in *The Memoirs of Sherlock Holmes,* where Holmes's Diogenes is described as "the queerest place in London...(in which are found) the most unsociable and unclubbable men in town."

While this may have been true in the Diogenes's Jurassic age, three-quarters of a century before Clifford first set foot in the place, it is no longer the case: for all its vaunted eccentricity and unorthodoxy, the Diogenes has an unmistakable aura of conventionality, of materialistic self-esteem and self-congratulation as palpable and thick as the ci-gar smoke that once upon a time filled the club's smoking rooms. The reason is simple. In the past thirty years, the expenses of running the club to a certain standard, of keeping the cooking no worse than de-cent and the wine cellar a bit better than adequate, and of seeing that the building's roof doesn't fall in, have skyrocketed to a point that has increased the dues beyond the reach of the club's charter constituen-cies: writers, teachers, theater folk, and artists; men and women whose style and cultivation generally exceed their financial resources. The Diogenes has therefore been obliged to look for money where money is: nowadays, over two-thirds of newly admitted members are lawyers, investment bankers, hedge-fund managers, management consultants, tax experts, and such, the sort of people who view life as one great big trophy case, and by whose workaday materialistic standards the right to wear the scarlet tie with the little gold lanterns is a coveted sign of having made it—almost on a par with membership in the Council on Foreign Relations or the Brook Club uptown. Fortunately, for most of these, getting in is the main, if not whole, point of the exercise, and they prefer to take their meals in more gilded uptown venues—so that, day in, day out, the Diogenes still belongs, as it were, to its traditional membership, who keen about the "onslaught of philistines" even as they raise their silver mugs in toasts to the improvement in the club's cooking. Nor is it regretted that the financial crisis of the previous two years appears to have materially reduced the number of Wall Street applications for membership.

Under the club's awning, Clifford pauses, turns, and takes a last look around the square: the little park, with its spiked iron fence lacquered to a spiffy gloss that picks up the fading daylight, the century-old streetlamps that now burn watts instead of whale oil, the imposing façades on four sides, ranging in style from austere 1820s Federal to exuberant 1920s Modernist, an architectural mélange that the neighborhood's vigilant arts watch has succeeded in having "landmarked"—to keep the district out of the hands of Trump or some other urban development barbarian with a friend at City Hall.

Visually and psychologically, it's like making a voyage back in time to a more measured and immemorial New York. Translate a paragraph of Edith Wharton or William Dean Howells or Scott Fitzgerald or Louis Auchincloss into sandstone and limestone and brick and glass and granite, and this is what you'll get. A placid backwater that has determinedly set its tradition-carved face against the onrush of the present, the roaring sea of hustle and bustle whose clamor can be heard in the background. Clifford seldom comes here without an agreeable feeling of relief, like someone who has narrowly avoided a traffic accident, without feeling a welcome sense that he's out of danger—at least for the next couple of hours—of infection from the stinking, noisome contagion of money and moneygrubbing and backstabbing that has desolated so much of the rest of his world.

Inside, the ornate clock set in the boss of the horns of a giant water-buffalo head, a trophy that club apocrypha claims was shot by Theodore Roosevelt, reads 9:17, as it has all through the nearly twenty years Clifford's been a member. A sign on an easel announces tonight's talk, "Goya in His Age," the speaker the art critic Robert Hughes.

Should be good, Clifford thinks as he starts up the stairs. A pair of members talking off to one side nod as he passes. He scans the bulletin board, then makes his way up another flight to the lounge, grabs a magazine and plops himself in a fat armchair. A waiter materializes.

"*Milano-Torino* as usual, Mr. Grange?"

"That'd be just fine, Reuben." The drink is a Negroni basically, but with *Punt e Mes* in place of the usual red vermouth, a trick Clifford's father picked up in Italy in '43, demonstrated for and served to his son on Clifford's eighteenth birthday, and which Clifford has since in turn taught to the Diogenes "mixologists."

Thirty minutes later, after a second cocktail and a perusal of two recent issues of *Country Life*, he starts to make his way upstairs to the dining room, then pauses on the landing, wondering whether Connie got his message about recording the cable show. He knows it's just an excuse to check up on her, but he can't help himself. He goes back downstairs, out the front door—cellphones are forbidden within the club—and calls both her numbers. Neither answers.

He checks his watch. It's getting on for six-thirty. What the hell is going on? Then it occurs to him that Jenny has late dance group on Wednesday evenings and that's probably where Connie is, with her cellphone turned off so as not to disturb the music. Relieved, Clifford goes back into the club and climbs the stairs to the third floor. When he enters the glass-vaulted dining-room, he heads immediately for his usual table. Three of the regulars are already seated: Schuyler Thackeray, a seventyish trust-and-estates partner at a famous old midtown law firm; Maud Struthers-Newton, a handsome woman maybe five years older than Clifford, in her mid-fifties, an art-history professor at Columbia, a specialist in Byzantine mosaics, well-enough preserved of face and figure to cause Clifford to surmise now and then, in an offhand and asexual manner, how she'd look without any clothes on, whether she has a sex life; on Thackeray's other side is Renee Newcastle, who has her own poetry imprint at one of the big publishing houses. Clifford's always found her somewhat exotic: she's fine-boned, mousy, and dark, with lovely deep-violet eyes, of an age that's hard to guess—perhaps forty-five, perhaps a bit older—and soft-spoken to the point of inaudibility. Even though he's in vocational limbo himself, he feels sorry for her; poetry has got to be a tough sell in this post-literate age.

Maud greets him in her customary challenging fashion: "Well, at last, Clifford! We wondered if you'd been kidnapped. Most irregular of you not to be here last week. Where were you?"

"Couldn't be helped. Fatherly duties," he replies.

"Really?" Maud says, with that tone of mild scorn tinged with faint incredulity that childless people reserve for those subject to the needs and whims of smaller beings.

"Yeah. Connie was indisposed, so I had to fill in. Believe me, I wouldn't have missed last week for any other reason! So—how was he? Tell me all. As bad as everyone thought he would be?"

"Worse!" Thackeray explodes. "A total disgrace! The club will never be the same!"

"I couldn't agree more," adds Maud. "I'm bound to say that in all

my years here, it's only the second time I've actually felt embarrassed
to be a member."

"Really? And what, pray tell, was the other time?" Clifford asks,
grinning. When Maud gets on her high horse, she's fun to needle.

"Don't be childish, Clifford. You know perfectly well. It was
when We-All-Know-Who had the temerity to bring Henry Kissinger
to the Yule Revel, of course!"

Clifford chuckles. "Of course. Lest I forget. Anyway, tell me about
the notorious Jackal. Did he spill any good beans?"

Last week's speaker had been an odd and controversial choice
for the genteel club: the notorious divorce lawyer Arthur Jekyll, the
one the tabloids call Jekyll the Jackal. Anyone listening to the club
gossips at the Snug Bar would conclude that Jekyll was easily the
club's most-despised member—although Clifford has yet to encounter
anyone at the Diogenes who actually admits to knowing the man. As
for how Jekyll ever got into the Diogenes—who proposed him, who
seconded him, who wrote letters, which governors had signed off on
him—is a mystery apparently beyond solution. How and why the
speakers committee had settled on him to open the new season is a
puzzle no less murky and the subject of much nasty speculation at the
club since the fall calendar was sent out back in June; the consensus
regarding the "how" part was that Jekyll probably "had" something
on someone on the committee; people like Jekyll always *had* something on someone, that's how people like Jekyll get where they are.
As for the "why," the feeling seemed to be that the lawyer could be
counted on to retail some really juicy tidbits about hanky-panky in
high or patrician places. After all, Diogenians were as fond of gossip
as the next fishwife.

"He spilled *no* beans!" Thackeray sputters. "Can you imagine the
fellow's cheek?" His bright little eyes sparkle angrily, the webbing
of scarlet in cheeks that are a virtual symposium on capillary breakdown. "You won't believe this, but the man had the gall and temerity to talk to *us* about moral equity and *noblesse oblige*! Can you
imagine? I mean, here we were, all on tenterhooks to hear about the

Richardsons, and what they're saying about that hedge-fund couple in East Hampton who sued the Maidstone, and the fellow wanted to talk about *noblesse oblige*! Jekyll wouldn't know *noblesse oblige* if it up and bit him in the fanny!"

"Few people these days would," says Clifford.

"That may be," says Maud, recapturing the initiative, "but there was still no excuse for a shyster like that to let us all down!"

"Maud, I share your ire if not your choice of words!" says Clifford. "I thought 'shyster' was a no-no. Even in these hallowed precincts." He sees Maud redden, so he adds, hastily, "In other words, the guy was a real weasel? Just like his nickname? Did he twirl his moustaches? Does he have a moustache? What does he look like, anyway? I sort of picture a narrow, sneaky fellow with a really bad comb-over."

"Actually," says Renee, in her quiet yet oddly deep and dark-toned voice, "he wasn't like that at all. I thought he looked rather genial. He reminded me of Gene Hackman. And he seems to have all his hair."

"Oh really, Renee!" exclaims Maud. "Don't always be such a pushover! The man looked exactly like an Irish bartender. A perfect thug! I've hardly ever seen anyone so common!"

"Moreover, he was very well-spoken," adds Renee, holding her ground.

"Tosh!" says Thackeray. "The fellow may have affected the locutions of a Harvard professor, but he's nothing better than a jumped-up city college type pretending to …"

"He did go to Harvard, you know," Renee interrupts quietly. "Both the college and the law school. I Googled him."

"Harvard?" Clifford asks, surprised. "Really? Funny, I'm like Schuyler here, I somehow think of Jekyll as strictly up from the gutter. City College, someplace like that."

"Nowadays," says Thackeray, "Harvard and the gutter are no longer mutually exclusive. When I see the sort of people who get in now…" He breaks off, obviously taken with a new thought—then, with a bright, satisfied smirk that puffs out his scarlet cheeks, adds, "And it's obvious, of course, that his real name's no more Jekyll than mine is Rockefeller."

"Really? Do you know what his real name is?" asks Clifford.

"From what Renee says, probably something like O'Hara," sniffs Maud. "Who knows, who cares?"

Thackeray's face brightens, his eyes glitter more fiercely, and he looks around the table in utter triumph as he says, "There was actually a pretty funny story going around the Downtown Association a few years back," he says. "It seems that one Family Court judge actually asked Jekyll if it was true he'd changed his name from Hyde! Jekyll into Hyde—d'you follow?" As if anxious to toast his own wit, he flourishes his now-empty mug at a passing waiter. Then he looks in a beetling way at his tablemates and adds, "Damned if I can see how a fellow like that ever got to be a member of this place! Of course, these days..."

He doesn't get to finish the sentence. "Actually," Renee interrupts, "he's been a member since 1977. I looked it up in the club book. I can't remember...when did you join, Schuyler? 1981, was it?" Her dark eyes betray a faint glow of mischief.

It's an uneasy moment, then Thackeray says, with a nod so faint as to be invisible, "I suppose I knew that, although I can't say I ever knew the fellow, and of course I took my law degree at New Haven, so I wouldn't know about Harvard. Come to think of it, I seem to recall that when he started out in practice, Jekyll was a kind of protégé of Martin Crockett, who once upon a time had quite a lot of influence around here. I'm sure none of you remember Crockett and Nevins—they merged into a big Chicago firm in the late '80s—but in its day it was a fine old-school firm, trusts and estates, mainly, as well as the old Madison Avenue Trust Company, and a few corporations. That is, until people like Jekyll sent it careening off its proper course and it ran aground and almost sank and had to be taken over by a firm of hicks looking to buy a silk stocking practice on the cheap. Back then, Martin practically ran *this* place;

he absolutely dominated the admissions committee through force of personality and one or two things he knew about one or two people. I've heard it said that he used to boast that his chairmanship of the admissions committee of this club made more rain for Crockett and Nevins than anything he ever did inside the firm. Still, one had to like the old rogue."

"That doesn't sound exactly old-school," says Clifford.

Thackeray glowers at him in a friendly way. "Old-school or no-school," he says, "billings are billings. Anyway, he liked to put his coming young men in here—which doubtless explains Mr. Jekyll contaminating our number. Poor old Martin—he must be spinning in his grave at how this particular 'coming young man' of his has turned out!"

"Well," says Maud, speaking as if from a lofty perch, "what *I* hear is that Mr. Jekyll helped a certain person on the speakers committee with certain domestic tribulations in a fashion that saved said certain person a great deal of alimony."

"Really, Maud!" says Clifford, waggling a jokey forefinger at her. "You really shouldn't be a party to such disgusting rumors. Our rulers here are above reproach."

"Oh, stop it, Clifford! Don't always make a joke! You know how people are. These days, *anyone* will do *anything* for money, including a great many members of this club."

"Honey," Clifford rejoins, "*most* of the members of this club, I dare say—present company excluded, of course."

Now Renee speaks up. "Well, actually," she says, "Mr. Jekyll did say one thing I thought was well put. It was right at the end, although by then you could barely hear the poor man, what with chairs scraping and people walking out once they realized he wasn't going to feed them gossip; I really felt embarrassed for the club. Anyway, what he said was—I think I've got it right—that 'Law is what gives morality its teeth, but morality is what gives dignity to law.' I did think that was rather well put."

"Oh, poppycock," says Thackeray, his voice full of scorn at the presumption of a poetry editor saying anything about the law. "The fellow probably stole it from somewhere. *Bartlett's*, I shouldn't be surprised."

"Well that's what I wondered, too," the editor says, holding her ground. "So when I got home, I Googled the phrase and I looked through all my quotation books and I couldn't find it anywhere." She looks around the table as she lets this sink in, then—evidently emboldened by having made one declaration on Jekyll's behalf—she risks all and makes another: "Actually, if it comes to that, I thought Mr. Jekyll was surprisingly well-spoken and articulate from beginning to end, much more so than I expected."

"I dare say we can thank his alma mater for that," Maud says with a prim smile. "A few years in Cambridge will teach even a cur to beg nicely." She directs her attention to Clifford. "You're not going to believe this, but do you know whom the unspeakable Mr. Jekyll had the nerve to cite? Here? At the Diogenes?"

She pauses for effect, then says, solemnly: "He cited Robert Bork!" She pronounces the jurist's name as if speaking the grossest, most pornographic obscenity in her vocabulary.

"Yes," seconds Thackeray. "Robert Bork! Here! In this club! Can you believe it?"

"No!" exclaims Clifford. "Never!" He thrusts himself backward in his chair in mock affright, one hand against his bosom, the other limp against his forehead, like an old etching of Edwin Booth playing King Lear. "Not Robert Bork! How dastardly!"

"Very funny," sniffs Maud. "But some of us...well, the man probably voted for McCain!"

In the Diogenian lexicon of contempt and derision, there is no worse epithet.

"I know, I know," Clifford responds, straightening up and putting on a good-little-boy face. "I'm sorry. Bork just doesn't happen to be a name that gets me going."

"Well, it should!" says Maud in a stern way. "But enough of this. How was your summer?"

"It was all right," says Clifford. He can tell what's coming next. It never fails. Like the first faint rumble of an approaching subway, he senses the approach of the question he dreads more than any other. Sure enough:

"And what are you working on?" Maud asks.

"Oh, this and that," he says.

Maud won't quit. "We're all very keen to have a new Clifford Grange film. It's been some time now, hasn't it? Don't tell me the well's run dry."

"It's just flowing a bit sluggishly."

"Well, put a boot in," Maud says. "We need people like you. It's seems months since I've read about anything I'd consider going to see. I mean, Almodóvar can only make so many films, don't you know? And Woody Allen's fallen completely apart! As have the French!"

"Maud, I'll do my best, I really will. I'm trying, believe me."

At that moment, blessedly, further conversation is cut short by a waiter passing through the room tapping on a xylophone. The general clamor subsides to a murmur, then silence, as heads turn toward the rostrum for the pre-lecture announcements.

Thirty-five minutes later, having heard a very good talk on Goya, Clifford waits for the applause to die away, and then, in the interval before the ritual Q&A, while chairs are being pushed back from tables and waiters summoned to refresh drinks, gets up and starts to make his good-byes.

"You're not staying for dinner?" Maud asks.

"Not tonight, sadly. I have to get home."

He doesn't, really—but something's pushing him. He leaves the dining room, and as he descends the stairs, he ponders for about the millionth time in his life what seems to him to be one of life's great truths: that men may be from Mars and women from Venus, but the real dividing line is the one that separates people who have had children from people who have not.

He's glad he came. It's good for him to get out of the house. Got to do more of it, he tells himself, get outside myself and my troubles, change my stripes and spend more time among the people in this country who don't give a shit about who had lunch with whom at certain New York and Los Angeles restaurants, who don't care who's "in," who's "out," according to *Vanity Fair* or *Women's Wear Daily*, and which picture won the weekend box-office derby with how much. Got to swallow my pride, cross the line, meet some new people. They say misery loves company—but if the only company available is the sorry-faced self-pitying sonofabitch in the mirror, it's time to make some new friends.

The day has changed for the better; the sky has cleared, the air feels fresher. Clifford feels intellectually recharged, and if his emotional tendency is still downward, it no longer seems in free fall, at least for the moment. Pausing for a light at Thirty-eighth Street, he calls home on his cellphone. This time, Connie answers.

"Did you get my message about setting the DVR?" he asks.

"No."

"I left it on both your cell and on the machine."

"When was that?"

"A little after four. You haven't checked the machine?"

"I thought I'd let Jenny do it. It's usually for her, anyway."

"Jenny's not home yet?"

"No. She went to Jean's after dance to work on their geography project. I'm picking her up at nine."

"Did you go to dance?"

"Why would I? I've been here all afternoon, catching up." Her voice starts to sound impatient. If there's one thing his wife hates, it's being grilled: how was work, how was the new second lead, the taping?

"No harm done," he says. "*Prime Suspect* is on the BBC channel at nine thirty. Will you set the DVR?"

"I will," she says curtly. "I'll do it right now—and I'll see you when you get here."

"I'm catching the 8:32. Don't wait up."

"I'm sure I'll be awake. See you then." Then she hangs up. No blown kiss, no small endearment. All business.

A few seconds later, she calls back. "I'm sorry if I sounded impatient," she says. "It's been a long day. We had a lot to get through."

"Well, I was starting to worry. Is something going on with the show? You sound kind of hot and bothered."

"No—well, actually yes: it's the studio. They're fiddling with the scripts and they're talking about shooting three extra episodes next week."

"You can handle it. Think of the overtime. I'll see you anon."

"Fine," she says. "Big kiss"—but her tone implies that the return of the hunter home from the hill isn't going to absolutely make her day. It's not that she sounds mad at Clifford, not at all, although it's not that she couldn't hide her mood if she wanted to, as good an actress as she is.

She definitely sounds impatient, however. If it isn't Clifford, might it be the show that's stressing her? To Clifford, that sounds unlikely. When they got back from Michigan, and she began to read through the teleplays waiting for her, there was hardly a snort. And one thing BME would never dare would be to spring surprises on its brightest star. As for shooting extra episodes, with all that entails in additional costs—not in a million years, not given the vigilance of the BBN bean counters, or the show's principal sponsor, Summerhill Farms, which has a net-profits interest and which keeps track of every last penny.

Something here doesn't compute.

But why worry? he tells himself. Next year, according to what's been made public, Connie will earn close to $30 million: $1,200,000 per episode of *Here's Constance!* plus on-time bonuses, plus a seven-digit annual royalty from her Summerhill Farms brands: mainly packaged-food lines. By comparison, Clifford's income from all sources will maybe touch $150,000, mainly residuals. He guesses that the combined Grange investment portfolios now add up to over $50 million: after the stock market collapse, his own is down to $1 million and change, which makes Connie's side—mainly treasuries and municipals—$49 million. And then there's Grangeford, which even now would probably list at close to $15 million before adding in a premium for celebrity ownership. You'd have to say that a family fortune that size is worth the aggravation that goes with accumulating it.

And it can only get better. Assuming the show runs another three or four years, makes it, say, to an eighth or ninth season, it'll be worth another billion—minimum—in syndication, and Connie will have a fifteen percent override on that plus a piece of any ancillaries.

But Clifford's not the type who finds comfort or pain in the contemplation of wealth, his own or someone else's. Given the way the world is now, however, he's slowly coming to believe his failure to do so is a distinct defect of character, possibly the one area in which his father failed in his upbringing. The general never impressed on his son the monstrous centrality and power of money in the American way. How could he have been expected to? General Grange's prime of life had been lived mainly in a different epoch, those postwar years when other qualities—discretion and learning, to name two—occupied the top of the charts. When the republic hadn't become as, well, stupid and envious as it now seems. The old man would have been appalled, inflamed, and infuriated by the present reign of Mammon and the terrible mess that Wall Street had got the nation into. He would be calling for scalps.

But Clifford has only so much mental energy for the state of the union. The state of his marriage is what he has to think about. Of course, he tells himself as he finds a seat in the club car, every marriage—every relationship—goes through bad patches. Why should his and Connie's be any different? As the train rumbles north, he reviews his marriage, breaks it down into x and y and z, as if he were diagramming it on a blackboard.

Money? No. Early onset menopause? Impossible! Their sex life? Possibly, but that doesn't feel like the right answer. After the first few months, when it seemed they did nothing but screw, until she finally got pregnant with Jenny, sex ceased to be a dominant chord in their relationship. Although the thought can't be evaded that his wife may be getting it somewhere else, the very notion seems insane! Connie would never take the chance! Not with all she's got going for her.

So what are we looking at, then? The dread Star Is Born Syndrome?—when one partner gets all the ink, fame, money, recognition and the other produces zilch—and finally goes crazy? Clifford's seen it happen to others; he's been told, more than once, by this or that old Hollywood or Broadway hand, that having a spouse become a star is like having that spouse take a lover—only worse. So maybe that's it. Connie is doing just fabulously; her comet rises ever higher in the stratosphere of ratings and recognition factor and Web site hits, all the indices of superstardom. It would be natural for her to succumb and become a kind of Connie Dearest, unable to distinguish between her onstage and at-home personas, a distinction that Clifford himself is beginning to have trouble with.

Besides, it's not as if she's exactly beating up on Clifford. On the whole, what the public sees and admires in the onscreen Constance is what Connie's family gets in the flesh: the model mother, model mate: easy, generous, reliable, trustworthy, patient, good-humored. Twinned personalities that Connie has heretofore had no trouble toggling between. They say all good things come to an end and perhaps that's what's going on with Connie. Still, all that Clifford has in the way of "evidence" are a few small, scattered tics and inconsistencies. Inconsistencies like tonight—for which there may be a dozen good explanations—if he can think of them.

The thing to do, he decides as they flash by Old Greenwich, is to wait this out and keep up his end. Pop a Zoloft now and then to settle the paranoia and suspicion. *I can do that,* he tells himself. He still loves and admires his wife; he respects her success and what's gone into it. He loves his daughter, loves being her father, loves watching her grow and change, loves giving her all that he has to give. He loves the domestic life at Grangeford: its patterns and rhythms give not only meaning to his existence, they impart a kind of armature, a governing logic that holds him up when his knees start to buckle. He loves the house itself, the old stone walls, the shingle and slate, the majestic old trees, the *oldness* and the *foreverness* of it all, loves the fantastic high-bluff view of the estuary and Long Island Sound.

In the face of all these advantages, what right has he got to complain? He's probably making too much out of too little, he decides.

Another twenty minutes and he'll be home. He squares his mental shoulders. Love and work, isn't that what Freud said were the main sources of happiness? Love and work: they're like the twin engines of the P-38s his father flew before switching over to Thunderbolts. Even with one engine dead, they could stay in the air and fight. *And so it will be with my marriage*, Clifford declares, *even if I have to fly the damn thing on one engine!*

The train begins to slow. As Clifford gets up and makes for the platform, a dreadful thought crosses his mind: no aircraft ever built can fly on *no* engines.

CHAPTER TWO

October 15

As the grandfather clock that has kept the time for four generations of her family starts to chime the quarter hour, the intercom on Annabelle Villers's desk buzzes rudely, interrupting her loving contemplation of the early morning landscape. The best time of day for the Great Smokies, she thinks, as, frowning, she swivels away from the window: "Yes, Mary Ella, what is it?"

"Belle, the First Gotham folks are here!"

"Already? My goodness!" Her visitors, an investment-banking team from First Gotham up in New York, weren't scheduled to arrive until 8 a.m.

"Something about needing to get out of Teterboro before a storm moved in. Shall I put them in the boardroom?"

"Do that, dear heart—and tell them I'll be right along," she instructs. "Make sure they have coffee and everything, you hear. I'm just going to freshen up."

She turns back for a final look at the spectacular panorama out-side her office window. In the limpid morning light, the dark primal beauty of the mountains is just perfect: rich green banded in deep purple shadow, a halo of sunlight picking out the tops of the west-ernmost ridges, the forested foothills' dark green and violet folds still draped in fading transparent swatches of fog. The view is magical and rejuvenating and brings back her fondest memories, intense recollec-tions of Tuscany, which has been her heart's secret yearned-for home for almost forty years, since she traveled there as a schoolgirl, and the hidden focus of her existence for the past three, the gathering point for her very best dream, the project that will sum up and make sense of her entire working life. Depending on what these First Gotham folks are about to tell her, she intends to bring Italy to the very shad-ows of the Great Smoky Mountains, to a magical site a bare dozen miles from Asheville, North Carolina, the thriving, pleasant city in which Annabelle has lived and worked practically her whole life.

Next year, she will turn sixty. For almost twenty years, the fam-ily company—Summerhill Foods—has owned her life, has been kin, project, purpose, and obsession. She's done all that she can do for the company; now it's time for the company to do something for her: to let her get on with the real business of living and to go back to her first and deepest passion: the art of the Italian Renaissance. Even though she's had a lot of fun doing it, and precious little frustration, truth be told, running Summerhill has been a duty. What she has in mind for the next and probably final stage of her life will bring her full circle. Of course, all that will depend on what the people waiting in her boardroom are about to tell her.

She goes into the small bathroom adjoining her office, splashes water on her face, and examines herself carefully in the mirror. The woman looking back at her seems more tired than she should, older than she should, considering that nowadays sixty's not all that old. She runs a tentative hand over her cheek. Her skin feels rough. Her hair doesn't look so good, either. Are those *new* wrinkles at the corners of mouth and eyes? She twists round and tries to examine herself over her shoulder. Her hips look *enormous!* Is she putting on weight?

She steps back and takes a second look and decides she isn't, that what her scale tells her is the truth, and that the mirror's just fibbing. She takes a moment to make a quick audit. On the debit side, she has a big frame and big features: the same chiseled, strong-chinned, country-gentry faces in the male family portraits down the hall in the conference room. In these parts, folks speak of "the Villers jaw" the way art historians routinely point to "the Hapsburg chin" in portraits by Velasquez and Goya. But she also has lovely, pale olive skin, a legacy from her Cuban mother, as is her hair: thick, dark, shiny with auburn highlights. She's built on a scale that discourages an over-emphatic personal style of dress. Nothing busy, nothing fancy, nothing too young: that's the formula followed by the personal shopper she uses, the owner of a downtown boutique who monitors the Paris, Milan, and New York collections for ideas.

Her taste is distinctly feminine. Annabelle prides herself that she *doesn't* look or dress like all those "Top 100" businesswomen in magazines like *Fortune*: tough, prim, manly, trained, and tailored within an inch of their lives and usually surgically improved. She steers clear of personal publicity. Unless it involves Connie Grange, Annabelle spurns all requests for interviews, photo spreads, seminar and panel appearances. She serves on no corporate boards save her own. Summerhill has no public-relations staff, nor outside PR firm; up to now it's been a private company, there's been no need for one, nor any need for Annabelle to stick her face in front, the way some CEOs do. Besides, down here in Asheville, folks still hold to the view that a lady gets her picture in the paper only three times: when she's engaged, when she's married, and when she cuts a ribbon at a church or charity function.

Good products, good relations with suppliers, workers, and customers, good advertising, and a powerful, effective brand identity and personification (namely Connie) are the keys to Summerhill's success. Let what's on the shelves wearing the Summerhill Farms/Constance

Grange Signature label do the talking and make the money: that's Annabelle's management credo.

She turns this way and that to check the Oscar de la Renta suit she's picked out for today. *Okay, darlin'*, she tells herself: *showtime.* She pauses by her desk to murmur a hasty prayer, crosses herself, and—for extra luck—touches the base of a small bronze crucifix set on a side table, a gift from her girlhood confessor. Then she blows a kiss toward a silver-framed photograph of a woman with a vivacious face, not quite *beautiful* but certainly pretty, whose direct gaze and friendly half-smile are framed by a coronet of dark, wavy hair. The photo is inscribed in a firm, clear, squarish hand: "To Belle with love and everything else. XXXXX. Connie."

Darling, darling Connie, she thinks, *from whom all blessings flow.* This photograph is Annabelle's favorite because it captures Connie's essence: her vitality and immediacy, that rare ability to project and connect. The way Annabelle sees it, Connie has become the soul and heart of Summerhill, as responsible as Annabelle herself for having taken Summerhill from a little bitty regional producer of snacks and chewing tobacco to what it is now, a brand-name jewel courted by A-list Wall Street investment bankers like those awaiting Annabelle in the board room. Connie, whom one media critic has described as "a combination of Oprah and Betty Crocker and Martha Stewart," *is* the brand.

She gives heartfelt and prayerful thanks for Connie three or four times a day, and more than that on Mondays, when she gets the previous week's sales and gross profit figures for the various Constance Grange Signature lines, and on Thursdays, when the Barrow Media people e-mail her the overnight ratings from which her marketing people will run the spreadsheets that will convert ratings points into sales and profits. Without Connie, the meeting that's about to take place this morning, or the one next week down in Bentonville, Arkansas, which will leapfrog Summerhill into the billion-dollar league, would never be happening, nor would Annabelle's vision for the rest of her life have the slightest chance of coming true.

Who could ever have thought it could turn out like this? Twenty years ago this coming November, on a foggy Sunday morning, the company King-Air bringing Annabelle's daddy's shooting party back from Albany, Georgia, crashed on takeoff, killing the nine people on board: two pilots and seven passengers, all men: Annabelle's husband, father, and brother, who ran Summerhill; the company's lawyer and the chief grocery and packaged goods buyer from a rapidly growing retail chain called Wal-Mart, which Annabelle's father had early identified as the kind of customer any business in its right mind wanted to be in bed with, and in which he had been an early investor. When it came to investments, Annabelle's daddy had a real nose for news: among his other early discoveries had been a smart young fellow in Omaha named Warren Buffett, who two or three times in the years since has come calling with an offer to buy Summerhill.

Back then, Summerhill was an enterprise typical of the U.S. economy once upon a time: privately owned, compact, and paternally run, with a strong regional identity. A making-and-doing outfit, and a driving force in its community. The workforce was fiercely non union, fiercely loyal. From top to bottom, Summerhill supported a nice standard of life for all who worked there; from the workers on the packing and canning lines to the Villers family, who had long been numbered as one of the pillars of Asheville life and society.

When her menfolk were killed, Annabelle was forty-one and childless, and was slowly going crazy in the life she found herself living. Two decades earlier, she had graduated from Chapel Hill, *magna cum laude* in art history, with her mind and heart set on an art career, to teach somewhere, or to work in a great museum. But the pressures from home were great, and so she'd deferred that dream and had done what was expected of a young woman coming from the culture that bred her. She'd come back home and married, thereby supplying the family with a husband to help run the company now, and it was taken for granted that she would in due course provide sons to run it in the future. Except there were no children. She had a hard time getting pregnant, then the pregnancy turned out to be ectopic, and in the end she lost both the baby and the ability to have children. She'd ended up just exactly where she'd promised herself she never would, as a company, country-club wife with not much more than a book club and twice-a-year visits to the great museums of the Northeast to keep her mind alive.

Then came the plane crash, and everything changed. Whenever she's looked back, which she hasn't done often because what would be the point, she's asked herself what prompted her to take over running the company. There were easier alternatives: she could have sold it to Buffett or someone else for enough money to keep her comfortable for the rest of her life and let her resume her art history studies, possibly even leave Asheville and go to live in New York or Boston or Washington to find happiness in the company of the old masters the way other well-fixed Asheville widows went to Palm Beach to find new husbands.

And yet she couldn't. That would be desertion. The people who worked at Summerhill were a Villers responsibility; they needed to be looked out for. So she took back her maiden name, rolled up her sleeves, and went to work. She made Summerhill the sum and substance of her existence. When she traveled now, she no longer made a beeline for museums and libraries; she visited supermarkets and malls to see what the competition was up to, what ideas she might pilfer. Her sole artistic involvement consisted of generous annual contributions to various North Carolina museums.

To the surprise of herself and many others, she had a knack for the business. Summerhill took off. It was, on the whole, a plum time for the economy, and Summerhill grew a bit faster than the GDP, which provided nice rates of return. By the tenth anniversary of the plane crash, Summerhill was probably worth $150 million all in; a nice nest egg by most folks' standards, and roughly eight times what Annabelle had paid estate tax on. She was privately very comfortable in any case, thanks to her father's providential investments in Wal-Mart and Berkshire Hathaway, but she couldn't quit. She reinvested one hundred percent of Summerhill's free cash flow in the business, upgrading facilities and product lines, enhancing productivity through incentives, picking the right spots to go into with new products, now and then making a small acquisition of a local or regional brand that looked like it would fit well. Summerhill grew and grew.

And then, six years ago this past May, her focus faltered. What happened was that the North Carolina Museum of Art over in Raleigh had put together a deluxe Italian Tour, one of those deals where a select group of the museum's friends, mother-henned by the director and the chief curator, would visit the great art cities of Tuscany and Umbria, and be received in the best villas and castles, often by families whose genealogies included popes and emperors. A couple from Asheville, really good friends, had signed up for the trip; they urged Annabelle to join them and without really giving it a thought, she agreed. It had been a long, gray, chilly winter. Summerhill was thriving; she could spare two weeks.

That particular spring, Tuscany virtually defined the word "glorious." The tour had been carefully planned and important strings had been pulled. The group visited seldom-seen private collections. It visited the studios of the Uffizi restorers. It dined at I Tatti, the old Bernard Berenson villa on the outskirts of Florence, now an outpost of Harvard, and lunched at La Pietra, Harold Acton's fabled estate, now part of NYU. It heard lectures on Botticelli and Duccio by the world's leading experts.

It only took two days for Annabelle to realize that what she thought had died in her never really had, that it had only been suppressed. She was powerless to resist the old siren song. Standing on her balcony at the luxury hotel Villa San Michele, looking out over the Arno basin, seeing Florence spreading away like a vast spiky jigsaw, the massive curve of Brunelleschi's dome, the upward thrust of Giotto's clock tower, the bridge where Dante had glimpsed Beatrice, Annabelle felt eighteen all over again; she felt she had come home.

On the group's last night, sitting by herself on the hotel terrace with a goodnight coffee and a grappa, Annabelle found herself thinking how wonderful it would be to create something like I Tatti and La Pietra right there in the foothills that, in most seasons, at certain times of day, looked exactly like the Tuscan hills outside her hotel window. A center for the study of Italian art and culture, that's what she'd create: a magnet for scholars, a jewel for the region, with housing for scholars, a library, study rooms of all kinds, possibly even a small, choice art collection.

The problem was, she realized at once, that what she had in mind was going to take a great deal of money, much more than she reckoned she could lay her hands on. A minimum of $300 million, she guesstimated, and probably closer to twice that, which was way beyond her means. Someone like Procter & Gamble or Frito-Lay or even Buffett would probably pay upward of $200 million for Summerhill, but after taxes and decent provision for the company's people, that would leave her pitifully short of her goal, even if she threw in her own personal resources.

Of course, she could try to sell the idea to like-minded wealthy North Carolinians, pass the collection plate, maybe see if the state could take a hand, but to do so would invite second-guessing or worse, as well as competition with the better-heeled eastern part of the state with its own highly developed cultural infrastructure. If she was going to get this done, she would have to virtually double the depth of her pocket, and the only way to do *that* would be somehow to bring about a huge uptick in the value of her company.

But how?

For a company the size that Summerhill was then, the avenues were few. Merger or sale wouldn't bring in enough money. A year or so ago, there had been feelers about one of those Midas-touch, minnow-swallows-whale leveraged buyouts, using Summerhill's clean cash flow and spic-and-span, virtually debt-free balance sheet as the fulcrum, but the idea never really appealed to Annabelle. Even if she got the richest possible price, she wasn't about to throw her people to a bunch of New York sharks who'd merrily trade Asheville jobs for a few extra points of what they called IRR, or internal rate of return.

And then, like a gift from heaven, Connie came along.

It happened a few months after Annabelle returned from her art tour. One afternoon, she was at home with a bad cold, feeling too sick to do anything but stare at the TV. Bouncing among channels, she came across a soap opera. She watched in a blank way for a couple of minutes, just to get a sense of what was going on, and in those two minutes her world changed forever. There was just something about one of the actresses, the one who played the second-banana role as the Good Sister. Annabelle watched the show intently to its conclusion and identified Constance Grange as the actress in question. She watched the show again the next day, and the day after that, and as she watched, a business idea, wholly unlike any that she had ever hatched before, began to take shape: *this girl could personify everything Summerhill stands for as a brand*! She thought it through over the weekend, on Monday did a bit of Internet research, then got the name of Connie's agent, and so began the amazing story.

It was, as she later told her board, a classic case of not knowing she was looking for something until she stumbled across it—the "it" being a personality who could carry Summerhill to the next level... and the next and the next. Connie was the right age—in her early mid-thirties—and she had the right kind of looks, nice but not startling, and, above all, she had the right kind of personality. There was something in her that, as Annabelle saw it, could be built into a unique blend of Martha Stewart's efficiency and focus, and Oprah Winfrey's honesty and spiritual quality. Moreover, Connie had something the others didn't: a convincing family life onscreen *and off*: a home, a husband, a small daughter.

But a personality can't be built in a media vacuum. There has to be a platform, a path to stardom. A hit TV show, for instance. Annabelle had a hunch that, given the way the country seemed to be going, a show that emphasized family values and family ties, but without the typical New York-Hollywood edge, without all that irony, could be a winner. The one thing there wasn't much of on television was what Annabelle thought of as "Nice with a capital N." Everything was either gory or smarty-pants. Or stupid. She was convinced that a sort of sitcom-cum-talk-show would work, with Connie, properly framed and presented, playing the hostess of a fictional cable-TV show for homemakers, dealing with her own offscreen problems and situations as well as those of her guests. With good scripts, and the right guest stars, *Here's Constance!*—as Annabelle envisaged it from day one—could catch fire, but she was also made aware that it might take as many as three years to find and build an audience. Annabelle had that kind of time, but not the kind of money, a minimum of $50 million for just one season, that her media consultants projected. To do this, she would need a partner.

She went over the lineups of the five big networks and concluded that Barrow Broadcasting Network, the smallest and most ambitious, would be the likeliest potential partner. Through her attorneys, she cadged an introduction to Ronald Barrow, the head of Barrow Media Enterprises, the parent of BBN, from a friend high up in Procter & Gamble. As she later told Mary Ella, "I went, I pitched, I conquered. Ronnie has the toughest, dime-squeezing mind in American media, but he goes absolutely gooey when it comes to family values, which he's on some fancy presidential commission about. Anyway, he liked what I was talking about and agreed to bankroll not only a pilot, but a full season's worth of episodes, provided I was willing to commit for ten minutes of advertising per episode at BBN's full rate-card. Which I was, even though it could add up to almost $50 million, but only in return for a one-third interest in the show's profits if and when we got there. The rest is, of course, history."

Just how many present-day zeroes that six-year history might translate into is what the First Gotham people have come to Asheville today to tell Annabelle. When she enters the boardroom, a crisp young woman a year or so either side of forty, in a stylishly stern pinstriped pantsuit, disengages from her colleagues and comes over to embrace Annabelle. This is Cecile Frost, a First Gotham senior managing director, vice chair of the big firm's corporate finance division, and the person in charge of the budding Summerhill relationship. Annabelle is very happy with First Gotham, the firm her accountants recommended. They call themselves "a boutique," specializing in fee-paying advisory work. First Gotham doesn't trade on its own leveraged capital, the way so many of its larger, more famous competitors have. As a result, the firm has come through last year's credit crisis with its resources and reputation intact.

"Sorry to be so early, Annabelle," she says, "but it was supposed to weather up and we figured better now than whenever."

Cecile interests Annabelle. The investment banker personifies what the polls and focus groups have identified as a key, core segment of Connie's "Blue America" audience—which accounts for just under forty percent of the show's repeat viewers. The first time they met, Cecile confessed to having Connie's show on permanent TiVo. Despite all the qualities of mind and spirit, the mental rigor that it presumably takes to become a star banker at First Gotham, a firm whose people are known as "the professional's professionals," there's a trace of vulnerability in Cecile. Annabelle's prepared to bet that under the brisk metallic façade is a woman who still hasn't gotten what she really wants out of life—and who is starting to suspect that she never will, not doing what she does now, not living the way she lives. She'd like to eavesdrop on Cecile's conversations with her mirror.

"Let me introduce my colleagues," Cecile says. "Irving, you know of course."

Irving Doolittle, senior executive associate for corporate mandates, is a worn, bearded man perhaps ten years older than Cecile. Professorial in appearance and manner, he projects the impression that Wall Street is intellectually beneath him, that if through mischance he hadn't been shanghaied into finance, he'd be holding down a tenured chair in comparative literature at Princeton, or making $100-a-bottle wines in Sonoma or New Zealand.

"Nice to see you again, Irving." Annabelle says. "How are you keeping?"

He grins, and makes to tug an imaginary forelock. "Tol'able, m'am," he says in an unconvincing "cracker" accent. "Jus' tol'able. But all the better for seeing you." Like Connie's husband, Clifford, Irving fancies himself to be a wit and skilled mimic.

"And this is Alfred Ornstein, whom you haven't met. Alfred's our senior VP for forensic accounting." Annabelle shakes hands with a wispy fiftyish man presiding over a stack of inch-thick spiral-bound memoranda embossed with the First Gotham logo. Forensic accounting is a notion new to Annabelle. And probably new, she reflects, to First Gotham and to Wall Street: hastily invented in the wake of the credit disasters.

The last person to be introduced is a young, squarely built, close-cropped African-American woman, who Annabelle decides can't be more than a year or two out of law school. "And, finally, this is Denyce Hargrove, who's been doing our legal heavy lifting."

"Nice to have you here, Denyce," says Annabelle. She smiles inwardly as she takes the young woman's hand. It's clear the cadre has been carefully put together to show that First Gotham touches all the right bases: gender equality, youth and age and affirmative action, and multiculturalism and multiethnicity, blond hair and gray hair and frizzy hair and kinky hair.

When everyone's seated, Cecile points across the room and asks, "That painting of Constance Grange is new, isn't it? I don't recall seeing it when Irving and I were here last month."

"It was just delivered last week," replies Annabelle. "Isn't it wonderful? It's by Stone Roberts, a local boy who's hit it big in New York. I'm crazy about it. I think it captures perfectly what Connie's all about. Essence of Connie, you might say."

"Indeed," says Irving, "just as a Van Dyck portrait of King Charles isn't just a representation of what that particular monarch looked like, it's also a portrait of *kingship*. It's symbolic! Back then, it was kings. Today it's brands, the real royalty of our age." The remark shows that Irving has been properly briefed, that he's been made well aware of the prospective client's keen interest in art history.

Annabelle looks around the table and smiles. "Okay, folks, enough of the badinage and the persiflage, as my daddy used to say. Cecile darling, make my day. Are you going to make me rich—and, if so, how rich?"

Cecile gestures to Alfred Ornstein, who distributes the bound memoranda around the table, then she launches into her pitch.

Ten minutes later Annabelle has her answer: if First Gotham is right, she is seriously rich. Seriously, *seriously* rich. Maybe not Forbes 400 rich—but close, very close. Roughly $900 million dollars rich.

Although Cecile and her colleagues use a lot of jargon, buzz-words like "asset virtualization," "tracking stocks," and "enterprise cores," what First Gotham's proposal comes down to is pretty simple. Summerhill's existing businesses will be split between two entities: one that will hold the Constance Grange assets and revenue streams, and another for all the non-Connie lines and products. Shares in the former will be offered publicly. Annabelle—and, if she chooses, her employees—will own the latter outright.

"Think of Summerhill as a store that has two cash registers," Irving explains. "One is painted red, the other blue. Into the red one goes the take from your Constance Grange operations. The blue one gets the rest. The red one is what investors want a piece of. They'll willingly pay, say, $25 for every dollar that goes into the red cash register, while they might pay no more than $10 to $12 for every dollar in the old blue one."

"Exactly," says Cecile. "After what they've been through, investors not only want, they *demand,* what we call 'transparency.' They want what's called a 'pure play,' a direct, unclouded share of the segments of your overall business that they like best. What they like best, they will pay the most for. In the case of an initial public offering—an IPO—of your Constance Grange assets and revenue streams, we think the market will accept a price-earnings ratio of twenty-five times."

"That sounds awfully optimistic," says Annabelle.

"Well, for one thing," says Cecile, "the market's showing a much better tone. Good stocks have performed well, and our sense of things is that people are really ready to gobble up a classy new name. You certainly fit that bill. Clean balance sheet, dependable growth picture, high level of shelf recognition and consumer preference, and, of course, you have Constance Grange."

"Connie makes that much of a difference?"

Cecile nods enthusiastically. "She certainly does. That's really what investors want nowadays: brands. That's the magic word. Coca-Cola, Apple, Mercedes. Brands create economic value; brands drive market valuation and consumer recognition. The essence of brand strength is image and marketing and *really* conscientious and careful stewardship. The ideal company today is a brand name, period, that outsources the stuff the brand name's stamped on. As long as the IPO puts investors' arms around Constance Grange, in a manner of speaking, that's all they'll care about. Constance Grange's fans love and worship her; they buy anything and everything that bears her name or face, and it'll be her fans who drive the market. Millions of investors lining up to put their money where their worship is, to buy a piece of their idol."

First Gotham proposes to put together an IPO of $800 million in "red register" common stock: $300 million to be sold by Annabelle out of her holding, $100 million by the Summerhill pension plan, and $400 million of new stock to help pay for a sparkling, spanking-new processed-foods plant that Annabelle plans to build some sixty miles to the southeast, near Gastonia, where there's excellent access to the interstate highways and a more reliable power grid. Next to her art institute, this new facility is the apple of Annabelle's ambitions. Not only will it significantly add to sales and profits, it will also be a major, statesmanlike gesture of corporate citizenship, proof positive of Summerhill's commitment to the state and the region. Annabelle's negotiated hard, and both the governor and the legislature have jumped through some pretty tight hoops to get her the concessions, tax abatements, and subsidies she's insisted on.

"If the economy and the general market continue to improve," Cecile concludes, "and our wealth-management people and economists think there's a seventy percent likelihood that they will, these figures could prove on the low side when we come to price the deal. The way we look at it, a couple of years from now, maybe three, *Here's Constance!* will go into syndication, at which point your revenue split with BME increases from one-third to fifty-fifty to two-thirds. That'll be priced into the deal. Of course, it's all contingent on things staying as they are or improving, both in the general economy and at Summerhill. But as I say, our investment people think we've definitely seen the worst, assuming there isn't another subprime disaster or Lehman Brothers lurking out there. I assume everything's tip-top here."

Annabelle nods. "We're very happy and comfortable with the forecasts we gave you. If anything, they should prove conservative."

"Fine," says Cecile. "So if the market doesn't go to hell, and nothing happens to Constance Grange, we're a go."

"The market I can't do anything about," Annabelle says. "But you can count on me to keep Connie off small planes."

"And away from Eliot Spitzer or Bill Clinton," says Irving, with a naughty look. Then he sees he's pushed it, turns sheepish, and adds, "Just kidding, of course. But I think you know what I mean."

"No offense given, none taken, Irving. And I do see what you mean. But I don't think we need worry about that. Connie is exactly what she appears to be. She has a good marriage and a fine family: a loving husband and a terrific daughter. She works hard, then goes home and cooks dinner, and never misses a PTA meeting."

"Music to our ears," Cecile says. "The family values angle is key. Constance Grange's value as a brand is probably tied to her role as a wife and mother to a degree that Martha's wasn't. Connie's more Oprah than Martha; there's a moral dimension there. But I'm not telling you anything you don't already know, Belle. As I recall, her contracts with you and Barrow protect you on that score. Isn't that right, Denyce?"

The young lawyer nods confirmation. "I've got the language right here. It's pretty boilerplate."

Denyce shuffles deftly through the papers in front of her, quickly finds what she's looking for, and reads: "Our success depends on the value of our Constance Grange brands and products. Our business would be adversely affected if Constance Grange's public image or reputation were to be tarnished....Constance Grange, as well as her name, her image, and the trademarks and other intellectual property rights relating to these, are integral to our marketing efforts and form the core of our brand name. Our continued success and the value of our brand name therefore depends, to a large degree, on the reputation of Constance Grange...et cetera, et cetera....OK, and here's the real kicker....Party of the First Part ('Grange') will not engage in acts of moral turpitude or do or commit any act or thing that will tend to degrade herself or other parties to this contract in society blah, blah, blah...willful gross misconduct...blah, blah, blah...or that will tend to shock, insult or offend the community..."

At that point, Denyce stops reading and looks up. "Then we get into the penalty part," she says. "Do you want to hear that?"

Annabelle shakes her head. "I know that it's pretty severe," she says. "Actually, it wasn't my idea. Ronald Barrow insisted on it. Apparently, it's standard in all his contracts. He's a very moral man. When he demanded it, my lawyers thought we might as well get it, too."

"And Mrs. Grange had no problem with it?"

"If you knew Connie, Cecile, you wouldn't have to ask that question."

"So she wouldn't mind if we incorporated something like it in our offering documents? I seem to remember something like that in the Martha Stewart Omnimedia prospectus. Could you check that out, Denyce? Perhaps we could borrow their language." She turns back to Annabelle and asks: "I'm not sure this is the time to bring this up, but have you ever thought of offering Constance Grange a stock participation in the new company?"

"You mean like options?"

"Options, a bonus in stock, some kind of buy-in. Whatever works best for all concerned from a tax point of view."

"No, as a matter of fact, I haven't. We *are* a family company. We've never had a nonfamily stockholder." As the words leave her mouth, she realizes how dumb and selfish she sounds, because if Connie isn't family, who is? "But that's not set in iron. Perhaps you could come up with some ideas on that score."

Cecile looks at Irving. "We'll be pleased to." Irving nods and makes a note on his yellow pad.

Why not set Connie up with, say, $75 million in stock? Annabelle thinks. *That can only be good for everyone.* She looks around the table. "Well, you folks certainly *have* made my day," she says. "Tell me: supposing that I give you the high sign, when do you see this happening?"

Alfred answers for First Gotham. "Probably mid-January at the earliest. You're on a September 30 fiscal year, which means the books close in a couple of weeks, and from what PricewaterhouseCoopers has told us, we can expect final audited numbers by early December. According to PwC, your company accounts are like driven snow."

"No offshore pork sausage limited partnerships, or special deals with Constance Grange under the table in the Cayman Islands?" jokes Irving, drawing a frown from Cecile.

"Is there anything else?" asks Annabelle.

"Well, if the details can be worked out, and it fits everyone's schedule," Cecile replies, "I think we'd like to do a major dog and pony show."

"'Dog and pony show'?" asks Annabelle.

"We like to make a series of pre-offering presentations to certain big investors face-to-face," Irving answers. "New York, Boston, Chicago, Dallas, San Francisco, Atlanta, Miami: places like that. Europe and the Middle East—Dubai—if it makes sense."

"Who'd be involved on our end?"

"Well, you, of course, Annabelle, so you'd better free up your calendar. A few of your key people, plus your accountants and lawyers." At this Cecile pauses, then continues, "I hesitate to ask you this, Annabelle, but do you think it might be possible for Constance

Grange to participate personally? At least in this country? It could do a lot for the deal."

"I don't see why not. I'll certainly ask her."

After another fifteen minutes of t-crossing and i-dotting, the meeting concludes. Annabelle offers to drive her guests to the airport. A van is brought around to the front of the building; Mary Ella has seen to it that there's a foam mini-cooler of Summerhill products for each guest.

There's time, so Annabelle takes the scenic route to Asheville International Airport; she wonders whether she should detour them by the site she has in mind for her art institute, but decides not to. Everything in its own good time. Make haste gradually.

As they're pulling up to the general aviation terminal, Irving leans forward from the back seat and asks Annabelle, "I'm trying to remember. Mrs. Grange's husband. He's a film director, isn't he?"

"He is."

"Wasn't his last picture a real bomb? What was it called?"

"*Crown Heights,*" replies Annabelle. "I didn't think it was Clifford's best, although I don't think it deserved the violent reception it got. It was a picture that took no prisoners; he tends to be that way. Too strong for most audiences, I imagine."

"I take it you didn't like it?" Irving's pushing Annabelle toward a place she doesn't want to go.

"To be honest—I didn't," she answers. "It was...well, it was painful to watch. We have enough division in this country as it is. Lord knows, people all have their faults, but I like to think we're better than what Clifford showed us. Although he's actually a very sweet man—and devoted to his family. My goodness, just look at all those airplanes! Asheville is certainly growing up!"

Inside the terminal, she shakes hands with Irving and Alfred, embraces Cecile and Denyce.

"Okay," says Cecile. "All systems are go, then?" She gives two thumbs up to Annabelle, who returns the gesture. They embrace, and as Cecile turns away, she adds, "You just keep doing what you're doing, and keep Constance Grange doing what she's doing, and come the first of the year, we're going to have a smash hit on our hands! And do keep us posted on any exciting new developments."

"Honey, you can count on it," says Annabelle.

CHAPTER THREE

October 21

At just after eleven, a NetJets Cessna Citation disembarks Annabelle and her baggage at Westchester County Airport, where a hulking black Cadillac Escalade is on hand to convey her from White Plains to the studio complex in the Brooklyn Navy Yard. At 12:30 p.m. on the dot, the SUV slides to a stop next to the converted loft building that now houses BBN Productions; a young production assistant is out front to greet Annabelle.

Before going inside, Annabelle pauses for a moment to savor the day. There's a fine fresh breeze off the nearby river, salt on the wind, a gull's cry. It's difficult to imagine that she's only ten minutes from Wall Street—or in the twenty-first century. Then she follows her escort through a security checkpoint and into a capacious freight elevator manned by an armed operator. At the fifth floor, the elevator shudders to a stop and Annabelle is conducted down a long, sunny hall to a door marked with a silver star decal so discreet it's practically invisible. The assistant melts away as Annabelle presses the buzzer. The door opens, and there's Connie herself, smiling, a cell-phone pressed to her ear, gesturing "Come in, come in!" She blows her guest a quick kiss, makes a swirling "Won't be a minute" gesture with her hand, turns away and goes back across the room to the window where she resumes her conversation in a low voice.

Annabelle waits impatiently for Connie to finish. She's so full of good news she's about to burst. The previous week, just ten days after the First Gotham visit, at Wal-Mart global headquarters in Bentonville, Arkansas, Annabelle had signed the biggest deal in Summerhill's history, a deal that she had initiated and that had taken three months to negotiate.

The deal will be announced by Wal-Mart after the New York Stock Exchange closes. Thank goodness for that, because the hardest part has been keeping it secret. Not even First Gotham knows. When she finishes with Connie, Annabelle will call Cecile at First Gotham and tell her the news, maybe even invite her to the Cosmopolitan Club for a celebratory cocktail.

This will be a huge new departure for everyone involved. For the first time in Wal-Mart's history, the giant retail chain will carry an exclusive personality brand: Constance Grange. The way the Wal-Mart people see it, it's a way into those "blue state" urban and suburban markets that had so far put up impossibly stiff opposition to "big box" stores. Connie appeals across all social and economic classes, and Wal-Mart is banking on that. The objective is to lure shoppers in with a range of new Constance Grange products that will be available only at Wal-Mart and that won't compete with Summerhill's existing lines. BME Media is also getting ready to roll out a Constance Grange monthly *Homestyle* magazine that will also be exclusive to Wal-Mart, which is also negotiating with BBN about becoming a preferred sponsor of Connie's show, although the star won't be asked to shill for Wal-Mart, or to act as a Wal-Mart spokesperson.

On the Summerhill side of the deal, Annabelle reckons the projected Wal-Mart contribution could kick her bottom line up twenty percent! And since it's Connie who's made this possible—without her, there'd be no Wal-Mart deal—Annabelle plans to increase Connie's stock participation from $75 million to $100 million, on a basis that will be virtually tax free, according to Summerhill's accountants. When she tells Connie about this, she may just faint!

Annabelle's also nursing exciting news of her own. Tomorrow morning, she's meeting with the chairman of NYU's art history faculty to review their suggestions for an international panel of experts to advise on her art institute. And the week after next, she'll be meeting with the leading museum architect of the moment in Milan.

Connie's "dressing room" is essentially a loft: a single huge space—it must be thirty by fifty feet—artfully divided by screens into a series of functional "rooms": lie-down, makeup, wardrobe, and so on. Windows that must be eight feet tall give a breathtaking panoramic view down the East River, from the Williamsburg Bridge to the Statue of Liberty. The décor is plain, pleasant, and functional. Very Connie, very personal, with lots of family photographs. The Grange Christmas card of two years ago: Connie, Clifford, and Jenny in Santa hats, in front of Grangeford, posed as if about to throw snowballs at the camera. Connie with Clifford and Annabelle at last year's Emmy Awards, the women smiling, Clifford trying his best to look genial, bless him. Connie and Jenny on horseback, at the Granges' summer place in Michigan. Connie and her daughter on a sailboat. The Granges on the beach at Sainte-Eulalie in the Caribbean, where they go every Thanksgiving. Connie and Ronald Barrow at a charity lunch. Connie and Ronald Barrow in Las Vegas, at last year's BME affiliates' meeting. Connie and Clifford on their wedding day, standing in front of the church flanking Clifford's father, the old general turned out in full dress uniform.

One photograph that she doesn't recall seeing before catches her eye. Slightly yellowed, it shows Clifford, then just a boy, standing next to his father. The Washington Monument rises vaguely in the background. To judge by appearances, the general was about the same age then that Clifford is now, in his early fifties, maybe a bit older. The likeness is unmistakable, father to son, son then to son now: the same lean, narrow, beaky features, the challenging dark-eyed stare. More softly molded in the boy, more pronounced and obvious in the man.

Finally, Connie ends her conversation and skips over to Annabelle. The two women throw their arms around each other. "Oh, Belle, darling, I am *so* happy to see you!" Connie exclaims. "Welcome, welcome, welcome!"

Annabelle steps back and studies her star. "My goodness gracious, girl," she declares, "whatever you're eating for breakfast, I want some! Constance Grange Signature Oat Grains, I trust?"

"You bet."

"Well, you look fabulous!"

"And so do you, and so do you!" Connie peers into Annabelle's face. "Is that a rosy glow I see? Is something going on that I should know about? Has Mr. Right finally come down out of those great big blue-green Smoky Mountains and swept you away?"

"I'm afraid not. But I'm not complaining. Now, I've got some news..."

She doesn't get to finish the sentence because the buzzer sounds, and Connie goes to the door and ushers in a brace of waiters, clad in what Annabelle recognizes as the Four Seasons restaurant's autumn livery, who wheel in two serving carts. Annabelle decides that her good news can wait until dessert. She picks up the photo of Clifford and his father and asks, "Have I seen this before? I don't remember it. It's darling."

"It is sweet, isn't it? It was taken in 1965, just after Henry got his second star and was assigned to the Pentagon."

"Amazing how alike they are. How is Clifford, anyway? And Jenny? And how was Sleeping Bear? Did you have a good time?"

"The lake was wonderful. For me, it's like being reborn and Jenny loves it. And Clifford's fine. I mean, you know, how he is: tell him to stop talking during a TV program and he'll start muttering about the Bill of Rights. We've had to make a rule. No politics at the dinner table. But all in all he was a very good boy at the lake. He knows how I love it there and he holds his peace."

"No improvement on Clifford's work front, I take it? No signs of a thaw with Ronnie?"

Connie shrugs and shakes her head. "None. I think Clifford's kind of given up. Did I tell you he now refuses to fly on any of Ronnie's planes? Frankly, I think that's not only insulting, it's stupid. You know how we always go to Sainte-Eulalie for Thanksgiving?"

"Of course."

"And you know that it's not exactly easy to get to?"

"I gather that's the point of the place. Don't you have to change planes in Antigua?"

"*And* in St. Maarten. Anyway, since he's boycotting 'Air Barrow,' as he calls it, my darling husband's going to miss an entire day on the island—unless he leaves on Tuesday. Which of course he can, since he has nothing to do. Nothing. I do wish Ronnie would grant him an amnesty if only for the sake of our family life. It's really amazing how scared of Ronnie everyone in Hollywood is. Of course, Clifford had no call to go after Ronnie the way he did. The movie stank and would have died without Ronnie lifting a finger. Anyway, there we are. Are you about ready, Bruno?"

"Just another minute, please, Mrs. Grange."

"Still, I gather Clifford manages to keep busy?"

"If you can call it that. He shuffles papers in his studio. Watches DVDs. He has this idiotic idea that someday, somewhere, someone's going to give him $300 million to make a four-part epic of Wagner's *Ring* set in Las Vegas. The high spot of his week is Wednesdays when he goes into the city to his club. At least it gets him out of the house, thank God, and leaves me one day to myself." She thinks over what she's said, and adds, "Look, I don't want to sound critical. But it does give me a chance to...to catch up with my letters and stuff without him clumping around in the background, whining about how unfair life has been to him. And of course when I suggest that he do something with the local college, teach a film course, something like that, he gets on his high horse and says he absolutely refuses to become what he calls 'a local talent.'"

"All set, Mrs. Grange," the waiter calls out. Silver and crystal sparkle in the fresh light pouring in off the river view; the napery is as fresh.

"Do you think there's anything I could do for Clifford?" Annabelle asks as they sit down. "Do you want me to say something to Ronnie? I'm going to see him this afternoon."

"Are you? What about?" Connie glances at her in a hard, suspicious way, and then her face softens as she dishes out the salad. "Anyway, that's sweet of you, Belle, but I really don't think that now is the right time. Everything is going so well. You know how Ronnie is. My guess is he's forgotten about Clifford's little tantrum, but if we bring it up, it'll only rub salt in the old wound. Do we really want to rock the boat?"

Annabelle shakes her head. "I guess not." *Not with Wal-Mart, the IPO, everything else that's going on,* she thinks. A rocked boat gathers no steam. *What a complex woman you are,* she thinks, studying Connie as she finishes serving herself. She has a face that inspires trust, opens hearts, invites confidence, compels respect, and yet, somehow, provokes a sort of sexual fantasy. A smart face, an honest face—and yet seductive. Alert, respectful, cheerful—and yet come-hither. But the key to Connie, in Annabelle's judgment, isn't her looks or physical presence, it's her aura. She is every inch and every decibel a lady: not upper-class, not snooty, mind you, but generous, poised, sure of herself. More than one writer with a long memory and a Social Security check in the mailbox has called her "the brunette Grace Kelly." Others—younger—describe her as "Diane Keaton without the ditz." There's nothing vulgar about Connie, nothing dirty or low. She projects what people used to think of when they said *"noblesse oblige,"* before the term became one of mingled snobbery and deprecation. And yet sex is definitely part of the equation, too. People always said Grace Kelly had the hottest pants in Hollywood, and while those kinds of rumors don't swirl about Constance Grange, her sex appeal is definite and lively—and lucrative.

For the next half-hour, the two friends make small talk. Finally, when they've finished the sorbet, plates have been cleared, and the serving carts taken away, Annabelle feels the mood and moment are as auspicious as they're going to get. She's relaxed, the old bond is securely in place, and she feels good about everything. She looks at Connie with affection and delight. *Ready or not, my dear, here comes $100 million.*

"Honey, I have something very exciting to tell you," she begins. "But you must promise not to breathe a word about this to *anyone*, not even to Clifford..."

And that's as far as she gets. Connie reaches quickly across the narrow table and places a finger on Annabelle's lips. "No!" she cries out. "No, no, no! Me first. I have something to tell you! I'm about to burst!"

And with a terrible smirk, an expression Annabelle has never before seen, Connie plunges a hand into the pocket of the smock she wears off the set, pulls out an oversized folded bit of cardboard, and thrusts it at Annabelle. Annabelle takes it, looks it over quickly, and feels the bottom of her world fall out. The expression on Connie's face, the tone of her voice, and, above all, the face on the card Annabelle's just been handed add up to a situational equation whose meaning is instantly, horribly clear.

The card Annabelle's been handed is an invitation to a "Black Tie & Champagne" opening at an art gallery in Coral Gables, Florida. She can tell at once it's the sort of gallery one finds in the hotel lobbies and shopping avenues of swank resorts, usually located between a jeweler and a florist, whose "art" can appeal only to a transient clientele with too much money and an anxious compulsion to spend. The art-world equivalent of a Wall Street bucket shop, a place a serious art lover wouldn't be caught dead in.

The title of the exhibition—ALEJANDRO: NEW AQUASCAPES— is embossed on the front in large, raised, scarlet letters. On the facing flap is pasted an artily lit color photo of a swarthy, Latin-looking man, black shirt open to display a thick gold chain twining through an obscene thicket of curly dark chest hair. He's posed in front of a painting, a large mural apparently, painted in a facile, unconvincing manner in garish, not quite Day-Glo colors of fish, coral, and other forms of aquatic life. The kind of stuff that sells by the yard in Florida. Her eye immediately dismisses the work as second-rate poolhouse art. She focuses her attention on the man, and her insides churn as she feels Connie's hand on hers, and then hears Connie murmur, in a low, confiding tone, "Isn't he sexy! Isn't he divine?"

The man in the picture could be forty-five, he could be fifty-five, it's hard to tell. He *is* definitely handsome—in a swaggering, cynical, been-around Latin way, with sleepy dark eyes, a strong nose, a mocking slash for a mouth, and thick, glistening hair swept back at the sides and gel-ruffled at the forehead. A gigolo to the life. Trouble with a capital T.

"Well, he certainly is," Annabelle replies. She's trying to buy time to sort this out and figure how to play it. *Dear God, please don't let this be what I think it is.* But she knows it is. How often has she heard her friends express their fears that their daughters will fall for the wrong sort. Annabelle feels not a shred of doubt that the man whose face adorns the invitation in her hand is the wrong sort, the kind of man you *never* want your daughter to meet, let alone the woman who is your meal ticket, who stands for the sanctity of home, motherhood, marriage, whose entire value as a brand name is based on those values. This could be big trouble. Big. Make that huge!

"He's very striking-looking," Annabelle says. She tries not to telegraph the feelings churning inside her. She's unable to raise her eyes to meet Connie's. She looks at the photo again, fighting for clarity. In her own ears she sounds completely unconvincing, so she continues, hastily, "Well, goodness!" she says uselessly.

Connie lowers her eyes shyly. It's a nice effect, perfectly calculated, perfectly executed, very professional. Then she looks up, eyes now blazing. "Oh, Belle, it's the most exciting thing that's ever happened to me!"

"Tell me all." *Please, please, don't tell me what I think you're going to.*

"Well, it started right after Labor Day..."

"Labor Day! That was over a month ago! And you've never said a word to me until now? You wicked thing!" Now it's Annabelle's turn to play a role. She reaches across the table and takes Connie's hands in hers. "All right," she says, "from the beginning. Every last detail."

"Well, as I said, it was just after Labor Day. The Wednesday, actually. Jenny and I had gotten home from Sleeping Bear that morning, but by early afternoon I was all alone at Grangeford."

"Where were Clifford and Jenny?"

"Jenny had rushed off to Fairfield practically the moment we got home. You know how kids are. Never a free minute. She was sailing over to Fishers Island with friends."

"And Clifford?" Clifford's the one Annabelle's worried about.

"He was wending his way back flying commercial—I told you, he won't set foot on one of Ronnie's planes—and he missed his Detroit connection and wasn't going to be able to get back until late that night."

"I see."

"Well, I was feeling itchy, the way I usually am when I get back from Sleeping Bear, feeling kind of betwixt and between. You know how I am with time on my hands."

"I keep telling you that you should have a garden."

"I know you do, but I hate flowers. Anyway, all of a sudden I remembered that there was a perfectly enormous house going up not far from where we live that one of the magazine's editors has been after me to look at as a possible feature for the lifestyle magazine. One of those twenty thousand square-foot McMonsters that people insist on building nowadays."

"Twenty thousand square feet? Goodness, that is quite a house. Who's building it?"

"Some woman in Miami whose husband left her a bunch of Spanish-language broadcasting stations. Apparently she only plans to occupy it for two, perhaps three, months a year in the autumn. To watch the leaves change, can you believe it! I guess the leaves on palm trees don't change color. Anyway, I dug out the memo I'd been sent—*Architectural Digest* and the other so-called 'shelter books' have been all over the owner and her architect and her decorator to do it—but our editor thought that if I was to push for it personally, we might get an exclusive. Anyway, it wasn't far away, maybe a half-hour drive from us, up in the hills on a little lake, and there I was with time on my hands. So I decided to go take a look."

"Without an appointment?"

"I reckoned I could peek in the windows, get a sense of whether it might be something we'd ever want to do. I figured if I went at five thirty, the workmen would've quit for the day and the place would be deserted, but there would still be plenty of daylight for me to look around."

"What about security? Don't they have guards?"

"In this part of the world, people stick up an ADT sign and figure that's that. At least until they move in the plasma screens and Sub-Zeros. I'd be gone a couple of hours, maybe a bit more, and I knew Clifford wouldn't get back 'til very late. So, at a bit after 5 p.m., I got into the Jeep and drove up there. Just as I expected, the place was deserted. I looked around, and then I tried the front door—and it opened. No alarms went off, so I went in. And then I heard music. Latin music."

"You heard music? Why didn't you turn tail? You could have gotten yourself killed!"

"I thought about it, but then I assumed someone had left a radio on. They do, you know. All the time: the Latinos especially. Up our way, construction crews these days are nothing but. Anyway, I went toward the sound, into a back room—and there Alejandro was. When I walked in on him, he was as surprised as I was."

"I'll bet he was!"

"So there he was, and he had his shirt off and...oh, Belle, it makes me squirm just to think of it! It was like every dirty book you've ever read—I'm almost embarrassed to tell you the story—but suddenly our eyes met, and then he looked at me, at my...well, we knew—we just *knew!*—and the next thing we were...well, you know."

I know! Annabelle tries to keep a smiling, confiding face. *I know!*

Connie pauses, eyes glittering, obviously remembering the moment. Then she goes on: "He has this sort of daybed and the next thing I know I was stretched out on it and, well...you can imagine the rest." She stops short and looks expectantly at Annabelle, obviously wanting approval.

Annabelle can only think: *You fool! You dreadful little fool! Doesn't this idiot know what she's doing? What this could do to everything? She fights for control. Get a grip, girl! Think! Reason! This needn't be the end of the world! It's just a problem. Problems exist to be solved. This is an old, old story. An old, old, trite story. Bad boys cast spells over good girls all the time, but good girls can be brought to their senses. Connie's a good girl. This needn't be the end of the world. It's just sex! Take away the sex, and it's nothing. I hope.*

"No wonder you're glowing," she says as calmly as she can, trying to sound undisturbed, sympathetic. "That's very exciting. I envy you." The words almost choke her. Then, the killer question, whose answer she dreads because she knows what that answer has to be: "So—I take it you're still seeing him?"

"Of course." Connie makes this sound like the most natural thing in the world. "He still has another month to go on the murals he's painting. But don't worry, dear, after he goes back to Miami, that'll be that. It's just a fling."

She studies Annabelle. "Don't look so shocked. I know what you're thinking, but you needn't. I'm very careful. I only see him on Wednesdays, my day off, and only in the afternoon, when...when you-know-who is in the city at his club, Conchita's off at her sister's in Astoria, and Jenny has dance until nine o'clock. Anyway, he goes back to Florida every Friday and doesn't come back until Monday night—and some weeks he doesn't come at all. His client—he's doing a lot of work in her other houses—flies him all over the place in her own jet."

"You're still taking a terrible chance. You know that, don't you?"

"I said not to worry! You're not going to believe this, dear heart, but he doesn't even know who I am! That is, that I'm *who* I am. That I'm...well, you know!"

"I see." How can that be possible? Connie's face is as well known as any in America. On the other hand, people in real life look nothing like they do onscreen. Which is true enough, but hardly any comfort. "Does he know you're married?" she asks.

"Yes. Well, I think so. If he's got eyes in his head." Connie holds up her left hand.

"You *don't* wear your wedding ring!"

"Why not? I wouldn't dream of taking it off! Please, please, *please,* Belle, I beg you: don't worry! It's just a fling! Haven't you ever had a fling?" She looks at Annabelle in a beseeching way, but a second later, something about her eyes and mouth changes, and her face says, unmistakably, *No, I guess you haven't.* The expression lingers for an instant, just long enough for Annabelle to catch it, before Connie starts to backtrack. "Belle, I *promise* you, it's nothing. Nothing! I swear!"

"That may be," Annabelle replies. She keeps her voice level: now is not the time to get mad, now is the time to get smart, to remain cool and think before speaking. She pastes a sympathetic smile on her face. "Believe me, I'm jealous. He's very handsome, very sexy. But I still say that you are taking a terrible chance. If this should get out..."

"How can it? Only you and I know!"

"Accidents do happen. This is the twenty-first century. People get caught. Look at poor Spitzer. Look at Clinton, or John Edwards. Look at Martha Stewart and that insider trading!"

"Not if you plan correctly and take pains! For instance, I *always* call Clifford on his cellphone to make sure he's on the train and then again in New York to make sure he's there."

"How can you be sure?"

"I'm sure, believe me! When I go to meet Alejandro, I wear a big floppy hat with my hair tucked up. And dark glasses. You'd have to have X-ray eyes to know it's me. And I always take my old Jeep with the black windows and the know-nothing license plate. I don't carry any identification. That is, I lock my wallet in the glove compartment."

"I see. And you're absolutely certain no one suspects a thing?"

"No one!"

"And you're sure Clifford doesn't?" The question is rhetorical. Over the years, Annabelle's provided a shoulder for dozens of wives and husbands to weep on. The spouse is invariably the last to know.

"Why should he? What possible reason would he have?"

"Well, he *is* about the most curious person I've ever known," Annabelle observes, keeping her voice level. This is like trying to deal with a spoiled, rebellious sixteen-year-old. "The two of you have been married for quite a while now, and ove0r such a long time, patterns and wavelengths develop within a relationship, and..."

"Belle, I'm telling you!" Connie practically stamps her foot. "He doesn't suspect a thing! You know how men are. They're so self-involved they never know what's going on around them emotionally! Clifford's so tangled up with his own self-pity, he wouldn't notice if I brought Alejandro to his studio and did it on his desk!"

"Fine. I'll take your word for it."

"I should think you should. I've never let you down, have I? Not once!"

Annabelle nods. "No—you haven't." She pauses. They're at the tipping point; she needs to be very, very careful about how she goes forward from here, with what she says.

"You know what I mean, dear heart. The last thing any of us wants is a scandal. I don't have to tell you why. What it could do to your image. All I'm saying is that it seems to me you're taking a terrible chance for an hour or two a week, no matter how good the sex is."

"Oh, Belle, *please*! You're not that cold-hearted, are you? Where's your sense of romance? And don't look at me like that!"

"I'm not looking at you like 'that,' or any other way, honey. I understand, believe me. I was married once myself. It just seems to me that you're risking a very great deal. You say you're not going to get found out, but how can you be sure? There's no such thing as absolute privacy anymore."

"Oh, Belle, *please!* You sound just like my *mother* used to!" She looks at Annabelle with beseeching eyes. It's a nice effect, very convincing. "You do understand, I know you do!" Connie shakes her head, and then continues in a purr. "Please? You're a romantic at heart. Just look at the way you feel about Italy and art!"

Connie falls silent. Annabelle says nothing. For several seconds, the two women seem to study one another, then Annabelle sees a new line of thinking take possession of Connie: her face hardens, she frowns, braces her shoulders, and says, in a really quite unpleasant voice, "Anyway, considering that I spend most of my life making money for you and other people, for you to complain if I ask for a little something personal for myself…"

Annabelle's been expecting Connie to go this way. Now this is no longer about a "fling"; now it's a matter of right, of principle. "Honey," she interrupts, in her best, soothing, sweet Southern voice, "I'm not complaining, just observing. What you do with your feelings and your body is your business, period. And I think you know me well enough to know that money's the last thing on my mind. But do remember how hard you've worked to get where you are. You have millions of people out there who believe in you, to whom you stand for something, who think you speak for them, who think you *are* them. If you get caught, if this should get out, if there should be a scandal, you'll break their hearts. That's all I have to say. It's got nothing to do with me. Or with money."

"'If' is not going to happen. Besides, you know Clifford…even if he found out somehow, do you think he'd make a scandal?"

"He might. But it's really not Clifford I'm concerned about."

"Who then? My audience? They'd understand. They're human beings, too, with human feelings and urges. Besides, what do you care about my fans? All they are to you and Ronnie is money in the bank!"

"I can't speak for Ronnie, but I know that's not how it is at my end, Connie." She looks at Connie sternly. "As a matter of fact, I resent you saying that. As for your fans, yes, they love you. They think of you as a friend, almost as family, but it's more than that. You represent much that they believe in. Values that they respect and cherish. Most of all, they trust you. If there's a scandal, they might see it as a betrayal of that trust. You have to think about that, Connie, you just have to."

Connie pauses before replying. Then: "Belle, believe me, I know all of that, and I've thought about it. And if I thought there was the slightest chance..."

"What about...what about *him?*" Annabelle gestures toward the gallery invitation lying on the table between them. "Men do boast among themselves, you know."

"Believe me, he won't."

Connie's tone tells Annabelle that there's no point in going further down this avenue, that it will only trap them in a maze of ratiocination. "If you say so," is all she can reply.

"Just please try to understand my position, Belle. I have practically nothing that's just *me*, now! I mean, my family has a claim, and you do, and Ronnie does, and the show and the magazine and the rest, and when I add it all up, there's practically nothing left of me that's just mine. Sometimes I feel like a pie that's cut up into little tiny slivers: you have your slice, and Ronnie has his, and Clifford and Jenny have theirs, and then there's the show and the magazine and the books and all those people who tune in...and, well, everyone's making money out of me, not that I'm complaining, seeing as how fairly you all have treated me, but still, why shouldn't I have this little corner of my life that's just mine?"

Annabelle can think of one billion-plus concrete reasons why not. But there's no point arguing dollars and cents with an inflamed libido.

Another avenue occurs to her: "I understand your feelings," she says. "But if Ronnie should find out...well, you know how Ronnie is on certain subjects. And about contracts."

"What do contracts have to do with it?"

Annabelle pauses. She knows she's taking a chance here, but there's no way around it. This is a card she simply has to play.

"You do realize that this could technically put you in violation of your contract? If it gets out and there's a scandal?"

Connie looks puzzled. "What do you mean?"

"There's a clause in your contract about...about your personal conduct. You do remember, don't you? Ronnie's lawyers insisted on it."

"You're not being serious!" Connie looks and sounds furious. "You and Ronnie would never..."

"You're only half-right, I fear. I would never invoke the clause. But I'm not the one who asked for it, and I can't speak for Ronnie. I don't have to tell you how he feels about...well, about something like adult...like infidelity. It's a matter of public record. And right now he's all puffed up about being named honorary chairman of the presidential task force on family values. Have you forgotten that? You and I were at the White House, remember? You even spoke. And very well, too."

"That's just some silly ceremonial thing."

"Not to Ronnie, it isn't."

"All right, let's suppose the worst happens. You're not seriously suggesting that Ronnie would invoke a personal conduct clause on me, are you? On someone who's making him two hundred million dollars a year?"

"You know how Ronnie is. And how rich he is. Two hundred million dollars will not come close to breaking his bank. He's someone for whom appearances count a great deal."

"This is ridiculous!" But for the first time, Connie doesn't sound completely sure of herself. The trouble is, Annabelle knows, with a great actress like Connie, one can never quite be sure of what is genuine and what is artifice.

"I hope it is," Annabelle says. "I just thought I'd better mention it. You know how lawyers can be."

"Anyway, what Ronnie doesn't know won't hurt him."

Annabelle shrugs. "As long as he doesn't find out—and goodness knows I certainly won't tell him! But if he finds out..."

"But he's not going to! How many times do I have to repeat myself?"

Connie leans back and studies Annabelle. "This really isn't about Ronnie, is it?" she says. "You're just putting him up as a straw man. It's really about you! I'm much more important to you—to Summerhill—than I am to Ronnie because you're much smaller than BME, right? It's you who's really worried, right, Belle?"

Annabelle maintains her calm. She shakes her head. "Please don't think that," she says, putting a touch of hurt in her voice.

The ground under her is starting to feel firmer. Like every adulterer Annabelle's ever read about, or heard about, or seen onstage or in a movie, or known personally or heard out, Connie's fighting for a rationale and she's not about to quit, but it's starting to be just talk. There's no point in going on this way. The trick now is to figure out how best to counterattack. Annabelle needs to get off by herself, think things through. She puts a consoling hand on Connie's shoulder. "Look," she says, "I don't want to quarrel with you. We're both grown-ups. Believe me, honey, I am your friend. And I understand. Just be careful, hear."

"Of course I will. You can trust me."

"I know that. And I do. Now—I have something to tell you. Something almost as thrilling for me as your news is for you."

For the next ten minutes, Annabelle explains the Wal-Mart arrangement to Connie. The latter's clearly impressed. Whether sufficiently so to reconsider this dangerous liaison she's entered into only time will tell.

But as for the $100 million stock bonus...well, Annabelle decides that can wait for another day. The Wal-Mart news will be posted on the wire and the Net shortly and will be a matter of public record.

The stock arrangement is Annabelle's little secret; it lies entirely in Annabelle's gift and discretion.

All that can usefully be said has been. It's an awkward moment. Then, fortuitously, there's a knock at the door, and a voice calls out, "Makeup, Mrs. Grange!"

As Connie gets up, Annabelle adds, "One other thing. It looks as if we've cleared the final hurdles for the new Gastonia plant. We hope to break ground next spring."

"That's wonderful," Connie says. "Will there be a ceremony? Will you want me to come down?"

"Of course I will. Gastonia's going to be all about you." She hugs Connie and murmurs, "Please, *please* be careful."

Connie steps back and looks at her. Her eyes seem almost teary with sincerity, an effect she can produce on demand. "Belle, sweetie," she says as she shows Annabelle out, "you can count on it!"

The rest of Annabelle's afternoon goes much better. Cecile and her colleagues are absolutely thrilled by the Wal-Mart news. Not merely as a coup for the Summerhill IPO, but because—by now Annabelle knows how Wall Street thinks—perhaps Annabelle might be willing to help First Gotham get a piece of Wal-Mart's investment-banking business. Afterward, Annabelle proceeds to the skyscraper just east of Columbus Circle that houses Barrow Media Enterprises. She's whisked through the elaborate security process in the lobby and taken to an elevator that speeds her nonstop to the sixty-fifth floor.

Barrow is seated behind his enormous desk. When Annabelle comes in, he stands up, but doesn't come round to shake hands. He stands virtually eye-to-eye with her, and she's certain the gossip is true: there's some kind of platform out of sight behind the desk to make him seem taller, the way some Hollywood stars are said to be photographed. The walls of his office are literally covered in photographs of himself with Presidents and other world or corporate leaders, every one—she suspects—doctored or shot from an angle that minimizes any discrepancies in height, so that Barrow looks, for instance, literally nose-to-nose with Clinton, who's in fact a big man, and every bit as tall as the current president, who occupies a silver frame of honor at the side of the desk, among Barrow's family photographs.

He gestures her to a chair in front of the desk.

"So," he says, "I gather all went well with your friends in Bentonville?"

"The news should be going out just about now."

"Frankly," he says, "I expect this will be a very considerable demographic coup. The White House, you know, has a deep interest in seeing its friends in Arkansas penetrate markets that have heretofore proven resistant. I was speaking to the president on this very subject just yesterday, when I was in Washington to chair a plenary session of the Commission on Family Values."

Annabelle has to chuckle to herself. Barrow, unlike most people, remains a great admirer of Alan Greenspan, and has adopted the former Federal Reserve chairman's deep, throaty timbre and ponderous, oracular way of putting things.

"Well, Ronnie, all I can report is that these folks have massaged the demographics six ways from Sunday—my goodness, they are thorough, and let me tell you, they don't leave one single solitary penny on the table—and just from where we are now they're projecting an incremental $150 million in same-store sales."

"Very gratifying. What other news? I gather you've just come from seeing Constance? How is the dear child? Did she tell you about *Runway?*"

"*Runway?*"

"The new fashion periodical we're rolling out to compete with *Vogue.* Constance will adorn the cover of our inaugural issue."

Connie had said nothing about *Runway,* but there are times when a little white fib can do no harm, so Annabelle replies, "She did. She's very enthusiastic."

"And I have even more exciting news. The vice-president is summoning a two-day panel to meet in Washington sometime late this fall on the present crisis in American marriage—I'm sure you've seen the figures about the rising divorce rate—and the wish has been expressed—'the Oval Office would be most grateful' was how it was put to me—if Constance could deliver the keynote remarks. Even when it comes to promoting virtue, we must never overlook the power of celebrity, must we, Annabelle."

"Of course not."

"Anyway, I'm very glad you found her well. All is well on her home front, I assume?"

Annabelle nods.

"Very good. The happy homes of this great nation are what make us unique, I always say. Her husband, I trust, remains supportive."

"Very."

"Excellent."

Barrow stands up. "I'm very pleased you came by, Annabelle. Unfortunately, I have to be out of here shortly; I have to introduce Nelson Mandela at the Council on Foreign Relations and before I flee, I must review some remarks I'll be making tomorrow night at the Harvard Club. Is there anything you need, anything we can do for you? Theater tickets, an airplane? Have you eaten at Per Se? It's really very excellent, very excellent. A car, perhaps, to take you wherever you're going?"

"That's sweet of you, but as it's a beautiful day, I think I'll walk back. I'm staying at the Academy Club."

"A fine institution. I've been a member there since 1984. So nice to see you again, Annabelle. I'll make sure you're kept posted on all developments at this end, and you'll do the same for us, I'm sure. And all of us at BME are very grateful for all your efforts."

Back in her room at the Academy Club, just off Fifth Avenue in the mid-Sixties, Belle flops back on the bed, stares at the ceiling, and begins to do some hard thinking.

Given this new problem, there is work to do, issues to be resolved, a strategy to be developed. Connie must not be allowed to continue with this madness; too much is jeopardized. Already Annabelle is asking herself: since she knows of Connie's affair, and since she can appreciate the degree of risk it poses to Summerhill's "core asset," what could a scandal mean for her IPO? She can't exactly ask Cecile to translate adultery into dollars and cents. Furthermore, now that she knows Connie's secret, and knows what public disclosure might mean, is she withholding what the lawyers and accountants call "material adverse information"? Should she postpone the IPO until the affair plays out? Should she consult her lawyers? If she does, how should she put it to them? If only she had done her schedule differently—gone to First Gotham first, before meeting Connie—the problem wouldn't exist. Or would it? She can't talk to her lawyers, she decides. They'll counsel disclosure; and no matter what they counsel, the facts will somehow come out, because there isn't a law firm in America that doesn't leak like a sieve.

So here she is, a mere ninety or so days away from achieving the essential giant step toward her life's and her heart's ambition, and now this!

No: not "now this." Now *what*?

Should she go back to Connie and try a carrot-and-stick approach: dangle the $100 million in stock on a conditional basis? Tell Connie: "Give up the lover and the money's yours. Continue with the affair and you can forget it!"

She dismisses this out of hand. Connie would only be insulted. So, too, in her star's shoes, would Annabelle.

Then it hits her: what about the lover? He needs looking into. Is he the sort he seems from his picture: cheap, flashy, a man with a price? Sooner or later, once he tips to who his new sex partner is, assuming he hasn't done so already—for all Annabelle knows, Alejandro could be secretly videotaping his and Connie's sessions (she imagines Connie all over YouTube; the mere thought makes Annabelle choke)—he'll come looking for a payoff. Every day, it seems, the tabloids are bursting with a new scandal in which a discarded lover or mistress goes public about a rich and famous former paramour. Bill Cosby, Michael Jordan: huge stars. Maybe he can be cut off at the pass and paid off now. On the other hand, if he's a kept man, as

Annabelle infers he might be, what about the woman who keeps him, the Miami woman whose house is the scene of the assignations? Suppose she finds out? What is she likely to do? Hell hath no fury...

A dozen scenarios suggest themselves, each more nausea-making than the previous one. *How am I going to get out of this mess?* That's what she's trying to figure out when the room phone rings. To Annabelle's amazement, it's Connie.

"Oh, Belle," Connie says, "our conversation upset me so. I could hardly get through the afternoon! Darling, please don't let's be this way, please! I hate it when we quarrel!"

"Please," says Annabelle, "we don't need to talk right now. Not over the phone. Where are you?"

"Still at the studio." Then a pause, what sounds like a sob. "Belle, I'm just sick about our conversation! I don't know what I can have been thinking to...to....well, you know! And I'm..." Connie's voice breaks off. Annabelle hears a tiny snuffle, a tiny choked sob, a tiny sharp intake of breath, and then: "You're right, of course. Anyway, I'm going to end it with...with...well, you know. What I means is, well, I was supposed to...but I called you-know-who and said I wouldn't be there. Tomorrow or ever again."

"You called him? On your cellphone? He could see the number?"

"Don't worry. I went to Rite-Aid and got one of those prepaid units." She's speaking so quietly Annabelle can barely make out her words. She says nothing, waits.

In a moment, she hears a faint snuffle, then Connie resumes, her voice thick with apology and contrition. "Oh, Belle, when I think of the chance I've been taking! You're so right! If Ronnie *ever*...if Clifford...I must have been crazy! I'm so ashamed! I'm never going to... well, you know what I mean. Never! I promise!"

"You don't have to promise anything, sweetheart. I know you'll do what's best." Annabelle says in her most soothing voice.

"You're not furious with me? I couldn't bear it if you were."

"Not in a million years, dear heart. These things happen. I'm glad you're being sensible."

"Oh, Belle, you're such a good friend. How could I ever..." and so on and so on. It's really very effective. Annabelle can *hear* Connie's tears; she can *feel* her remorse.

That is, she hears, and she feels—but what she can't escape is an instinct that tells her that Connie is lying. That this is all an act. That Connie has about as much intention of giving up her "fling" as Annabelle has of giving up her dream of the art institute.

But what if she isn't lying? Maybe she has seen the light, has reconsidered and repented. But if she is lying, as Annabelle can't help suspecting, well, then, Houston, we still have a problem—which means there has to be a contingency plan. A just-in-case.

Because the problem itself is a real one. Annabelle is absolutely certain of that. Connie's audience might tolerate lewd, immoral behavior in a president or a governor, or in a Hollywood starlet of the moment, but not in Constance Grange. This audience will take this as a personal betrayal, and will wreak its vengeance at the checkout counter and with the TV remote.

Okay, Annabelle thinks: say Connie does what she says and dumps Alejandro. Is that the end of it? For all Annabelle knows, hot sex is as addictive as drugs. For a straight arrow like Connie, the first jolt of illicit sex might prove to be addicting, the way people say that crack cocaine is: just one hit, and you're hooked. Alejandro could prove to be just the first of a series that could run on for however long it takes Connie to reach menopause.

But she can't worry about that. First things first. Stay with the here and the now. How can she determine if Connie's really lying?

She thinks for a while, and then the answer comes to her. She picks up the phone. A minute later, she's put through to the prominent Asheville lawyer who's handled her family's business for close to forty years.

"Heber, I need the name of a good private detective in the Northeast. I have a friend—a college classmate—who thinks her husband's steppin' out on her. She wants to get the goods on him."

Her lawyer's response is immediate. "Tell her to get in touch with Harris Associates up in Providence, Rhode Island. Ask for Peter

Harris, and use my name. Harris is the best. You remember that ugly business with the Reynolds girl and that UNC basketball player a few years back?"

"Of course."

"The trustees used Harris to get the goods on the bookie who set it up. Peter's expensive—but in a class of his own. If you can't get him, well, there's Kroll, and there's Terry Lenzner, both good outfits. Where'd you say your friend lives?"

"Connecticut," says Annabelle. Then she asks, "I assume this Mr. Harris can act quickly?"

"Honey, you give him the green light, he's like NetJets. He'll have an operative deployed within an hour." There's a pause, and then the lawyer on the other end says, "Hold up a minute there. I just thought of something. No point in getting your friend to spend a lot of money with Harris if it don't count."

"What are you talking about?"

"Just a legal thing that I suddenly thought of, that I need to check. You say this friend of yours lives in Connecticut, right? I'll be back to you in five minutes. Ten at most."

Leaving Annabelle puzzled, he rings off. Eight minutes later, he calls back.

"Okay, you can go ahead with Harris. I just wanted to make sure Connecticut still has fault divorce. Somewhere I heard they'd changed the law up there, but apparently not yet."

"What do you mean by 'fault divorce'?"

"Divorce the old-fashioned way, the way we were all brought up. Not just agreeing to disagree, the way it is now most places. Divorce for cause, doubtless a carryover of them old Yankee Puritan traditions. You take the chance; you get caught; you pay the price. The scarlet letter for adultery, or puttin' people in the stocks for being drunk in public."

"We can skip the history, Heber. What's the bottom line?"

"The bottom line is, in that state, the party with the goods, provided they are the goods, that is, hard evidence and not just say-so or gossip or circumstantial speculation, can go into open court and—at a minimum—ruin the other party's reputation and empty their bank account. Nothing seals the deal like a juicy set of dirty pictures. For the people directly concerned, the fun part about fault divorce is the money, whereas for you and me it's the scandal. In a fault state, if a divorce gets adjudicated, the judge can take the misconduct into account when he decides who's going to get how much. In no-fault states, he can't. That's why most divorces in fault states get settled quietly. Folks don't fancy seeing their dirty laundry washed in public. Or their dirty pictures put on display for all to see, especially now with this YouTube thing. Or their Dun & Bradstreet reports on the front page or the evenin' news so that the world knows how much—or, usually, how *little*—they're worth. That's why most states nowadays are going to total no-fault, even though the divorce bar hates it."

"Why is that?"

"Simple arithmetic. It destroys their leverage. You remember that fellow Wigand over in Kentucky, the one who blew the whistle on Brown & Williamson, the one who was on *60 Minutes,* who they made that Russell Crowe movie about?"

"Refresh me."

"Well, what happened there was, the tobacco companies were keen to discredit this fellow, so they had all kinds of investigators diggin' up stuff, and they found out that when Wigand got divorced there had been some a really juicy complaint against him, wife-beating or some such, but they never got to use it because Kentucky's a hunnert-percent no-fault state and any evidence was sealed in the court records so tight it might as well have never existed. They lost their potential leverage. You follow?"

"I suppose so."

"Well, as I said, I thought I heard your friend's home state had gone to total no-fault, which means there's no point in hiring someone as expensive as Harris to gather evidence that don't count or can't be used, but it turns out I was wrong. There's a total no-fault bill *pending* up there, but that's all it is."

"Why is that?"

"Church and state. Catholics hate divorce, as we all know. And it seems the Catholics still have a lot of clout up that way—huge. There's a big Hispanic bloc, but even more important is that the cardinal up there, fellow name of Santiago, Cuban, I think, has the ear of them Indians that own that big casino and are the biggest financial power in the state now that the insurance industry's gone to pieces. Apparently you can't get elected dog-catcher up there without that Indian money. Which puts Cardinal Santiago in the catbird seat. Vote for divorce and forget about any help from the tribes, is pretty much what he's let it be known. And that is why the no-fault bill stays bottled up in the legislature."

"Cardinal Santiago, you say? Is that Joseph Santiago?"

"I b'lieve that's the name. Why? Do you know him?"

"If it's Joseph Santiago, he was a friend of my parents."

"Of course! He was that high-falutin' priest—wasn't a cardinal then—who came out to do your daddy's and Frank's funeral. It's the same fella, isn't it?"

"Sounds like it. Unless he has a twin with the same name. He was kind of a protégé of Daddy's. I haven't seen him in years."

"Well, ain't that a coincidence?"

Yes indeed, thinks Annabelle. *Possibly a useful coincidence? It never hurts to have an ear at court.* "I see," she says. "Anything else?"

"Well, just this: even if Harris does his job and gets the goods, he's just the first step. They play rough up there, especially if there's any real money involved, which means your friend'd do well to sign up a top divorce lawyer who knows all the tricks."

"You have any names in mind?" Annabelle's question is merely a courtesy. Her mind is already off on a different tack.

"Well, there're a couple named Cohen, and Peter Bronstein, of course, and Felder, and Arthur Jekyll."

"I'll keep them in mind. Thanks, Heber."

"Well, good luck to your friend. These things can be a bitch, if you don't mind my sayin' so."

They sure can, Annabelle thinks as she rings off. She utters a tiny shriek of fury and frustration, kicks off her shoes, and throws herself violently back on the bed. The idea of having a private detective spy on Connie repels her. Still...

She picks up the phone and the paper with Harris's number, and then puts them down again. For a moment or two she just lies there thinking. *God bless it!* Why does it have to be that no matter how hard and honestly you work for something, no matter how efficaciously you pray for it, no matter how greatly luck appears to be running with you, whatever the object of your hopes, your passion, your desires happens to be, if there are other people significantly involved, they're going to screw it up for you. Philosophers will tell you that "character is destiny," but what they neglect to point out is how ninety-nine percent of the time, "the character that determines your destiny isn't yours, it's some other SOB's." That was her father's view. If he said it once to his daughter, he said it a hundred times. Well, she can't just sit here gnashing her teeth. The reason folks hire lawyers is to get advice worth taking. She picks up the phone and dials the number for Peter Harris.

CHAPTER FOUR

November 12

"Mr. Jekyll's just on the phone, Mr. Hyde. He'll be with you in a moment. Please make yourself comfortable."

Inwardly, the receptionist finds it hugely amusing that a Mr. Hyde has arrived to consult with her Mr. Jekyll, but she doesn't show it. Her English accent is ever so precise, genteel, dignified and so is her manner. She's entirely of a piece with the décor, the new arrival thinks, smiling to himself, straight out of *Gosford Park*: the same Central Casting bullshit notion of "Olde Englande" that he's encountered in a half-dozen film-industry and Wall Street offices: horse-brasses and gilded mirrors, a gouged and creased leather chesterfield sofa and armchairs, lots of chintz and sporting pictures and views of spire-punctuated meadows and dales and babbling brooks, a glass-fronted bookcase containing tired old sets of the *Waverley* novels and Macaulay. All in all, the visual equivalent, expressed in carved dark wood and polished metal and old leather and molded gesso of the Anglicized nomenclature—Devonshire and Canterbury and Oak Hill and Westbury—in which sleazy bucket shop operators, whether on Wall Street or Rodeo Drive, drape themselves in order to convey an impression of genteel old-money respectability.

He takes off his glasses and vigorously polishes them with the end of his necktie, then crosses the small anteroom to examine a watercolor hanging on the opposite wall, a pleasing if innocuous view of a cathedral seen across a wide meadow. A label on the mount identifies it as the work of John Constable. The new arrival doesn't agree.

The receptionist recognizes the scarlet and gold pattern of the visitor's necktie; her employer has one just like it, which is hardly surprising, considering that it's to discuss "an important matter of club business" that this visitor has made the appointment. The receptionist doubts it. People come here to talk about painful family matters; people discuss club business in clubs. She suspects that "Hyde" also may be a *nom de guerre*. If so, at least the new arrival has a sense of humor, which isn't usually the case with her boss's visitors.

"Can I get you something to drink, Mr. Hyde?" the receptionist asks. "Tea, water, coffee, a Diet Coke?"

He doesn't seem to hear. She repeats his name—"Mr. Hyde?"— and he turns around with a confused look, as if he's uncertain to whom she's speaking, which convinces her that she's right about the false name.

"Oh, uh, no thanks," he replies. "Sorry. I was wool-gathering."

If he sounds discombobulated, he is. He wishes he hadn't come; he's wondering whether it's not too late to bolt—to make some excuse and get out of here. The last thing he needs to do is to get involved with someone like Jekyll. Not yet, at least.

He looks around, then sits down, then gets up again and goes over to the mirror hanging on the opposite wall, an elegant roundel set in a heavy, richly carved gilt frame topped with a fierce federal eagle, all beak and arrow-clutching talons with a stars-and-stripes shield at its breast. He examines himself in the glass and doesn't like what he sees. Is he putting on weight? What's this puffiness around the chin? Too much wine at dinner, he decides. Then he takes a second look and decides he doesn't look so bad after all. He sucks his stomach in and prods his mid-section with stiffened fingers. *Feels hard.* This morning the scale registered one hundred fifty-seven pounds, only a pound more, actually, than at his annual check-up back in May. Not bad for a man of fifty-one. Still, he resolves to cut back on that second glass of wine before dinner. Well, maybe not the second, but the third for sure.

He smooths his hair back, trying not to let his long fingers press down too firmly as they pass over the thinning area just back of the crown. He sets the knot of his tie just so and returns to his seat. The receptionist behind the desk smiles at him; he smiles back. *That smile must get some workout,* he thinks. Working here must be like working for an oncologist. The clients and would-be clients will be people like himself, whose guts have been hollowed out or are in the process thereof. Like cancer, only worse, because no virus, no germ, no spirochete can do to someone's insides what another human being can—especially someone you love or have loved. Well, that's why people use Jekyll. Everyone says the guy is the Tiger Woods of get-even. If your objective is the financial destruction of the opposition, its social obliteration and financial immolation, the dirty washing hung out for all the world to relish, it's generally agreed that Jekyll's your man, a lawyer who leaves them for dead, and then some, and charges twice the going rate for the financial equivalent of body bags. Look at what he did last year to that guy who had been head of a big New York bank: from the cover of *Fortune* to eight months in rehab and a Chapter 7 bankruptcy, all courtesy of Arthur Jekyll, every last miserable detail and digit laid out in the *Post* and *The Star* and on the Web.

He turns around to examine the portrait hanging over the sofa. Its label identifies the painter as "Charles Willson Peale (1741-1827)" and the subject as "Chief Justice John Marshall (1755-1835)." *Figures.* He moves on to the glass-fronted bookcase on the sidewall; on the shelf under the Scotts and the Macaulays is a small group of unmatched volumes, two or three in plain gray buckram collectors' cases. There's a first edition of a novel by Howells, *A Modern Instance,* which he's never heard of. He replaces it and pulls out another, an inch-thick buckram box that contains four printed tracts by John Milton, first editions by the look of the paper and the typefaces: the one on top is *The Doctrine and Discipline of Divorce,* dated 1643; the other three deal with the same subject. He fancies he knows a bit about Milton—*Paradise Lost,* of course, and *Comus* and the more famous poems, but he's never heard of this stuff. He starts to read, then hears a door open behind him. The receptionist suddenly stops clacking away at her computer keyboard and a man's voice says, "Mr. Hyde?"

When he turns around, his first reaction is: Maud and the others at the club table were right: this guy really doesn't look like he's supposed to; there's nothing vulpine or lupine about him. He really does look like a goddamn Irish bartender: square, blunt features under thinning mouse-brown hair fast becoming gray that's neatly parted high on the left temple (no comb-over, thank God, the visitor thinks); the eyes knowing and attentive with a trace of a twinkle, hardly the reptilian glitter one would expect; the mouth's a plus, too: perfectly average, without that snapping-turtle downturn that lips tend to curve into after a few decades of biting off other men's nuts. All in all, a perfectly friendly, inquiring face, which means it's a mask, obviously: a screen behind which a sharp, devious, vicious imagination can operate without giving its game away at the get-go.

The bartender look ends at Jekyll's collar. From there on down, it's strictly the "Manhattan Power Look," as the glossy magazines call that certain way of dressing: the style seen at the Regency Hotel or Michael's at breakfast, the Four Seasons or Le Cirque at lunch, "21" or Elaine's or Elio's or Primavera at dinner: a long-draped, slick-cut double-breasted suit tailored in an unctuous navy-black fabric. The visitor has often thought how appropriate it is that the New York power guys—the elite of Wall Street, the professions, the corporate media (everyone at BME dresses like this), and real estate and all the hotshot wannabes that paddle frantically in their wake—dress like undertakers, because the sons-of-bitches are burying the culture.

The rest of Jekyll's getup consists of a white-collar, striped-body shirt, a fat-knotted Hermès power tie, heavy cuff-links set with red stones, glistening loafers, Milan probably, what they call "bench made." All in all: probably $7,500 on the hoof, maybe more, he calculates, completely befitting the sort of man the gossip columns report on constantly, who has a usual table at so˙ many smart restaurants that it sometimes seems he's having four dinners simultaneously; who has a Mercedes limo—maybe a Bentley—and a timeshare on a Gulfstream to get him from place to place; who drinks $1,500-a-bottle Chateau Petrus when he's not drinking blood, who's automatically brought the "special" pasta at Rao's, whose cellphone is seldom silent, who has Liz Smith and Don Imus and Larry King and *Page Six* and the White House on auto-dial and a due bill out on anyone who's anyone, who can get whatever he wants within the compass of no more than two phone calls, who can pick up the phone at 7:50 p.m. and get a client third-row-center seats for whatever is the hottest show in town.

The lawyer holds out his hand. "How do you do, Mr. Hyde. I'm Arthur Jekyll." He gestures at the pamphlet in Clifford's hand. "A false start, I'm afraid. I started to make a collection of the literature of divorce some years ago; I thought it would invest what I was doing with the dignity of literary association, then found that there was nothing to collect, apart from this scattering, so I abandoned the chase."

His light baritone voice has a rasping quality. It's accentless, the vowels clipped, the consonants emphatic. Nothing "street" about it, certainly nothing "Noo Yawk."

"Frederick Hyde," says the visitor, returning the handshake. His voice rings squeaky in his ear and he wonders if his grip feels as damp and tentative to Jekyll as it does to him.

Jekyll peers closely at his visitor. "Have we met before? At the club?"

"I don't think so. I'm not there all that often. Most of the time I'm in Santa Fe."

"Of course. That's the residence you give in the club book. It must be very pleasant, living there."

"I don't get to the club that often."

"Nor I," says Jekyll, smiling. "As a matter of fact, although I've been a member for what seems forever, in the past twenty years I've only been there twice that I can think of: once, a long time ago, for a memorial service, and then, oddly enough, just eight weeks ago, when I was the Wednesday-night speaker—to the ill-disguised wonderment of all. Now, please—come this way."

They proceed down a short hall, passing three closed doors and a small open area set aside for files and document processing. The atmosphere is hushed and sanitary, as pin clean and shiny as a scalpel.

"We're a small shop," Jekyll says. "One paralegal, one IT specialist, one in-house forensic accountant—and myself. And Ms. Grosvenor out front, of course, my indispensable first line of defense. The fact is, our computers do most of the dog work. If only they could teach these machines judgment, it would be a perfect world. Ah, here we are."

Jekyll occupies a large corner office with fine views north over the park and west to the Hudson. It's a fantastic view, in the visitor's eyes only slightly marred by the looming towers of the BME Center at Columbus Circle, which brings Ronald Barrow to mind for a brief, dyspeptic flash. He takes in the rest of the office. What really strikes him is how moderate and modest it is. He'd expected every surface to be covered with the artifacts of self-esteem, self-validation, and self-promotion usually encountered in the offices of self-important men—like that little prick Barrow. Jekyll's office sports none of the visual equivalents of dropped names: diplomas, civic awards, and certificates; framed letters from presidents or other great personages; photos taken with famous clients, or signed by celebrities. The absence of such is a definite plus, the visitor thinks. But—on the debit side—there don't seem to be any photos of family, friends, or pets, nor anything that looks like personal memorabilia. *Does the guy have a family?*

The books on the shelves seem an interesting mix. Law books, of course, but also an Oxford University Press one-volume Shakespeare with a beaten-up binding, a broken set of cloth-bound Dickens, a half-dozen Trollopes, a row of *Library of America* volumes in well-creased shiny black jackets, and a cluster of books with "golf" on their spines. A putter stands in a corner, along with a tin-flapped practice putting cup.

Off to one side of the wide partners' desk that dominates the office is a snazzy laptop that no doubt incorporates all the latest bells and whistles. Other state-of-the-art equipment is disposed elsewhere around the room. A string quartet—Mozart? Haydn? early Beethoven?—is playing softly on what sounds like a very good sound system. On one wall hangs a large Pioneer Elite plasma TV, about the size of a nice Cézanne, that the visitor knows cost a bundle, because he has one just like it at home, a gift to his wife from a grateful sponsor.

Jekyll sees him looking at it. "A small indulgence," he explains, almost apologetically. "I sometimes get trapped here on weekends, and I don't like to miss watching golf. Are you a golfer, Mr. Hyde? Do you play in Santa Fe? Las Campanas, perhaps? I hear it's a fine course, very testing."

"Um, uh, no, no, I don't. My old man did, though. He was a complete golf nut. He died on the golf course, as a matter of fact!"

"If there's a worthier way to go, I don't know what it is. May the good Lord be as kind to me when the time comes. Your father never tried to convert you?"

"Never."

"A wise man. No field of human endeavor has thrown off richer and more catastrophic Freudian resonances than father-son golf. Trust me, I know whereof I speak. A good many of the more emotionally crippled men I've dealt with in this office have owed their sorry mental estate to competing against their fathers on the golf course."

"You may be right, but that wasn't true of us. My old man tried hard to do a good job as a father. He didn't want any filial resentments lingering on after he was gone. He always used to say that hell is the condition of having to know through all eternity what your children *really* felt about you. Hey, is that what I think it is?" The visitor points to a large, gold-framed document hanging off to one side of the plasma monitor; it appears to be a very old copy of the U.S. Constitution.

Jekyll nods. "A second printing, alas, but a very good example. My pride and joy," he says.

"Wow! That's really something!"

"I think so, too." Jekyll smiles. "The fact is, you've stumbled on my dirty secret. When I'm not taking the bread off the table of widows and orphans and saving the day for wronged men and women, I'm a closet constitutionalist. Constitutional law fascinates me. It's my secret pleasure, my binge food. I'd give all I have to argue a case before the Supreme Court, not that I ever expect to have the opportunity."

Jekyll pauses, doubtless to let this improbable notion take effect. Then he asks: "Anyway, enough of this; we're both busy men. What can I do for you, Mr. Hyde? You're here in connection with an Article X matter, is that right?"

The visitor nods. Article X of the by-laws of the Diogenes Club stipulates, "It being one of the purposes of the Club to encourage creative collaboration, no member shall reasonably refuse the request of a fellow member for professional advice and counsel on a work of clear artistic, literary, or philosophical purpose, provided the request does not offend normal standards of decency or strong personal or political convictions."

The rule was adumbrated to encourage artist-members and writer-members to give each other a hand on artistic undertakings and enterprises. It was certainly not put in for the uses of Jekyll's visitor, who's here under a doubly false flag: not only has he misrepresented his purpose, he's using another member's name. Either is grounds for expulsion. If Jekyll reacts badly, and reports this incident to the club, "Hyde" will surely be asked to resign—and then what will he do with himself?

Well, these are chances that had to be risked. He certainly doesn't want his real name in Jekyll's office log, which for all he knows is open to every pair of eyes in this office, and therefore a potential conduit to the gossip media. It's common knowledge that the press routinely pays off the paralegals and secretaries of top divorce law-yers to sell out their employers and their employers' clients. Now that he's finally face to face with Jekyll, however, there's no need for further subterfuge. He takes a deep breath, then says, "Well, actually, Mr. Jekyll..."

"Please. Call me Arthur."

"As you wish. Well, um, well, Arthur, the fact is, I'm afraid I'm here under a bit of a false pretense. My name isn't Hyde. I happened to know he's in the Far East, so I borrowed it. Actually, my name is Grange. Clifford Grange. My wife is a woman called Constance Grange. Perhaps you've heard of her?"

"I have, of course. Who hasn't? I take it you're the film direc-tor?"

"Guilty as charged."

Jekyll breaks out into a great, wide, beaming smile. "Well, well, well," he says. "I am very pleased to meet you. Honored, in fact. What was the last film of yours that I've seen? Ah, yes, *Crown Heights*. Three or four years ago—could it have been that long?"

"Four years come July," Clifford replies. He shakes his head at the memory. "Tell me, how the hell did you see *Crown Heights*? Those bastards at BME Films left it in the theaters for about three minutes."

Jekyll smiles. "When I read in *Variety* that the film was going to be recalled, it made me curious. I have my spies in Hollywood; in my business, you have to. One of them sent me a pre-release DVD."

"You're lucky. I hope you've still got it. Most of those discs were melted down for scrap. Someday it might be worth as much as that copy of the Constitution over there. So what did you think?"

"It was a very daring film, if I may say so. I gather certain people found it offensive?"

"Merely Jews, blacks, Catholics, Irish, and Italians. And let's not leave out WASPs, who hated the main character."

"Which suggests that you must have done something right, to have offended so many. What are you working on now?"

Clifford shakes his head. "Nothing, I regret to say. Nothing seriously, at least. It would be a total waste of time and creative energy. The fact is...well, for the past couple of years, I've been blacklisted."

"Blacklisted?"

"That's my call," Clifford says with a shrug.

Jekyll doesn't seem as shocked as Clifford would have expected. "Goodness," he says mildly. "I thought that sort of thing went out with Senator McCarthy and the House Un-American Affairs Committee."

"Don't you believe it. Now that a half-dozen people control ninety percent of the media—the Internet excepted—censorship is alive and well everywhere you turn. In my case, it's my own damn fault. I'm sure you know who Ronald Barrow is?"

"I do indeed. Barrow is Mr. Sanctity-of-Marriage, you might say, and therefore I am his arch fiend. What he claims in his posturing way to keep together through his National Marriage Foundation, not to mention this ludicrous presidential commission on family values, I rend asunder."

Clifford snickers. "And I thought I was the little runt's enemy of choice. What happened in my case was that when the political correctness crowd took after *Crown Heights*, and Barrow caved and pulled the picture from theaters and cancelled the DVD release, I blew my First Amendment stack and said some things I shouldn't have. Loudly, eloquently, and in public. That is, I let my boyish temper get the better of me and got personal on the subject of Barrow on *Charlie Rose,* no less. About Barrow being so short, because I knew that would really get to him. And it did."

Jekyll smiles. "You may have wisdom on your side. My old mentor, Martin Crockett, used to say that ninety percent of the world's problems can be traced to three sources: sex, money, and short men."

"He had a point," Clifford says. "Anyway, Barrow put the word out—hell, maybe all he did was look cross—that anyone who worked with me was never going to work with him—or BME, or BBN, or B-whatever, and the short story is, my professional goose was cooked, and now it's in the deep-freeze."

"I see. Well, nothing goes on forever. And they say this is a free country." Jekyll sighs and looks at the ceiling. Then he returns his gaze to Clifford. "Now, how can I help you?"

"I'm not sure you can. I have to tell you, I'm nervous being here. You're sure that what I tell you won't get out of this office?"

"Well, there is such a thing as attorney-client privilege."

"That may be. But your cases have a way of finding their way to *Page Six*."

"Only when I want them to," says Jekyll in that mild but firm way of his. "Still, I can understand your concern. Your wife being who she is, if it were known that you were coming to see me, people might get the wrong idea."

"Actually," says Clifford, biting down hard, "what really worries me is that people might get the *right* idea."

For a moment, Jekyll says nothing. The expression on his face doesn't change save for a slight tightening around the eyes and mouth. Finally, he nods, more to himself than to Clifford. "I see," he says. "I'm sorry to hear that. Perhaps you'd better tell me about it."

"Well," Clifford says, speaking faster now, as if to get the words out before he changes his mind. "It would seem that my wife is having an affair. Actually, make that: my wife *is* having an affair!"

"Do you know this for a fact?"

"I do know it for a fact."

"You have proof?"

"I do." Clifford hesitates. *In for a penny.* "The works," he continues. "Dirty pictures. Triple-X camcorder stuff—all in living color."

"May I ask how these were obtained? By a private investigator, I assume? I wish you'd come to see me before you did that. Those people aren't always reliable."

"No worry on that score. The goods were gotten by me. Me, myself, and I, up close and personal—on my own camcorder through a lighted window."

"I see. Do you have them with you? Perhaps we should look at them."

Clifford shakes his head. Mad and hurt as he is, he can't bring himself to the point of letting Jekyll or anyone else see Connie... with...that...that guy.

"The stuff's safely hidden away at home. In my office safe. And there it will stay. That way, it doesn't end up on Gawker or YouTube or some X-rated Web site. Unless, of course, in a thirst for vengeance that I don't quite feel as yet, I decide that it should. But that will be my call."

"I understand," says Jekyll. "Now—do you know who her paramour is?"

"The other guy? He's some kind of a painter, apparently."

"A house painter or an artist?" Jekyll asks. His expression makes clear that his experience of paramours embraces both categories.

"An artist. That is, I think he is: there's paint tubes and cans and brushes and stuff like that lying about the room. He's working in a big house that's under construction about fifteen miles from where we live."

"Does he have a name?"

"Not that I know. I haven't wanted to be seen asking questions in the neighborhood. My personal nickname for him is Donkey Dong. I assume I needn't amplify on that."

"You certainly needn't. And rest assured that I am fully cognizant of the consequences of any of this finding its way to the public. Now, please take it from the beginning. Leave nothing out that might be pertinent. I ask only one thing from you: complete forthrightness. I've been at this business too long. I am a connoisseur of prevarication and dissembling and every other kind of lying and humiliation ducking and false witness you can imagine. People have tried to feed me more red herrings than there are real fish in the sea. If you want me to help you, I need to know everything. To be either disingenuous with me or selective with the facts will prove both offensive to me and unproductive and very expensive for you. Can we agree on that?"

"Fair enough." Clifford gathers himself. According to *Page Six*, Jekyll charges $2,500 an hour, so he's already a couple of grand in the hole. "Message received," he says. *Keep this as factual as you can*, Clifford tells himself: no sarcasm or irony, and no tears either, no lamentations, no keening or rending of garments. He doesn't want to be misinterpreted: he's hurt and he's angry, but he can't—and he won't—let those feelings incapacitate his sense of what's at stake overall. He feels a degree of sexual humiliation, but nothing like what he would be going through had this happened, say, ten years ago. He feels entitled to some kind of retribution, but he's not sure what kind, and he can flatter himself that he's not out of control with a thirst for revenge. He's simply here to explore his options with the divorce lawyer who by common consent is the smartest, toughest, and most ruthless—therefore the best. Maybe Jekyll can come up with some kind of "neutron bomb"—which would punish Connie but leave their life together intact. If things get rough, he'll have locked up Jekyll before Connie can hire him.

"Okay," he says. "Connie and I will have been married fifteen years come Christmas."

"In church or by a judge?"

"At Saint George's, Stuyvesant Square. By the rector."

"Any children?"

"One. A thirteen-year-old daughter named Jenny. Actually, her baptismal name is Guinevere. She hates it."

"Tell me about your life at home."

"Well, the first word that comes to mind is boring. The second is nice. The third is stable—up to now. Connie works her tail off four days a week. She leaves for the studio at 6:30 a.m. and gets home around 6 p.m. Wednesdays she has off. On the weekends she and Jenny do their *Gilmore Girls* routine, which consists of equal parts of shopping, giggling, and spoiling each other's day."

"Social life?"

"Well, it's not that we're reclusive, but we tend to limit our socializing to where it has to do with our daughter: kids' awards dinners at the yacht and tennis club, stuff like that, or stuff that's strictly professionally motivated. A few charity events—mostly when it's something the Great God Barrow's got a hard-on about—and of course she does the wave-the-flag stuff, stuff that goes with the territory: trade shows and affiliate get-togethers. Our life inside the gates is strictly private. Connie wants it that way and so do I. No publicity, period. No *People,* no *Us Weekly.* Paige Rense at *Architectural Digest* has been begging Connie for years to 'do' our house, but no soap, although now that Barrow Publishing is doing a shelter book of their own, she may relent. Of course, a scandal would change everything; we'll have paparazzi where we now have rhododendrons. And you can say 'kaput' to her career."

"How about when just the two of you are alone together?"

"It's fine. Listen, I know movie-star marriages where it got so bad they'd start hitting the bottle the second the clock chimed six, and by seven were hitting each other *with* the bottle; I know marriages where silence was the rule. I know every kind of bad or flawed celebrity marriage, and believe me that's not—that *wasn't*—us. Connie doesn't bring the show home with her and when she's around, I keep my grievances to myself. At least I try."

"Fine. Now, turning to recent events, how did they unfold?"

"Fine. Okay, we got home from Michigan..."

"Michigan?"

"Sorry. I should have said that we spend August at a place on a lake in Michigan that Connie's been going to since she was a girl. That's one of our two big family vacations."

"And the other?"

"Every Thanksgiving we go to the Caribbean for five or six days. To Sainte Eulalie, which is in the Lesser Antilles. It's super-private."

"So I've heard. Now, back to Labor Day this year."

"Okay. Well, on the Wednesday morning after Labor Day, we closed the lodge at the lake and came home. That is, the girls did. My flights got screwed up so I didn't get back until close to midnight."

"You don't fly together?"

"They were flown home on one of Barrow's jets. I won't fly on a Barrow airplane. As a matter of principle."

"I see."

"Anyway, when I got home, everything seemed normal. Jenny was off on an overnight sail to Fishers Island and Connie was in bed, fast asleep."

"She'd been home for a while then?"

"Between Barrow helicopters and Barrow jets, they were home by noon."

"I see."

"Anyway, when I got home—we're talking late Wednesday, September 3—Connie seemed a bit irritable. I put it down to my waking her up—she was definitely not keen to snuggle—and to my insistence on not flying Air Barrow. The next day, all was quiet, since Connie was away most of the day, looking at a bunch of houses in our vicinity that they're thinking of using in the new magazine."

"Including, I assume, the house where the...the paramour is working?"

"Which, of course, I didn't know at the time. Anyway, over the next few days and the weekend, we kind of circled each other warily, what with Connie being so touchy, which I attributed to Jenny's being away—you have no idea how close those two girls are—and the prospect of going back to work in ten days. Anyway, Jenny got home Sunday night, and Connie got herself all involved in back-to-school shit and I managed to lose myself in the general shuffle. Which brings us to Wednesday, September 10, which I am now starting to think of as a day that will live in infamy, although I didn't then!"

"Tell me about it."

"That was the day Connie was scheduled to take Jenny to the city for a whole bunch of doctors' appointments and so on. But when she woke up that morning, she said she had the flu, so I filled in for her—which is why I missed your talk at the club. She was up and about when we got home late that evening—Jenny and I had done the whole father-daughter bit after the doctors: shopping, theater, dinner—and said she felt a whole lot better, and she looked a lot better. The next day, she was still home—she had the week off, shooting wouldn't start again until the following Monday—and although she seemed A-okay physically, she was really cranky, as if her previous irritability had been taken to the nth power. Which is to say: she jumped all over me."

"Had your daughter started school?"

"In a manner of speaking. Field hockey practice had started, which left Connie and me alone in the house with Conchita. Anyway, by now I've learned to make allowances, and I figured it was the lingering effect of her brief bout with the flu, or maybe it was PMS or whatever, but I just went and hid in this little studio outbuilding I have down at the end of the property. The week and the weekend came and went, she went back to work, Jenny started school, and I figured serenity would return, but when she was in the house, I'd now and then catch her looking at me like I was something she'd stepped in. I'm telling you all this because I don't want you to think I hit the panic button right away. But by the following weekend —that'd be the weekend of the thirteenth of September—I was beginning to feel that what at first seemed like mere irritability on her part was turning into something...well...pathological. That something was seriously wrong."

"How so?"

"To begin with, I was now feeling a slight but distinct change in what you might call the climate of our marriage, a shift in barometric pressure, in the feel of the air. My old man used to say that marriage is like living by the sea. You become hypersensitive to the tiniest changes in the color of the sky or the feel of the evening air, the wind in the rigging, the way the sound of a ship's bell or a foghorn carries. Small signs that can ultimately mean 'Here comes Katrina!'"

"I see."

"Obviously, being a guy, my first reflex was to wonder if something wasn't up in the sex department, but—hell!—where would she find the time, or the opportunity? Besides, sex has never been that big a deal with her. And she gave off none of the overt signals. I mean, she didn't suddenly start lapsing into dreamy silences, or develop an unaccountable silvery laugh, or sigh a lot. There weren't phone calls hastily answered and just as hastily hung up if I drifted into the bedroom. I didn't find any unexplainable bits of paper lying around, phone numbers I didn't recognize, unfamiliar initials inside hearts scratched on trees, stuff like that."

"So what ultimately aroused your suspicions?"

"The following week, on Wednesday, September seventeenth, I was in the city for Robert Hughes's talk at the club. It was around four o'clock, and I was just about to go into the club when I remembered that I'd forgotten to set the DVR to record a program on BBC, so I called home to ask Connie to take care of it for me. I couldn't raise her: either at home or on her cell, which I thought was pretty odd because she's *always* home on Wednesday afternoon, but I figured her cell was out of range or out of power, whatever. But then I called again, around six-thirty, just before going upstairs to dinner, and she still wasn't home."

"And she usually is?"

"Always. She and I are not merely *creatures* of habit, we are *slaves* of habit. It's one reason we get along. I'm a military brat. I grew up with reveille, the sunset gun, the orders of the day, the mess calls, retreat, taps, all that stuff. Her old man was an Iowa banker, but he also worked a big farm. You know: up with the cows, et cetera."

"And when you got home, did she have an explanation?"

"Of course. She'd driven over to the Whole Foods near Stamford, and then done some more shopping, and the battery in her cell was out. But I didn't believe her. I don't know why, I just didn't. And then, a couple days later, something else got my attention. Well, actually Jenny called my attention to it by complaining about it."

"And what was that?"

"Connie has always made a big deal about no—that's N-O in capital and neon letters—work on weekends, about keeping the time sacred and apart for her family. But over the next two weekends, suddenly, she spent time—a good bit of Saturday, most of Sunday—dealing with matters—studio paperwork, BME stuff—that she had to get out of the way, but that she always used to take care of on Wednesdays, her day off, while Jenny was at school and I was in the city."

"So...?"

"Well, by my lights, when someone stops doing something they've always done at a certain time or on a certain day, or both, and starts doing said something at a different time, on a different day, it's usually because they've found something else—or something better—to do with the earlier schedule."

"A reasonable premise."

"So—I asked myself—if Connie's no longer doing what she used to do on Wednesdays, what's she doing instead?"

"You might have asked her."

"Ask Connie a direct question she doesn't want to answer, she'll talk circles around you. I figured I could find out for myself. And then there were the other mysterious phone calls."

"Mysterious phone calls? I thought you said there weren't any?"

"Not *to* Connie, *from* Connie. To *me*. On my cellphone. On the train. On the street in Manhattan. I'd get on the train, and before we passed Darien, she'd be calling, and again around Mamaroneck. Or I'd be walking down Park Avenue and...brrrinnng!"

Jekyll slides his reading glasses off and examines them, thinking. Then he tips them back on. "I see. Your theory is that she was calling to check—to be certain—that you were where you were supposed to be."

"You and I have read the same detective stories. Yes, that's how I figured it."

"I suppose it is possible that she was concerned that it might be *you* up to something?"

Clifford shakes his head. "Are you kidding? She takes me completely for granted. And for good reason. Anyway, I decided to run a little field test. The next Wednesday—that would be September 24—I announced that *I* had a stomach flu and was going to skip the city and the club and stay home, especially since it was pouring outside. I wanted to see how Connie reacted."

"And how did she?"

"Not well. The look that passed over her face when I gave her the news was definitely less than loving. Anyway, I crept back upstairs to bed—or pretended to—and then I heard the kitchen door close, so I went to the window and there she was, in the rain, under this big tree about halfway down our lawn, talking into her cellphone. Right then I knew that I could move my darkest suspicion from the wings to center stage: whatever was going on, whoever it was going on with, it wasn't problems with the show, or anything like that. So then I asked myself, assuming Connie's up to something: *where?*"

"The first question most men in your position would have asked would have been: *with whom?*"

"Oh, that was on my mind, too, believe me. But the way I figured it, unless I came up with the where, there was no way I was going to be able to come up with the who. Besides, I figured that whoever it was, it would be someone I didn't know."

"What about a professional connection? Someone she works with?"

"On a Barrow set? Forget it."

"It wouldn't necessarily have to be someone on her show."

"I suppose not. But that would mean either Connie was going into the city to meet whoever, or whoever was coming up our way to meet her, or they were meeting halfway, but none of that computed. For one thing, too dangerous. Christ, in the city, she might even bump into me! Or someone else she knows, or be spotted from a cab. It happens. And if it was somewhere around where we live, where would they go? Our house? Not a chance! One of the romantic country inns up our way? Another no-no: they have valet parkers, desk clerks, and waiters itching to get on the phone to the tabloids. The back seat of a car? At her age? Finally, I just couldn't see Connie sneaking around New Rochelle or Fort Lee. She's just too well-known. Given one thing and another, I figured I was looking at a ten-to-twenty-mile radius from where we live. No more than a half-hour drive. And probably a private house."

"That's a lot of territory."

"You're telling me! And a shitload of houses! So I asked myself: How am I going to pinpoint a needle in a haystack that enormous?"

"Before you continue," Jekyll says, "let me ask you: do you think your wife has had any inkling of your suspicions?"

"Not the slightest. Not then, not still. You know how women are. They think we men are so out of touch with our own feelings that we can't possibly be in touch with theirs. Anyway, to cut back to the chase, it took me almost a month to get my ducks in a row. My first thought was to give her one of those cellphones with a GPS—I told her she could use it to keep track of Jenny and me, hah, hah, hah—but when I tested the waters, she rejected the idea pretty vehemently. Then I had a better idea. Do you remember that cops-and-robbers picture of mine called *Hearts of the City*?"

"Of course. I liked it. It was full of ingenious touches."

"Ingenious is my middle name. Anyway, when I was making it, I did some research on surveillance and investigative techniques, and I got to know a guy who has a spy shop way over on East Twenty-eighth Street who I used as a kind of off-the-books technical advisor. I went to see him—that was on the third Wednesday in October, the fifteenth, Louis Auchincloss was the speaker—and told him a cock-and-bull story about a project I was working on—as if!—and he gave me what I needed: a kind of a knockoff of that LoJack system the cops use to track stolen cars, GPS, WiFi software for my laptop, and a transmitter the size of a coat button, which I stuck on the inside of the rear fender of Connie's Jeep when I got home. Over the weekend, when she went off shopping with our daughter, I checked it out and it worked fine. Do you follow me?"

"I do. I'm familiar with these systems."

"I bet you are. Anyway, I could hardly wait for D-Day to roll around."

"And that would have been what date?"

"The following Wednesday, October 22."

"That was quite a while ago."

"It's taken me all this time to calm down, think about it, about what it all could mean—and get up my nerve to come here—and I'm still not sure I should have. Anyway, the fateful morning dawned bright and clear and off I went to the city, quote unquote, if you get my meaning, right on schedule, leaving my lady wife in a really good mood, for reasons that no longer need go undefined. Add to that the fact that Belle Villers had been in town just the day before—she and Connie had lunch at the studio—and if anything or anyone can be counted upon to bring sunshine into Connie's existence, it's Belle."

"I assume you refer to the Annabelle Villers who is the CEO of Summerhill Farms?"

"The very same. Belle really discovered Connie and made her what she is. They've gotten to be very close. Poor Belle. If she knew something like this was going down, she'd shit in her knickers! Because all it needs is for some Brink's watchman or carpenter who's forgotten his toolbox to walk in while my wife and Donkey Dong are going at it, and the next thing you know, it's all over the Internet and the media and Connie the brand is kaput and with her, Summerhill, because Belle has bet the farm on Connie. Belle deserves better."

"You sound fond of Ms. Villers."

"I am. And I think it's reciprocal. Belle's a mensch. Anyway, to get back to my sorrowful narrative: on Wednesday morning, October 22, I set off for the city at my usual hour, right around 10:30 a.m., with my laptop tucked away in my shoulder bag, along with my own trusty digital camcorder, a cool little job I had specially modified for shooting in super low light to check out night locations back when

I still had work. I parked the car in my reserved space across from the station and got on the good old 11:08, but this time I didn't ride all the way to Grand Central. I waited for Connie to call to check on me, so she could hear train noises in the background, which she did about the time we were pulling out of Greenwich and again just after Larchmont, then I got off at Pelham and took a taxi to White Plains, where I rented a basic anonymous Toyota with New York rental plates. I turned off my cellphone so she couldn't call me, just in case—this 'empty battery' bullshit can work both ways—and drove back and parked a couple of miles away from our house behind a strip mall. This would have been around 1 p.m. I plugged my laptop into the cigarette lighter, got the GPS running, and waited."

"Suppose she'd already left?"

"I knew she wouldn't. There was a guy coming at noon about a new stove, and a Mothers' Sports Night Committee lunch at another parent's house after that, and then it was odds-on she'd come home to pretty herself up. So I figured I was looking at an ETD of 3 p.m. at the earliest, so I buried my nose in one of my old man's favorite P.G. Wodehouses, with one eye on the laptop, and waited. Sure enough, a little after 3:30, the laptop started to beep and the game was afoot, as Sherlock Holmes would say. It was just like the movies: blip, beep, blip, beep, blip, beep across a scrolling map. I felt like Jack Bauer on *24*. All I had to do was not get too close. I followed her from Grangeford to number 127 Winding Crest Drive, which is just this side of the New York state line back in the hills, a total distance of 17.6 miles.

"Having established that 127 Winding Crest Drive was where Connie had gone and had parked—the blip was no longer moving—I parked down the road about a half mile and walked back through the woods with my camcorder. It being October, the light was starting to falter, and what with the woods being thick, I wasn't much worried about being spotted."

"You weren't worried about security? You mentioned Brink's. A watchman? Some kind of alarm system."

"I figure that if Connie wasn't, which she obviously wasn't, I needn't be. Usually, at this stage of a job, the security outfits just put up a sign and figure that'll do it. Motion sensors and security cams are the last things they put in. Anyway, I stealthily made my way through the trees and at the back of the house I saw two windows lit up. I edged up through the trees—my heart must have been doing five hundred beats a minute!—and I was able to get close enough to see in. Let me just say that any fears I might have had about being spotted were groundless, because Connie and Donkey Dong were totally preoccupied. I don't think I have to draw a picture."

"*In flagrante*, in other words?"

"About as *flagrante* as I expect it gets," Clifford replies. "They were going at it front, rear, on top, on the bottom, the entire playbook. No bodily crevice or orifice left unexplored. A vivid and living testimonial to all that personal-trainer stuff Connie does to keep in shape. And that's not the whole of it, I regret to say. There was... well, a chemical element involved, too."

"'Drugs, you mean?"

"Poppers is my guess. Amyl nitrate. To finish the story, I ran the camcorder for about ten minutes, and then I downed tools and snuck back off through the woods. I drove the rental car to Manhattan, gave it back to Avis, and was at the club just in time to have three stiff ones to settle my nerves before Louis Auchincloss, which may explain why to this day I can't remember a word he said."

"I'm surprised you could stay calm enough to do that. I'm not sure I could have."

"I couldn't take the chance of not showing up and someone calling home to see if I was sick or something. Then I caught my usual train from Grand Central. I was home right on schedule. End of story."

"That was three weeks ago," Jekyll says, counting on his fingers. "What about the following Wednesday? Or the one after that?"

"I didn't have the heart to go for a second or third take, but I'm sure she was there. As a matter of fact," Clifford looks at his watch, "she's probably on her way there as we speak."

Jekyll shrugs. "Is there anything else you think I should know?"

"Well, I don't know if this matters or not, but Connie's master contract with BME and with Belle is a personal services agreement that contains a morals clause."

"A *morals clause!* My goodness, I must say, between your being blacklisted and your wife's contract, you and Mrs. Grange seem to be living in a kind of 1950s time warp."

Clifford grins, "You mean you don't write morals clauses into your prenuptial agreements?"

"I don't write prenuptial agreements," Jekyll replies. His smile is downright sinister. "If I did, I'd never be able to break them. My work is strictly postnuptial. It's more fun that way."

"Well, there's nothing funny about this. Basically it says that if she does anything to bring public disrepute or scandal upon herself, anything that adversely affects her value as a personality or a brand —which means, by extension, her value to BME or Summerhill, including syndication—she pays a heavy price, including a clawback. And of course she gives up any future rights and royalties from brand-name products, which I estimate could be in the neighborhood of $50 million. Bottom line: a scandal that irreparably damages the brand— and mind you, we're not talking some teeny-bopper idol here, but a grown-up audience that spends grown-up money—could end up costing my wife and all who sail in her the better part of a cool billion dollars."

"I see. Well, goodness. Is there anything else?"

"Yeah," says Clifford, fishing a blank check from his pocket. "I want to pay you what we'll call a preemptive retainer. I may not end up doing anything *with* you, Arthur, but I sure as hell don't want to end up finding myself *against* you. If Connie decides to dump me and run off into the sunset with Donkey Dong, it's a hundred to one that you'll be *her* first call. How much should I make this out for? Would ten grand do the job?"

"We can discuss that later," Jekyll says. "Now, what can I tell you about myself?"

"I guess I pretty much know what I need to. I mean, you're not exactly an unknown quantity."

"Well, there is one thing you should know. I'm in this business because I happen to harbor an exalted view of the institution of marriage. That is to say, I think marriage deserves a better chance than society and legislatures give it. I think marriage and the marital vows people exchange mean something. I abhor those who abuse or treat them casually, including the several generations of judges and legislators and social thinkers who have defiled, undercut, or otherwise degraded an essential social institution. Finally, I could see by your face and manner, at least when you and I started to talk, that the sensational aspects of my practice trouble you. Today, publicity and the intrusiveness of the media are givens of my profession. If I can exploit them or leverage them to my clients' advantage, I will. I have no qualms about humiliating or disgracing an opponent in public if it will help my client's case. If it should deter others from deception and fraud, that's a bonus. Should you decide to go ahead, I will do my best for you, and proceed without mercy."

"Well, that's good to hear. Let me ask you something. As a writer-director, I've always tended to overdo what we call 'the backstory.' What's yours? Did you have an epiphany? Bolt of lightning knock you off your high horse on the Damascus Road?"

"Something like that. In 1981, I was an associate at a very prestigious although hidebound midtown firm called Nevins Crockett. It was the sort of place where Daniel Webster wouldn't have made partner before the age of forty. I was then thirty-seven years old and working mainly for the managing partner, Martin Crockett. I was like a Supreme Court clerk with judicial rank: doing most of the work, whispering from behind the arras, and getting myself positioned to take over some of our bigger clients when the day came and, eventually, the leadership of the firm. That was not just my ambition, it was Martin's intention. His getting me into the Diogenes was an integral part of that strategy.

"Then fate intervened. Our most profitable client was East River Bank and Trust. Banks are manna to law firms, because they generate so much business, everything from loan documentation to trust deeds. It seemed the East River CEO's son was about to be involved in a nasty divorce involving the usual elements, almost stereotypical: a young wife who felt herself sexually shortchanged, an assistant golf professional with roving hands, a lot of money in the background, a Palm Beach setting. He wanted us to handle it. He made it clear that if we wouldn't, he'd take his business to Milbank Tweed, which already had a family law practice, and which certainly could take on the banking end, since they already acted for Chase Manhattan.

"Martin wasn't keen. He hated the idea of divorce work. Ordinarily, we would have referred our client to Sol Rosenblatt, Eli Bronstein, Shad Polier or another of the leading divorce practitioners of the day, first-class attorneys and decent men with whom we had worked before, but here we had no choice. So Martin asked me to take it on."

"Asked—or ordered you?"

"Does it matter? I was his fair-haired boy and, of course, I was bursting with ambition, as rising men in their late thirties generally are. Back then, remember, thirty-seven was still considered young— at least in the law. I also think Martin may have seen in me certain qualities I didn't know I possessed—or flattered myself that I didn't possess. Let's just say they added up to a certain ruthlessness that might have been happier on Wall Street, although I really never had a taste for that kind of work. It probably helped that I came from the kind of quarrelsome, uncaged family that is today called 'dysfunctional,' an upbringing that left me with a taste and an aptitude for mind games—for sowing confusion, discord, misdirection, unhappiness, and misjudgment in order to protect myself from my abominable father. It turns out that mind games are as essential to a successful divorce practice as they are to a career in high-stakes poker. I suppose I should also divulge the Palm Beach factor."

"Palm Beach?"

Jekyll grins. "Palm Beach. I was born and raised there—I was what the smart set down there considered a 'townie'—and it left me with a pretty clear-eyed view of what the American rich are really like. Whoever it was that defined the upper crust as 'a bunch of crumbs held together by dough' was right on the money, if you'll forgive the pun. I was, so to speak, an outsider with an inside perspective, since my father was a reasonably successful realtor to the gentry, which required him to lick their boots, parrot their repulsive political opinions—and, on any number of occasions, sleep with his clients, male and female."

"Ouch!"

"Putting the Freudian aspect to one side, let me simply say that Palm Beach is a place I deeply loathe, and not simply on account of my childhood and upbringing there. It is a place that incarnates everything that is most repellent and contemptible about American materialism and social ambition. It was bad enough in my day, and it's become even more grotesque, morally speaking, in the intervening half-century, the prime example—as I see it—of what this country is *not* supposed to be about, a sinkhole of money, a gilded cesspit, the national and global capital of blind valueless wealth worship, thousands of people luxuriating in the delusion that wealth is a synonym for wisdom and character. Dorothy Parker once said, 'If you want to see what God thinks of money, look at who He gives it to.' She clearly had Palm Beach in mind."

"That bad, eh? I've never been there."

"Clifford, if I may call you that—and I hope you'll call me Arthur—Palm Beach is beyond the imagining of any halfway decent, halfway intelligent human being. So, as you might guess, it added salt to that particular legal stew. The bottom line is that I did Martin's and our client's bidding, did it with skill, enthusiasm, and a certain irrepressible cruelty—and the rest is history. When the other side flew the white flag and prostrated themselves, I knew I had found my destiny."

"Or it found you."

"Perhaps. Anyway, thus was born Jekyll the Jackal. Or, as Dominick Dunne called me on what used to be called Court TV, 'the scourge of Worth Avenue.'"

"Worth Avenue?"

"The main shopping street in Palm Beach. Dominick's is an appellation I wear with pride, the way your father probably wore his medals. I did a little tally a month or so ago. Of my hundred biggest, ugliest cases, no fewer than forty-four have involved people with at least one legal residence in Palm Beach. Nineteen of these clients kept their houses there, indeed, seven ascended to the Forbes 400 as the result of my efforts. In the other twenty-five, I was able to force the sale of $130 million in Palm Beach residential property, as well as bring about several mergers, two Chapter 11 filings, and two Chapter 10s, not to mention uncountable millions in fees to pill pushers and psychiatrists. There have also been thirty-seven club resignations—four being the most by any one individual—twelve nervous breakdowns, seven cases of out-of-state tax fraud uncovered and prosecuted. I believe myself to have precipitated eleven cases of aggravated assault after the fact, all duly punished with the full and wrathful majesty of the law. Finally, there have been eleven suicide attempts, of which six succeeded—not a bad batting average. And—as I think I may already told you—one homicide for which I'm entitled at least to partial credit, in my view. All in all, not a bad record. In the state of Florida—and Florida's not the only one, mind you—I fancy I've been as potent a force for wealth redistribution as anyone in politics and anything in the tax code."

Jekyll's tone is self-mocking, but underneath, Clifford detects real pride. "At the risk of sounding like I'm sucking up to you," he says, "I must say you don't come across as very jackalish to me."

Jekyll grins. "Perhaps you'd prefer another animal. Take your pick. I've also been called a weasel, a hyena, a shark, a barracuda, and a piranha. If your preference is ornithological rather than ichthyological, you have your choice of vulture or buzzard. Also vampire—with or without the modifier 'blood-sucking'—and leech. Those of a herpetological bent may choose from adder, cobra, viper, asp, python. All in all, a veritable zoology of vituperation. And there may well be other vermin that have escaped either my notice or that of my clipping service. I have also been likened to a number of weapons of mass destruction, not only by people whom I've confronted professionally, but frequently by people with whom I've never exchanged words of any kind. Cruise missile, B-52, a walking fragmentation grenade, human IED—to name four. Other attorneys regularly characterize me with references to the excrement of various mammals, but that's merely professional courtesy. Indeed, as far as I'm concerned, the worst slur ever thrown in my direction, the one I found most wounding, was when a learned judge described me to *Newsweek* as 'making Roy Cohn look like Justice Holmes by comparison.' That hurt. On the other hand, the *Hollywood Reporter* said once that I was the Hannibal Lecter of divorce—which I consider high praise."

"If you don't mind me saying it, you do kind of resemble Anthony Hopkins—although a friend at the club says you remind her of Gene Hackman."

"You think so? I've always rather fancied the notion that if a movie was made about me, I'd be played by Jack Nicholson. I think he's more my style—intellectually. Anyway, as you can see, I'm basically an amiable fellow, despite my fearsome reputation. It's just that I do what I do with zeal and, it would appear, a certain amount of skill and ingenuity. I pride myself on what elsewhere might be called craftsmanship. I seem to have an instinctive feel for what people like least about themselves, and what they fear most—which, in ninety-nine cases out of one hundred, is losing their money. Mammon is the straw that stirs the drink, because ninety-nine percent of the particular psychology in which I traffic is grounded in money worries. I think it's fair to say that we live in an age where money is the defining element of almost anything people aspire to. Either to help themselves get it— or to prevent someone else. To have more—or at least not to have less. And, of course, in terms of my work, let us not forget that while money is a dreadful basis for friendship, it is an excellent—you might say, an essential—basis for enmity."

"Okay. Now, since it's on my dime, let me ask you one more thing: if you're such a great believer in the institution of marriage, have you ever tried it?"

"Sad to say, no. I never really had the time. Too busy unraveling other people's marriages to weave one of my own, I suppose. Ah well, perhaps someday…"

"So you have no regrets? I'm just curious, mind you."

"I suppose I do, but I really can't think of any that seem to fall within the realm of the possible. Would I prefer to have ended up on the Supreme Court? Obviously. What lawyer wouldn't? Would I prefer to have sat on great boards and represented famous corporations? Not at all. Too boring—and, if one ends up representing, say, an Enron or a Tyco or a bucket shop like Bear Stearns, worse than that. I don't like what I do, but I don't despise it either."

"Sounds like you're the guy for me. *If* I decide to do anything."

"That will be your call. What you will get is first-rate advice and counsel on matters of family law—and, if you want it, aggressive representation."

"Fine. That's what I'm here for—and I have to say I'm starting to feel better, a whole lot better, about having called you." Which is true: Clifford is definitely feeling more relaxed about coming here. His guard is lowering; his cynicism melting. "Maybe before I get out of your hair," he says, "you can give me some general idea of my options."

"To do that, I need to know certain facts. Where is your legal residence?"

"We live in Connecticut. Outside Darien—not far from the Sound."

"I see." Jekyll thinks this over, and then smiles. "Well, Mr. Grange, assuming your evidence is as airtight as you say it is, you are in a position to allege what is called 'marital misconduct.' Which can make things very expensive for your wife."

Clifford shakes his head vigorously. "Money's the last thing I'm thinking about."

"Most people say that. At least, at first. Down the line you may feel different."

"I doubt it. But you're the expert. Why don't you take me through it? I don't want to do anything I don't fully understand."

"Fine. We begin with the happy fact that you and your wife live in a state whose divorce code recognizes marital misconduct—what we call 'fault'—as a legitimate and compensable cause of action."

"And what exactly is meant by 'marital misconduct'?" Clifford asks.

"Provable violence, alcoholism, or drug addiction, and—as in your case—adultery. I should emphasize that the right to allege fault is merely an option under your state's divorce code. You can use whatever evidence of fault you may have, but you don't have to if you don't want to. Here, let me give you the exact wording." The lawyer turns to his computer, taps out a series of commands on his computer keyboard, and reads out loud: 'Spouses do not *need* to prove "grounds" to obtain a divorce'...blah, blah, blah...'Fault can be considered by the court in determining the financial orders (alimony and assignment of property)'... etc... etc.... 'Fault generally makes a difference in the court's award when the fault is substantial and it substantially contributes to the breakdown of the marriage or the loss of marital assets.' Obviously the former would be the case, and as regards the 'marital assets,' we might choose to argue that your wife's share in the economic value of her 'brand'—as her sponsors and advisers doubtless call it—is itself a marital asset that would be seriously affected or destroyed by her misconduct."

"Only if I go public."

"If you file for a fault divorce, I don't see how that could be avoided, although her lawyers would undoubtedly move to have the proceedings sealed. But let me finish: 'The Court has the power to assign to either the husband or wife all or any part of the estate of the other. Any property, therefore, regardless of when or how acquired, can be redistributed by the Court.'"

Jekyll turns away from the screen: "So, as you can see, you're potentially in a strong position—a very strong position. At least for the moment, that is. But this may change, and I would therefore urge that if you decide to act, you do so immediately."

"I don't think I follow you."

"The legislative wolf is at the door. There is considerable pressure on your state assembly to follow the lead of most other states and go one hundred percent to no-fault, which would obviate the advantage you now enjoy."

"There is? I didn't know that—and I read the local papers pretty carefully because those SOBs up in Hartford are always trying to screw us on the property tax. Anyway, suppose the state goes to no-fault? Does that mean that adultery no longer counts?"

"Effectively."

"How the hell can that be? What right does the state have to cancel my marriage vows, which seems to be what you're saying? Connie and I got married in a church, not by some judge, and we swore before God to be faithful to each other."

"I understand your reaction, but that's the way it'll be if the code gets amended."

"What about the First Amendment? What about separation of church and state? I thought the Constitution says that church and state are separate, which to me means the state has to keep its goddamn hands off *The Book of Common Prayer*, which is where Connie's and my marriage vows are set down."

"Basically, the Constitution does say that—more or less. But there are also questions of federalism—powers specifically granted to the several states—that are a given."

"Says who?"

"Well, the Supreme Court, actually. Although recently, what past courts have given, the present court appears disposed to take back."

"Yeah, but…I mean…how can this happen, federalism or no federalism? The whole point of exchanging marriage vows is the idea that if one party breaks them, down comes the hammer: the wrath of God or the wrath of someone like you. Which this no-fault crap eliminates?"

Jekyll nods, then adds, "Some states that have gone over to no-fault—Michigan and Louisiana come to mind—have subsequently had second thoughts. The evidence strongly suggests that no-fault has been economically devastating to women, especially mothers—which I must say I find somewhat deliciously ironic, given that it's feminists who've been the loudest proponents of no-fault. They claim it restores women's independence."

"Freedom to be dirt poor, you mean? What a stupid law!"

Jekyll shrugs.

"What about the Eighth Commandment? Thou shalt not commit adultery?"

"I'm afraid the Supreme Court has ushered all Ten Commandments out of the courtroom."

Clifford shakes his head—then grins. "And of course you divorce lawyers must hate no-fault, since it picks your pocket. As you say, fault gives you the leverage to push people into fat settlements. You can blackmail them."

"Let us just say that fault divorce helps people think rationally, in terms of what Tocqueville called 'self-interest properly understood.' Fault provides plaintiffs with a useful means for obtaining just compensation for grievous emotional and sometimes physical injuries that have been inflicted upon them. The value of evidence is a function of the legal constraints placed upon its use. As I said before, since scandal is our era's opiate of the masses, guilty parties will frequently prefer to settle rather than see their private misconduct placed on public exhibition. Fault divorce thereby also helps ease the legal logjam, since cases get settled rather than tried. Anyway, Clifford, what matters is that as things stand, on the basis of what you've told me, and given the evidence you say you have, and the divorce code currently in effect in your state, I see no reason why you shouldn't achieve an appropriate custodial and financial settlement should you go forward with an action for divorce or separation."

"By 'custodial,' you mean take Jenny away from her mother? I'd never do that!"

"I'm sure you wouldn't. No sensible—or decent—man would, and you seem to me to be both. But you would be entitled to have the court award you an equal voice in matters of upbringing, schooling, and so on."

"Management by two-person committee, you mean? I'm not sure that would work with Connie. Or with Jenny."

"That would be up to the three of you."

"Okay—now, 'an appropriate financial settlement,' as you put it. Meaning what, exactly? That stuff you read me says I'd be entitled to half, at a minimum, right?"

"Correct."

I'd never touch her money, Clifford's thinking. *Never! I do have my pride.* On the other hand, this could add up to a whole lot of money. A whole lot. He does some quick figuring. This could add up to $25-$30 million, and probably more. A whole lot more. Enough for him to bankroll a couple of films.

"Even though Connie's the big earner?" he asks. "That hardly seems fair."

"Fair doesn't come into it."

"Okay, how would the court do the calculations? Sooner or later the show will go into syndication—where the really big bucks are. What about that? What about her value as a brand?"

"Provided we can assign a demonstrable and reasonable present value to those earnings, and provided we can make a case that your support as a homemaker—don't make a face, Clifford, I'm simply talking tactics—has been essential to her success as an actress and therefore to the creation of the brand, you would be entitled to fifty percent of that income stream, although you'd probably negotiate a lower percentage.

"Actually," he hears Jekyll say, "you could probably do just as well, perhaps even better, merely by threatening a public divorce action, provided that the threat reaches *all* the right ears."

"You mean Barrow and Belle Villers?"

"As you yourself pointed out a while ago, were Ms. Villers to become aware of your wife's liaison, she would doubtless be very upset. Ditto Mr. Barrow, one would think. What's your wife worth to them? Several hundred million, I should think. Probably more. A billion? What's your guess?"

"A billion sounds about right."

"And what's your guess as to what they'd pay to forestall a scandal?"

Clifford shrugs. "I don't know. $100 million? You tell me? You're the expert on legal stick-ups."

"I should think at least twice that. I usually open the bidding at two-thirds of whatever assets are in play."

"Jesus Christ, Arthur, that would be $600 million! More!"

Jekyll shrugs.

"And how does that work? At some point, do you go backchannel and tell Belle and Barrow, 'Okay, pay us, say, $600 million by 5 p.m. or the *National Enquirer* is going to show your thirty million viewers a bunch of pictures of your billion-dollar snow maiden humping Donkey Dong? Is that the strategy?"

"Somewhat coarsely put—but yes, that's more or less the approach. At some point."

"In other words: blackmail?"

"In essence, Clifford, most civil litigation comes down to legalized blackmail."

"Okay, now let's get real. How much do you think I could get if everything falls out just so?"

"A safe estimate would be $200 million."

"Jesus!" With that kind of money, Clifford could green-light himself. And not for peanuts budgets either.

"The money would be paid in over time, of course. However, should you want to go forward, I urge that you do so without delay. Fault divorce is here today in your state, but it could be gone tomorrow."

"You said that. So what's the deal? What's holding the no-fault amendment back?"

"Do you know who Cardinal Joseph Santiago is? The Archbishop of Southern New England?"

"Sure. Who doesn't? Up our way they call him 'God's croupier.' He's like the chaplain to those Indians with the big casino."

"Forest Fields. The tribe that is fronting the operation is called the Nissanquasetts."

"'Fronting?' I thought they owned it."

"Their name may be on the deed, but that's about as far as it goes— or so I hear. Most if not all of these so-called 'Native American' casino ventures follow the same pattern: a tribal name on the door, shadowy overseas money backing the play, smooth Washington and statehouse lawyers and lobbyists easing the legislative path—and in the case of the Nissanquasetts, a prince of the church to boot. One even hears that the Vatican fronted the seed money and the work in Washington necessary to gain 'recognized' tribal status for the Nissanquasetts. Of course, the official story is that they've been devoted children of Rome since being converted to Catholicism in the late seventeenth century by a follower of La Salle who apparently mistook the Housatonic for the Mississippi and zigged when he should have zagged.

"In the case of the Forest Fields venture, Santiago, a man who gets around, is said to have played a central role as a facilitator, using a Kraków bank where the Holy See is said to have influence, although most of the important capital is rumored to be Russian and Pakistani, with a lashing of heroin money from Palermo."

"You mean like *Godfather III*?"

"As I say, a man of infinite parts is Cardinal Santiago, lavishly well connected in both God's realm and Caesar's, expert in financial matters, a protégé of Marcinkus, the man behind the Ambrosiano and Sindona affairs, although Santiago managed to emerge from those imbroglios untouched. His Eminence is the primary if not the entire reason that your state has not gone to one hundred percent no-fault. Up to now."

"Explain, please."

"His diocese is seventy percent Hispanic. It's a potent voting bloc."

"You're right about that. I think I heard the next election's going to give our state capital a Latino mayor."

"In other words, Santiago holds a powerful political and economic nexus in his wiry fingers. Through him your state's oldest and wealthiest inhabitants, the Nissanquasetts, make common cause with its newest and poorest. Santiago's diocese has a twelve percent unemployment rate, mainly Latino, and Forest Fields has supplanted the insurance industry and Sikorsky as your state's single largest generator of political contributions."

"I see."

"Now, as regards no-fault, you're aware that these have not been good times for the Catholic Church. Quite apart from the sexual abuse scandals and a number of financial irregularities here and there, Rome is deeply concerned about the rising U.S. divorce rate. Divorce is, of course, anathema doctrinally."

"That I understand."

"So it follows that the Catholic church is strongly opposed to no-fault divorce, because no-fault, at least in theory, makes divorce easier to obtain and socially more palatable...."

"So the Cardinal opposes the no-fault bill, right? Which means, with his financial clout...am I getting warm?"

"You are. Any politician in your state who gets on the wrong side of Santiago will find the bottomless Forest Fields purse zipped shut. In politics today, no money equals no way. It was Santiago, you know, who pushed through your state's Defense of Marriage Act, over the opposition of the speaker—I should say, the *former* speaker—of your state assembly."

"Defense of Marriage Act? I didn't know there was such a thing."

"Indeed there is. The act—almost forty states have passed such legislation—stipulates that the only legally valid marriage is that between a man and a woman, which is Rome's view. To the church, opposition to no-fault is the logical legislative corollary. Rome regards no-fault as the thin edge of the wedge, the camel's nose, the first step on the road to Sodom. Now, what has happened so far is this: your lady governor has her eye on the U.S. Senate, it is said; perhaps beyond. Although not Catholic herself, she knows where her wafer is buttered, if you will, and her closest advisor, and likely successor, your attorney general, Isobel Hewitt, *is* a Catholic, indeed a former nun—and very close to Santiago. *QED:* the governor has sworn to veto any no-fault bill that the state assembly tries to pass, and Santiago has put it about that any member of the assembly who votes for no-fault will never receive another farthing of support from Forest Fields. As a result, the no-fault legislation has languished in committee for some time now. And will languish there for the foreseeable future, assuming His Eminence continues in rude good health and stays away from the altar boys."

"Not exactly separation of church and state, is it? But suppose Santiago drops dead and no-fault passes? Where's that leave me?"

"Up the proverbial creek without the leverage you now possess as a matter of legal right. Under your state's pending no-fault legislation, as drafted, your moral and legal claim with respect to any misconduct on the part of your wife would be eliminated, would simply be taken off the table as a cause of action. So would the financial claim."

"Wow! But suppose we go to Plan B? Skip the legal botheration and go straight to blackmail? 'Pay up or I sell what I've got to the *National Enquirer*?'"

"Without the force or warrant of the law to back up the threat, I'm not sure. *You* could threaten to leak what you've got to the papers, but there are real risks there, including the possibility that the other side might castrate you with a libel suit. At the very least, they'd challenge your evidence on technical grounds."

"Such as?"

"They'd begin by pointing out that you're a well-known movie director who's known to be cutting-edge, technically."

"So?"

"I have no doubt that if you were to produce your digital evidence, the other side would claim that you'd simply utilized Photoshop or some other comparable image-editing software and spliced your wife's head onto some stock pornographic footage. It's the sort of thing that any halfway competent person with the right programs can pull off in an hour. I could do it myself. Indeed, there've been one or two times I've considered it."

"I see. So, tell me this: why wouldn't they try to discredit my evidence in a regular divorce action?"

"I'll come to that. The short answer is, they probably would. And I'd lay one hundred to one that a judge would find sufficient merit to suppress your evidence. As a matter of fact, a very similar objection was raised in a California court not long ago—and the judge was persuaded to throw out 'evidence' not dissimilar to what you've got. After all, what corroboration have you that these aren't fabrications?"

"Look, *I* took these pictures!"

"That's what *you* say."

"But I did, damn it!"

"Of course you did. You know it and I believe you. But did anyone *see* you take them? That's why private investigators work in pairs, never mind what the movies show."

"Yeah, but..."

"I'm merely playing the devil's advocate, Clifford. But if I were your wife's attorney, I'd challenge them. I'm sure you remember the DNA debate in the O.J. Simpson trial, and the confusion *that* caused. Confusion breeds doubt and doubt is the mother of 'not guilty.' Or, in your case: 'no money.' Without corroboration, by the time the other side's forensic technicians get through analyzing and breaking down and disputing the digital evidence you've described to me, our case will be finished. In my opinion, it is therefore essential for you to obtain corroborative evidence and testimony."

"You mean hire a private detective?"

Jekyll nods.

Clifford shakes his head. "Jesus, Arthur, I'm not sure. I mean, the idea of some guy watching Connie and..." His voice trails off.

"Believe me," Jekyll says, "I understand your position. I just want you to understand the situation in its totality. I can recommend an excellent firm of private investigators: Harris & Associates. Peter Harris and his people could stake out a cat from ten feet without the animal knowing it. And they're absolutely discreet—that I guarantee. I could call Peter now for you. Would you like me to?"

Jekyll starts to reach for the phone on his desk. Clifford holds up a hand.

"Not yet, please. I want to think this over." He looks helplessly at Jekyll. "I'm sorry to seem so wishy-washy, especially given what Connie's done—is doing—to me—but it's hard for me to deal with the idea of bringing in...some, uh, some stranger to...well, you know..."

"Of course, I do. You're a decent man on whom a gross indecency has been inflicted, but not enough to destroy your sense of what's appropriate."

"It's just that...well, Connie is the mother of my kid. If this all blew up in public, I don't think Jenny would ever forgive me."

"You don't have to complain," says Jekyll. "Think it over. You know where I am if you need me." The lawyer checks his watch. "I'm sorry," the lawyer says, "but I have another appointment out of the office." From his desk drawer, he extracts a business card. "In case you change your mind, here's where to reach Peter Harris. Just say I told you to call."

"I'll think it over. But I probably won't do anything. My guess is, if I just leave bad enough alone, it'll go away or burn itself out, this thing with Donkey Dong. It's just a fling. It has to be. So I have to ask myself: why make a fuss and break up my marriage and totally screw up our daughter?"

"A good question."

"Of course, I might change my mind. You've suggested a few hundred million reasons why."

"Well, think it over." Jekyll starts to push himself away from his desk, and then sits down again. He looks at Clifford, his expression grave. "One thing I do want to say, Clifford: the way you're reacting to your situation seems to me to be, frankly, astonishing. Over the years, I've met with literally hundreds of people who've caught their spouses being sexually unfaithful, and I have to tell you that nearly every last one of them was burning and shaking and foaming at the mouth with the wish to get even. Revenge and retribution: that's what they want, no matter what the cost to anyone—including themselves. The women, especially—and it doesn't seem to matter if there are young children involved. They make Medea look like Mother of the Year by comparison!"

"I doubt that Connie would react that way. I sure as hell know I wouldn't."

Jekyll smiles at him. "I'm sure neither of you would mean to, but in my business, you run into all kinds of deeply bitter, emotional inversions. There's no more virulent form of hatred than love turned inside out. Jung had a theory—I think it's called the shadow theory—that what we dislike most in other people is what we can't stand about ourselves. It certainly applies to my work. My average client usually can't decide whether he or she hates the estranged partner more than he or she hates themselves for having fallen for such a person in the first place."

"That may be," Clifford says. "Don't let me fool you. That is, don't mistake patient for passive. Or passive-aggressive, if it comes to that. I'm just trying to be practical. The truth is, you make a list of all the basic cuckold emotions—sexual humiliation, vengefulness, jealousy, anger, the urge to kill someone—and I've felt them all this last month and I still do. Traces, at least. Hell, I briefly—*very* briefly—thought of driving up there and confronting the guy, but then I thought, hey, he's pretty buff, he'd probably beat the crap out of me. So then I thought, well maybe I should get a gun and shoot him dead, assuming he doesn't take the gun away and shoot *me*. But finally I thought, why spend the rest of my life in prison for a piece of garbage like that. I'm just trying to be practical. To balance out all the whys and wherefores."

"Patience is nearly always the wiser course. Within limits."

"And then there's this: maybe I deserve it. I can't have been a whole lot of fun to be living with the past couple of years. For Connie, it could be like sharing a bed with a eunuch, because that's how I feel: impotent, as if my nuts have been cut off. Do you know what it's like to be at the top of your game and then suddenly you can't get work?"

"I can only guess."

"I tell myself, maybe the stuff I want to do isn't any good, that maybe it's shit, that maybe *Crown Heights* showed I've lost it all—but then I see the crap that gets bought and made and put onscreen or published, and I....You get the picture.

"Besides, how can I not be grateful to Connie? Without her, where's the bread on the table? The bottom line, Arthur, seems to be that after all the other shit that's gone down in my life—a lot of it of my own making, I freely admit—this business with Connie doesn't seem like the end of the world. It was much worse when I was eaten up with suspicion and curiosity. Now that I know what's going on, I'm not saying I like it, but maybe I can live with it."

"Well," says Jekyll, "whatever you decide, I'm here."

"I'll keep you posted," Clifford says. "Funny, isn't it?"

"What?"

"How the cuckold's antlers can also be the horns of a dilemma."

"Nicely put," Jekyll says. "Look, don't be so hard on yourself. And put away that check. This meeting's on the house. If we work together, that'll be something else."

Riding down in the elevator, Clifford reviews the bidding. The way he sees it, he can do nothing, which is contrary to his nature. Or he can do something, which—given the way the rest of his life has been going—will doubtless turn out to be contrary to everyone's best interest, starting with his own. And what exactly would "do-

ing something" entail? Well, he could confront Connie. He's written
a dozen confrontation scenes in his head, acted them out mentally,
relished his performance, admired his skill at dialogue, pacing, setting
the marks. Mentally had her at his feet, weeping, begging forgiveness;
in his imagination had watched her, proud, full of bluff and insolence,
futilely trying to fence her way verbally around his rapier thrusts of
insight and wit and condescension; had watched her internal confidence shatter like an imploding building and watched as the smile, the
lilt, the grace, the sureness, along with the roses in the skin and the
diamonds in the eye, became muck and dust. Watched disgrace and
shame turn her into a weeping shell begging his forgiveness: useless
to herself, useless artistically, commercially.

Or he can go to war—and that presents a whole other calendar
of horrors.

But it also presents the possibility of enough money to set Clifford free: free to create, free to speak his mind. A freedom that will
bring to a close alienation, dependence, parasitism, ostracism, and the
further diminution of Clifford Grange.

There just isn't any quick and easy answer.

Maybe the right thing—right now—is to do nothing. Wait and
see, let time and circumstance run the table. After all, leaving aside
the money and the comfort, he does like—has always liked—being
married to Connie; he loves his daughter; he likes family life, likes the
way they live, likes the things they do together. He values the takings-
for-granted his and Connie's years together have built up, intimate
certitudes that may be bruised right now but that Clifford doubts
are irreparably fractured by this adventure of hers. What was it that
French king said? That Paris was worth a mass? Well, this marriage
is worth a fuck.

Whatever doubt he feels about a course of action, he no longer
thinks that he did a bad thing by coming to consult Jekyll. At least he
knows where he stands, what his options are. And there's something
else, a feeling that he finds as comforting as it is unexpected. Renée
was right: the man is definitely not a total shark. He's like the Wizard
of Oz, operating inside and behind that terrible reputation the way the

genial Frank Morgan character did in the movie: "A very good man, but a very bad wizard," as the Wizard says when he's unmasked.

And there's this: Jekyll is the first person he's really been able to talk to since his father died. A man Clifford feels he'd like to stay in touch with, no matter how this business with Connie plays out. Is that likely? Is that possible? Maybe the acquaintanceship can be sustained via the Diogenes.

Outside, on Seventh Avenue, Clifford thinks about hailing a taxi, and then decides to walk down to the club. He's not displeased with his own performance at Jekyll's. He fancies that he came across as a pretty cool customer.

For the present, there's no need to act, he tells himself. Let matters stand as they are. See what happens. Thanksgiving's coming up, and the family's annual visit to Sainte-Eulalie, and Clifford thinks there's a good chance the sun and sea and sand will gentle Connie's soul. Out of sight, out of libido.

He'll keep a watchful eye on her, of course, but he'll also keep his emotional distance and let the future cut its own channels at its own pace. What the general liked to call "The old Doris Day ploy." *Que sera, sera,* what will be, will be. Yes, indeed: in life and love and peace and war: for better, for worse, for something in between.

Whatever.

As he thinks that, an ugly image rushes back into his mind, a memory of two figures on their knees, a beast with two backs contorted and distorted with lust, and with a sudden rush, the old anger comes back from its brief holiday.

CHAPTER FIVE

November 25

Clifford, bleary with just four hours' sleep, crosses the flyblown lobby and pulls a credit card from his wallet. As he hands it to the clerk, he sees that it's black, with the name of Connie's production company at the bottom. The receptionist looks at it dubiously; he's obviously never seen an American Express card like this one. Having seen the sort of people who wave theirs around in Manhattan restaurants, Clifford feels somewhat sheepish, since he has a perfectly good green one in his own name. When it comes to stuff like this, he tends to be a reverse snob.

The clock behind the reception counter reads 6:07 a.m.; his flight to Antigua won't depart for another two hours, but anything to get out of his miserable room and this concrete-block fleabag. A good working definition of hell is to be forced to connect through Miami International Airport on the Wednesday before Thanksgiving.

He's lucky to have found even this lousy accommodation. Yesterday was one of those trips from hell; the bad airline luck that began with his trip home from Sleeping Bear is still holding. It started with "equipment problems" at JFK, which meant he missed his Atlanta connection, leaving him two choices: hang around through the next day in Atlanta, an airport that terrifies him, or go via Miami. The latter at least sounded closer to the Caribbean, so he opted for it, and his choice proved unlucky, because the flight was diverted by weather to Orlando, and he didn't arrive in Miami until 1 a.m., half in the bag on airport cocktails and generally feeling like a displaced person. It's been the sort of experience that makes any claim that America once had a functioning airline industry, that people once looked forward to traveling by air, even dressed up for it, seem like an urban legend, a remote fairy tale of the kind one tells incredulous grandchildren. Clifford counts himself lucky to get a taxi driver who knew a hot-sheet place where he could lay his head. The only saving grace was that he'd bent his rigid principles to permit his luggage to go on ahead with the Grange women in a Barrow jet. It occurred to him that he may have compromised himself by allowing his luggage to fly Air Barrow—but what does a suitcase know from principle?

He thinks about his wife and daughter, asleep on Sainte-Eulalie right now, in the same villa the family always takes, overlooking turquoise waters and shining sands, and how he should be there himself, with the day presenting no problem more vexing than which trunks to wear, which thriller to read, and how early the first rum punch might be decently drunk. And he wonders if principle is really worth it.

"Where do I catch the courtesy van, please?" Clifford asks the clerk as he signs the credit card slip.

"We don' have no courtesy van, mister. I call you a cab, okay?"

"That'll be fine." He locates a ten-dollar bill and hands it across the counter. It's a heavy tip, but for all Clifford knows, the poor guy will leave this stinking job and go straight to a second eight-hour gig, and after that possibly even to another. The life these Latino immigrants are fleeing must be unimaginable for them to put themselves through this.

He goes over to a ratty plastic-covered sofa and sets down his only baggage—a carry-on with his laptop, a couple of magazines, a few toilet articles, and a paperback thriller by Lawrence Shames, a writer who in Clifford's opinion does Carl Hiaasen "Florida crazy" even better than Carl Hiaasen.

"Your taxi be here in fi', ten minutes, mister," the clerk calls over.

"Thanks." Clifford closes his eyes and waits.

A few minutes later, there's the sound of a vehicle outside. Thinking it must be his cab, Clifford starts to get up, then sits down again as a young man trudges in, lugging a bundle of newspapers. False alarm. He watches the man cut the bundle and fill a *Miami Herald* coin box off to one side of the reception counter, next to the Pepsi machine. He and the clerk yammer at each other in Spanish for a moment, then he goes out.

"How much is the paper?" Clifford asks the clerk. "I don't suppose you have *The New York Times*?"

"*Times,* no have. Maybe at airport. *Herald* seven'y fi' cents. You wan' change?"

Clifford buys a paper, casually scans the front page and almost drops the paper. Right in the middle of the front page, accompanying a story headlined "Local Artist Slain," are two photographs: one of an EMS team wheeling a gurney bearing a body bag past a neon sign that reads "Lupo's"; the other a formal photo of a man in a white tuxedo jacket, a man whose face is by now as familiar to Clifford, waking or dreaming, as his own.

It's Donkey Dong.

A jagged shockwave of nausea ripples up his gut. He feels dizzy, close to hyperventilation. He sits down heavily, puts his head back, closes his eyes, and takes a series of great heaving breaths.

"You okay, mister?" asks the clerk.

"I'm fine," he manages to gasp. "Just a dizzy spell." He gets control of himself, opens his eyes, and studies the photograph.

Donkey Dong smiles at the camera in a cocky fashion, sporting sexual overconfidence like a boutonniere. He's in a white dinner jacket with flashy black piping on the lapels, a flamboyant wing-collared shirt, a floppy maroon tie, more scarf than cravat: the sort of gigolo outfit a desperate older woman buys for her fancy man of the moment to show both appreciation and contempt. The picture is evidently cropped from a larger image; a woman's arm, the hand sporting a large jewel, rests on the man's right forearm.

He turns to the story. The subheads read "Murder in Coral Gables," then, in smaller type, "Possible Drug Connection."

He gulps down the text. The victim is described as "Miami-born artist Alejandro Vargas, 37"—so that's Donkey Dong's real name!— "a popular figure in certain South Florida circles, particularly as the frequent escort of socialite and Miami art scene fixture Estrellita Homberg, 66, widow of media and banking tycoon Gustavo Homberg, who is reported to be in grief-stricken seclusion at her Bahamas villa, where Vargas was to join her for the long Thanksgiving weekend."

He reads on. The story notes that the deceased was "a lively, regular presence on the south Florida social scene," that he "moved with ease in many different circles," that he had "achieved some success" as an artist-decorator, and had in fact returned home just the day before, "from the Northeast," where he was executing a private commission for Mrs. Homberg at "a summer house" she is building in Connecticut. The rest of the story is pretty boilerplate, a plot line right out of *CSI:Miami,* the outcome predictable: a parking lot at midnight, muffled steps, an arm around the neck, a quick sweep with a knife, a dead man. According to the paper, the Dade County police are "pursuing leads" while they riffle through a buffet of motives that include jealousy and money, as well as the possibility that this is just another one of those unfortunate fatal flare-ups to which people in hot climates are prone.

He rereads the story. After the jump, inside the paper, there are two more photographs: one at some kind of formal dance, the other in a box at a jai-alai fronton: both show Vargas with a flashy, bejeweled, blonde, sixtyish woman with hard, dark eyes, obviously the woman who belongs to the arm on page one; she's identified as the decedent's patron, Mrs. Homberg. A nearby sidebar provides scant biographical information on the deceased: arrived in 1990 as a legal immigrant from San Salvador; worked at a Palm Beach Publix sacking groceries, moved south to study at Southwest Atlantic Junior College of Art, supporting himself by acting in small-time Spanish-language porn films. The article implies that he seems to have found his vocation as a protégé, catnip to rich women of a certain age and income who supported his art. The inference is clear, that his current patroness is merely the latest in a long list. Interestingly, Vargas was due to become a citizen next year.

Clifford lets the paper drop and thinks: this is a typical Miami story right out of Shames, Hiaasen, John D. MacDonald, "Scarface," the Versace killing. Gaudy, ominous, violent, loud, degraded, ruthless Miami. There's just something about the city, a kind of swamp-evil, hot, noxious, toxic, brackish, and rotten. A place where the temperature of air and blood both frequently touch one hundred degrees, where the senses are deafened by ear-busting salsa rhythms and rackety hip-hop and the clank of Baccarat crystal and the glitter of bling and the yammer-yammer of demotic Spanish. Forget all that Chamber of Commerce bullshit about how cultured the place has become, with art fairs and concerts, and how socially competitive with Palm Beach and Delray it is. Miami's still what it's always been, no matter the demographics: big flashy houses, big flashy cars, big flashy boats. Bejeweled women barely not hookers hanging on the arms of tough old scrawny men in sports shirts who once knew Meyer Lansky; men with one-hundred-fifty-foot sportfishing yachts afloat on seas of drugs, parked at marinas guarded by gel-slicked hoods with Uzis tucked in the jackets of iridescent jogging suits. A magnet for thrill seekers and chance takers feeding off a smorgasbord of high and low swindles, corruption and deception. Vargas country.

Screw the sociology, he thinks, because his screenwriter's mind has just come up with another worse thought: is there anything that might connect the late Señor Dong to Connie? Could this be a contract hit arranged by Donkey Dong's patroness? *Please God, make this nothing more than it seems: a random bar fight, a random knifing.*

Enough with the Law & Order *shit, he tells himself. Repeat after me: there is nothing here to connect this guy to Connie. Niente, nada!* And his apprehension fades away before the force of a sudden inspiration. A terrific idea. On the cruel side perhaps—but too good to resist. There's no way he can't pull it off. Sainte-Eulalie is cut off from the world, save for one satellite phone in the Great House for emergencies. That's the point of the place: total escape. No TV, no cellular connection, no cable, no papers. If you need to keep in touch with the news, with your money, with the in-crowd, your doctors, you're better off elsewhere. Go to Saint Barts, to Nassau. On Sainte-Eulalie, there's no way Connie can know about Vargas, not before Clifford gets there.

"Hey, mister, you' taxi here! Mister—you hear me?"

Clifford opens his eyes and stows the paper in his shoulder bag.

In the terminal, the newsstands are just opening for business. He tears the story out of the *Herald,* stows it away in a compartment of his shoulder bag as a keepsake. Then he buys a *New York Times,* a *New York Post,* and a spanking-fresh second copy of the *Herald.* When he deplanes in Antigua, right on schedule, he leaves the New York papers in the seatback pocket, but keeps the *Herald,* which he's thoroughly reread on the flight. Two hours later, an Island Airways De Havilland lands him on Sainte-Eulalie. Looking out the window, Clifford spots Connie and Jenny waiting beside a Plantation Bay Mini-Moke. They both look terrific. Golden and happy.

Back at their seaside cottage, Jenny immediately heads up the beach to join her clique, kids whose families, like hers, have been coming here year after year. Clifford watches her go, and then says to Connie, "Christ, I'm glad to be here. Finally!"

"I'm glad you are, too," she says, smiling. "Of course, you *could* have been here yesterday," she adds. "But I'm not going to say anything. You have your own way of doing things and I respect that."

He looks out over the beach to the gentle turquoise water. "God, I love this place! Paradise! How about a swim?"

"Let me visit the loo first," she says. "It must be that conch salad Jenny and I had last night."

She starts to head inside.

"Want to look at the paper?" Clifford asks innocently. "I'm afraid all I have is a *Miami Herald*. The New York papers hadn't come in by the time I had to board."

"Sure."

"Here you are." He tosses the paper gently on the bed, making sure the paper lands with the bottom half of the front page facing up.

"Beggars can't be choosers," says Connie. She picks up the paper without looking at it. "I won't be long," she says, and disappears into the bathroom.

As Clifford changes into a swimsuit, he visualizes Connie scanning the front page and seeing the photo of Donkey Dong. He would give all he has to see her face.

Perhaps three minutes later, he hears the toilet flush. A moment later, she comes out.

She tosses the newspaper back on the bed. "Shall we hit the water?" she says. Her face is composed, her smile steady, her voice even. It's a magnificent performance, provided one knows to appreciate it. She puts on her dark glasses and makes for the beach. Clifford follows, studying her from behind. It's only through minuscule nuances of bearing and stride, of the slightly too gingerly way Connie's holding herself, the careful way she places her feet just so in the sand, as if she's packed with explosives that a careless misstep might set off, that someone who knows her body language intimately might "read" the feelings that must be boiling inside. At the lawn's edge, she shucks her T-shirt and drops her sunglasses on it. Nearing forty, she still has the smooth figure of a college girl.

She turns and looks at her husband. "Ready when you are," she says, smiling.

Even though he's on guard, her expression so closely resembles genuine affection that it produces a kind of emotional epiphany in Clifford. A remembered quality, that once upon a time was always present when he thought of his wife, when he talked with her, when he looked at her, when a happenstance—the tilt of her chin, the set of her shoulders, the way a hand rested on a hip—evoked a reaction, call it tenderness, he will always associate with the old Connie, the original Connie, the Connie he loved and courted and made pregnant and started to build a life with. Memories of almost painful intensity flicker within Clifford for just an instant, no more than a few beats in his chest, in particular a moment recollected from what today seems another life: of a another sunny day at another brilliant beach, when they were just beginning to court and spent a Memorial Day weekend on Cape Cod. The ocean had felt ungodly cold, and Clifford had hung back at the waterline, but Connie had plunged in. He remembers her coming back up the beach, glistening, literally sparkling with water droplets. Is the bond still there, that certain strength of union, that fond and reliable consolation? The old emotional indispensabilities? He's not sure, but he knows what he hopes. And of course in the middle of all this confusing welter of renewed affection is a distinct stab of regret at the little joke he's just played on his wife.

"Lead on," he says.

She lopes across the narrow bone-white beach and into the water. She plunges into the slight swell and strokes seaward, straight out, toward the bobbing white floats that mark the safe boundaries of the club beach, swimming with a strong crawl stroke, learned and honed over all those Michigan summers, all those races in freezing lake water. She just keeps going, out and out, until he begins to wonder whether, grief-driven, she intends to swim until her energy gives out and she drowns. But then, nearly at the float line, she stops, turns, treads water, waves vigorously, and calls out, "What are you waiting for? Come on!"

As he wades in, Clifford wonders whether it might be relief, not grief, that his little joke has brought to Connie, whether his little joke may in fact turn out to be on him. She may well have looked at the newspaper and immediately thought: problem solved. How can he tell? Never one to leave well enough—or bad enough—alone, Clifford decides to press the point. As he swims out to join his wife, he ponders his next step.

That evening, before dinner, while Connie's still drying her hair in the bathroom he calls to her, "What did you do with that *Miami Herald*? I can't see it anywhere."

"Look on the bedside table? The maid probably put it there."

"Nope."

"I guess the maids took it when they tidied up the room. Sorry."

"Goddamn these people!" he swears. "I wanted to keep it. Did you happen to read the murder story on the front?"

"No. Why?" She comes back into the bedroom. "Newspapers are at a premium around here. I'm sure they haven't thrown it out. Do you want me to call housekeeping?" Her husband can't detect a single suspicious note in her tone of voice. "Don't bother," he says. "I'm sure I can track it down on the Internet when we get back."

"What was so interesting about that story, anyway? I would think the last thing you'd want to read about on vacation are killings and blood."

"You know how I'm always fishing for ideas. Something to jump-start my stalled career, including begging you to plead my case with Ronnie."

"I've told you I would—when the time is right."

"Which is likely to be when? The twelfth of never?"

"Don't be silly! I told you I would and I will."

The exasperation in his wife's voice sounds genuine. Clifford tells himself not to push it. Connie has cheated on him and hurt him, but whatever he feels counts for nothing against the possibility of being able to work again. "I'm sorry," he says. "I know you know how I feel. And I know you've got my back with Barrow. Anyway, about that piece in the *Herald*: I thought it kind of lends itself to a *Scarface* angle; you know how crazy the suits in Hollywood are for remakes."

"I would think that the last thing we need is another *Scarface*, given the shape the world's in."

"Apparently blood and chainsaws are catnip to the video game crowd. There was something in that story about how the dead guy worked in porn. That's a weird angle you could really do something with. I wonder if he had a really big dick? Maybe they chopped it off and stuffed it in his mouth." His choice of words is exact. Connie hates profanity and obscenity. She's always telling him to watch his language.

"Yuck! Don't be disgusting. Let's go have a rum punch. Jenny's waiting."

After dinner, their daughter goes off to join her mates, and the Granges go out on the Great House patio for coffee and a nightcap. Clifford stares up into the wide, starry canopy of heaven, thoughtfully sipping his drink.

"You know," he says finally, injecting into his voice just the merest hint that the postprandial Plantation Bay Special, his third of the evening, is kicking in, "I just can't get keep that damn *Herald* story out of my mind! Apparently, it was some kind of love triangle deal: the guy was being kept by an older woman, but must have been fooling around and got caught, and while the story doesn't say it in so many words, the inference is clear: sugar mommy lost her cool and put a hit on the guy. Which he probably deserved. Guy like that'll probably fuck a snake!"

"Clifford, stop it, for goodness sakes! Are you drunk?"

"Just enough to make sense," he replies. "You know, maybe this is really the way I ought to go if I'm going to get my career back. Set my sights lower. Sex and violence, that's what they want today, no politics or good versus evil or moral hazard or any of that high-toned bullshit I used to go in for. I wonder..."

"Clifford darling, stop it! This is pointless!"

"Well, what other choices do I have? As I said earlier, maybe if you'd do the noble spouse bit and intercede with your little friend Barrow on my behalf..."

She cuts him off: "Believe me, I've thought about it. If only I had a better reading on Ronnie."

He looks at her with a hard, careful candor. "I would think that if anyone could read the little cocksucker, it'd be you."

"Can't we talk about something else?" She reaches out and puts a hand on his. "Let it go, sweetie. If the right opportunity comes along, I'll speak to Ronnie. I swear I will."

"I doubt that," he says, "not when everything's going so well for you. Still, it's a nice thought. What is it that I read somewhere? That a little hypocrisy is the price we pay for civilization?" He knows he's pushing it, but he can't help himself.

She pulls her hand back. Her eyes are angry. "Are you trying to make me mad? Because if you are, you're succeeding. How can I make you understand that it's not Ronnie who's your problem! He's probably forgotten that you exist! It's *you* who's the problem! Don't you see that? You act like you're Christ on the cross when the fact is that, in Hollywood, you're no more than a third-string Woody Allen. Or should I say Norman Maine?"

"Ouch!"

"I'm sorry, but that's how it is. Now, please let's not spoil our vacation. Let's declare a truce. How about another drink?"

He shakes his head. He should apologize, but all that's left to him, the way this has turned out, is to stand his ground, even if it worsens the mess he's making.

"How about a stroll by the water?" She sounds like she means it, but he can't sort out whether it's Connie the private person or Connie the public actress who's talking. Again he shakes his head, feeling that he might as well play out the hand. "I think not. I think I'll just sit here and trouble deaf heaven with my bootless cries."

"As you wish." She sounds really fed up. She gets up and walks quickly away.

Clifford watches her go. Should he wait a minute or two, and then follow her? No, best to give it a rest. He could use another drink, but decides against it. Instead, he waits ten minutes, and then returns to the cottage. She's not there. He goes to the edge of the terrace and looks down the beach, where he sees her sitting on a bench that's been carpentered around the trunk of a tall palm. He goes inside, undresses, and gets into bed.

A half-hour later, he's reading when he hears her on the cottage patio. She comes to the bedroom door, looks at him without a word, and then turns away. He hears the scrape of a chair.

Damned if he'll make the first move, he goes on reading for a while, then turns out the lights without having said a word.

But he doesn't fall asleep. Finally, he eases out of bed and crosses the room to where he can see her. She's just sitting there, staring out at the long trail of fluorescence cast by the slowly rising moon. He stands there, hugging the shadows, like a cockroach avoiding a flashlight beam, and studies the moonlight on her hair, on her bare shoulders, wondering what she's thinking. Then he returns to bed. It creaks faintly as he settles. He wonders if she hears. If she knows he's awake. When he puts his head down, sleep tries to take him but he fights it off. There's more to be said. He'll wait her out. She can't sit out there forever.

Finally, as he supposes he always knew would be the case, he gets out of bed and in his shorts walks out on the porch and comes up behind Connie. She's sitting rigid, staring out to sea. He places his hands on her shoulders. She doesn't flinch—nor does she melt.

"I'm sorry," he says. "Sometimes I think I'm going nuts. Make that: I *am* going nuts. I need to work. That's the problem. You understand that, don't you?"

She reaches up and places a hand on his. The shimmering silver-gold track of the moon stretches all the way to the horizon.

"It's all right," she says. "I do understand. Plus you've had a long day." She rises wearily. "Let's go to bed."

Inside, he watches her undress. Through half-closed eyes, a fake slack and sleepy expression, he studies his wife the way a kid observes, from behind a tree, a crowd of grown-ups at a lawn party. He watches her hang her clothes up, put away her underthings, cross the room, naked, and can't take his eyes off the rough unruly bristling dark tangle at her crotch, completely out of sync with the perfectly put-together rest of her. You see that, and you *know*, as he has known, as Donkey Dong would have known the instant he set eyes on Connie, because guys like that always do know, a woman with a thread hanging loose, that if you know to tug it, an entire careful tapestry of restraint and reserve will unravel. All it takes is the situation, the moment, the man. When she and Clifford began to "date," her ardor astonished him; it was as if he'd unlocked a chastity belt—and then somewhere along the way he lost the combination.

She slips into bed. "I'm sorry if I pissed you off," he says.

"Well, you did," she says, "but no matter."

"Truce?"

"Truce." She slides close to him; he feels her hand at his groin, exploring. Feels himself begin to stiffen in spite of himself.

"Umm," she murmurs. "What's this?"

"You might call it a token of my respect and affection." He's a goner.

"Why how very upright of you, good sir." She kisses his neck, and then pushes him over on his back, pulling his shorts down. She shifts her body and begins to go down on him, making little moaning sounds, hands and lips sliding up and down. He feels his ejaculation start to move up the pipeline, all pleasure and existence concentrating at the very tip of his cock, his mind emptied of all intelligence and cognition. He hangs on for dear life, but he can only manage a few seconds before he feels like he's falling off the goddamn planet. Connie senses he's about to let go and starts to take her mouth away, but he puts his hand firmly on the back of her neck, holding her head where it is, and comes half in her mouth, half on her cheek and chin as she twists her head away violently and pushes him back.

"For God's sakes, Clifford," she mutters. She plucks a tissue from the nightstand and wipes her mouth. "You know I hate that," she says.

"Sorry," he says. "Don't know what came over me—no pun intended." Then, quickly, "My turn now," and before she can react he plunges his head between her legs, holding her under her thighs so she can't wriggle free, teasing her with his tongue in fast little circular licks. He remembers exactly what to do, exactly how she likes it. In a few seconds she's his, that is, she's the prisoner of her own irresistible excitement; a minute later, no more, she begins to shudder, a quick series of abrupt spasms, gasps like slashes in her breathing pattern, then, "Oh, *mi amor*," she groans as she comes. "*Que amor!* Oh God, stop! Stop, please."

No more than ten, fifteen seconds from start to finish, but he doesn't stop. He keeps it up and she comes again and again, until finally she can't stand it any longer and pushes his mouth away. After she gets her breath back, she pats him affectionately on the shoulder, the way one absently strokes a pet, murmurs, "Thanks, I needed that," and falls asleep.

He reaches across her and turns out the light. For a long time, he lies by her side, feeling angry and screwed over. *Amor*, he thinks. *Amor! Gotcha!*

When morning comes, he knows it's time to quit the needling. He's had his fun. He's raised a welt or two. He flatters himself that he's stung her inside where it may not show but still smarts. So where to go from here? There's only one practical answer. Shut up and put up. His only real relief and sanctuary are his family and his home. What can he have been thinking? No more games, then. He's pushed this as far as he can.

But of course his next thought is: *what if she starts up again—with someone else?* The old anger starts to simmer.

Well, he won't think about that now. Like Scarlett O'Hara, he'll think about it tomorrow.

And that's what he manages to do. The rest of the short vacation is fabulous. They play, talk, walk, even make love again, and it's all seamless—except for the half-dozen times a mischievous voice inside Clifford hisses, "*Amor! Amor!*"

The following Sunday, they fly home. This time Clifford's complex, principle-dictated route functions perfectly, and he gets home just a few hours after the ladies. In Miami, he buys a copy of the *Herald* and searches for further news on the Vargas murder.

Monday morning, back in the real world, with Connie at work, Jenny at school, and a third cup of coffee to intensify his anxiety level, he heads down the lawn to his studio. The grass, now brown, glistens with frost—winter is definitely tapping at the window.

The little building is an unapologetic, unmistakable knock-off, right up to its misshapen conical roof, of the architect Philip Johnson's much-photographed New Canaan retreat, although instead of being in a wood-enclosed field, it's oriented to command a splendid raking view of the Sound, with Long Island in the far distance.

Connie built it for him a year ago as a birthday present. It's the one place on earth where he's still generally happy and secure, sealed off from his private calamity. The studio is his bunker, bolt-hole, snuggery, sacred grove, *sanctum sanctorum*, bubble chamber. *If one didn't know better*, he reflects, looking around, *one would say this was the workspace of a feverishly employed man.* The scarred surface of the desk is practically invisible under a jumble of papers: bills, film journals, mail-order catalogs and come-ons, clippings, Post-it notes, announcements and club correspondence from the Diogenes, at least a half-dozen yellow legal pads in various stages of scribble and sketch, souvenir mugs and prize cups holding pencils and pens, framed photographs, stacks of CDs and DVDs, the disarray surmounted by a handsome nineteenth century brass lamp with double green-glass shades. Behind the desk is a high-backed eighteenth-century English barber's chair that Clifford works in. Today, it too is piled high with papers.

On a counter next to the door that opens to the small bathroom, there's a coffee machine and a microwave; underneath, a small refrigerator and open shelves for the necessaries. An old handheld Arriflex movie camera on a folded tripod is propped in a nearby corner.

Between two windows on the left-hand wall is a mélange, neatly hung, of framed memorabilia of Clifford's father. It has photos, including one with Spencer Tracy taken in Korea during the actor's VIP visit, ribbons and medals, letters and commendations, a scorecard from the day the old man shot his then-age—seventy-eight—on a Vero Beach public course. Only five years later, he was dead.

Facing the door is a solid wall of shelves holding books, videotapes, and laser discs. In the angle of the wall is a tall, locked, glass-fronted corner bookcase that holds Clifford's bibliophilic treasures: original screenplays, some autographed, the most cherished being a shooting script of *All About Eve,* one of Clifford's favorite pictures.

This was signed by the principals: the director, Joe Mankiewicz, the stars, Bette Davis, Anne Baxter, Celeste Holm, George Sanders, Gary Merrill, Hugh Marlowe, and Gregory Ratoff. There are also first editions of novels that became what are in Clifford's opinion important or merely good movies, from Dickens to Elmore Leonard, along with movie books, many autographed, and a morocco-and-gilt-bound set of his own scripts that Connie had made up for him a few years ago, but which stops with *Summer Heat,* the film that preceded *Crown Heights.* On the shelf below, lying on their sides, are a bunch of leather boxes, more or less matched to the bindings of the scripts, that hold videos and DVDs of Clifford's films. He never plays them. At this point, with his professional life in shreds, it would just be too painful. Finally, on a bottom shelf, pushed in haphazardly, is a series of Diogenes membership books.

The first order of each day's business is usually to choose music. Wagner, he thinks, to get the week off to a big start: maybe Stokowski conducting excerpts from *The Ring,* over the top. Clifford's feeling inspired, lively-minded. Invigorated by the crisp day outside and by his four days on Sainte-Eulalie. A good morning to resume work on his "Wagner Project." He's feeling mentally and creatively strong. This is going to work.

But before that, there's one thing he has to do. He goes online and checks out the *Miami Herald* Web site for the days he was out of circulation on Sainte-Eulalie. There's no Vargas news worth reading. The police are still looking for the killer. Okay, time to share the good news with Jekyll. He picks up his cellphone and seconds later, "Mr. Hyde" is put through.

"Great minds work alike," Jekyll says. "I was just about to call you."

"Really, what about?" But before Jekyll can explain, Clifford says, "I'll bet my news tops yours?"

"I doubt it."

"Oh, yeah, well, try this. My problem has been dealt with. By an angry guy with a knife. In Coral Gables. Donkey Dong is *mort!*"

"He's dead? You don't say!"

"On my mother's grave. Killed in a barroom brawl—actually a parking-lot brawl—last Tuesday night. The cops were still looking for the killer, last time I looked. I'll fax you the story from the *Miami Herald*."

"You needn't bother. I'll look it up online."

"You needn't bother. I already checked. What I've got is what there is. For the record, the guy's name was Vargas. Alejandro Vargas. He painted murals in rich people's pool houses, but basically I think his day job was gigolo. Arm candy for the woman who owns the Winding Crest house. If you use a little imagination, it's not hard to imagine that she found out about...holy shit, what am I saying!"

"Probably what I'm thinking. *Cherchez la femme*. You're wondering whether his patroness may have discovered his relationship with your wife and acted to deal with it with extreme prejudice. I think you can discount that."

"Why do you say that?"

"If she had found out about Mrs. G., I think we'd somehow have known. Someone like Vargas is likely to have several women on the string. As for a professional hit, it sounds very improbable. However, let's count our blessings. This situation could have mushroomed. Tell me: is the other party to the Vargas relationship aware of this development?"

"The other party is. I saw to that—all very subtly. You'd've been proud of me."

"And how did she respond?"

"Cool as the proverbial cucumber. But she's wounded, I'm guessing—not that she'd ever let me see it."

"It's also possible she's relieved. These relationships are usually quick to wear out their welcome."

"I thought of that. Anyway, what's your news?"

"Well, coming on top of yours, it's probably anticlimactic, but your legal position is no longer as strong as it was when it was last discussed."

"Come again?"

"There has been an amazing, wholly unexpected development. You'll recall that we discussed the no-fault bill that's been pending in your state assembly?"

"The bill the cardinal's got bottled up, right?"

"Exactly. But it's bottled up no longer. Last week, either with His Eminence's complaisance or without—there seems to be some confusion on the matter—the bill suddenly came out of committee and was passed by acclamation. You now live in a no-fault state."

"You're shitting me!"

"Regretfully, I am not. It was what is called a 'midnight raid.' The Tuesday before Thanksgiving, the state assembly was in its customary late pre-holiday session, clearing up unfinished business before the Thanksgiving break, when the speaker was suddenly informed that key opposition to the long-pending no-fault bill had been withdrawn."

"'Key opposition?' You mean the governor? And informed by whom?"

"As to the latter, no one's saying. As regards the former, the governor's thrown her body on the grenade, but I think we're really talking about his Eminence, Cardinal Santiago, even though he just happened, conveniently, to be in Rome when the amending legislation was brought to the floor. On his return, after the bill had become law, he did shed a few fatalistic crocodile tears."

"So what you're telling me is, if I had called you just now to say let's drop the hammer on...well, you know, the woman in the case... I'd be up shit's creek?"

"I'm afraid so. Certainly as far as using evidentiary material in court or in a lawsuit."

"How the hell can they do that, Arthur? I mean, what they're basically saying is that Connie's and my vows to be faithful don't count for shit, right? Don't I have certain First Amendment rights?" *And fuck the First Amendment. So much for CG Films with its $200 million production budget.*

"I'm afraid not. Anyway, I hope you didn't spend too much money with Peter Harris."

"Not to worry. I figured let sleeping dogs lie—"

Before he can finish the sentence and tell Jekyll that he never called Harris, he hears the lawyer say, "What's that, Ms. Grosvenor?" and then there's a muffled silence, obviously a hand over the receiver. When Jekyll comes back on, he sounds distracted, his concentration evidently elsewhere. "Clifford," he says, "I'm sorry, but I'm afraid there's a call I have just *got* to take. Hanky-panky at the highest level that has obliged me to tread loudly, since in this particular instance fate has handed me a very small stick. Yes, Ms. Grosvenor, tell them I'll be right on. Good-bye, Clifford. All the best."

Jekyll rings off.

Well, that's that, Clifford thinks. *Those fucking bastards!* He can't recall feeling so helpless, and helpless is a frame of mind Clifford Grange *really* doesn't do well.

He'll miss Jekyll, too. He's an interesting guy, a peculiar bundle of contradictions. Still, perhaps they can keep in touch. Let a little time go by, then call and suggest lunch at the club, that's what Clifford resolves to do.

As for going forward himself, now what? Close the book on this sorry episode and move on, right? Get the Wagner Project up to speed. And keep a close eye on Connie. Very close. And try to tamp down the anger.

His intercom rings. It's the housekeeper. The BME people are here to install the big new TV. *Always something,* Clifford thinks as he goes up to the house. *Well, if the world wants to fuck you, it damn well can!*

ACT TWO

•

The Harps of the Blessed

"Whenever the enlightened, wealthy, and spirited of an affluent and great country seriously conspire to subvert democratical institutions, their leisure, money, intelligence and means of combining will be found too powerful for the ill-directed and conflicting efforts of the mass. It is, therefore, all important to enlist a portion of this class, at least, in the cause of freedom, since its power at all times renders it a dangerous enemy."

—James Fenimore Cooper,
The American Democrat, 1838

CHAPTER SIX

February 22

It's Sunday night, the Monopoly board has been put away, the cocoa cups washed, and the women of Grangeford, who have to be up and at 'em first thing Monday, have gone upstairs to bed. Clifford isn't sleepy, and—as usual—he hasn't got a whole lot on his plate, so he decides to have a nightcap and watch a movie. He goes into the library, makes himself a Scotch, and examines the neatly arranged DVDs in the bookshelf. His fingers settle on *The Day of the Jackal*, an old favorite. As he pulls it out, it suddenly occurs to him that he's reneged on a commitment he made to himself late last year: to get in touch with Arthur Jekyll and propose lunch.

The following morning, he waits until the coast is clear, goes down the lawn to his studio and telephones Jekyll. The lawyer's surprised to hear from him. "Don't tell me there's been a flare-up?"

"Not to worry," Clifford says. "All is totally copacetic. Which means, as someone famously said, that I'm basically sullen but not mutinous. Ours is a model modern marriage. She goes to the office and I do the washing up. She makes the money and I spend it. Just kidding, actually. No—the reason I'm calling, Arthur, is to see whether you might be free for lunch sometime. We could meet at the club."

"What a nice idea. Can I get back to you?"

"Absolutely." As Clifford says this, he has another thought. "By the way, Arthur, when we last talked, something you said led me to believe that you were under the impression I had hired that private detective you told me about. What made you think that?"

There's a pause. The attorney is evidently searching his memory. Finally Jekyll says, "I must be getting old, but I can't imagine why I said such a thing. You never spoke to Harris?"

"I didn't. I thought about it, but in the end decided not to."

"Well, then, no harm done. How are you otherwise? Any news on the film front?"

"Sad to say, the stalemate continues. As far as the movie industry is concerned, I think I've ceased to exist. And you? Keeping yourself gainfully occupied?"

"Busy, busy, busy. Starting with Bear Stearns, then Lehman Brothers and the rest, the market in subprime matrimony is in a state of total capitulation. A great many Wall Street couples are re-examining the economic basis of their marriages with a view to getting something while there's still something to get. I can hardly keep up. Anyway, I'll get back to you shortly about that lunch."

Clifford decides to punt on Wagner. He'll get to that tomorrow. He needs something profound, so he puts on a CD of a late Beethoven quartet, and then gets his pads and pens in order and his computer up and running. He deals with the few e-mails he gets, checks his bank and brokerage accounts, reads the trades online, which causes him to ponder the latest project attachments of a couple of directors whom he thinks utterly untalented, catches up on Nikki Finke's Hollywood blog, and scrolls through last Friday's Gawker posts. When he's finished, he pops on the screen saver—Jenny as the Sugar Plum Fairy in her grade school's *Nutcracker*—and settles back in the fancy new

Aeron office chair his wife and daughter gave him for Valentine's Day to figure out what will get the old juices flowing, or at least to try.

In this he isn't entirely successful, but he manages to putter through the day. Around six, his womenfolk return from their toil. They have an early dinner, a pleasant evening, then it's early to bed, and the next morning is more of the same for Clifford.

Until midafternoon, when his phone rings. It's Jekyll.

"I'm sorry to bother you," he says, "but in light of our conversation, I've come up with something that might interest you. When can we get together? Will you be coming into the city as usual tomorrow? Could we meet?"

"I'm planning to, so just name the time and place. The club?"

"I'd prefer a place free from prying eyes. A client of mine has a suite in the Waldorf Towers—number 38E—that we can use. Will that be all right?"

"Sure." *This all sounds very mysterious.* "But why the cloak and dagger? Want to give me a hint?"

"I'll tell you when I see you. Waldorf Towers, 38E, have you got that? You can enter on the Fiftieth Street side. I'll leave your name— that is, 'Hyde'—at the desk. Will noon be too early?"

"I'll see you then." Clifford hangs up. He's puzzled. This development calls for a reflective cappuccino, which means a trip back up the lawn to the espresso machine in the kitchen. As he busies himself with grinding and tamping and frothing, his eye roves idly over the refrigerator door and notes a new addition to the usual potpourri of schedules, recipes, and reminders.

It's a four-by-six photo that had to have been taken a week ago at the state capitol, the occasion being the announcement that Summerhill Farms will build a massive new processing and packaging plant on the outskirts of the city. In the photo, Belle and the governor are side by side in the center, flanked by Connie and by Cardinal Joseph Santiago, Archbishop of Southern New England, who by all accounts is the person mainly responsible for bringing about Belle's decision to cancel her plans for a new facility in her home state and to build it instead in New England. The plan is expected to cost some $400 million and to generate approximately a thousand new jobs in the area.

The way Connie got the story, Santiago had telephoned Belle back in December last year, just after the Summerhill IPO was announced. Apparently the two had known each other for a long time. He told Belle that he'd read the preliminary prospectus with great interest, and that his Native American flock's pension and tribal funds were thinking about taking a substantial position in Summerhill shares. He had also noted Summerhill's strategic alliance with Wal-Mart, with whom his own flock at Forest Fields were having serious discussions about Wal-Mart putting a "big box" store on the casino property. Had Belle considered the advantages of a New England processing and packing facility? Was she irrevocably committed to Gastonia? North Carolina was a prosperous state, but Connecticut was struggling. Santiago had delivered a compelling hard sell on the advantages of his home diocese: proximity to important Summerhill markets, reliable, cheap Hispanic labor, plentiful water and electricity, etc. In addition, he indicated that he could persuade the state to come up with a package of tax and other incentives at least equal to whatever North Carolina had put on the table. Then Santiago followed up with a personal visit—he flew to Asheville in a shiny new Forest Fields Gulfstream—and performed a mass of remembrance for Belle's parents and husband in Asheville's famed Basilica of Saint Lawrence, which clinched the deal.

The local press celebrated this as a major coup for the governor and the cardinal. Belle caught the sharp end of the stick: unshirted hell from the North Carolina political, industrial, and media establishment, but she had played her own trump card—her plans for an art institute—which had brought the state's cultural and educational leadership to her defense and had gone a long way toward silencing her critics. Clifford supposes he's happy for Belle, although he's frankly not so happy with her. All she reserved for Connie in the IPO was a lousy $25 million in restricted stock grants, which he thinks was kind of chintzy of Belle, considering how *Forbes* says Belle's now worth over a billion, and considering how much of that is due to

Connie. $100 million would have been more like it. That the stock is up some forty percent since the offering is small consolation. But what's done is done. Move on.

The next day, Clifford knocks on a door on the thirty-eighth floor of the Waldorf Towers and is admitted by Jekyll. He settles on the sofa and looks around. The décor is pure corporate: dull verging on drab, all muted beiges and grays, dreary textures, noncommittal reproduction furniture, the art on the walls uninteresting and impersonal, the lighting dim.

"What is this place?" he asks.

Jekyll smiles. "Until recently, it was on the books of a large Oklahoma oil company, although it functioned principally as the place of assignation for that company's CEO and his so-called 'executive assistant.' Ex-CEO, I should say, as well as the now considerably less well off ex-husband of a client of mine. She's keeping it while a new Park Avenue apartment is being redone in keeping with her transformation from a Muskogee housewife to a very rich Manhattan divorcee, albeit a somewhat moth-eaten one."

"Some love nest. What's a place like this go for?"

"Around $100,000 a month, even in hard times."

"Wow. Okay, Arthur, what's up? Why the subterfuge?"

"I need to speak to you in absolute confidence, and I want to do so in a place we can't be seen together—not for the time being—or overheard. The recording devices I had placed in this apartment when it was under previous stewardship have been removed and I know it's clean. Now, let me begin at the beginning, with our conversation of last December, December 2, to be exact, when you had just returned from the islands and called to tell me that Mr. Vargas was no longer on the scene. Apparently, there was a misinterpretation on my part: I was under the impression that after our first meeting last year, you engaged Peter Harris to conduct a surveillance of your wife. But from what you told me just this past Monday, I gather you didn't?"

"Correct. I tried to tell you when I called you after I got back from the Caribbean, but you cut me off. The fact is, when I left your office after I came to see you, which was when—mid-November?—I thought about it, but I never called Harris. What made you think I did?"

"Well, it appears someone did." He lets that hang in the air for a second, seeming to savor Clifford's look of astonishment, then continues. "Let me recapitulate. You came to see me on Wednesday, November 12. The following Monday—that would have been on the seventeenth—it chanced that Peter called me on another matter. As we wound up our conversation, I happened to mention—quite innocently and very discreetly, I can assure you—that he might be hearing from a client of mine with respect to a surveillance in your area."

"You did *what*? Jesus, Arthur, I—"

"I'm sorry," Jekyll interrupts, in a formal voice, "but what I said to Peter was perfectly proper. He and I have worked together for years and we have a long history of mutual referrals. In the event, he asked me if I was referring to a job at 127 Winding Crest Drive. I said I was. He thanked me, saying that he hadn't realized the referral was through me. I assumed you had your own reasons for not naming me, so I let the matter pass and Peter and I ended our chat."

"But I didn't call him."

"I realize that now. So after you and I spoke on Monday last, and you reiterated that you never called him, I telephoned Peter, and on the pretext of getting my own office records in order, asked him about the Winding Crest job: when he received the assignment and when it was completed. He checked his diary and informed me that he was on the job as of October 21 and that the surveillance was completed on November 10."

"October 21? That's impossible! You and I didn't even..." Clifford's voice trails off, he looks at the ceiling as if searching the air for an answer, then asks Jekyll, "You're sure he said October 21?"

"I can play you the recording of my conversation with Peter if you like."

"October 21! Jesus! That means..."

"My reaction precisely, Clifford, when Peter told me the date. That meant that he was on the job on October 22, which by your own account..."

"Was a date that will live in infamy. That's when..."

Now it's Jekyll's turn to finish the thought. "That's when you conducted your own surveillance mission. A fact that wasn't lost on me, and which has very disturbing implications. Clearly, someone else had an interest in certain goings-on at 127 Winding Crest Drive."

"Well, it sure as hell wasn't me, because..." Clifford's voice trails off as he grasps the significance of what Jekyll has just said. "Of course, it could have been another house on Winding Crest." To his own ears, the supposition sounds stupid and unconvincing, so he tries another tack: "How about if the guy was carrying on with someone else in our part of the world? Guys like that, they get around, and up where we live, there must be a thousand desperate housewives."

"I take your point," says Jekyll. "Still, I haven't heard anything, not on the grapevine, nor from any of my hedge-fund clients, a number of whom live in your neck of the woods and are prone to gossip viciously about one another. No—I think we can be certain."

By now Clifford's mind is on another, more dire tangent: "So if Harris was on the job on October 22," he asks, "does that mean...?"

"I think it's very possible that not only your wife but you yourself would have come under surveillance, yes."

"Oh, Jesus!" Clifford's shoulders slump. He shakes his head in disbelief at the notion that someone else knows not only about Connie but that he knows. He asks, weakly, "So who do you figure called Harris? And why was Harris on the job so long?"

"Well," Jekyll says, "to answer you in reverse order: I suspect Peter was retained to ascertain that the liaison was ongoing. As regards his client, I first thought of the late Mr. Vargas's Miami patroness, especially if she suspected that her boy toy was stepping out on her. Certainly, hard evidence of the sort you described to me could incite a quarrel with Mr. Vargas, followed by an uncontrollable urge to see him punished for his tomcatting. Possibly followed by his untimely demise, Miami being one of those places where every service is available for a price. The personality profile fits. I did some online research on Vargas's patroness, who is well known to the *Miami Herald* and the social glossies of the area. She appears to be cursed with a fiery temper. There was at least one incident in a nightclub when she belabored another society matron with her handbag."

Clifford starts to interrupt, but Jekyll holds up a hand. "The more I think about it, however, the less I like that theory. For one thing, I know Peter Harris, and I know how he works. He's only as effective as his nose is clean. He would have opened a file on Vargas that would include any subsequent information relating to him. Peter's research people are nothing if not thorough; they would certainly have picked up the *Miami Herald* account of the homicide, which identified Mrs. Homberg by name. Peter would have put two and two together and contacted the Dade County authorities. Call it instinct, but I'm inclined to rule out Mrs. Homberg. I think Peter's client was someone else."

"So who then? That little prick Barrow, checking up on his star?" Clifford thinks over what he's said and answers his own question. "No—that's nuts. Barrow would've gone nuclear by now."

"I agree. But you're getting warm."

"Cut it out, Arthur. No games, okay? This is serious."

"Indeed it is. Anyway, I had a brainstorm. Let me try it out on you, see if you find the narrative as convincing as I do."

"Shoot."

"All right. On October 21, the day Harris's services were engaged and the day before your incursion on Winding Crest Drive, I believe you told me that your wife had lunch at her studio with Annabelle Villers."

"That's right. Christ, Arthur, you're not suggesting—"

Jekyll raises a hand. "Hear me out. On October 21, what do you think they may have talked about over lunch?"

"How the hell should I know? What do women ever talk about? Kids, shopping, cabbages and kings, Connie's show, I suppose."

"What about love affairs—broadly defined? Do you think they talk about those?"

"Those, too, I guess. Hey, wait a minute! You're not suggesting that Connie told Belle about....She'd never dare!"

"Don't be so certain," Jekyll says. "When it comes to affairs of the groin, women—in my experience—are twice as likely as men to confide in friends. I sometimes wonder whether women don't have affairs mainly in order to be able to confess them to a bosom friend. It's the intimacy thing. Women are absolutely fixated on intimacy as an essential constituent of the examined life."

Clifford smiles. "Are they now?" He shakes his head. "I wouldn't know. My wife is a wonderful and talented person, and a bonny and boon companion and helpmeet, not to mention a good and loving mother, but intimacy isn't her top priority. Nowhere near. Unless sex equals intimacy, which I somehow think it doesn't. Connie has a very clear grasp of where and by whom her bread is buttered, and as for Belle, she's strictly all business. Hearts and flowers do nothing for her. I guess what I'm trying to say, Arthur, is that we're not talking about a couple of high school girls whispering and giggling over the teacups. This relationship is tied up with all sorts of business angles."

Jekyll smiles. "A forty-year-old woman with a sexual crush is not all that different from a sixteen-year-old. Take it from me. Suppose you instructed your wife not to confide her most intimate secrets to her best friend because it might cost money. How do you think your wife would react?"

Clifford looks at Jekyll. His mouth shapes itself in a thin, knowing smile. "Point made," he says. "I guess. Yeah, she'd tell me to stuff it. Especially now, when her success has made her used to getting what she wants."

"So, let me continue. This is all hypothetical, mind you, but it has a certain ring of probability to it. Assume that your wife confessed

her carnal bliss to Ms. Villers. The latter probably did remind her
diplomatically—your wife after all is, as you put it, her meal ticket—
of what was at stake. She would probably also have wormed out the
essential information as to when and where, just in case. That is, if
your wife didn't tell her out of hand.

"Now, how would you rate the likelihood that at some point, either late in the conversation, or possibly later after giving the matter
some thought, your wife would rethink her indiscretion and quickly
seek to offset it by agreeing to terminate a relationship she would
have no intention of ending."

"It's a fair supposition. Connie definitely does not want to get
crossways with Belle. Belle is her best friend."

"That was my impression. I think it likely that she would have
waited until after Ms. Villers had left, and then recanted over the
phone, so as not to betray her words with her face. Even as skilled
an actress as Constance Grange can slip now and then. Now, take
it the next step. If your wife did in fact do this, would Ms. Villers
believe her?"

"She might. She might not. I guess it all comes down to that intuition thing that women are supposed to have."

"Let's say she didn't. Let's say that she decided to check up on
your wife, so to speak. Would that be in character?"

Clifford nods. "Belle didn't get where she is by winging it. She
plays her hunches, but she subjects them to a major reality check.
Yeah, you're right: Belle likes to have all the facts before she makes a
move. She would go for some kind of confirmation."

Jekyll smiles. "That was my guess. But how? The only rational
way would be to have your wife put under surveillance. How to make
sure your wife meant what she said? She'd ask someone, perhaps her
own lawyer, on some pretext, for the name of a discreet investigator.
That she ended up with Peter is odds-on. His name's at the front of
the Rolodex of every first-class lawyer in whatever field."

"Harris could act that quickly?"

"Absolutely. I think it's an absolutely safe assumption that Harris had the Winding Crest house under surveillance by the following day, when both you and your wife went there."

Clifford's hardly listening. "So," he says, almost as if talking to himself, "assuming Belle found out about Connie and Donkey Dong, what would she do about it?" He looks up at Jekyll. "Jesus, you don't think..."

"It's unarguable that if my version of events is correct, then we have another woman thinking bad thoughts about Mr. Vargas, possibly wishing him out of the way."

"You have to be kidding! Belle wouldn't in a million years...and what about me? I was there, too, and definitely not thinking nice thoughts."

"I don't see you hiring an assassin. Not that I don't think you may have fantasized about it."

"Yeah—but what about getting rid of me? Two for the price of one."

Jekyll smiles. "You're still here, aren't you? And there's this consolation. If I were Ms. Villers, and Harris had reported your October 22 incursion to me, I might well have expanded his brief to put you under surveillance. After all, you're the wild card in this particular hand. But even if she had, Peter ended the job on November 10, a full week before you came to see me, so there's no way for her to connect the two of us. And even if she could, it wouldn't matter, because no one involved has any interest at all in seeing any of the people involved be identified publicly. In any case, all of that brings me to this. You may have seen it before."

He reaches into his jacket pocket and pulls out an envelope from which he extracts a folded newspaper clipping, which he flattens on the table between himself and Clifford. It consists of several paragraphs of text topped with a photograph that Clifford recognizes immediately as the same one recently added to his icebox door, the photograph of the announcement of the new Summerhill plant on the steps of the state capitol. He looks at it, then raises his gaze and looks questioningly at Jekyll.

"I know what this is," he says. "What's your point?"

"You know who the four people in the picture are?"

"Sure. Even if it wasn't right there in the caption. Connie, Belle, the governor, Cardinal Santiago. He's an old friend of Belle's family."

"Excellent. Now, when you came to see me after you found out about your wife's adultery, it was to learn what your options were. Correct?"

"Correct."

"Assuming that Ms. Villers was Peter Harris's patron, and that she learned from him that he had observed you..."

"How would he know who I was?"

"He might not, but I'm sure his people captured you on film, and Ms. Villers would have recognized you. That being the case, and since you know Ms. Villers well—at that point, assuming you were in her shoes, what would you have done?"

"I would have sat down and tried to figure what my options were."

"Exactly. She would have examined her nonviolent options, homicide being a bit extreme for most people, no matter how much money is involved. Although I suppose I should admit that from what I have learned, Cardinal Santiago might have been in a position to render service in procuring the disappearance of poor Mr. Vargas."

"Are you kidding?"

"Not at all. There have been periods in the church's history when arsenic has been as essential to its primacy as incense. As you may be aware, before coming to Hartford, Santiago served as Archbishop of Miami. In such a position, he would have gotten to know all sorts of people with all sorts of capabilities. And by the looks of him, he would have been quite at ease hanging out with the Borgias. But let's put that to one side. The essential point is that from what I know of Ms. Villers, in addition to weighing up her own alternatives, she would also inform herself as to what *your* options were."

This makes sense. Belle does like to walk around all sides of a problem; it's what's made her a world-class negotiator. She's very much a belt-and-suspenders type, or whatever the female equivalent to that is. "I guess so," he says.

"That being the case," Jekyll says, "this starts to make sense." He taps the newspaper clipping. "Ms. Villers knows about your wife's infidelity and she knows that you know. The main question now becomes, what can you—Clifford Grange—do about it in a way that may compromise, even kill off, the goose that lays the golden eggs?"

"Assuming I want to do anything, which I don't. Besides, the point is moot now, isn't it?"

"Not to Ms. Villers, not back then. Knowing you as she does, she may doubt you'll do anything, but she probably knows you're angry about your own life, and angry men don't always stop to count ten. Who knows what such a person under extreme psychosexual stress is capable of?"

"Jesus, Arthur, that's not very complimentary. You make me sound like an axe murderer!"

"Relax. I'm simply putting myself in Ms. Villers's shoes. So she does what you did: consults an attorney and finds out that your state's divorce code includes fault divorce, but that there is a legislative conversion to no-fault that's hung up in committee. And she finds out why said legislation is stalled and—and more important—by whom."

"Santiago, you mean?"

"Exactly. And—here's where happy coincidence strides onstage—when she learns that the person holding up the legislation is none other than an old family friend, she wonders whether there might be a way to get the no-fault legislation unblocked, which will put you out of business, so to speak, and very neatly. It would then have been logical for her to wonder next whether there might be a way to induce Cardinal Santiago to withdraw his doctrinally based objection to the no-fault bill. She—"

Clifford practically jumps out of his seat. "The plant!" he exclaims. "The one this picture's all about, the one that was originally going to be built in North Carolina! She tells Santiago she'll move the plant if he gets out of the way on no-fault, right?"

Jekyll's grin fills the dreary room. "That certainly is what it looks like. A French king once opined that Paris was worth a mass and became a Catholic. Why wouldn't a prince of the Catholic Church react the same way to a trade involving massive corporate investment and hundreds if not thousands of new jobs in his diocese, which happens to be the state's bleakest quarter? In Santiago's position, it would have taken me perhaps thirty seconds to make up my mind. I doubt it took His Eminence half that amount of time."

Clifford has to smile. "Arthur, that's fucking brilliant! You should have been a goddamn detective-story writer." Then his face darkens. "And, of course, the sons of bitches are going to get away with it."

"Not necessarily. Ms. Villers may know what she knows, but she doesn't know that we know what she knows. That's a very useful tactical edge. Which brings me to my main point. I think that what we have here is yet another situation where the rich and powerful have conspired to play fast and loose with the system in the interest of financial profit, which I personally find offensive. I think you and I are in a position to do something about it."

He pauses to let that sink in, and then adds, "And, to be selfish about it, in a manner that might afford me the greatest satisfaction of my lifetime. Do you recall that I told you the first time you came to my office that I would give my eye teeth for the chance to argue a constitutional case before the Supreme Court?"

Clifford nods.

"Well, this could be it. But it's up to you."

"Up to me?"

"What I have in mind is to bring an action against the state. It could be the jurisprudential equivalent in church-state matters of *Roe v. Wade*. For sake of argument, let's call this action *Doe v. Hewitt*, Ms. Isobel Hewitt being your state's chief legal officer."

"And who's Doe?" He knows the answer before Jekyll can answer and points to his own chest. "Me, right? Are you nuts? Forget it!"

"I think you should hear me out. If you're not convinced, then, so be it. Nothing ventured, nothing gained."

"Arthur, you want *me* to sue the state? Do you know what that will do to Connie?"

"Trust me, if you go along with what I have in mind, your name— and your wife's—will never come into it."

"That's what you say!"

"Just listen, please. Tell me, are you familiar with the 'takings clause' of the Fifth Amendment?"

"You mean—as in, taking the Fifth so as not to incriminate one-self?"

"No. The takings clause has to do with the appropriation of private property for public use. The Fifth Amendment provides, and I quote, 'that no person shall be deprived of life, liberty or *property* without due process of law,' due process being the overarching con-cern of the Fifth Amendment, which then goes on to recite the so-called 'takings clause,' which holds that private property may not be taken for public use—however defined—without—and I quote—'just compensation.'"

"Didn't we just have a big case about that in New London?"

"Very good. The case was called *Kelo v. City of New London*. The docket number, should you care to look it up online, is 545 U.S. 469 (2005)[1]. At issue was what is called 'eminent domain,' an extension of the takings clause whereby government condemns and seizes private property in the interest of what it deems the greater good. The ques-tion in *Kelo* was the local government's power to use eminent domain to transfer land from one private owner to another, as opposed to a transfer from private hands to a public authority for broad public use, such as a park or a highway, which had been the traditional purpose of eminent domain. *Kelo* involved an effort by the city to condemn and tear down a bunch of single-occupant waterfront houses in order to clear the land for a high-end development that promised a better tax yield and a fancier and more cosmetic demographic. The Court held in a five-to-four decision that the general benefits a community enjoyed from private-sector economic growth qualified such redevelopment plans as a permissible "public use" under the takings clause of the Fifth Amendment."

"Do you buy that?"

"I have my doubts, but that's neither here nor there. As I reflected on what seems to have gone down between Ms. Villers, Cardinal Santiago, and various persons in your state legislature in connection with (a) the conversion to no-fault, and (b) the relocation of the Summerhill facility from North Carolina to Connecticut, it suddenly occurred to me that in your case we have an instance of what might be called 'moral eminent domain.'"

"I'm not sure I follow you."

"Well, eminent domain customarily relates to tangible property. But there's a school of constitutional reasoning that holds that 'property' need not be limited to real estate. In *The Federalist Papers*, Madison speaks of personal liberty as a *property* right. 'Just as we have a right in our property,' he writes, 'we have a property in our rights,' or words to that effect. And of course there's intellectual property. Anyway, to cut this short, the more I've thought about it, the more it seems to me your state's sudden switch to no-fault—was tantamount to a seizure of your property rights."

"I assume by 'property rights' you mean that theoretical $200 million that we talked about, that we figured Belle and Barrow might stump up as hush money?"

"Actually, I was thinking on a somewhat more elevated plane, basically about your right to sue, to obtain due process, but, yes, 'your' theoretical $200 million does come into it. I think that's what a court might have awarded in a properly argued and negotiated divorce action under your state's old divorce code, an action that can no longer be brought under the amended code. To deprive you of that right to sue—the possibility of a fair economic settlement—might be construed as tantamount to a 'taking.'

"Then, from there, I found myself wondering whether certain of your First Amendment rights hadn't also been abridged. When you and I were talking about the change in your state's divorce law, you asked how it could be that the state could, so to speak, overnight effectively cancel out the wedding vows of someone married in church like yourself. I thought it was an excellent, interesting question. The wedding vows are in *The Book of Common Prayer*, which lays out the various Episcopal rites and sacraments that are the core of worship. The Constitution grants us absolute freedom of worship. Absolute, that is, as long as it doesn't include cannibalism or sex with children or other perversions. Now as you and I see it, vows only count if they mean something. To make a vow—call it a 'promise'—is to take a sort of risk, as I see it: namely, the risk of eternal damnation on some level—Dante condemns adulterers to the second circle of hell, an early stop on his journey, but hell nevertheless—and in this life, if one breaks that promise, there's the risk of damage to purse and prestige. Otherwise, what's the point?"

"What you'd argue," Clifford says, his interest piqued, "is that by going to no-fault the state in effect fiddled with my right to worship as I please?"

"Actually, my First Amendment argument would unspool as follows: you and Mrs. Grange exchanged vows in a purely religious marriage, performed in a church by a priest. The vows included an oath to be faithful, as set forth in *The Book of Common Prayer,* which is to Episcopal practice what the Constitution and Bill of Rights are to American law. Fidelity is a core value of marriage, marriage is a sacrament, and sacraments are the cornerstone of worship, freedom of which—the freedom to believe, the freedom to perform the sacraments—is constitutionally protected."

"Yeah, but what about the separation of church and state?"

"I asked myself that question. In many countries, the church-state dichotomy is dealt with by dual marriage ceremonies. People of faith get married twice: once at the altar and a second time before the duly constituted secular authority. That way, there's neither legal nor moral nor religious confusion. But that's not true in this country."

"Well, you still have to get a marriage license."

"Which has nothing to do with the form or content of the marriage ceremony. A marriage license is basically a sexual license to drive. Actually, if you ask me, the point of a marriage license is to keep the state in the picture if divorce follows. As regards church and state, by allowing binding marriages to take place in church without requiring a secular ceremonial counterpart, it seems to me that the state is, by standing aside so to speak, validating those marriages across the board. In my opinion, and the opinion of any halfway rational human being, no-fault effectively hollows out the oath of fidelity—which is a promise both to the betrothed and to God. If the state does that, I think one might argue that the state, in a meaningful way, has unconstitutionally abridged freedom of belief."

"And you think this holds water legally? Sounds like a stretch to me."

"The freedoms the Constitution secures for the individual, the Congress and the states are forbidden to limit. In other words, the right of individuals to participate in sacramental marriage would seem to me to lie beyond the reach of the state to proscribe, limit, or substantively modify, provided that such marriages don't involve the happy couple smoking peyote or having sex on the altar with five-year-olds. My argument would be that religious marriage is a form of worship that is entitled to the same constitutional protection as any other sacrament: the Eucharist, baptism, and so on. After all, can one sacrament be less equal in the eyes of the law than another? Does the state have the right to impose its drinking laws with regard to wine offered at communion to minors? Nor may the state alter or proscribe the sacrament of baptism by immersion, even if some risk of drowning is alleged. Nor can it alter the sacrament of ordination. The state can't stand next to the deathbed and muffle the absolving priest; it can't legislate away fear of the Last Judgment, can it?"

"Very fancy reasoning, Arthur. Still, it sounds pretty far-fetched."

"Possibly. But if argued in conjunction with the Fifth Amendment, it may gain additional weight."

"Maybe so—but aren't we talking apples and oranges? Or maybe Christ and Caesar? Marriage is one thing, divorce is another."

"Really? I would assert that the negotiated agreement—divorce—that ends a marriage is as inherent to that union as the exchange of vows that began it, just as the entrance to a room is, if passed through from the other direction, the exit. Tell me, do you ever read *The New Criterion*?"

"I see it at the club sometimes."

"An excellent magazine. Well, while I was mulling your situation, I remember an article I'd read in it on judicial activism. It was by Robert Bork. You know who he is?"

"Sure."

"Now I'm not crazy about Bork's politics, but he has a first-rate legal mind, and what he says is generally worth thinking about, even if you disagree. In any case, in the course of his article, there was one line, really no more than a throwaway, that I vividly remember drawing me up short, because it touches so cogently on what I do for a living. He was making fun of the sort of judicial freethinking that's made a mockery of American jurisprudence, at least in his opinion, and to illustrate what he was thinking of, he said—and I think these are more less his exact words—that if you go by the thinking of 'activist' Supreme Court justices like the late Justice Blackmun, who wrote *Roe v. Wade,* or several of the present bench, then you could also think, quote unquote, that no-fault divorce is a constitutional right.

"As I say, it was just a throwaway line, uttered sarcastically and clearly intended to indicate the author's scorn for a certain kind of knee-jerk liberal judicial demagoguery, but to someone like me, who sees marriage and divorce in pretty much zero-sum terms, it posed an interesting question. If you take Bork's proposition to the next logical step, and assume that no-fault divorce has no *a priori* constitutional legitimacy, mightn't there be circumstances in which no-fault divorce might be unconstitutional? And that prompted me to investigate what, if anything, the Supreme Court's had to say on the subject of divorce. I blush to admit that in all my years of practicing divorce law, I never had. I worked right through Monday night researching it, and my hopes were answered. Guess when the Supreme Court last took a really hard look at the fundamental judicial and constitutional issues involved in divorce?"

"How would I know? Divorce is a big deal in this country. Don't half of all marriages end in divorce? But from the way you put it, it must have been a while ago."

"How about 1888?"

"You're shitting me."

"I am not. You can look it up. And that means that almost a dozen decades have passed since the Court last examined a legal and social matter that has grown to be a monstrously large fact of American life. Over that same span of time, one is hard put to think of other social tendencies of this magnitude that the Supreme Court hasn't examined and reexamined and often significantly redefined—or, if you prefer to put it in Borkian terms, meddled with. The Court's been all over marriage, from intramarital sexual conduct to the right of persons to marry under what the framers would have considered pretty peculiar circumstances, and of course now you've got the whole gay marriage issue. How odd that divorce should have escaped judicial scrutiny all those years."

"You get no argument from me. I'm just here to listen. So what did the Court decide back in 1888?"

"The case was docketed as *Maynard v. Hill*. The particulars in it needn't concern us. Basically, the Court decided that marriage is a so-cial 'relation,' quote unquote, which it is the exclusive constitutional prerogative of the individual states to define and administer—which includes defining and administering the legal basis for terminating marriages as well as certifying them. No surprise there; that's what Federalism is all about. But when I read Justice Field's majority opin-ion in *Maynard v. Hill,* I found exactly what I was hoping for. Not a First Amendment argument, but an approach that as far as I can see validates my Fifth Amendment premise, especially for the kind of bean-counting Supreme Court we have now. Here, read this."

He produces a sheet of copy paper and passes it to Clifford. A passage has been highlighted in Day-Glo yellow. Clifford takes out his reading glasses, gives them a quick once-over with his tie end, and reads: "Marriage...has always been subject to the control of the legislature. That body prescribes the age at which parties may contract to marry, the procedure or form essential to constitute marriage, the duties and obligations it creates, its effects on the property rights of both...and the acts which may constitute grounds for its dissolution...but if the act declaring the divorce should attempt to interfere with the rights of property vested in either party, a different question would be presented.'"

Clifford reads through it once, then rereads it, then puts the paper down. He looks at Jekyll and shrugs. "So?"

"'Rights of property,' Clifford, '*rights of property!*' An opportunity to raise the 'different question' with respect to those rights to which Justice Field's opinion refers."

"And you think mine might be those sort of circumstances?"

"I do. I feel so strongly about it that I want you to engage me, at my sole expense, as your attorney in a constitutional challenge to your state's conversion to one hundred percent no-fault divorce. I intend to take this to the Supreme Court."

"Are you nuts?"

"Don't look so skeptical. I've—"

"I'm not skeptical," Clifford interrupts. "I'm dumbfounded! You? The Supreme Court! I mean, don't get me wrong, Arthur, you're as smart as they come. But...well, I'm speechless!"

Jekyll looks at him patiently. "As I was about to say, I've heard you on the subject of the First Amendment. I sense that you venerate the Constitution every bit as intensely as I do. I know how you despise the power of money in our society; half your films address that issue in one way or another. You obviously believe that the institution of marriage is sacred, and while I might not put it in exactly those words, I think we both feel that marriage as an institution is too crucial to the working of a proper civil society to be trifled with for someone's private profit."

"You get no argument there. Anything else?"

"If my legal reasoning is as well-founded as I think it is, I think the Court will hear this case. Starting with the Warren Court, the justices on the whole have preferred to make social policy to interpreting law, and my guess is the present Court's no different, although it's still finding its ideological feet. Chief Justice Smiley hasn't yet had the kind of big, noisy, defining case I'm sure she's looking for: a *Brown v. Board of Education*, a *Dred Scott*, a *Roe v. Wade*. Here's one where the ground is for all intents and purposes judicially unplowed, or hasn't been since 1888. Who's to say they won't jump at it? As a matter of fact, I'm pretty certain I can get this to the Court without going through all the legal hoops. And even if we don't get there, at the very least we'll be making it very, very hot for some people who deserve it for twisting the system inside out to protect their purses. Doesn't that appeal to your sense of mischief?"

"Maybe so." And it does. Still, he has to try to be reasonable. "Just look at it from my side. Arthur, I just can't take the chance! Say I go along with this and sign on as Doe. You know how long that secret will last? About a day! There are no secrets anymore! Anything that's confidential, there's fifty million assholes on the Internet trying to pry loose what it is—and generally succeeding. What if Murdoch's people get on the case? If the press finds out this is about Connie and me?"

"The press won't find out."

"Oh, bullshit! Stuff like this always get out! What did I just tell you? There are no secrets anymore. Rule number one of modern life is: you're going to get caught. Someone'll find out who Doe is, some paralegal, researchers, consultants, transcribers—and they'll shop me to *Page Six* or Fox, or some fucking blogger will pick it up and put it all over the Web..."

"Clifford," says Jekyll, interrupting in a calm voice, "that simply will not happen. Do you think I'd propose this to you if there was the slightest risk of exposure? There will be no indication anywhere, or at any time, whether the plaintiff in *Doe v. Hewitt* is male or female, husband or wife. There will be no one other than myself and yourself with access to the true facts of the case. You have my word on that. Just we two."

"So you say. But what about your paralegals and so on?"

"Thanks to modern technology, what with computers and the Internet, I can do the work—the research, the drafting, the filing— myself. Only two people will be actively involved: you and I."

"Actively involved? Hey, no way!'

"Why not? I'll need to perfect my argument and my delivery, and who better to coach me on that but you, the consummate actor's director? You'll have a great time."

Clifford thinks about this. When he next speaks, his tone is less certain. "And you really think the Supreme Court will want to listen to this?"

"Why not? The Court has time and again limited or expanded the power of the states to regulate practically every other crucial aspect of the marital relation."

"Maybe the Supreme Court's like ninety-nine percent of the people in this country and doesn't give a shit about no-fault divorce."

"That may have been true a few years ago; I don't think it still is. The tide is running with us. Ours is an age that has suddenly rediscovered marriage to be a central component of the American way. There've been proposals for a constitutional marriage amendment. There's the Federal Defense of Marriage Act that disobliges the states from recognizing same-sex marriage, although a number of states, your own included, have chosen to ignore it. Now, of course, given the anti-gay marriage initiatives that were passed in the last election, we can expect to see more legal scuffling."

"Where's the Supreme Court come out in all this?"

"So far—nowhere. The Court has declined to face the matter. But, federal involvement in domestic relations is a truly hot-button issue, so I expect that sooner or later the Court will have to hear a case."

"And what about straight people? Are we left out of all this? Once again, the forgotten majority."

"There aren't many 'straight' cases, so to speak, that raise a judicial question sufficient to tempt the Court."

"I see. Should I be proud? Not to change the subject, but doesn't it take months if not years for a case to be heard?"

"I've considered that. We can petition the Supreme Court for expedited adjudication. Provided the state agrees to co-petition, our chances for an early hearing are good."

"And why would the state do that?"

"I believe they can be made to understand that it's to their advantage. What de Tocqueville would call 'self-interest properly understood.'"

Now Clifford grins. "Arthur, I'm not even going to ask how you intend to do *that*."

"Trust me," says Jekyll.

Clifford sighs, then looks at Jekyll with mingled suspicion and amusement. "There's something I have to ask you, Arthur."

"Anything."

"It's just this. I kind of feel I'm in a movie I've seen before. About the wicked, no-account courthouse hack who achieves professional redemption. There was one a few years back with Paul Newman."

"The Verdict," says Jekyll. "I thought it was very average." He hesitates, then adds: "Having seen that film, Clifford, I have to say that I find the comparison slightly insulting. I am not a drunk. I am not insolvent. I do not fancy younger women. Well, *much* younger women. I am also not Paul Newman, although I suppose that if I were, it would make up for other deficiencies."

"Maybe so. Newman did get nominated for an Oscar. I guess what I'm really trying to ask is, how much of this has to do with some kind of itch you need to scratch, some Daniel Webster jones you want to feed?"

"I beg your pardon?"

"It's just a feeling I have about you. Maybe you're out to make amends for a life—a life in the law—misspent. Maybe you think you can use me—my situation—as the stepping-stone to some kind of personal redemption. We all know the story: guy goes into the Supreme Court as Jekyll the Jackal and come out as Oliver Wendell Holmes."

"That's certainly part of it," Jekyll replies calmly. "I'd be a liar if I said it wasn't. Any lawyer who really cares about the law relishes the prospect of arguing an important case before the Supreme Court. But I can tell you in all candor that I really don't think this is an ego trip. I think this is about right and wrong."

"Let right be done, huh?"

"I beg your pardon?"

"*The Winslow Boy*. It was my old man's favorite movie. The original one, I mean—with Robert Donat."

"I see," Jekyll replies. "Yes, I suppose you could say that."

Clifford smiles sadly. "Arthur, I'm over a barrel. I'm tempted, I really am. But is it really fair for me, with all the best will in the world, to shove my and everybody else's chips into the pot to test your theories about constitutional law—a field in which you are not exactly well-known—or to help you regain your self-esteem or whatever the hell else you think you stand to gain? You see that, don't you?"

Jekyll doesn't answer.

"I was brought up with the Pledge of Allegiance," Clifford continues, "in the version that includes God, because if your old man's a combat pilot, you pretty quickly gets on a first-name basis with the Good Lord. By the time I was six, I knew the words to 'My Country, 'Tis of Thee' and 'America the Beautiful' and 'The Battle Hymn of the Republic,' and I still do. I revere the Constitution; I worship Jefferson and Washington and Franklin and all those Adamses and Hamilton and Madison and Lincoln, but I'm also a guy who's slowly learning the big lesson of the twenty-first century: namely, that life is all about me, myself, and I, about getting what *I* want when *I* want it. When push comes to shove, I've got to be just like every other one of the three hundred million of us in this great nation: looking out for Number One and expecting the rest of the world to look out for me. As it says on the money, *e pluribus unum,* which today means: out of the many—me!"

"I can understand your feelings," Jekyll says calmly. "On the other hand, I'm surprised that you'd sit idly by and let what is probably the largest bribe paid in your state's political history go down without a murmur. And here's something else you might think about. It's what used to be called *noblesse oblige,* which has now become a term of derision if not downright opprobrium, even at places like Harvard. If this country's most-advantaged citizens, the people with the most chips, don't stand up for what's right and principled, there's no hope. The past three decades have seen exactly the reverse. It's time to break that pattern."

Clifford shrugs. "Arthur, goddamn you, you're playing me like a goddamn banjo! You sound just like my old man. And maybe that's the real point. Maybe I owe this to my old man, to what he stood for. Win one for the Gipper. For God, Mother, and Apple Pie. Suppose I sign on? What's your timing?"

"My guess is that, what with everything else I have going on, it will take me about six weeks—say mid-April—to clear my decks and get everything in order."

"And if, in that time, I have second thoughts, we can always back off, right?"

Jekyll nods. "Of course."

Clifford smiles. "You know, Arthur, I hate to say this, mainly because of what it says about me, but as interesting as I find all your legal lacework, what I kind of like best is what you said earlier: the idea of making it hot for Santiago and the rest of them, making them squirm a little. I still feel shortchanged. I tried to make Connie squirm—she's the one who really deserves to—when we were in the Caribbean, but it didn't really work out the way I planned, and Barrow's still out there, so maybe the only way left to get the job done is by proxy. Play a little mind game. Let them know that we know what we know and watch them wriggle."

A smile from Jekyll, who then says, "And of course there's always the $200 million."

"Yes, there is that." Clifford shakes his head and says, smiling in defeat, "Arthur, you've got my number, haven't you? You've spotted my Achilles' heels, both of them. I'm an idealist, but I also have a vocation, which is to make movies. And then there's this: I may never get what I want out of life, so why not help someone else get what they want? Goddamn it! Okay, you win. I'm on board. At least provisionally, for stage one."

"Perhaps you should think it over."

Clifford grins. "Arthur, you've set the hook. Reel me in fast before you lose the fish. If I think it over, forget it. I'm not good at thinking things over. When I do, I usually wimp out, so I gave up sober reflection years ago, and the older and angrier I get, the better it is for me to act quickly. Now—let me out of here before I change my mind!"

But when he's outside, on Park Avenue, he feels a sudden shiver at the ribs, and in spite of himself can't help thinking: *what the hell have I let myself in for?* Still, it feels pretty good. For the first time in what seems like forever, he's actually being given the opportunity to put his abilities and experience to work. Not only that, but he stands at least a chance of getting back at someone—and by now it doesn't really matter who.

CHAPTER SEVEN

April 1

But for the cassock, the priest seated behind the anteroom desk, pink
and blond with a good deal of puppy flesh about the face, might have
tumbled off a riotous ceiling in a Venetian palace. *Ganymede in a dog
collar,* Jekyll thinks, as the young man concludes a brief muttered
phone conversation, then rises and asks Jekyll to follow him.

"I'm afraid His Eminence has been detained across the way," he
explains as he shows Jekyll into the cardinal's office. Then, as if to
add a deeper note of gravity: "He's with the governor."

The thought of the two most powerful political figures in the
state huddling amuses Jekyll. He briefly wonders whether his visit
has anything to do with the cardinal's meeting. He doesn't see how.
There's nothing to connect him to Constance or Clifford Grange or
Annabelle Villers.

He looks around. Santiago's lair is about the size of Jekyll's own
Manhattan living room, perhaps twenty feet square, with a clere-

story high up on two walls through which, on a bright morning like this one, the sun pours in agreeably. It's a bare, Spartan space that gives off a harsh, penitential kind of sanctity. It reminds Jekyll of a fresco by Carpaccio of Saint Jerome's study that he saw in Venice years ago, complete with the same sort of engaging paraphernalia: books, scrolls, ink pots, religious objects. On the bookshelves are ranged liturgical and patronymic commentaries, the previous pope's autobiography, the present pope's latest call to arms, a history of the church in America, several volumes of devotional verse, and, fittingly, from what he knows of Santiago, a set of Machiavelli in the original Italian. Two paintings hang on the walls. One is a smallish Madonna in Glory, with a certain clumsy, backwater charm, identified by its label as the School of Sano di Pietro, circa 1450. It's from the collection of the local museum, which Jekyll knows to have been endowed by its early tool-company benefactors with a decent group of Italian old masters collected back in the capital city's glory days as a hub of manufacturing and insurance. The other painting is a martyrdom of Saint Sebastian about four feet tall, a brutal picture, the saint pierced like a pincushion by uncountable arrows. The label identifies it as Paduan, about 1500. Spare, intellectual, everything just so, just as it should be: but it doesn't fool Jekyll. Like his own, this office has been carefully assembled to convey a specific impression that's simple and monastic: a holy man's cell, very medieval and pure in spirit, inhabited by one of mankind's better angels. Jekyll's willing to bet that there's a second, secret, twenty-first-century office somewhere hereabouts where the hard, practical work gets done. An office that will have computers and Bloomberg screens armed with sophisticated investment and real estate software, and secure, direct lines to trading desks around the world. His Eminence may be a great figure of his faith, but Jekyll's done his homework, and he appreciates that this is a man who can do derivatives calculations in his head, who knows the yield book as well as he knows his rosary.

In front of the refectory table that serves the cardinal as a desk is an uncomfortable-looking, backless wooden chair, with arms like the wings of a lyre. Jekyll settles himself in it and inspects the desktop. It, too, is Spartan: its surface bare except for an inkwell, a pocket missal, breviary, and bible bound in identical scarred, stained dark-green leather, a carved ivory jar, quite yellow with age, that holds pens and pencils, a blank notepad, and a scarred metal gooseneck desk lamp. Affixed to the wall behind Santiago's chair is a waist-high narrow shelf bearing a signed photograph of the Holy Father and a handsome bronze crucifix on an ivory stand.

He closes his eyes for a few seconds; he's tired; he had to get up very early to be sure of being on time. Tired but keyed up. The game's finally afoot and this is the part he relishes: the first salvo in what he expects will be a protracted exchange of mind games. That idiot Rumsfeld has gotten few things right, in Jekyll's opinion, but he was on the mark when, in connection with terrorism and the Iraq War, he spoke of what we know we know, and what we know we don't know, and what they don't know we know, and what they don't know we don't know. A perfect summation of what Jekyll has planned as a Ponzi scheme of supposition, half-fact, red herrings, and false starts, of many surmises and few certitudes, each successive layer building on its predecessor.

He hears the office door behind him, and a raspy voice says, "I apologize for being late, Mr. Jekyll. I had business in the capitol."

He gets up and turns to meet the cardinal and is immediately struck by the presence of the man. Physically, Santiago isn't imposing, but he exudes an inner intensity that's almost palpable. His face is right out of El Greco, lean and intense, the gaze piercing, the features seamed, attenuated, and refined by years of striving and cynicism and ambition and fervor. The skin sallow and taut over the cheekbones, the dark eyes conveying an impression of enormous cumulative weariness, a sort of elegant, exquisite fatigue. His Eminence is in mufti today, turned out in a perfectly tailored black suit, a scarlet over-vest below the dog collar, and a discreet pectoral cross of gold and enamel that looks very old and very valuable. On one wrist is a gold watch, on the other a gold bracelet, and on the right ring finger a gold signet.

After shaking hands, he goes around his desk and seats himself and studies his visitor silently for a moment, then says, finally, without preamble, "So, Mr. Jekyll, how can I help you? I gather you wish to discuss the recent amendment to the divorce code. You implied that you represent a professional group. Isn't your business more properly over in the capitol building?"

"I won't beat about the bush, Eminence. I believe that you and I are on the same side of the table when it comes to no-fault divorce, which is what I've come to discuss. I'm sure that you were as disappointed as I in the recent action of your state assembly."

"I was. As was the Holy Father. But there are boundaries that must be respected, and I'm afraid that this is one of those. In the event, this state's conversion to a no-fault divorce code was made while I was out of the country. I consider it to have been a form of betrayal and have made my feelings—and those of the Holy Father—very clear to my good friend, our governor."

"Oh, come now, your Eminence. I mean no disrespect, but I wasn't born yesterday. It's an article of political truth in these parts that on such a matter no such drastic shift could have taken place without your by-your-leave, whether you were physically within the state at the time or not."

The smile with which the cardinal greets this is thin and dangerous. "Let us just say that acquiescence after the fact is different from yielding beforehand. In this instance, we were confronted with a *fait accompli,* however unpalatable it may have been—or may still be—in terms of doctrine, or to myself personally, or to those in Rome to whom I report. You yourself are recognized as a practical man, Mr. Jekyll. I am quite aware of who you are, and of your reputation. So you will understand that there are times, especially given certain difficulties the church has had to deal with in this country, for us to be practical, especially when it concerns issues on which the electorate seems broadly agreed. I doubt that, in my situation, you would have done differently. We make it a policy not to meddle in the state's business, just as they stay out of ours. Separation of church and state, Mr. Jekyll—just the way it says in the Constitution."

Jekyll lets his eyes widen. "The Constitution, you say? Your Eminence is reading my mind!"

Santiago looks puzzled.

"It just so happens," says Jekyll, "that what I seek Your Eminence's good counsel on also involves the Constitution. I have a client, you see, whose constitutional right to freedom of worship appears to have been seriously infringed by your state's conversion to no-fault divorce. I'm not going to go into the specifics now; it would take too long. I assure you, however, that this matter is no jurisprudential will o' the wisp. I do have a memo outlining the principal arguments that I'll leave with you. And after I leave here, I am scheduled to meet with your state attorney general, Ms. Hewitt."

Santiago's hands go up. "Mr. Jekyll, this is all beginning to sound absurd. You cannot possibly expect someone in my position to get involved in a matter that's clearly a business for the courts?"

"Oh, but I do. As I expect you will, once you've heard what I have to say."

Santiago looks utterly baffled. He's obviously trying to figure out how to get back on the offensive.

"Here's the thing," says Jekyll, pressing his advantage. "I will shortly bring an action against this state that I intend to docket as *Doe v. Hewitt,* 'Doe' being my client, 'Hewitt' being this state's chief legal officer. It is the kind of case that will ultimately have to be decided by the Supreme Court. That being so, why not sooner than later? I have come to Hartford today to try to persuade Ms. Hewitt to join me in petitioning the Supreme Court for expedited adjudication, which the Court is empowered to do. Supreme Court rules specify that a writ for direct appeal can be justified, and I quote, 'upon a showing that a case is of such imperative public importance as to justify deviation from normal appellate practice and to require immediate determination in this Court.' That was the basis for the Court's hasty and—in my opinion—ill-considered and unjustified intervention in Florida in the 2000 presidential election. We might also seek a writ of *mandamus*, but that needs further looking into. Are you with me, Your Eminence?"

"I don't see how I can possibly help."

"Ms. Hewitt is said to be a close friend of yours—some even say protégée. I'm sure a word from you will carry great weight."

"That may be, but haven't you ever heard of the separation of church and state? Interference by me would be unconscionable. And very likely unconstitutional."

Jekyll shrugs. "Your role, in the basic sense, would be more procedural than political, strictly speaking, and hardly constitutional. All I seek is a joint stipulation by Ms. Hewitt and myself as to the material facts and the constitutional relevance of my client's case, together with a petition to the Supreme Court to give it an expedited hearing. I'm not asking you to be a signatory, although down the line you might wish to file a brief as *amicus curiae*. If she and I are jointly as persuasive as I expect we will be, we should be able to get a hearing in Washington as early as next fall, early in the Court's next term."

"Mr. Jekyll, this is ridiculous! Even leaving myself out of it— which I can assure you is exactly how it is going to be!—have you considered the fact that Ms. Hewitt was instrumental in drafting the new divorce legislation and that she facilitated its passage in the assembly? How can she possibly participate in a legal challenge to legislation that she helped ratify?"

"Eminence, believe me. If I prepare you properly to help her understand that everyone's best interest, and not merely the interests of justice and right and the American way, will be best served if she goes along with what I'm proposing, I guarantee you she will cooperate."

Santiago shakes his head. "This is pointless," he says. He rises from his chair and extends a hand. As if irradiated by the sunlight flooding through the high windows, the ruby stone of the cardinal's ring glows like a talisman. "There's no point in going on with this, Mr. Jekyll. I think we can regard this matter as concluded. So now, if you'll excuse me, my assistant will show you the way out. I have much work to do."

Jekyll disdains the proffered hand. "I really do think we need to discuss this further," he says. "My client is a morally furious individual who feels cheated and betrayed, the victim of a conspiracy that strikes at the very heart of liberty. In such a state, people tend to do things—say things—that create wide ripples of collateral damage: to reputations, to institutions, to political futures. I happen to share my client's outrage, and I intend to use every resource at my disposal, fair and foul, to secure a fair hearing and an appropriate settlement."

He speaks carefully, weighing each word before pronouncing, being especially careful to avoid any hint as to whether the client is a he or a she. "My client prefers—we prefer—to pursue this through the courts, because only in that fashion can this matter be adjudicated, and subsequently settled, in a discreet, anonymous fashion. No names need be named, and you have to believe me that in view of the interests involved in this situation, at every level of public and private concern, that is a most desirable—you might say 'essential'—outcome here. But if this can't be achieved, and in my opinion it can only be brought about with this state's full cooperation and complicity, then we may have to find recompense in the public arena. I need hardly remind you what that might be like, given the metastatic properties of the Internet when it comes to gossip and factoids. No one escapes."

Again, a thin smile from Santiago. "Mr. Jekyll, I have to say that I have absolutely no idea what you're getting at."

Jekyll smiles back. "Is there somewhere we can talk privately?" he asks. "Someplace absolutely secure, where we can be absolutely candid with each other in the certainty that what passes between us will not be overheard? Perhaps downstairs in the basilica?"

The cardinal looks at him; his angular features are composed and amused, but his eyes have taken on a stony, lethal luster. "You're an insistent man, Mr. Jekyll, and an obsessive one. And I will confess that you've engaged my curiosity." He stands up. "Please follow me."

The great church is virtually empty in midmorning: the usual black-clad old women in a pew, praying, a young woman with Inca features kneeling before the altar of a candlelit side chapel, a sexton busy with a dry mop in the narthex, a couple of teenagers in the shadows, murmuring.

Santiago leads the way to a remote pew. "Will this do, Mr. Jekyll?" Without waiting for a reply, Santiago turns toward the altar, crosses himself, and murmurs a brief prayer. Then he returns his burning gaze to Jekyll as he sits down. "Now, sir, please, make it brief."

"I'll try, Eminence. I've told you about the lawsuit I wish to file. What I'd like to unfurl for you is a narrative, a narrative formulated by myself and my client and known only to myself and my client. After you've heard me, I think you'll agree that it's essential that it be kept in the strictest confidence, and made known only to the absolutely necessary minimum of other ears. On our side, it has been discussed exclusively by my client and myself—although our conclusions have been memorialized in a safe place in the event...well, in the event that either my client or myself, or both of us, should become incapacitated or otherwise unable to pursue the matter to its just conclusion. I trust I make myself clear."

There's no reply. Jekyll goes on. "In a minute, I'm going to show you a photograph. They say every picture tells a story. This depicts a modern miracle, so to speak. I'm sure you're familiar with the miracle of the Holy House of Loreto?"

No response.

"Well, as you know, the Holy House was the humble abode in Nazareth in which the blessed Virgin received the angel bearing the news that she had been chosen by God to give birth to His son. After that, it began a series of miraculous relocations, transported by angels, as the legend has it. From Nazareth to Dalmatia in the thirteenth century, and then—only three years later—to its present location in Italy. The story I am about to tell you is similar, although it involves a much larger structure miraculously moved not from Nazareth to Loreto but from Gastonia, North Carolina, to a site some fifteen miles north-northeast of where we sit. And brought there not by angels, but by a combination of political, commercial, and spiritual powers. Would you please look at this?"

Jekyll reaches into his briefcase, extracts a photograph, and lays it flat on the space between the two men. It's the same photograph Jekyll discussed with Clifford.

Still no reaction from Santiago.

I'm sure you recognize the occasion this records," Jekyll says, "so I won't bore you with that. As I said a moment ago, every picture is said to tell a story. Let me tell the story that I think goes with this one," and he proceeds to set out the sequence of events he hypothesized to Clifford at the Waldorf Towers. He keeps his voice level, but makes clear by his tone his conviction that he's addressing a hostile audience.

When he finishes, there's a momentary pause, then Santiago says, in a voice just as calm but just as pointed as the one in which Jekyll addressed him, "This is ridiculous! Of course, I had a hand in persuading the CEO of Summerhill, whom I have known since she was a child, to consider locating her new facility here. For very good and honest commercial and financial reasons. As you surmise, I read about the plant and called her to try to persuade her to build it here. North Carolina is a prosperous state. We are not. The erosion of our manufacturing base has been tragic. My flock is desperately poor. Anyway, as I say, Ms. Villers is an old friend, and she listened to me, thanks be to our Father in heaven."

"Really? I always think of Ms. Villers as an executive who pays close attention to costs. The differences in actual as well as projected operating profit and construction hardly seem to justify relocation. Indeed, Summerhill is reserving almost sixty cents a share for costs associated with giving up its original North Carolina site and building the plant in Connecticut, a few miles north of here. As a stockholder of Summerhill since its initial public offering, I have an interest in these matters."

At this, Santiago chuckles. "Mr. Jekyll, I have no idea how many shares you own, but I doubt that they come to more than a pittance relative to the Summerhill holdings of this diocese, as well as other accounts to which I have an advisory relationship."

"By which I assume you mean Forest Fields?" asks Jekyll. There's no reply.

Jekyll lets matters jell for a moment or two, then says, "Here's what I think *really* happened, Your Eminence, to put it crudely: I think that Ms. Villers offered to move her plant here in exchange for your withdrawing your opposition to the state's no-fault divorce bill and giving your friend the governor the green light to stand back from her threatened veto."

"And why would she ever do that?"

"Who knows?" Jekyll says amiably. "I think there was a very good reason, but I leave it to you to puzzle that out. I think you and Ms. Villers came to an understanding, and that you then had a quiet word with Attorney General Hewitt or the governor, it really doesn't matter which—and they took care of the legislative heavy-lifting while you hightailed it to Rome that week where, from behind the Holy City's thick walls, you could weep crocodile tears of chagrin."

Santiago sounds calm, composed, as he answers, "A very pretty fiction, Mr. Jekyll, but pointless. Your surmise has no foundation in fact or actuality. Nothing you allege has the remotest truth in it! I know nothing of the matters you allege. Now, this interview is concluded. I have work to do."

"Of course, Eminence. I apologize for taking so much of your time. I'm merely trying to be helpful. These have been difficult times for Rome. I needn't rehearse the sorry history in great detail: priestly malfeasance in ways ranging from molestation to misappropriation, financial pressures, the Banco Ambrosiano scandals, a failing demographic—and then of course there's *The Da Vinci Code* with its assertions of dark truths cabalistically suppressed by the Vatican."

"It's a ridiculous book."

"Of course it is, Eminence, but correct or incorrect, it's hard to argue with tens of million copies sold. My point is, I doubt the church—whether we're speaking of yourself or of the Holy See—has much enthusiasm right now for another scandal. Especially one with intimations of political subornation if not outright bribery."

There's a smile in Santiago's voice when he answers. The man's a tough nut. "This is all very entertaining, Mr. Jekyll. As I say, you should have been a thriller writer, the way you can weave such a narrative, such a fantasy. I must be going. Please excuse me."

"There's just one more thing," says Jekyll. He hands over another photograph, a picture recently obtained from a friend in the office of the Dade County Medical Examiner: an especially gruesome autopsy photo of the late Alejandro Vargas. It's a long shot, but Jekyll sees no point in not playing it.

"What is this? Am I supposed to know this man?"

To Jekyll, his puzzlement sounds absolutely genuine. "His name was Vargas," he says. "He was murdered late last year in Coral Gables."

"Vargas, you say? The name means nothing."

"Really? Ah, well. I must have been mistaken. Thank you very much for your time, Eminence."

The two men part at the entrance to the basilica. It is not a cordial moment. Santiago watches the lawyer set out across the square toward the capitol building, then goes back inside, to the elevator, which takes him not to the office in which he received Jekyll, but to another, higher up in the north transept, accessed directly from the elevator cab by a steel door controlled by an electronic touchpad.

Here is the church modern. Spare steel and glass furniture of museum quality, all the electronic and digital paraphernalia needed to monitor a complex network of interests, including—just as Jekyll had guessed—a shoulder-height array of Bloomberg screens displaying world financial markets and a continuously updated closed-circuit feed that displays the daily "drop" and "win" at the Forest Fields casino complex, broken down by game. Tacked to a wall-length bulletin board are preliminary architects' drawings and plans, along with budgets, for a major expansion of the casino.

On the wall behind the desk is a portrait of Richelieu, Santiago's model and idol. He goes over to it and studies it admiringly, taking in the foxy, shrewd expression, the sharp alert nose, the oddly sensuous lips beneath a carefully tended gray moustache, the perfection of lace. *How would you deal with this, Monsieur?* Then he turns away, goes to the window, and looks out. At this elevation, five floors above plaza level, he can look straight across to the silver dome of the state capitol. Below, he can make out Jekyll striding across the broad paved expanse toward the capitol building, on his way to call on Isobel Hewitt.

He ponders the situation, processing quick win-loss calculations as he tries to deal with this wholly unexpected development. He wastes no time and energy trying to figure out how Jekyll has managed to put two and two together, what set the lawyer on the scent. All that matters now is damage control. For a brief moment, he considers the other photograph Jekyll showed him; he has no idea what that's about and concludes that it was probably a lawyerly trick of some kind designed to confuse and unbalance. So, what next? Obviously there can be no retreat, no undoing of what's done, he reasons. As his wily Florentine colleagues are fond of saying, *"Icche c'è c'è"*: what there is, is what we have. He thinks for a bit, then picks up a telephone and makes a series of calls. Afterward, he remains beside the window, seated on the wide sill, thinking.

He's still there an hour later when he sees Jekyll pass through the columns of the capitol portico, talking animatedly on his cellphone as he moves toward a waiting limousine. The cardinal smiles and turns away from the window. Moments later, his own phone buzzes. He listens, then says, "I think it's the only practical course. You have my full assent."

He puts down the phone. As always in the life of an active, involved man, there is other business to be dealt with. Let those responsible for this particular mess deal with it. It is now out of his hands.

CHAPTER EIGHT

June 13

After he finishes with the newspapers, Clifford checks the Weather Channel online. The forecast for the Hudson Valley calls for rain. The radar screen shows ominous ragged green patches moving in from the southwest. He decides to make an earlier start than planned.

Clifford's pleased to be getting out of here. He doesn't do "alone" well, especially on weekends. He's hardly ever been left entirely to his own devices at Grangeford for any extended stretch, and though it's only been three days since his women deserted him, just this brief interval of 24/7 solitude is turning out to be intolerable. He's lonely. Jenny left Thursday for a weeklong end-of-school house party at a classmate's country place at the other end of the state in the Berkshires; Conchita, the housekeeper, has gone off with her sister for a long package-deal weekend in the Poconos; Connie—whose show is in reruns until the fall—is out west, at the BBN affiliates' meeting at Laguna Niguel, south of Los Angeles. She won't be back until Monday night.

So when Jekyll called yesterday to see whether Clifford could meet him at the lawyer's country place on the Hudson, Clifford gladly agreed, even though it's a two-hour drive. He isn't expected until 2 p.m. at the earliest, since Jekyll's taking the morning off to play golf. But with rain on the horizon, Clifford might as well leave earlier. If he's early, so what? He can always nose around the towns in Jekyll's neighborhood, maybe find an amusing antique store or bookseller to stick his head into, check out some of the big houses around Rhinebeck. By 9:30 a.m., he's on the road.

He's looking forward to the day. This is the first time Jekyll's asked to get together on a weekend. Clifford is curious to see how Jekyll lives, and this may be the only chance he'll get. Apart from their regular Wednesday sessions in the borrowed apartment in the Waldorf Towers, e-mail, fax, or phone have more than sufficed since they started working together on *Doe v. Hewitt*. He's no longer concerned about leaks. The way Jekyll has this ship caulked, nothing's going to get out. The landlines and fax lines are swept daily, they stay off cellphones, and the computers are checked out and firewalled on a regular basis by a firm of hotshot Web consultants.

It's hard to believe that *Doe vs. Hewitt* is really happening, but it is: it's docketed for argument before the Supreme Court this coming October. Jekyll has pulled it off, just as he said he would, and somehow "persuaded" the state attorney general to co-sign the petition for exigent but not emergency adjudication. In late May, not longing before adjourning for the summer, the Court agreed to hear the case.

The debate practice at the Waldorf seems to be working. Jekyll gives Clifford notes and "talking points," and Clifford plays the several justices, male and female, peppering Jekyll with questions and arguments. He's finding certain justices easier to impersonate than others: based on the records and recordings he's assembled, Jekyll thinks Clifford's De Vito and Mornington-Kaplan are spot on, but that his Cleveland smacks too much of a minstrel show, and both agree that his Chen is going to need a lot of work, not to mention his impersonation of Justice Ramirez, the most enigmatic figure on the Court. Clifford's enjoying himself, really enjoying himself. This is like rehearsing a show or a film. A lot of give and take, all aimed at finding "the moment" and how to get in it and stay there.

Jekyll's been proven right on another score. The nation has really gotten into Doe v. Hewitt, just as Jekyll foresaw: for the pundit class, it's all about the issues, everything from feminism to the economics of marriage; for the people in the street, and the blogosphere, it's the gossip, a multimillion-player guessing game about who the "Does" really are. At this point, the speculation assumes, in nine instances out of ten, that Doe is a wife. By 11:30 a.m., Clifford has reached the Hudson. He stops for coffee and a sandwich, then tools around the area for another hour until he feels he's exhausted the area's possibilities. By now, it's starting to drizzle. *What the hell*, he decides: he'll head for Jekyll's now. What's an hour among friends? He thinks about calling ahead, decides not to. Either Jekyll's home or will be shortly. Clifford will be perfectly happy to sit in the car and go over his notes.

On the way over, he finds himself thinking how this relationship is turning out to be more interesting, maybe even *better,* than he ever would have expected. He's starting to think of Jekyll as a friend, and it's been a while since Clifford's added one of those. Maybe it's because Jekyll's kind of a loner, too. Doesn't need—doesn't want—a lot of people in his life. The lawyer's a funny guy. Here he is, up to his elbows day in day out in the worst kind of human swill, and seeming to relish it, and yet there's a deep vein of common sense in the man—and under that an unmistakable schist of decency. From Jekyll's offhand remarks about books, music, and films, he strikes Clifford as pretty refined, too, although he really has no idea what kind of life the lawyer leads "off camera." His social life, for example: what's that like, with whom does the guy hang out? "I don't go to parties in stores," he's told Clifford, who knows exactly what Jekyll means—a good half of the party venues reported in the Manhattan press seem to take place at Bergdorf Goodman or Hermès—and Clifford feels the same way, and he certainly shares Jekyll's view that "a social life consisting of functions you pay to go to is hardly worthy of the name."

It's a little before 1 p.m. when he turns into Jekyll's driveway, which is marked only by a small sign that reads "65," half-hidden by uncut weeds; if he hadn't been told where to look for it, he'd have easily missed it. The drive curls through a grove of alder and maple to an unpretentious house situated on a high, moundlike bluff: a two-storied white clapboard affair, the shutters gleaming with fresh green paint, decent-sized but certainly not grand, with an attached two-car garage, both doors down, and, just off to one side and a bit lower, a connected outbuilding that might be a studio or guest cottage. Off to the right, Clifford catches a distant view of the Hudson.

There's a car in the driveway, a dark-blue Lexus hybrid with New York plates. Funny, Clifford would have figured Jekyll for more of a Mercedes type. Anyway, Jekyll must be home; the weather probably caused him to quit after nine holes. He goes up to the front door and gives the brass knocker a couple of brisk raps. From inside, he hears Jekyll call out, "Coming!"—then footsteps, and the door opens, and there's Jekyll, looking very suburban in khakis, a golf shirt, and loafers. "My goodness," he exclaims. "Clifford! What are you doing here? I wasn't expecting you for another hour."

"I came over early," Clifford explains. "Wanted to see what it's like over here where the virtuous folks live." On the floor just inside the door is a wheeled suitcase. "You going somewhere?" he asks Jekyll. And then he senses that there's someone else in the house. "Look," he says, "if I'm interrupting something, I can easily go around the block and come back. Just tell me when."

"No, no, come on in," Jekyll says. He pauses, then adds: "There's someone here I think it'd be a good idea for you to meet."

Clifford follows his host inside and into the living room. The best words for Jekyll's country décor are "utilitarian cozy." One or two decent antiques, the rest mix-and-match plain vanilla, nothing fancy, nothing expensive. Comfortable overstuffed chairs and sofas, a leather ottoman, a big TV set with a full array of supporting ordnance, a crammed revolving bookcase crowned by a high-tech halogen lamp, a miscellany of tables supporting low brass lamps with green glass shades, a small, faded Oriental rug that, in decent condition, might be worth a fair penny, shelves sagging under heavy art books; every other flat surface bears its fair load of newspapers, magazines, and CD and DVD boxes. It reminds Clifford of his own studio. A civilized man's bunker from which to fend off the barbarians.

On the corner love seat, a drowsy brown cat is being idly stroked by one of the most interesting-looking women Clifford has ever seen.

When the two men enter the room, she pushes the cat away and gets up, coming around from behind the coffee table, which is covered in legal pads and marked-up documents.

She's almost as tall as Clifford, with more angular features, a more oval face, dark brown eyes and olive skin, and dark hair worn shoulder length. A prominent nose, her mouth decisive without being thin-lipped. The effect is Latin, or maybe Middle Eastern. She's wearing very little makeup, the lips barely tinted, just a faint pale hint of color. Her figure, on the slim side, is okay: nice shapely breasts, nice defined hips. She's dressed mannishly: a button-down shirt not very different from his own—blue instead of yellow—tucked into well-cut khaki trousers, a pale green sweater loosely draped across her shoulders—draped just so, with the elegance and careless precision Clifford associates with Frenchwomen and their scarves. The sweater, together with her shirt, sets off her dark auburn hair and her good coloring. Rimless reading glasses hang from a plain fiber cord around her neck. He guesses she's a year or two older than his wife: probably in her mid-forties.

"I was mistaken, Natalie," Jekyll says to her. "It turns out the car I heard wasn't your taxi. Natalie, this is Clifford Grange. Clifford, this is Natalie Sloan. *Professor* Natalie Sloan, that is."

"I know who Mr. Grange is," she says. The hand that takes his is long-fingered and strong, the nails buffed but clear. "We've even met. At a party at the New York Film Festival. Five or six years ago, perhaps? You were introducing your film *Hearts of the City*." Her voice is unaccented, her pronunciation unhurried, the voice of someone eminently comfortable with who she is.

"Could have been," he says. He must be getting Alzheimer's, not to remember a woman as remarkable as this. "That would have to have been at least six years ago. My last hurrah at the festival. I haven't been invited back since."

"I'd just moved east from Berkeley. One of my students took me. You spoke afterward. It was a very interesting picture."

"Natalie teaches law at Cardozo," Jekyll interjects. He pauses and looks at Clifford, obviously thinking over what he's about to say, deciding between the truth and something else, and then continues. "She's working with me on...well, on *Doe v. Hewitt*. Some of the more recondite jurisprudential aspects." He turns to Natalie. "Clifford's an old friend, my dear. He's using his enormous theatrical experience and knowledge to help me with my presentation before the Supreme Court. You might call him my debating coach."

"I see." She turns to Clifford. "I don't suppose Arthur's confided the identity of his mystery client to you?"

"Alas not," he says. "I hear *Us Weekly* is offering a $1 million bounty for a positive identification, and I could use the money." At that moment, there's the sound of a car in the driveway, followed by the toot of a horn.

"Ah," says Jekyll, "that will be your taxi, Natalie. Here, let me get your bag."

Natalie Sloan extends a hand. "It's been nice to meet you, Clifford. Perhaps we can repeat the pleasure—if Arthur lets us. He likes to keep his friends in tight little compartments." Then, before Clifford can reply, she turns away and follows Jekyll out the door.

Clifford plunks himself angrily on the love seat. When Jekyll returns, he asks, "Arthur, what the hell are you up to? Who the hell was that?"

"She's beautiful, isn't she? And her legal mind is every bit the equal of her looks. Very in the Anouk Aimée mold, don't you think?"

"You'll get no argument from me on that. But you and I had a deal. No one else was supposed to be working on this. Goddamn it, Arthur! I have half a mind..."

Jekyll puts up his hands. "Please, Clifford," he says. "Calm down. Natalie is a distinguished legal scholar. I need her help as much as I need yours. Here, look at this." He picks up a printed document and hands it to Clifford. "'Venus at the Bar: New Initiatives in Family Law,'" Clifford reads, "'by Natalie Judith Sloan, LLD, Professor of Judicial Ecology, Benjamin L. Cardozo School of Law, Yeshiva University.'" He looks at Jekyll.

"So? And what the hell is judicial ecology?"

"The study of law in its broadest social and cultural context, I suppose. Why don't you ask Natalie the next time you see her?"

"Because there isn't going to be a next time."

"Oh, calm down! There's nothing to get either excited or worried about. Trust me." Jekyll gestures toward the west-facing windows. "Come over and look at this view."

The panorama of the great river is breathtaking. It's like a thick glistening serpent undulating southward, with ripples and eddies for scales—now gray, now tinged with green, as the unsettled murky light keeps shifting. Clifford's mind is elsewhere: "Okay, great view! Now—Arthur—don't change the subject. How many times do I have to hear you say, 'Trust me'? You swore to me that you and I'd be the only people working on *Doe v. Hewitt*. That was how you sold me on this goddamn project! Does that wom...does she know who Doe is?"

"No, Natalie does not know you're Doe. You have my word on that. She has no reason to, nor do I see any reason that she should. And may I point out that it's not my fault that you arrived ahead of schedule and without warning. It was never my intention that you and Natalie cross paths."

Clifford is riled. For the first time, he's seeing the Jackal side of Jekyll: devious, win at all costs. "You mean what I don't know won't hurt me. Don't try that tree falls in the forest bullshit on me."

"Clifford, calm down, please. Come with me now. I want to show you something."

"All right—but be warned, Arthur. I'm pissed and I'm on my guard! I have half a mind to call this whole charade off. After all, it *is* my case."

Jekyll says nothing. He leads the way through the kitchen, out the back door, and along a covered walkway to the small shedlike building Clifford had noticed on arrival. What started as a drizzle is quickening. Jekyll produces a key ring and works a series of deadbolts, then leads Clifford inside. The interior is a single small chamber, no more than fifteen feet square, so chock full of stuff there's barely room for the two men: along one wall are waist-high bookshelves, the shelves stuffed with legal texts, the tops cluttered with yellow legal pads still in shrink-wrap, reams of computer paper and boxes of pens and pencils, a compact CD player, a fax machine, a two-button cordless phone, a coffee machine, and a small refrigerator. Under the window in the wall opposite the door is a card table with two folding chairs side by side. On it is a computer hooked to a cable modem and a cordless phone; underneath is a multifunction printer-scanner. In the center of the room stands a podium with a reading light and a kitchen timer.

"This is my war room," says Jekyll.

"So I see," says Clifford.

The wall opposite the podium has been corkboarded from floor to ceiling. A three-foot space at either end is given over to serried ranks of paper affixed with differently colored pushpins. The main part of the wall is taken up by nine eleven-by-fourteen-inch photographs: six men and three women whose faces Clifford feels he's coming to know as well as his own. The photos are arranged, from left to right, in the order the Justices are actually seated, as the audience in the courtroom will see them. The seating protocol goes back and forth, back and forth, with the most junior Justice farthest to the Chief Justice's right (the spectators' and advocates' left) then the next junior farthest to the other side—and so on and so on.

Clifford goes over and examines the photos one by one. On the far left will sit William Chen, the most recent appointee, a disciple of Richard Posner, the iconoclastic former chief judge of the Chicago-based Seventh Circuit, like his mentor a proponent of cost-benefit legal thinking. Next to Chen is Justice Esther Mornington-Kaplan, former chief counsel for NOW and a keen student of gender-related law. Then a square-jawed, white-haired man with a snapping-turtle mouth: Lewis Hartman, a former solicitor general, and in Jekyll's view, the Court's resident nitpicker, a stickler for small points and fine shadings. Hartman is considered the Court's swing vote. Next is John Henry Newbegin, the Grand Old Man of the Court, a throwback to the glory days of Warren and Douglas. Newbegin is said to be dying of cancer of the esophagus.

In the center is the new Chief Justice, the Honorable Shirley Smiley, former dean of the University of Michigan Law School, former presiding judge of the Supreme Court of the state of Michigan, former chief judge of the Court of Appeals for the Fifth Circuit. She's a pleasant-looking woman, with bright eyes and generous features that hardly accord with her reputation as a tough-minded conservative. The feeling is that the Smiley Court has yet to define itself as a collective jurisprudential personality and to establish a philosophical compass that appellants can reliably steer by. So far, Smiley's most radical step as Chief has been to get rid of the comic-operetta gold stripes on the sleeves that were her predecessor's trademark.

The next face over belongs to a wide-browed, importantly dew-lapped African American, who smiles at the camera over a perfectly tied black bow, a snowy shirtfront, and gleaming ruby studs. Herman Cleveland, a former Ohio State All-American and NFL All-Pro tackle, a Ford appointee and perhaps Washington's best-known and most sought-after widower-about-Capitol-Hill. Law-trade scuttlebutt claims that "old Herman has more tuxedos in his closet than citations in his head." By coincidence, Devoria Dugdale, the Court's other African American Justice, is seated next to Cleveland: she is as forward-looking and affirmatively acting as her colleague is a throwback to the '50s in style and mindset, and is known to consider Cleveland lazy and deferential; backstage gossip asserts she routinely refers to her colleague as Uncle Tom; Cleveland in turn is said to have more than once described Dugdale as "uppity" in the card room at the Cosmos Club.

Next comes the Court's most controversial figure, Arturo De Vito. "The incomparable Justice De Vito," Jekyll calls him. "Incomparable in his own eyes if no one else's." A fixture on the talk-show circuit, De Vito possesses by some degree the sharpest and wittiest mind on the Court. He is mercurial, sardonic, erudite, orotund, operatic, and vain. According to Jekyll, "Justice De Vito uses the word 'moral' in discourse with about the same frequency as Donald Trump uses the first-person singular." Finally, farthest over on the Court's left, is the Court's first Latino Justice, as well as its resident enigma and cipher: Justice Edgar Ramirez, whose judicial profile so far has been so low as to be virtually invisible.

"Oyez, oyez, oyez, the famous 'nine scorpions in a bottle,'" says Clifford. His study of the photographs has revived the hold the *Doe* project has on him. His pique has subsided. He turns to Jekyll. "Okay, Arthur, this time you're forgiven, but you only get one free pass. Next time, I'm out." He gestures toward the photographs. "A pretty fearsome lot. You think you can handle them?"

"With your coaching, and Natalie's jurisprudential input, I have no doubt that I can. Not a working day goes by without me reflecting intensely on the psychological, philosophical, and judicial predilections of these nine people."

Clifford has noticed that Jekyll's vocabulary seems to have gotten weightier; the lawyer's using a lot of long words; he even sounds pompous. By now, Clifford has heard a bunch of recordings of Supreme Court arguments; the give and take between justices and attorneys is usually conducted in pretty plain English. He makes a mental note to see that Jekyll tones it down. "I'm sure you do," he says. "Now— what's up? Why am I here? You said you needed to talk to me."

"Just this. I've been pondering whether it might be advantageous to go public with the fact that you—Clifford Grange—are helping me—Arthur Jekyll—prepare for my Supreme Court appearance in *Doe v. Hewitt*. Strictly in a professional sense."

"Why?"

"For one thing, if we 'out' our relationship, if the world sees us holding hands in public, there's much less chance they'll figure you're my mystery client. It's what is called 'hiding in plain sight.' It will also obviate the need for us to have a cock-and-bull story ready in case our collaboration is discovered—accidents happen even in the best-arranged households—so there will be no skein of lies or contradictions to get tangled up in, merely something just a bit less than the whole truth."

"You sound to me like you're running scared."

"I'm simply being cautious. And then there's this: by going public, we present Ms. Villers with a viable way of buying you off without letting on what she may or may not know. That's an option I feel I owe you."

"Say that again?"

"I've been thinking it over. Santiago will surely have informed Ms. Villers about my visit with him. If so, she may have deduced that you are Doe."

"How?"

"It's obvious. Thanks to Peter Harris, she's aware that you know about your wife's affair. Your circumstances fit those of the petitioner in the appellate briefs we've filed with the Supreme Court, which is something that only she's in a position to work out. She's a resourceful woman, and I have no doubt that she's casting about for other ways to deal with this issue, since she has to be every bit as concerned about accidental leaks and public disclosure as you. In her shoes, I'd be considering how to buy you off, to settle the case before it gets to Washington. Much as I look forward to arguing before the Court, I owe it to you to give Ms. Villers her chance. If it becomes a matter of public record that you and I are collaborating, she will be able to treat you as an emissary to me, to approach you with a plain face to act as an intermediary in negotiating a settlement with me—and through me, my client *Doe*. If I'm right, you might soon find yourself considering an offer of upward of $200 million."

"Yeah, but what about you?"

"If she coughs up, you can compensate me adequately."

"But this is *fun!*"

"Granted. I've never had a better time. But this isn't all about me. You should think it over."

"I'll do that. But tell me one thing. This hide-in-plain-sight ploy. How would you do it? *Page Six?*"

"I think I'll use dear old Marge Brown."

"Does anyone still read her? She must be a hundred! The last column of hers that I saw read like a Beverly Hills AARP newsletter, and that was at least two years ago."

"She has enough of a following for our purposes. And she's malleable, poor old thing, possessed of infinite self-importance, proud of her friends in high places, and therefore a woman who, as they say in your trade, 'takes direction.' As you well know, gossip isn't gossip any more, and hasn't been for a long time. It's a branch of public relations. In the old days, one thought of gossip as invasive, as dealing in information and speculation that its subject would prefer *not* be circulated. Gossip today, certainly of the Marge Brown variety, is almost entirely concerned with matters people *want* to be known about themselves; matters that they in fact pay to have disseminated or planted by publicists or other schemers. Marge's, quote unquote, gossip column might more accurately be described as a bulletin board for publicists."

"I see. So—assuming I decide to go along with you—when should I expect the shit to hit the fan? This is likely to cause quite a stir chez moi. Connie's always hated no-fault, for all the usual knee-jerk reasons, and of course she's Mrs. Family Values, thanks to Barrow. I can also tell you she's quite aware of *Doe v. Hewitt*. Bottom line: she reckons she's got some skin in this game. Once she knows I have your ear, she's never going to leave me alone."

"I'm having dinner at Elio's with Marge Brown tomorrow night. Her column runs on Tuesdays and Thursdays."

"I see." Clifford laughs. "Ready or not, here she comes. Now, you also said you had something you wanted to work on. No time like the present. Incidentally, there's something else that's been bugging me."

"Yes?"

"Well, I wish you'd reconsider about excluding the 'eminent domain' angle from your argument. I think it works, especially if you pair 'moral eminent domain' with 'moral hazard.' Chen might really go for that."

"I agree that it makes for a compelling-sounding argument, but tactically I'm loath to ask the Court to revisit a finding that's so recent, even though the financial particulars are different. But I'll think it over. Now, let me tell you what's on my mind. I woke up the other night with my head full of a line of questioning that I expect that the enigmatic Justice Ramirez might throw at me. Why don't we run through it?"

"Fine."

It's almost five when they finish and Clifford prepares to head home. As they pass through the living room, the lawyer suddenly exclaims, "Damn!"

"What is it?"

Jekyll snatches up a manila envelope lying on a side table. "I meant to give this to Natalie. I'm afraid the surprise of your early arrival distracted me."

"Is it important?"

"Just some material on shame as a governing concept of social order and how it might be evoked in law. An essay by Martha Nussbaum of the University of Chicago. No matter, it can wait."

Impulsively, Clifford finds himself saying, "Look, I'm headed for New York right now to see an old Louis Malle movie at Film Forum. Where's Professor Sloan live? I'll be happy to drop it off at her place."

He can't believe he's saying this. He had absolutely no plans to go to the city. But it has stopped raining, so why not?

"You're sure?" Jekyll asks.

"No problem."

"All right. Let me call her on her cellphone."

To conclude the business takes no time at all. "Natalie lives in Brooklyn, in Dumbo. Hard by the Brooklyn Bridge on Water Street. She doesn't have a doorman, so call her when you're a block or two away and she'll buzz you in or come down to meet you. Here's her cell number. I'll let her know you're coming. Do you need directions?"

"Just give me the address and I'll plug it into my GPS."

Jekyll writes it down, along with the phone number. "I really appreciate this. You're sure it's not out of your way?"

Clifford shakes his head. "Hey," he says, "what are friends for?"

By the time Clifford turns off the Brooklyn-Queens Expressway at the Cadman Plaza exit, it's just before seven and starting to rain again, lightly. He pulls over and dials Natalie Sloan's number; she answers promptly and he tells her he's five minutes away. She says she'll be downstairs, waiting. He reckons he's maybe a mere two miles, at most, from his wife's workplace in the Brooklyn Navy Yard. The thought carries a frisson of adventure, of riskiness, even though it's the weekend and Connie's twenty-five hundred miles away.

Her building turns out to be a converted warehouse that looks to be close to a hundred years old. She's waiting inside the front door. When he hands over the package, he says, "You know, they say it's going to let up later on, and I'd rather drive back home when it's not raining. If you're not doing anything, how about dinner?"

She looks at him, momentarily puzzled, then with a slight smile, "Are you sure? Didn't Arthur tell me you were coming to the city to see a film?"

"It'll be on for a couple of weeks. I'll catch it later. Besides, since we're in this together, it might not be a bad idea to compare notes. Is there any place decent to eat around here? Isn't the River Café somewhere in the neighborhood?"

"It is. Just at the end of the street. But it's impossible on a Saturday night, even in summer, and mostly tourists, anyway. There's a nice little place around the corner on Front Street. This early, I'm sure they can take us."

Clifford digs an umbrella out of the Jaguar, and they walk to the restaurant. It's half full, and they're given a corner table. There's no one in the place who looks remotely familiar to Clifford.

At the table, they order quickly and begin to talk, starting out the way people in such situations always do, feeling their way around what they do, what they like, what they read, what they listen to, and who they voted for. Listening to Natalie, Clifford starts to feel that this is destiny, that somehow he's run into a mind-mate. It's a feeling nicely helped along by the bottle of wine he orders. To him, it seems that Natalie speaks his language, likes what he likes, sees life in pretty much the same way. Listening to her, looking at her, he can't help thinking of Connie and making a comparison. Increasingly, his wife seems like two separate people, the star and the private person, while this woman seems—well—whole and entire, as some poet said.

"Arthur tells me you teach judicial ecology. Can I ask what that is?" he asks at some point.

"Well, you know what ecology is?"

"I guess so. The study of the way we function in relation to the world we live in? Or—more properly, what we do to the world we live in. What I'm not sure I get is the 'judicial' part."

"What I do is investigate the way the different elements in what we call 'the law' conceptualize themselves in relation to the rest of modern life. You might say that what I do is mix up law and political economy and sociology and psychology and see how it all falls out."

"Hmmm. Interesting. So how'd you get mixed up with Arthur? I wouldn't think the kind of law he practices is exactly ecological. Unless you consider it a form of pest control."

"Don't be so sure of that. Divorce is a central constituent of the social context in which we live in this country. And you? What brought you and Arthur together?"

"We're both members of the Diogenes Club. I happened to be between engagements, as they say, and Arthur wanted coaching for his appearance before the Supreme Court. Emphasis, language, gesture, that sort of thing. I've done a lot of work with improvisation—I even taught it at the New School, back before I became a nonentity—and he thinks it might help him put on a better performance."

"Why do you say 'nonentity'?"

"It's a long story. Let's not ruin dinner."

She smiles. "Very well. So do you think Arthur will shine?"

"I wouldn't be surprised. He's a great pupil. And he wants this really badly. Tell me—have you known Arthur long?"

"About ten years, actually," she replies.

"So how'd you meet the great man?"

"I was married right out of law school. To a real bastard—although I didn't find that out until the honeymoon. A bastard with a rich father and a taste for hookers. Very low-grade hookers. After ten years, no children, endless humiliation, and boredom so suffocating I could barely breathe, I wanted to get away from him, to have him out of my life. *Completely* out of my life. I did serious research as to what lawyer would most likely achieve that for me. Arthur came out on top, not even close. Even though I needed someone like him, I expected to hate him because of his reputation, but he grew on me. He also made me financially comfortable for life."

Time for a field check, Clifford thinks. "I don't suppose he's dropped any hints about who Doe is? I'm dying to know," he asks her. It amazes Clifford how smoothly, how easily the fibs come.

She shakes her head. "Nary a one. Arthur compartmentalizes things. He's like an old-fashioned Communist spymaster running a bunch of agents: he divides them into cells, none of which knows about the others. I'm sure he didn't intend for us to encounter each other. And then there's another thing about him. He lets out all sorts of meaningless little secrets in order to create the impression he's a gossip, but if it matters, *really* matters, he's absolutely closed. He allows to get known only what he wants to be known. The big stuff never gets out. If you or anyone ever finds out who Doe is, it won't be through Arthur. I'm crazy about him!"

"You sound like you have a crush on him."

"Hardly. I don't have 'crushes.' But I like him, and I admire him. He's just so good at what he does. You must know what I mean, because your wife's that way. She's amazing. I saw her on *Inside the Actor's Studio*. She was very good."

"I didn't see that show, for some reason. I keep telling myself I need to watch the DVD. Anyway, Connie's a pro. She takes it very seriously and works hard at it." Clifford's voice is noncommittal. No one ever got anywhere complaining about one's spouse.

"Can I ask you something?"

"Anything. Anything at all."

"Does your wife know you didn't watch her with James Lipton?"

Clifford smiles his best charming smile. "What do you think? Of course she doesn't. I told her she was fabulous. Hey, don't look at me like that. I didn't have to watch. I know how good she is."

"So what are you working on now?" she asks. "Apart from Arthur, of course."

That goddamn question again. This and that, he tells her. Not much, he tells her. He glides over his recent career history, not exactly leaving anything out, but steering clear of the anger, resentment, and self-pity. He makes it sound as if he's on a self-imposed creative hiatus. "Although to do so has its risks. Take last week: I was in the city, walking west on Fifty-fifth Street. Outside of Michael's, which is a restaurant packed with everybody who thinks he or she is somebody in the media or showbiz, I ran into this guy who'd been a minor writer on a couple of my pictures, someone I hardly know, and he looked at me with this kind of snarky, cheap grin and cracked what he doubtless thought was a really clever joke: 'Hey,' he said, 'are you who you used to be?'"

"You're joking!"

He smiles. "Of course I am." Except that he isn't. It's a true story. "How about coffee?"

She nods, and takes a hard, analytical look at him. "Somewhere in there, I think there's a streak of melancholy. Am I right?"

"You mean the old 'Laugh, clown, laugh!' bit?" He pauses, and then says, "Why? Is that something women find attractive?"

"I certainly do. Perhaps because I've got one myself. A yard wide."

"You do? I never would have thought that. How come?"

She shrugs. "The soul has its reasons. The truth is, I quite enjoy being sad. Tell me, have you ever been to Lisbon?"

"Never."

"Do you know what fado music is?"

"I suppose I do. That Portuguese stuff, right? Kind of wailing, lost-my-best-friend music?"

"I guess you could call it that. I think it's the best sad music in the world. I love it. I have since the first time I ever heard it."

"Which I assume was in Lisbon?"

"No—I've never been there, either," she says. "I'm saving it for the right time, or the right person. But when I was in Cambridge, at Harvard Law, a friend took me to a concert by a woman called Amalia Rodrigues. She was kind of Julia Child of fado, a high priestess of her art. The man who took me was an investment banker; this was back when you could say that with a straight face. Anyhow, he was quite civilized in spite of what he did, very generous, and I guess he was trying to impress me with how cosmopolitan he was by taking me to this concert. As I sat there listening, it suddenly came over me how small he seemed—how small my life taken as a whole seemed—next to the possibilities of feeling that were in that music. By the end of the evening, I'd decided to get rid of him and go someday to Lisbon—but not until I really needed to, not until I was really sad, so sad I could barely get out of bed."

"Really? Why the sad bit?"

"I figured that a place that could give birth to that music must be the best place in the world to be sad in. A place just to go to and stay up all night and listen to fado and drink brandy and go to bed alone with the sun coming up and sleep late and get up with the kind of hangover that keeps the sadness going and do it all over again."

"And that time has never arrived? You're lucky."

"Am I?" She looks at her watch and says, "Golly, where did the time go?"

He checks his own. It's barely nine-thirty. "Don't tell me you turn into a pumpkin this early?" he asks.

"There's a panel I'm on at Rutgers tomorrow. I have a 7:15 train out of Penn Station. Shall we get the check? Can we go Dutch?"

"Not a chance." He's scrambling mentally for a way to keep this going. In his imagination, he's already halfway into her bed, more than halfway into a crush. He's had plenty to drink, maybe too much to perform up to par, fully—but he recalls hearing somewhere that it's easier to get a woman to sleep with you if you're a bit tighter than she is, and maybe it's the booze, but he's suffused inside with the suave and satisfying confidence of a man who's about to get what he wants because he thoroughly deserves it.

The check comes, and without thinking, Clifford takes a credit card from his wallet, puts it down, looks at it, and picks it up. It's his black corporate American Express one, issued to Constance Grange Associates LLC.

The last thing he needs to have happen is for the cashier or waitress to make a connection and pass the word to *Page Six* that Clifford Grange, husband of the domestic goddess, has had dinner *à deux* with a beautiful woman at an obscure restaurant in Brooklyn while his wife was in Las Vegas.

He substitutes his own plain-vanilla green card. Natalie doesn't appear to notice. Clifford hopes not, but when he suggests a brandy, she refuses.

Outside, the streets are empty. It's dark now. The rain is still coming down. They walk back to Natalie's in silence. At the entrance to her building, there's a pause, an awkward flicker of time, then—to break the clumsiness—Clifford says, "Well, I guess I better hit the road."

Natalie looks at him. "I know what you're thinking, Clifford. I'm thinking it, too," she says quietly. "You'd like to me to invite you upstairs for a drink, maybe even for the night, wouldn't you?"

"I wouldn't say no."

"I've been considering it. You're attractive and I'm lonely and I think you realize that."

"Lonely? You? You don't show it."

"That may be. And you're intelligent and funny and you have feelings that you seem unafraid to show. And you're also half of the most conspicuously, publicly happily married couple in the country." She grins at him. "Don't think I missed that business with the credit cards."

"I'm sorry about that."

"Don't be. In some way I'd like you to come up. But I think we both know where that would lead, which funnily enough doesn't trouble me. I've certainly had just enough to drink, and God knows, I haven't slept with anyone in months—so all that's working for you, too. But I don't like one-night stands."

"It wouldn't have to be."

"Oh yes it would. If it became something else, the risks would multiply. If it got out...well, just think what a scandal, any kind of scandal, might do to your wife's image. It could ruin her career. Do you think I'd ever want to be a party to that?"

"No, but..."

She puts up a forefinger. "Clifford, listen to me—please. It's not that I don't sleep with married men, because I have before and I will again, no doubt, because there aren't many attractive and interesting unattached straight men out there, not ones that I've been able to find. But your case is different. Besides, I just couldn't do it to Arthur."

"Arthur? Why does he have to be involved?"

"This case is important to him. I think it may be the most important thing that's ever happened to him, because in the end it's going to determine how he feels about himself and his life. He deserves the best we can give him—and that means no distractions, especially not an interoffice romance—or affair or whatever you want to call it— between the two of us. I don't think either of us is under any illusions about what it could mean to Arthur's case, which is predicated on the sanctity of marriage, if it should get out that the famous director who's working with him, a man whose marriage is the very model of what a marriage is supposed to be in these morally helter-skelter times, is involved in a bit of what the public will regard as hanky-panky. You see that, don't you?"

"Of course. I suppose."

"Don't be sorry, Clifford. I like you. As I just said, you're smart, funny—what's not to like?" She reaches out and touches his hand. "Look, if it's going to be, it's going to be—but not now, not here, all right? Maybe another time. Maybe after this is finished, after it gets wherever it's going to go, all right?"

"What can I say?" He shrugs. "I…"

She puts a forefinger to his lips. "I have to go to bed now. Don't look so mournful. We'll see each other again, I'm sure we will." She raises up on her toes and kisses his cheek. "Goodnight, Clifford. You don't know how lucky you are to have a great marriage—or maybe you do. Don't ever lose sight of that."

Alone on the street, he feels a kind of aching loneliness, mainly sexual yearning. *How few people I have in my life*, he thinks, *really have*. Connie and Jenny—they total now maybe one and a half, tops, for all the attention they pay to him. Jekyll. Maud, Renee, and the people at the club table, and a couple of bar acquaintances there. One or two old industry pals who haven't forgotten—mainly because they're in the same career boat themselves, bailing with both hands. People he says hello to in Jenny's solar system: teachers, coaches, other parents—no one close. People to whom he pays money for work done, goods and services rendered, whom he addresses with an egalitarian bonhomie that both sides pretend is a form of friendship. And now maybe Natalie Sloan.

And there's this, too—the evening, whatever it's failed to deliver, has opened his eyes in one direction: he realizes irrevocably how much he resents Connie. Before this, there were ways around her success, her money, her aura. From here on, it can only get worse. Come September, Jenny will be off to boarding school: Andover. Andover,

Andover, Andover. It's all she can talk about. And then he and Connie will be left alone together at Grangeford, to stare at each other across a luxurious, upholstered no-man's-land evening after evening after evening. Right now, the prospect is unendurable.

He closes his eyes, again thinks briefly of trying to call Natalie, and decides against it; the cellular equivalent of a cat howling under a window is not a role he fancies for himself. One thing's for certain, he doesn't feel like the long drive back home. Fortunately, there's a hotel in the East Village that's owned by a member of the Diogenes who always keeps a room or two free for stranded members. He gets the number and moments later, he has a room for the night. He drives over, puts the Jaguar in a garage, checks in, and then goes back out and wanders around until he finds a bar on Third Avenue that looks promising, and proceeds to get good and thoroughly soused.

Somehow he makes it back to the hotel. When he wakes up the next morning, there's not a hint of hangover, and the world seems full of sweet chirping. As he exits the garage, it seems to him that he feels better about life and about himself than he has in years. He'll make a fresh start at home. He'll put out of mind his doubts about his marriage. He'll try to forget about Natalie Sloan. He mentally pats himself on the back for his resoluteness. As he pulls on to the FDR Drive, heading north, he starts to whistle *"Que sera, sera,"* and a minute later, as his spirits mount into bluebird mode, he's singing his lungs out.

CHAPTER NINE

August 18

The jet enters the clouds and shudders violently. Annabelle jounces
up against her seat belt, her heart leaps from her chest to the vicinity
of her tonsils, and she digs her fingers into the arms of her seat. The
plane bounces again, then settles back on course, the engines regain
their purchase and so does Annabelle's pulse.

She's on her way to visit the Granges at Sleeping Bear Cove. For
four years now, Connie has begged Annabelle to spend a weekend
with them at the lake, and for four years now Annabelle has accepted, only to have to beg off because of a crisis at a glass plant,
an FDA problem, a sinus condition, the death of a beloved aunt. To
tell the truth, she hasn't lamented these missed opportunities. Fond
as she is of the Granges, and as few as the occasions are to see her
goddaughter Jenny, there's just something about the prospect of
being off in a vacation community in the dark north woods that un-
nerves her. How a twitchy person like Clifford Grange can handle
it, she can hardly imagine.

It's really Clifford she's flown north to see. It's clear to her that he's the Doe in this *Doe vs. Hewitt* business, being led by the nose by the awful divorce lawyer who virtually blackmailed Santiago into forcing the state to cooperate. Nobody in Hartford wanted the kind of scandal that Jekyll was capable of causing. How had he made the connection? As for Clifford being Doe, who else could it be? Especially now that a link between Clifford and Jekyll has been reported in a New York gossip column. The latter was plainly a subterfuge, but Annabelle finds herself in a situation in which the circumstantial evidence is overwhelming, but where nothing can be shown to be fact. Still, in today's media climate, supposition more than suffices, and this *Doe v. Hewitt* business has got to be stopped before it ruins everything for everyone.

Sooner or later, someone's going to stumble on the truth. Hardly a day goes by now without one or the other of those supermarket scandal sheets, or their TV equivalents, or some nosy Internet Web site, speculating as to the identity of "petitioner Doe" and their spouse. Annabelle thinks it's no less than a miracle that not even a whiff of suspicion has attached to the Granges. A month ago, *Us Weekly* ran a feature on Connecticut couples who might be the Does and came up with a list of twenty-two, which mercifully didn't include Connie and Clifford. The article had led to denials and threatened lawsuits, and soon exhausted its fifteen minutes of furor. But the fear remains that somewhere out there there's someone, some workman, security guard, passing truck driver, gas station attendant, someone who saw or noticed something last fall, who'll hear about *Doe v. Hewitt* and make a connection and exercise the great American prerogative of unmasking someone more rich and famous. A stop has to be put to this—and now. And the only way Annabelle can imagine doing this is to buy Clifford off.

It's a risky approach. Anyone who's heard Clifford on the subject of wealth and the rich and the influence of money in American life and politics would know that. If it wasn't for his professional situation, she'd never consider trying. But she knows he's desperate to get back to making films, and the prospect of being able to finance himself may prove decisive.

The first question is, how much will it take? According to Jack Welch's book, the former General Electric CEO personally offered Jerry Seinfeld $100 million in GE stock to stick around for just *one* more season, and Connie has at least three, maybe four left in her—according to Barrow's people—so is that some kind of yardstick? Seinfeld may have been worth $100 million to GE/NBC, but $100 million was peanuts by GE standards, and Constance Grange proportionately means so much more to Summerhill and BBN. Annabelle has calculated how much in aggregate she and Barrow stand to lose if Connie's brand value is ruined and she has come up with a figure of over $1 billion. Will twenty percent of that—$200 million—get the job done? Is there any way she can hope to get Ronald Barrow, who's a notorious public prude, to share the cost? If he won't, how much can Annabelle afford on her own?

As things now stand, not much more than $100 million, depending on a call she's expecting from London—because she has something on her plate that may eat up practically all her resources.

She reaches into her briefcase and takes out a large, slender buckram-slipcased volume that has been her constant companion since April, when it arrived in Asheville as a part of a major Anglo-Italian art library bought by Annabelle for the research arm of the institute. It is the privately printed catalog—one of only twenty copies—of the Hentzau-Lucarelli collection in Vaduz, Lichtenstein, assembled mainly in the mid-neenteenth century, which is the greatest single aggregation of Italian old masters still in private hands. All the great names, from Duccio to Caravaggio, that grace the great public collections of the world.

In April, when she lunched in London with Julian Cuthbert, the English dealer with whom she's been working on collecting for her art institute, she asked whether he thought the Hentzau-Lucarelli art, or any part of the collection, might be available. He answered that it was out of the question, that collectors from Frick and Mellon to Goering to Russian oligarchs had made passes and been spurned. That was that, she thought—until Cuthbert called a month later from Geneva. He had opened the conversation with typical Brit flipness. "Do you have $1.5 billion, old girl?"

"Do I *what*?"

"Don't beat around the bush, my dear Annabelle. I know you do. I checked your last proxy statement. Now, here's the thing. I've just spent a most entertaining two days in Vaduz. It seems that the Hentzau-Lucarelli collection is owned by a Lichtenstein nominee trust that is said to be a front for an important European family, possibly royal. Today, there are approximately twenty beneficiaries, most of them under fifty, a majority of whom would prefer to see the cash value these things represent put to work saving the rain forest or doing good work in the Sudan. The trust is advised by a lawyer in Zug, Switzerland, in whom I have made, over the years, a considerable investment, as it were, by supplying him with pleasures both sporting and sybaritic that I needn't go into. A connection I valued mainly because of his influence with certain Greek shipping interests. I had no idea of the Hentzau-Lucarelli connection. So I hotfooted it to dear old Zug, and, over a really quite decent '61 Petrus, learned that the decision to sell the collection had only just been taken by the heirs in solemn conclave assembled. They want to do it quickly. What with the auction market looking shaky just now, I think a reasonable offer might preempt all comers."

"Reasonable being...?"

"What I just said: $1.5 billion or the equivalent in euros."

"I don't have anything like that."

"Of course you do. I read your last SEC filing on the Internet. Dear girl, there will never be an opportunity like this in the lifetime of anyone you and I know. I have seen the private files on the collection, which include completely up-to-date reports on authenticity and condition by the best people in the field. Just imagine these things in Asheville. Imagine the green and envious faces in New York,

Washington, and Boston when these great works find their permanent home in the very shadow of the Great Smokies. But time is of the essence. Gene Thaw has been said to be nosing around Vaduz, and if he gets the scent in his nostrils, he'll call Acquavella and Bill will enlist Mr. Cohen in Greenwich, or maybe even the Chinese, with whom he's gotten very chummy, and that will only complicate matters irredeemably. I also hear that Richard Feigen was in Zurich last week, asking some pretty pointed questions, and no one in this business has a better nose for news, as you Americans say, than he."

"I understand. Still, the price you're talking about averages out to close to $50 million an object."

"I simply will not let you speak of 'averages' in conjunction with works of this quality. Take the Hentzau-Lucarelli Duccio annunciation. It's the same size as the Stoclet picture for which the Met paid $45 million, but infinitely more complex and interesting. And I could go on from there. 'Averages,' pshaw!"

"How long do we have?"

"At the outside, no more than a week, I should think. On your behalf, I've put down $10 million in earnest money."

"A *week*!"

"When it wants to, love always finds a way. Go look at that catalog and call me back."

"Julian, a billion five; I haven't got that kind of money."

"Of course you do. Just sell some shares."

"I can't. Not legally, not in this time frame, so soon after the offering. I'll have to borrow the money."

"Borrow it, then. Would you like me to call a friend in Dubai on your behalf?"

"No. Let me see what I can do. But no promises, all right?"

After hanging up, Annabelle had fetched the catalog. By the time she turned the last page, she was hooked. It was everything the dealer had claimed. She *had* to have these pictures. She picked up the phone and called Cecile Frost and asked if she could see her that very evening. Then she instructed Mary Ella to get onto NetJets to arrange for a flight to New York, and by noon the next day, Annabelle had herself a deal with First Gotham.

It involves her selling $200 million of her Summerhill stock, the legal maximum, with First Gotham providing the $1.3 billion balance through a loan secured by the collection itself and by Annabelle's remaining stock, which at current prices is worth a bit over $1 billion. The prospect of owing this much money makes Annabelle nervous.

Her determination to devote her time and energy to the art institute when it opens next year in temporary quarters is firm. But she can't do that and give her company the attention it deserves, so she has confidentially authorized First Gotham to prepare a valuation of Summerhill with a view to exploring, also on a top-secret basis, the sale of Summerhill to another company, a giant like Kraft Foods or LVMH or one of the few big leveraged buyout shops that are still alive and well. It's First Gotham's view that Summerhill has a "private market value," allowing for certain cost reductions and the incremental profit contribution of the new plant outside Hartford that will go onstream next year, in the neighborhood of $6 billion, which would make Annabelle's personal holding worth in the neighborhood of $2 billion—provided nothing goes wrong, which makes it more important than ever that *Doe v. Hewitt* be put to sleep, given the havoc a scandal could wreak on the value of Annabelle's collateral.

There's no turning back. Cuthbert has been given the go-ahead to negotiate for the acquisition of the Hentzau-Lucarelli collection and is in Vaduz right now with her offer. She checks her watch. 10:32 a.m., Central time, which means 5:32 p.m. in Lichtenstein. He should be calling any minute now.

She stares out the window. The cloud cover is thinning, with breaks that here and there disclose dark forests dotted with blue-black lakes. A landscape entirely unlike the Great Smokies. She closes her eyes and begins the yoga exercise she's been working on with her personal trainer, inhaling and exhaling with a deep, level swiftness, binding herself so tightly to the pillar of breath that the flight attendant has to speak her name twice. She looks up to see the young woman holding out a cordless handset. "You have an urgent call being patched through from Europe, m'am. A Lord Cuthbert. Do you want to take it?"

The call takes a little more than a minute. When she hangs up, she is breathless. In no more time than it has taken her to say "Done," she has eclipsed all the collectors of the present, and moved into the Maecenean stratosphere of Mellon and Frick, Widener and Wallace. It takes the rest of the trip for Annabelle to get a grip on her excitement.

The Sleeping Bear airport is a surprise. She's expected a dozy, rustic, country landing strip, but there's what looks like a very up-to-date control tower and four gleaming private jets and a helicopter parked on a side runway. She also immediately spots the vintage red Mustang convertible she's been told to look for, but the figure standing beside it, waving vigorously, isn't Clifford, who she's been told would be meeting her. It's Connie. *Darn!* Annabelle had planned to use the drive to Sleeping Bear to feel out Clifford.

Connie gives her a big hug. "I'm so excited you've come, darling! Finally! I thought we'd never get you up here. You're going to love it."

"You didn't have to come. I could just as well have taken a taxi."

"Not to worry. I had to drive Clifford over, anyway. He's gone to Ann Arbor for the day."

"Ann Arbor?"

"You won't believe this, but he hired a plane so he could go over and look up something at the University of Michigan Law Library."

"Why, for Lord's sake? Clifford isn't a lawyer."

"He might as well be. It's the case that everyone's talking about: *Doe v. Hewitt.* I know you don't read the New York gossip columns, but if you did, you'd know that my darling husband has been conscripted by that awful Arthur Jekyll—the one they call the Jackal—to coach him."

"Actually I do know about it. Our local paper runs Marge Brown's column once a week. I gather Clifford is helping Mr. Jekyll in some way."

"Jekyll is going to argue the case before the Supreme Court in early October and he's drafted Clifford to direct him almost as if he was in a play. Jekyll may be a famous lawyer, but he's hardly ever actually argued a case in a real courtroom, let alone the Supreme Court—I gather almost all his cases get settled out of court—so he asked Clifford to coach him. Make him more effective and—my guess is—more genteel. When Clifford taught at Northwestern, he also coached the debating team."

"I'm surprised Clifford let himself get roped into something like that. I gather Mr. Jekyll is pretty unsavory company to be keeping."

"He didn't have much say in the matter. It's some kind of ridiculous club thing. One for all and all for one. But I have to say this: at least it's given Clifford something to do. He's thrown himself in head over heels. Last summer, Clifford just moped around. It nearly drove me crazy! This year, I don't have to worry about keeping him busy. He sits on the porch scribbling on legal pads and listening to this dreary Portuguese music on his little stereo."

"Portuguese music?"

"I think it's called fada, something like that. It's very gloomy. You know how Clifford is. He gets these enthusiasms. Lord knows what it'll be next!"

"No news on the Ronnie front, I gather? About Clifford's career, I mean. Have you had a chance to speak with him?"

"I haven't. But I will—when the time seems right."

Not for the first time, Annabelle finds herself wondering whether Connie sincerely wants to help her husband, whether she doesn't like the situation just as it is. On the other hand, if Clifford's still in career purgatory, he'll probably be inclined to listen to a serious offer to drop Doe v. Hewitt. "Tell me," she says. "I don't suppose Clifford might know who the Does are? The entire country is burning up with curiosity."

"You know, he hasn't said a thing. I don't think he knows. I don't think anyone does—except Jekyll and, of course, his client. I just wish the whole business would get over with; it's made life absolute hell for some of our friends. I don't suppose you saw that story in *Us Weekly* about the couples in our state that might be the Does? They came up with over a dozen names, mostly rich hedge-fund types from Greenwich."

"Were you and Clifford on it?"

"No—thank heavens!"

For the next dozen miles, the two women chitchat about this and that. Finally, after running alongside a glistening stretch of lake for the best part of a mile, Connie swings through an arched gateway fashioned from birch branches and announces, "Well, here we are."

The Grange "lodge" is a low-lying, half-timbered lakefront house on Sleeping Bear Cove, an arm of Lake Michigan pinched off from the mainland at its narrow end as if by giant fingers. There's a deck looking out over the water, and a dock extending some fifty feet into the lake; a small sailboat and two canoe-looking craft are tied up there. On three sides rise noble palisades mantled in sixty-foot-tall firs that plunge straight down to the water's edge.

As they pull up to the house. Jenny Grange hurtles out the front door, flaunting a blue prize ribbon the size of a tea saucer and reminding Connie that mother-daughter tennis starts at two sharp. There's a quick lunch of sandwiches, and Annabelle is made to change her clothes and then it's off to a round of activities that leaves Annabelle exhausted even though she's only a spectator. When they return to the house around five, they find that Clifford has returned. He embraces the three women in turn.

"Connie tells me you're becoming quite the legal scholar," Annabelle says. "I want to hear all about it." As Annabelle asks the question, she notices a faint scowl cross Connie's face.

"And so you shall," he replies smiling. He turns to Connie. "Sorry about missing the parent-child sail-off. But you're a better crew than I am, anyway, so I'm sure our darling daughter the trophy hunter didn't miss me. What's for dinner? Shall I fire up the grill?"

"Can't you remember anything? It's bonfire night!"

"I'm sorry. My mind was—"

"I know where your mind was!" Her irritation is evident. "May I remind you that this is supposed to be a vacation?" She snorts, and turns to Annabelle. "I swear, he might as well be married to that awful Jekyll!"

"Hey!" says Clifford sharply. "Wasn't it you who only yesterday was praising Jekyll for giving me something to do and getting me off your back?" Then he throttles down. "Sorry." Obviously wanting to defuse the moment, he grins at Annabelle. "Hard to serve two masters," he says. "But I try. I can see they ran you ragged, too. Okay, as the man said, let me get out of these wet clothes and into a dry martini, and I'll be rarin' to go."

It's just after ten when the last ragged chorus of "It's a Long, Long Trail A-Winding" dies out over the lake and the Grange party sails home. Connie and her daughter plead justifiable exhaustion and plunge off to bed with barely a goodnight. Clifford proposes a nightcap to Annabelle, and she accepts.

They carry their brandies out onto the deck. It's a truly majestic northern night: blessedly silent, the air crisp, the moon high, the sky clear, everywhere an impression of tallness and expanse, with only a couple of moving lights on the water to signify the human presence.

"What a charming place this is," Annabelle says.

"Isn't it? We had my old man up a couple of years before he died, and he said it was as if the '50s never ended. Up here, they still like Ike. Still, if you put that Midwestern WASP taste for frenetic physical activity to one side, it's pretty cool. Actually, it kind of brings to mind that old hymn, the one that goes, 'Where every prospect pleases, and only man is vile.'"

Annabelle takes a deep draught of the night; the air's as fresh as it is back home in the mountains; she's beginning to feel herself again. "So how are you otherwise, Clifford? Connie says you're very caught up in this Doe business."

"Not with her unstinting endorsement, as you saw this evening. But I'm really getting off on it."

Annabelle's feeling her way. It's a tricky, fraught moment. "Tell me about it," she asks, trying to get a better sense of how best to take this.

Clifford's in the same position. He knows a thing or two that she knows, but not enough. Does she know about Vargas, for instance? He hasn't been able to expel Jekyll's supposition that, impossible as it seems at least from a character point of view, Annabelle may have had something to do with the fellow's death. "Basically, I'm rehearsing Jekyll for his half hour in the Supreme Court spotlight," he says, riposting. "I do the justices in diff'rent voices, to paraphrase Dickens, and by now I've got them down pretty pat. At least Jekyll seems to think so."

"What's he like, Arthur Jekyll? He has a terrible reputation."

"He's actually not a bad guy. Intellectually, he's pretty impressive, which surprised me, based on what you hear about these big-time divorce lawyers."

"That is surprising. I don't suppose he's given you any inkling of who his client is."

Clifford grins. "Not a clue. Although obviously there's a bunch of money involved. A few hundred mil is what I'm guessing. My guess is it's some Wall Street type who's made off with a whole bunch of the taxpayers' bailout money. From one or two things Jekyll's said, I gather he's concerned about the client's safety."

Now what is that supposed to mean? Before she can ask, Clifford continues: "I suppose if you screened the Forbes 400 you might come up with a list of likely suspects. Personally, I haven't got the time—or the inclination. Hey, you want to come on October 17 to hear my boy strut his stuff at the Supreme Court? I'll bet I can scrounge a house seat for you. Connie's promised to be there."

"I'm not sure I can. I'll try."

"Do. It should be quite a show, assuming we ever get there."

"Why do you say that?"

"Jekyll's a wheeler-dealer at heart. From one or two things he's said, I can't escape the feeling that Arthur's expecting the other side to make his client an offer the client can't refuse."

Is Clifford playing me? Well, she has no choice to go with it. "Are you saying that he might recommend such an offer to his client?"

"That's the subliminal message I'm getting."

"Have you any idea how much he thinks it would take?"

Clifford shakes his head. *Don't push it,* he tells himself. "Not a clue. My sense is there's a whole ton of money at stake here, maybe hundreds of millions."

"Goodness," she says, and shakes her head, stalling. Annabelle's on the spot. *Should I make an offer now?* She decides no. She needs to regroup, to do some thinking, sleep on it. *Time to take this in another direction.* "What are you working on for yourself?" she asks.

He shakes his head. "Not much. What's the point?"

Annabelle likes that. If Clifford really has given up, he may be an easier sell. She needs to keep this going. "You can't quit completely. You're a talented man."

"Honey, if I'm the only one who thinks my talent is owed something, my talent better file for Chapter 11." He pauses—as if suddenly struck by a fresh idea. "Hey, maybe you'd like to back me. You're loaded."

Is he jerking my chain? She can't tell. Clifford's face is friendly, open. She laughs. "It sounds very exciting. I'm afraid, however, that films just aren't my thing."

He grins. "No apology required. Cheers!" He clinks his snifter against Annabelle's. Out on the lake a bird emits a sudden harsh whoop, causing Annabelle to start. Clifford looks at her, reaches over, and pats her hand. "Honey, you seem kind of tense. This place hasn't worked its magic on you yet. A good night's sleep will cure all." He stretches his arms above his head, as if he's reaching for the moon. "I don't know about you," he says, "but I'm beat. What do you think? Beddie-byes?"

He puts down his brandy and gets up. "See you in the morning. Sleep as late as you like. There's yet another father-daughter breakfast regatta tomorrow, and if I miss that, Madame will have my head. The missus will be manning the skillet. How do you like your eggs? I'll leave her a note."

"Scrambled."

He pecks her cheek and bids her sweet dreams.

When Annabelle comes out the next morning, she finds Connie in the kitchen.

"Clifford and Jenny are gone at least until ten," her hostess reports. "Poached eggs all right? What's that?" She points to the book under Annabelle's arm, an old brown volume.

"I just have to show you this," says Annabelle. "I've done something completely reckless, but I couldn't help myself! But this has to be strictly between us—at least for the moment. You must promise: not a word, not even to Clifford. Promise?"

"Of course."

Annabelle hopes she can't take Connie at her word, and if the past is any guide, she can't. People who have big secrets of their own to hide will usually betray those of other people. She wants Clifford to know, to have an idea of what's at stake here; her art institute project is the sort of thing he'll sympathize with. It's not just about money, which may make him more receptive to an offer. Still, she feels she can't tell him herself for fear of appearing too obvious. Better to use Connie as a conduit—so, over coffee, she takes Connie through the catalog, item by item. She can see that Connie's overwhelmed. "Isn't it unbelievable?" Annabelle says. "It will be like being in the Louvre or the Uffizi. But I had to raise a great deal of money to swing it."

"I imagine you did," Connie says. "Still, it's what you love most, and if you have the money, why not? Nothing on earth will ever give you as much pleasure."

A bit after ten o'clock, there's a halloo from the lake. A small boat with a pink sail is approaching the dock, Jenny at the tiller, Clifford manning the sheet.

"Now," says Annabelle quickly, "not a word, promise?" She tucks the catalog away in her tote bag under her swimming things.

"Cross my heart and hope to die."

"So how'd you do?" Anabelle asks the intrepid sailors.

"Fourth," says Jenny. She makes a grumpy face, and then looks crossly at her father. "Daddy screwed up at the lee mark and we had to go round again." She disappears into her room.

"Ah," he says, "the thrill of victory, the agony of defeat. I screwed up royally—but I console myself that I will be forgiven when the time comes to shop for clothes for prep school. Anyway, this afternoon we have the big softball game. And a shot at redemption. Who's for a swim?"

The next morning, Clifford drives Annabelle to the airport. She's certain he's set this up, but it's just a hunch. She decides not to play hardball and not to get too specific. Just create a framework and see what happens.

"Clifford, I have a *huge* favor to ask you. I almost brought it up last night, but—I don't know—it seemed better to wait."

"How mysterious. Ask away. For you, honeybunch, anything."

"My lawyers have been approached by the attorneys from the other side."

"The other side? You mean Hewitt? That doesn't sound right."

"Not Hewitt, silly. The *other* side! Your man Jekyll's spouse."

"That doesn't sound right."

"All I know is what I've been asked to do."

"And what exactly is that?"

"Apparently, the other side is anxious to avoid a public scandal and see this matter closed before it gets out. They read of your association with Jekyll, and they knew of my connection to Connie, so they naturally assumed that I'd be on good terms with you, and they have asked me to ask you to ask your Mr. Jekyll—"

"Run that by me again. Sounds like Tinker to Evans to Chance. You've been asked to ask me to ask Jekyll...well, what exactly have you been asked to ask me to ask Jekyll?"

"Simply this. What figure will his client accept in return for dropping the case before October, when it is scheduled to be argued before the Supreme Court?"

"Which you think he'll tell me? Why should he?"

"Obviously I can't answer that. I'm only a go-between. I don't know Jekyll. Whoever these people are, they seem to feel this is the best way to explore the possibility of a preemptive settlement. Will you do it? As a favor to me, if for no other reason?"

Clifford smiles at her. With his free hand, he pats her shoulder. "Will do, but I can't guarantee satisfaction."

Now what is that supposed to mean? Annabelle asks herself. All she can do is soldier on. "I only said I'd ask," she says.

When he gets back to Sleeping Bear, Connie and Jenny are newly back from their tennis tournament. The family passes a pleasant evening. All agree that it has been a pleasure to have Annabelle with them, even if for such a short visit.

The next day, Clifford goes out on the lake alone to fish. When he's around the bend from the house, safely out of sight, he gets out one of the disposable cellphones Jekyll now insists he use and calls the lawyer.

"Herself has come and gone," he tells Jekyll.

"And?"

"And, a bit of this and a bit of that. We had a couple of those you-know-what-I-know-or-maybe-you-don't back-and-forth conversations you like so much. The bottom line is this. In a variant on the old 'I have a friend who's pregnant,' gambit, she represented herself as having been asked by, quote unquote, the other side to ask me to ask you if there's a number your client would accept to drop our suit. Of course, she didn't say 'our.'"

"Which doesn't mean she hasn't guessed."

"Of course, she has—at least if you ask me. We were just fencing with each other. Anyway, what do you want me to tell her—if anything?"

"That's for you to answer. You're the client."

"Well, I think Belle's in a bit of a squeeze. When we went to bed last night, my darling wife was up to the brim with pillow talk. You're right about women not being able to keep other women's secrets. It seems Belle has committed to buy a very fancy collection of old masters for that art institute she's building outside Asheville. Big-time stuff: Botticelli and Duccio were a couple of the names mentioned. Connie got the impression that this spending spree has left Belle without much of a safety cushion, which means we could be talking a billion dollars, maybe more."

"That would be just about what her shares are worth. If she could sell them."

"What do you mean?"

"Under securities law, she's both an insider and a controlling person. There are limits as to what percentage of her holdings she's free to sell."

"She's apparently worked out some kind of a loan deal with her investment bankers. Anyway, what do you think I should tell her? I have a sense that $200 million would really be pushing it and I really don't want to break Belle's bank."

"She may have some kind of sharing arrangement with Barrow."

"It's a thought—but I doubt it. She'd have to lay out all the whys and wherefores for the little SOB and I don't see her chancing that. My instinct is to stall. Call her in a week or so, and tell her that your side is thinking it over. See if we can bring the fish to the fly. Besides, after all the work we've done together, I kind of want to see how this story ends."

"We may not prevail, you know."

"Stop talking like that! We're going to win. No doubt about it. Think *Winslow Boy*. Right is going to be done."

"I wish I shared your optimism. Ms. Hewitt is a formidable opponent."

"So were the New England Patriots in 2008."

"You should think about Ms. Villers's disguised offer to negotiate very carefully, Clifford."

"And I will, I promise. But I really don't want to squeeze Belle to the point she jumps out the window, and anything much south of $100 million won't get the job done, not with what movie budgets are like nowadays. Hell, I might even want to make *Doe v. Hewitt* into a picture, all these plots and subplots and he said-she said, which means we ought to let it take its course. Say, Arthur...?"

"Yes?"

"How's Natalie Sloan? Do you ever talk to her?"

"Of course."

"Give her my...best, will you? I hope I'll see her again sometime."

"I'll be happy to. I imagine the next time I'll see *you* will be the Wednesday after Labor Day."

"Roger wilco, over and out. Oh yeah, one other thing..."

"Yes?"

"You know, Arthur, this is turning into a buddy picture, you and me. Butch and Sundance. I always wanted to make one of those. But most of all, thanks for getting me involved in this. I think you've saved my goddamn life!"

CHAPTER TEN

October 13

Out where the sea falls off the edge of the world, night is giving way to the flaming edge of first light; the sky is the color of hellfire. A ship making its way along the horizon looks like a cinder. High up, the contrail of an airplane carves a wide circular track, like a skywriter. Clifford rolls down the window of his rented car, a big, old, finned Cadillac like his father used to drive, and feels the wet Florida night heat blast his face as he scans the shoreline. In the early light, the livid salt sky too hazy for this early hour, he can't seem to see his father, but he knows the old man's out there somewhere. He always is at dawn, picking shells, talking to himself.

Clifford gets out of the car. The glare off the ocean is blinding. A molten orange road sign off to the side flashes PALM BEACH in bright neon highliter green.

"Where are you, Pop?" he calls out. "Pop! Pop! Answer me!"

Then—finally—he sees the old man down by the water, picking his way along the edge, poking at the softly lapping wavelets with a short stick with a crooked end that at first looks like a cane but turns out to be a golf club. Even from this distance he can read the writing stamped on the blade; it's the old Spalding Pro-Flite five iron his father cut down for him when he was six and they used to go out at twilight together and play a few holes on the airbase's nine-hole course.

Clifford stares and stares. He can't seem to move, as if his feet are glued to the sand. From this distance, the general looks more bird than human. A heron or egret: lanky, pale-crested, bright-plumed, hungry-eyed beneath the stiff grizzled tufts of a martial brush cut, head bobbing as he goes: alternately studying the beach for shells, then lifting his gaze to stare out to sea. He stalks the water's edge with deliberate, stiff grace, each foot placed just so as he makes his way, his balance so precise and perfect that his footsteps barely dent the packed sand. Now and then he pauses and bends slightly to poke at a bit of shell or a shiny pebble with the golf club, then unfolds himself erect again and stares briefly out to sea with a remote, impenetrable contemplation.

Clifford clambers over the low concrete ridge that separates the parking lot from the beach. "Pop, Pop, I'm over here!" he calls out. "Hey, Pop, come on, we have to go! It's our tee time!" As he draws closer, he's no longer certain that it's his father he's speaking to. The old man's features are confusing. He looks a bit like Jekyll. The figure continues his perambulation, shows no sign of having heard. Clifford starts across the beach, but the old man's moving faster. Another dozen flailing steps. The old man is practically out of sight, disappearing into the eastern blaze.

"Pop!" he cries. "Pop! Wait!" But the spindly figure doesn't hear. The sun continues to mount its fiery arc. Everything's burning up. "Pop! Pop!" At last, the old man seems to hear his son's desperate cries and turns around.

But now the face isn't either the general's or Jekyll's. Haloed by the orange glow of dawn on auburn hair, so that it seems framed in flames, it's a young woman's face, strong-featured, intent, intelligent, inviting. Familiar in a way—but Clifford can't come up with a name. He turns toward the young woman, wants to call out her name, fights to remember what it is, still can't. She raises a hand in a tentative wave, smiles...

Click! The dream is swallowed up in a blaze of yellow and light, the inward screen goes blank. Someone has turned on the lights in the hotel bedroom.

"Surprise!" a familiar voice calls out as Clifford crawls toward awareness.

"Jesus," he mumbles, pushing himself upright, fighting to get his bearings from the compass points marked where, why, when, who. As he looks toward the source of the voice, he gets it sorted out: Washington, the Jefferson Hotel; to hear *Doe v. Hewitt* argued before the Supreme Court at 10 a.m. today; Connie—standing in the door-way, smiling.

"What the hell are you doing here?" She's supposed to be in Ve-gas at some big BME function. He reaches for his wristwatch on the night table and knocks it to the carpet. "Jesus, what time is it?"

"Don't sound so grumpy! You think I'm not going to stand by my man on his big day? Ronnie fixed up a plane for me, my own personal red-eye, and here I am."

"You should have called."

"Why? Might you have been up to no good? I thought it would be fun to surprise you."

"Sorry, I'm still waking up. Jesus, I hope I can get you a ticket. It's a sell-out. Wait a minute, you're in luck. Belle called last night. She can't make it. You can have her ticket."

"Not to worry. I already have one. Ronnie called Justice De Vito, who's an old friend. There'll be a ticket in my name at the door.

"I'll be back in two shakes," she says. Minutes later, she returns, turns off the light, and slides into bed next to him. She isn't wearing anything. He knows what's going to happen, knows that's not what he wants—not today. "So how was Vegas?" he asks. "Everyone positive?"

"The usual. They think the economy's finally getting better. Come here."

She curves herself to him. He lies there, prone and taut, eyes squeezed tight, hands extended by his sides, as if frozen in ice. He receives her kiss in as good grace as he can manage, hears her take a deep breath and purr, then feels her hand begin to steal up his thigh toward the fly of his pajamas. He rolls away, kicks free of the covers, and sits up on the edge of the bed. "Got to pee," he says. "Be right back."

"Hurry," she murmurs as he gets up and crosses to the living room. He can tell by her voice she's sleepy. Another five minutes and she'll be in the Land of Nod and the threat will have passed.

"You want a glass of water?" he calls from the bathroom. She doesn't respond. He moves stealthily to the bedroom door. She's asleep; her breathing is regular, a series of tiny, light snuffles: she'll be out until he wakes her. He retrieves his watch, goes back into the sitting room, and plops down heavily on the sofa.

His head is spinning. He's having trouble processing the moment. Connie's precipitate appearance has caught him off guard and unprepared. With each succeeding month since he learned of her affair, Clifford has managed to chip away at the old anger, but it has taken work, emotional hard labor, a real effort at suppression of his own frustrated, furious discontent with his own situation. *Doe v. Hewitt* has helped with the latter—but not entirely. The slow fury he now feels building inside him is proof that it may all have been a pretense, that he's never forgiven her, that he still wants to see her punished. But punished in a way—what did Jekyll call it, "a marital neutron bomb"—that would hammer Connie morally, shame her deeply inside, and yet leave all the comfort and ease of Clifford's Grangeford life intact, not to mention the emotional integrity of his family.

Obviously this is impossible. He can have one—or he can have the other. Which is why he'd decided to try to handle the situation strictly at his own end, and up until five minutes ago, when the bedroom light jerked him from a lovely, dreamy sleep, he actually believed he'd made real progress. And now here it is again, the old anger. Which only intensifies his ire.

Another three hours till showtime, he thinks. He's not sure he can stand the wait.

Clifford checked into the Jefferson Hotel last night around seven and by eleven was pretty well in the bag. All the way down on the Acela his mind had swum in a sea of vivid imaginings centered on Natalie Sloan, whom he hasn't seen or spoken to since their dinner in June. He's found himself thinking frequently about her. She's in Washington now, he knows, and he'd hoped to get together with her. The way he'd worked it out in his club-car fantasy was that when he got to Washington, he would call her at the Madison, the hotel where Jekyll says she's staying, find her alone and unengaged, invite her to a quiet dinner somewhere, where he'd behave with more subtlety and have less to drink than the first time, and utterly charm her. Then they'd go back to the hotel for a nightcap—his or hers, it wouldn't matter—and then upstairs. And that's what he'd done on arrival, in the first flush of sober resolution: rung the Madison. But there had been no answer. And no answer the next time he called, nor the next time after that, nor every fifteen minutes after that—until it suddenly got to be 11 p.m., too late to try again, and himself by now definitely feeling little pain, having drained the minibar's limited supply of scotch and moved on to vodka, and so he finally gave up and, too flustered to work out what he might get from room service, made himself a nourishing minibar supper of nuts, chips, and a Twix washed down with the one last miniature of Stoli, and then fell into bed.

He looks down at the sofa. Stacked beside him is a fat pile of magazines and papers. *Doe v. Hewitt* here, *Doe v. Hewitt* there. Here, there, everywhere. Ee-i-ee-i-oh! An entire industry of comment and analysis dangles from *Doe v. Hewitt* like bats in a cave. To read the op-ed pages, to watch the punditical gab-fests on the tube, is to come away with the impression that the very moral and ideological fate of the republic hangs on the outcome of this case. A good deal of the jabber has little to do with the specifics or specific merits of *Doe v. Hewitt*. It's Fox News and its right-wing cadres up in arms against MSNBC and its liberal cohorts: the mudslinging has been great fun to watch.

Jekyll thinks it's a riot; he relishes the statistics: how many *Doe v. Hewitt* Web sites there are, how many Google hits, law school workshops, "bleeding-heart" symposia, *amicus curiae* briefs et cetera, et cetera, et cetera. He especially loves the polls. "Do you realize," he told Clifford the last time they talked, "that as we speak, four hundred ninety-seven of the five hundred thirty-six sitting members of Congress have found themselves obliged to declare a position on *Doe v. Hewitt?*

"In a way it's ridiculous, but perhaps it isn't. The uproar does seem to prove my point: no-fault has turned out to be a loaded and legitimate issue. People are using our case to leverage their own commitments to this or that aspect of marriage broadly defined—especially the issue of same-sex marriage, with which our pleading has no conceivable connection other than its punditical utility. Even if we lose, to have shown that is something."

"Arthur, you're not gonna lose," Clifford told him—for about the millionth time.

That had been three days ago, and Clifford was still highly confident. Jekyll may be a novice at this, may never have argued a case in a court this high, but it's hard to imagine anyone being better prepared. Jekyll has learned from him. He's much quicker on his feet than when they started, sharper in his responses, his timing and pauses much, much better. After the next-to-last rehearsal, Jekyll told him, "You know, Clifford, if something should happen to me, if I should get hit by a bus, say, you'd be perfectly capable of arguing the case. Perhaps I should qualify you to replace me *pro hac vice,* just in case."

"What the hell is that?" Clifford wanted to know.

"It means *for this occasion only.* Supreme Court Rule 6 provides for argument *pro hac vice* and allows cases to be argued on a one-shot basis by attorneys qualified in the courts of a foreign state. I have friends in overseas jurisdictions who owe me big favors. I'm pretty sure I could get you admitted to the bar of Grand Cayman or Andorra with a phone call. How about it?"

"Arthur, please, don't scare me. Nothing's going to happen to you. Just don't walk in front of any buses, okay?"

Well, then was then and now is now. Rehearsals have ended and they're looking at curtain time. No wonder Clifford sensed a certain apprehension in Jekyll when the two men last spoke. Clifford felt it himself—along with a touch of sadness. These past months, Clifford's felt creatively alive again. Everything he loves and knows about film, about teaching, about theater and debate has fed into this effort. He's given a good account of himself; that he knows. Done the research, thought through the lines, deftly developed the characterizations; just like he told Annabelle, he's done all the voices.

He reaches down and picks up a magazine. All three of the country's biggest-selling newsweeklies have put *Doe v. Hewitt* on the cover this week: *Time*'s cover banner asks, "Is Adultery the New Pandemic?", *Newsweek* has "Marriage: A Waning Institution?", and *U.S. News & World Report* displays "Best States for Divorce: The Experts' Ranking." He puts the magazine back down. He's too tired to read. He closes his eyes, leans back, drifts off.

He awakens fifty minutes later on the sofa to a dull light seeping in. Once again, it takes him a few seconds to figure out where he is. He needs air, to clear his mind and settle his nerves.

And, one other thing, he wants to pray. His father always prayed before flying a mission. A prayer before a trial at arms, that's the thing. Pray to the god of battles, as Nelson did on the eve of Trafalgar. Pray for Jekyll, pray for victory, pray for right to be done. Yes, indeed: get the god of battles into the act.

He quietly gets dressed and goes out. Downstairs, he leaves an eight-thirty wake-up call for Connie. Outside, it's what he thinks of as "typical Washington weather": overcast, humid, oppressive. His stomach is starting to act up and his skin feels clammy. He knows the symptoms: stage fright. And if he's got it, what about Jekyll? He hopes the guy has brought along some beta-blockers. He thinks of calling Jekyll to wish him well: Godspeed, "break a leg," *ave atque vale,* "another openin', another show," and so on. But he decides to leave Jekyll alone with his own thoughts and his nerves.

He wanders through the neighborhood. *There has to be a church somewhere around here, goddammit!* Sure enough—up ahead he spies one. It turns out to be Roman Catholic: Saint Mary and Martyrs. He hesitates, looks at his watch, figures, *What the hell, I'm an Episcopalian—we're theological first cousins.* He mounts the steps and goes in.

The interior is dim and empty, the gloom punctuated by candles flickering restively on dark chapel altars. Instinctively, he pauses at the font and twitches a knee, but doesn't cross himself the way he used to while touring Italy. He walks halfway down the aisle, sits himself in a pew, and begins to pray: *Dear Lord, give Jekyll the tongue of angels, string for him the harps of the blessed, and in Thy mercy let right be done. Please, God—let the good guys win just one, okay?*

His concentration is disturbed by a movement further down the aisle. In the dim light, a curtain parts and a figure leaves the confessional booth and walks toward the back of the church. There's no mistaking who it is: *My God,* Clifford thinks. *It's Hewitt.* He recognizes her from Jekyll's photo array: the black, high-collared jacket and white blouse, clerical in appearance and impact; the brilliant white helmet of hair; the fine-boned, strained face, fierce and attenuated, not beautiful but striking: what people call "handsome" in a woman. A face full of the ferocious righteousness and moral certitude that Jekyll admires. The lawyer has vetted Hewitt every which way, hoping to find some leverage, but there's not an atom of scandal or hypocrisy in her past.

He quickly inclines his head and hides his face in praying hands as she passes up the aisle, not that she would have the slightest idea that he's who he is. That he's Clifford Grange, that he's Doe. After she passes, he counts to a hundred just to be safe, and then leaves the church. Outside, the overcast sky has changed color; now dirty yellow streaked with brown, and the humidity feels like one hundred fifty percent. He walks quickly back to the hotel. 8:30 a.m. D-Day in an hour and a half.

In the lobby, he calls upstairs and tells Connie he'll wait for her downstairs. At the newsstand, he buys *The Washington Post, USA Today, The Wall Street Journal, The New York Times, The New York Post* and *The Washington Times*. He settles himself on a couch in a corner and scans the front pages. Most are dominated by various polls. According to Fox News/*Washington Times*, 61.3% of those polled believe "Petitioner Doe" to be female, 36.4% believe Doe to be male, 2.1% are undecided. ABC/*USA Today* reports the following views concerning fault versus no-fault divorce: among males aged eighteen to fifty-five, the key demographic, 24.2% are in favor of fault divorce, 49.3% prefer no-fault, the balance is undecided; among women in the same age brackets, 47.2% favor fault, 37.4% favor no-fault, with the remainder holding no opinion; the Gallup poll shows that 22.2% of males polled favor criminalization of adultery, versus 47.8% of females. The right-wing *Washington Times* displays the headline "High Court to Hear Gender Equivalent of Battle of Gettysburg." *The New York Post* has polled people concerning the nature of the misconduct in question.

Today's *Washington Post*'s lead editorial compares no-fault to the increasing practice of condemning church property for more lucrative commercial use and praises *Doe* for opening up this judicial avenue. As for *The New York Times*, its op-ed page, wholly devoted to today's argument, is all over the place. Their lead conservative columnist equates no-fault divorce to declining elementary school test scores and blames everything on overpermissiveness. The liberal counterpart, a Harvard professor, female, declares: "Marriage is not only overrated in our society, but also overworked as a panacea..." A Harvard professor, male, considers no-fault as a further, blasphemous incitement to Islamic fundamentalism. Finally, a famous divorce lawyer cites no-fault as evidence of "a growing desensitization with respect to infidelity." On the opposite page, the lead editorial states that "it would appear that *Doe* represents a big step on the path to America becoming a post-marital society."

From New York the *Page Six* column reports: "Today's hot ticket among the bold-face types is one for the ages: an oral argument in Washington before the Supreme Court. Namely, *Doe v. Hewitt*, the by-now legendary lawsuit that has the cognoscenti and chatterati from Santa Monica to East Hampton guessing at who the fabulously wealthy principals are. The Court has seen a demand of tickets unprecedented since *Roe v. Wade* was argued back in 1973. Expected to attend are Oprah Winfrey, Barbara Walters, Constance Grange..." *The New York Daily News* headlines a column by its proprietor that seems to touch every conceivable ideological base.

He thinks about ordering coffee and a roll, but doubts he could get a crumb down. His mind turns to Jekyll, over at the Cosmos Club, which has a reciprocal arrangement with the Diogenes. The lawyer will have risen early out of a combination of habit and nerves. He will have finished brushing and combing; he'll be knotting the tie he will have finally chosen from the five he's probably brought down, dismissing this one as "too New York," that one as "too flashy." By ten, he'll be at the Supreme Court for the traditional briefing by the Clerk of the Court on Court procedure and protocol (always "Justice so-and-so," never "Judge"). He hopes Jekyll picks a suitable tie. Many attorneys appear before the Court in morning-coat and striped trousers, but jackals don't wear morning clothes and so Jekyll will be wearing dark gray flannel, newly tailored for the occasion, and a plain white shirt.

At nine-twenty a bellperson comes over. "Your car is here, Mr. Grange." Just at that moment, Connie comes out of the elevator. She looks wonderful: fresh and splendidly turned out in a dark Carolina Herrera suit. Always perfect timing, always on cue, always hits her marks. Amazing. Clifford feels the atmosphere in the lobby alter perceptibly as people turn away from their conversations and look up from their papers and laptop screens to stare at the star in their midst.

"All set?" she asks brightly, thrusting her arm through his in what he feels is an unwelcome assertion of ownership.

It's a quarter to ten when the limousine drops Connie and Clifford off. Clifford's excitement has intensified with each passing stoplight. He's sliding back into that shell of intense concentration and apprehension he remembers from openings, festival screenings, and Film Forum premieres. Connie's busy chatter about Las Vegas goes virtually unheard. She doesn't seem to notice that her husband's focus is entirely elsewhere. Or perhaps she does—he breaks into his own thoughts to wonder—perhaps this, too, is like the old days when she used to chat him up to cheer him up until the very moment when the lights went down. The instant he asks himself the question, he knows the answer: this isn't like the old days; the old days are gone.

He's never been to the "Marble Palace," as the Court building is often called. A throng streams across the broad plaza, up the steps, and between the august columns, passing beneath a pediment that might have been transported from the Acropolis. In front of the plaza, watched by a half-dozen bored District cops, a desultory line of pickets shuffles back and forth, waving placards marked SAY NO TO DOE!

But it's the gauntlet of reporters and photographers that runs from the bottom of the broad steps to the top that signifies that this is a day out of the ordinary. When they spot Connie, they go berserk. "Over here! Hey, Constance. Hey, give us a smile! Who you rooting for?" As Connie stops to talk to a *Vanity Fair* writer she knows, Clifford spots Natalie Sloan flanked by a middle-aged couple. The three are intently studying some kind of legal-looking document. As Clifford starts to wave to her—a tiny, conspiratorial wiggle of the fingers of his right hand—she looks up and sees him. She's turned out very severely: a gray flannel suit over blouse and pearls, her auburn hair pulled back in a tight bun. She returns his wave with a smile and a tentative waggle.

In the foyer, a VIP desk has been set up. The ushers are struggling to keep order, no easy task with a throng consisting mainly of people whose eminence, in their own eyes, or at least those of their publicists, is beyond question and their right to precedence therefore absolute. The young man assigned to show them to their seats leads Connie and Clifford across the Great Hall and through airline-type electronic security gates set up to detect weapons and recording devices. In the doorway, Clifford pauses momentarily to take it all in.

The sight is breath-stopping. Clifford's not easily impressed, but nothing he has read or heard, neither his books and tapes, nor the photographs Jekyll's shown him, nor his imagination, has prepared him for the effect this place has on him. The courtroom's classically august architecture, so perfectly bespeaking the monumental moral gravity of the business that Americans come here to transact, or at least tell themselves that they do, seems to play on the moment, to work its cool marble magic on his nervous energy, his passion, his anticipation. It's a knockout; it has nothing to do with Hollywood law, Wall Street law, O.J. Simpson law, *Law & Order* law. This isn't Dominick Dunne or Perry Mason country. Here—the very marble seems to declare—is done law of a different, incomparably loftier order of philosophical magnitude and judicial dignity. Here law is an instrumentality of civic virtue, of truth, of first causes and ultimate purposes. Under-the-table deals don't get cut in this chamber. In this chamber, the fix isn't in. This place is about absolutes, about Right against Wrong.

The great room is some ninety feet square and forty-odd feet high, with walls and columns of European and African marble. The raised stage on which the justices sit is flanked by a pair of tall bronze screens. These had formerly shielded an area reserved for VIPs—presumably to prevent the proceedings from being affected or disrupted by the sight of the great and famous—but the recently arrived Chief Justice has had them moved away in the interests of "transparency."

The nine empty Justices' chairs face the room, seeming to be sizing up the gathering audience. Clifford mentally fills them with the people on the wall of Jekyll's "war room," from his left to his right:

Chen, Mornington-Kaplan, Hartman, Newbegin, Chief Justice Smiley, Cleveland, Dugdale, De Vito, Ramirez.

He stands up to get a better look around the room. There are three distinct sections to which spectators are led or herded, as the case may be: the main courtroom where he and Connie are sitting; a sort of loggia off to his right, three or four rows deep, with a restricted view of the courtroom and a raking sightline of the bench; the old VIP section, now allocated to less exalted although still ticket-worthy members of the Washington-New York-Hollywood *nomenklatura*. A railed-off passage at the rear of the courtroom remains open to the public: a narrow channel through which is fed a steadily moving stream of tourists who want to be able to say they've been there, seen that.

This morning, all seats are rapidly filling up early. The side rows mostly with somber, self-important-looking people in suits. There's a lot of lawyer and lobby interest in this case: three separate chapters of the American Bar Association have filed *amicus* briefs in *Doe v. Hewitt*, as have some fifty other organizations and individuals, so many that the Court has finally decided to hear none this morning, but to consider them separately in conference. It's like being in church before a wedding or funeral. People are standing and talking while they wait for the action to begin; others are unabashedly rubbernecking the arriving celebrities, and others are just sitting quietly. He turns toward the dais and looks for Jekyll. The counsel tables are placed directly facing the bench, to either side of the slant-topped podium— with its red and white warning lights. At the left-hand table, he can just make out the back of Jekyll's head. At the right-hand table, the brilliant pale mane of Isobel Hewitt gleams like alabaster.

Four minutes to go. Celebrities continue to fill the main section, their imminence signaled by cries and bursts of white light from the vestibule. Toni Morrison arrives with Maya Angelou. He recognizes Cameron Diaz, angry-faced Don Imus, then Geraldo. A still further increase in the buzz level as John Travolta enters the courtroom; the actor is reported by *Entertainment Tonight* to be in negotiations for the screen rights to the case. *Negotiating with whom for what?* Clifford has wondered. *These are* my *fucking rights!*

The governor and the speaker of the assembly of the Granges' home state pass down the aisle, followed—a minute later—by a looming hawk of a man in clerical robes with a peep of scarlet at the throat: Cardinal Santiago, trailed by two younger priests. He identifies the Kissingers, the Greenspans, Barbara Walters, and a couple of Manhattan restaurant impresarios he used to know. Two minutes to go now. The chairman of the Federal Reserve goes by, then a couple Clifford thinks may be Ben Bradlee and Sally Quinn, with Liz Smith and Susan Sarandon and Julia Roberts close behind; then Michelle Pfeiffer, followed by two men in early middle-age, talking earnestly as they pass down the aisle: "John Grisham and Scott Turow," he hears a man in the row behind tell his companion, and barely have the writers taken their seats when there's a flash of white linen and Tom Wolfe materializes. Suddenly a terrific salvo of light and noise breaks out in the vestibule: Oprah's arrived. She's with Bill Cosby, and they're followed by Steven Spielberg and his wife, and Tom Cruise with his.

The minute hand on the clock high above the bench moves almost straight up on ten o'clock, the distant clamor from the vestibule rises to a sharper spike than any so far. There's movement at the front of the courtroom. All eyes, as one, turn in that direction. Two men in cutaways have appeared from a side door, followed by several aides. These, Clifford knows from his reading, are the Marshal of the Court, the Chief Clerk, and their assistants. They take their places at two outward-facing tables beneath the bench and look upon the packed courtroom with lofty, neutral faces. The buzz dies away.

The minute hand touches the hour. The wide curtain behind the bench parts, and Chief Justice Smiley appears, a tall, strong-striding woman with a wide, friendly face. She reminds Clifford of a lady golf pro. On her right arm is an old man, frail, and obviously ill; with her left hand, the Chief Justice holds up the oxygen line that runs from her colleague's nostrils to a wheeled oxygen cylinder pushed by a clerk: this would be Justice Newbegin.

On Smiley's other side, jovial, beaming, built to Easter Island scale, is Justice Herman Cleveland. Two more ranks of three Justices follow, then all nine fan out and take their seats, followed, like matadors, by their individual *cuadrillas* of clerks and legal assistants, on hand to fetch law books and refill water jugs as needed. The assistant marshal responsible for operating the timing system, as rigid and dictatorial as a chess match's, finds his place. The Chief raps her gavel, the functionaries and all those in the courtroom rise as one person, and the Marshal intones the ceremonial welcome.

"The Honorable, the Chief Justice and the Associate Justices of the Supreme Court of the United States. Oyez! Oyez! Oyez! All persons having business before the Honorable, the Supreme Court of the United States, are admonished to draw near and give their attention, for the Court is now sitting. God save the United States and this Honorable Court!"

Clifford's throat catches. Once a military brat, always a military brat. This is the way he always felt watching his father salute the flag at reveille and taps, the way he was brought up to feel about this country and what it's about. Then he feels the old, familiar theater thrill: the lights dimming, the actors in the wings avoiding each others' eyes as they run through their initial cues and prepare to take their places, the curtain about to rise. The Chief Justice runs quickly and efficiently through some routine administrative business, looks out over her reading glasses at the packed courtroom, turns her attention to the counsel tables, and finally fixes her gaze upon Jekyll. In a pleasant, everyday tone, she says, "Case number 97-231, in the matter of Doe versus Hewitt. Mr. Jekyll, you may begin when you are ready."

CHAPTER ELEVEN

When Jekyll rises and goes to the lectern, Clifford crosses his fingers so tightly they turn white and he utters a devout silent prayer: *May God indeed save the Honorable Court—and all who come before it.*

"Madam Chief Justice, and may it please this Honorable Court," Jekyll says, and then his voice breaks. *Opening night jitters,* Clifford thinks. *Come on now. Get in the moment.* Jekyll takes a sip of water and begins again. This time his voice is clear and strong.

"Madam Chief Justice, and may it please this Honorable Court, our argument is not about the pros and cons of divorce. We are not asking nor inviting this Honorable Court to participate in a sociology colloquium. What we will argue today centers on our perception of the First Amendment and the Fifth Amendment. At issue, as we see it, is the nature and character of marriage under God, and the constitutional power of legislatures and governments to interfere with that nature and that character. Our pleading is also about property. Personal, private property and the protection thereof from seizure.

The property to which I refer is nontangible. It is spiritual, but we will argue that we possess a constitutionally protected property in our faith just as we have intellectual property in our inspiration—which may also be God-given. And it is, above all, about moral equity.

"In our society, the forces for moral equity fall into two categories: external and internal. The internal and personal forces—shame, responsibility—can be powerful but are also susceptible to our appetites and to other interests of self. Only law, the last resort of a society's moral character, remains beyond the reach of appetite. This case asks the question: will the law endorse the view that personal appetite is entitled to legal—and thus, by implication, moral—precedence over values that have been agreed upon and commonly held in our society since the time of Moses? We say it should not.

"This case involves so many instances of infringement of Petitioner's constitutional rights that I hardly know where to begin. In altering its divorce statute from fault to no-fault, the state has reneged on a bargain with its citizens that goes back to the First Amendment, which is that the federal and state power will not infringe on an individual's freedom of worship."

Clifford sees Justice De Vito's jaw tighten, and words start to form, but Jekyll also notes the Justice's expression and beats the voluble De Vito to the punch: "By 'worship,' I think we'll agree, is meant the practice of organized religion on a sacramental basis inoffensive to society at large—we are not talking about *Reynolds* here, or *Employment Office vs. Smith*, but about *The Book of Common Prayer*. In Petitioner's faith, in the Episcopal Church, that is, marriage is a sacrament..."

"According to T.S. Eliot, a—quote—dignified and commodious sacrament," De Vito interrupts. He's a storehouse of quotation, Clifford and Jekyll have figured out, and he likes to show off the goods on his shelves.

"Certainly to those who receive it, Mr. Justice De Vito," says Jekyll, voice level, betraying no more than a faint note of amusement. "An exchange of vows, made freely and without coercion by two consenting individuals, vows that included, in this instance, a pledge of mutual fidelity. By moving to no-fault, the state has negated the force of that pledge and impinged after the fact on a private religious and moral understanding between two persons that is legally endorsed by the state."

Clifford listens intently with his director's ear. *Take it slower, measure your phrasing. Your voice goes off when you try for too much—stay with the pitch, don't push it. It'll come, it'll come.*

"Excuse me, Mr. Jekyll." Justice De Vito again. "Do I detect that you're moving this in the direction of breach of contract under guise of religious freedom? Presenting us with contract law in sacramental clothing? Inviting us to confuse a judge's robe with a priest's cassock? As you know, the Court has time and again disallowed the application of the First Amendment to matters of contract, implied or otherwise."

And they're off. For the next twenty minutes, Jekyll spars with various Justices, landing a few, taking a few on the chops.

Many of the questions asked by various Justices strike him as incredibly, indescribably trivial while Jekyll seems possessed of a convincing eloquence that their rehearsals together barely hinted at. Clifford begins to wonder if Jekyll really needed him, whether getting him involved was merely the lawyer's way of humoring a wavering client. Whether that's so no longer matters. Clifford's no lawyer, but it sounds to him as if Jekyll, for all his inexperience, is giving as good as he's getting and may even be ahead on points. As when Jekyll answers a question of Justice Mornington-Kaplan's by quoting an earlier Supreme Court opinion that "religious beliefs worthy of constitutional respect are the product of free and voluntary choice, in this instance mutual," and glosses the citation by adding, "By its silence on the matter, the state accords legal standing to a marriage performed in church by a priest just as it accords such status to a marriage performed by one of its own judges, and accepts the terms and understandings on which all such marriages are entered into, even if these may have taken place out of state. Unlike France, for instance, we do not require that a marriage be formally contracted before both civil and religious authorities to enjoy full legal standing." The look on the Justice's face seems to appreciate that Jekyll has scored a point off her.

This makes Clifford feel better. Mornington-Kaplan has been a tough study for him, the Justice who, of the nine, Clifford finds least congenial, a dry, humorless presence next to whom he would hate to find himself seated at dinner.

His tapes and transcripts have prepared Clifford for the less than Olympian tone of the give and take, the informality of expression. Until then, he had anticipated a level of discourse to match the Court's architectural majesty: grave, chiseled, marmoreal. But when he actually listened to recorded argument, to the plain talk in which Sarah Weddington argued *Roe v. Wade*, in which Theodore Olson argued *Bush v. Gore*, their voices and everyday locutions, he heard a *vox populi* clamor, people in robes arguing the way people in shirtsleeves did: a mixture of pontification, irony, resentment, certitude, and near-profanity.

Now Justice Hartman, chimes in; he has a high, chirpy voice, very precise: "Is it your contention, Mr. Jekyll, that legislation must follow liturgy when it comes to making family law?"

"With respect, Mr. Justice Hartman, obviously not," Jekyll replies, with a patient smile and tone of voice to match. He seems steadier, more confident with every syllable. "Nevertheless, religious observance, the free expression of faith, is as much defined by the avoidance of sin as by a striving for grace. Sin has—must have—its cost in this life as well as in the next. Criminality is sin as defined by law. We speak all too easily of accountability in our society—probably because we have abandoned any intention of enforcing it. That may be called a public choice, but the choice is not the government's to make, or the lawmakers' to decree, but for the conscience of the electorate, collectively and individually, in the law."

Hartman looks as if he's just found a $100 bill on the pavement. "Collectively, Mr. Jekyll? But isn't government the expression of the collective wishes of a majority?"

"With respect, Mr. Justice Hartman, we hold that the government and the law aren't quite the same. For one, we have seen the government, the Bush administration comes to mind, repeatedly test the law, as this Court itself ruled with respect to due process for the Guantánamo prisoners. The law may establish the ground rules for good government, but government isn't always good, and when that happens, we go to law to protect ourselves from governments of our own making. We're arguing that the law is the final resort for those socially pandemic problems and crimes that society's private collectives—its churches, fraternal organizations, guilds, and the other entities at which de Tocqueville marveled when he came to analyze this nation's unique qualities—find insoluble."

Good on you, Arthur, Clifford thinks: *in a pinch, always cite de Tocqueville*—advice remembered from his own college debating days and passed along to Jekyll during their rehearsals.

It doesn't take long for Justice Mornington-Kaplan to gallop back into the fray on her high horse. "Are you asserting that adultery is a crime, Mr. Jekyll?"

Jekyll turns her aside deftly: "The state—certain states—say it is. Personally, I'm not sure what jurisprudential status to accord adultery, Madam Justice. Neither are the American people. According to one recent survey, thirty-five percent of those polled consider adultery a crime. According to another, twenty-two percent think adultery does a marriage some good. Petitioner is happily spared the responsibility for arguing that question and this Court from adjudicating it. I will merely point out, however, that while, in moving to no-fault, the state has in effect eliminated adultery as a grounds for divorce, adultery remains on the state's statute books as a crime—a second-degree misdemeanor, to be accurate. As it does on the statute books of twenty-six other states, nearly all of which have also converted to no-fault."

Mornington-Kaplan starts in with a rejoinder, but De Vito interrupts, obviously in the coils of a joke too good to waste: "If I may paraphrase my learned colleague's question, Mr. Jekyll, is the thrust of Petitioner's First Amendment pleading to stand Shakespeare's famous sonnet on its head and argue that it is *not* the state's business from the marriage of *untrue* minds to remove impediments?"

An uneasy titter ripples through the courtroom. On the bench, a couple of the Justices allow themselves an uneasy smirk. Clifford feels a twinge of trouper's sympathy for the justice. De Vito's joke is clearly lost on a good half of those present, and it wasn't all that bad: carefully thought out and husbanded for just the right moment. It surely would have cracked the general up.

"He ought to be working Vegas," Connie whispers to Clifford.

"He probably thinks so, too. It certainly pays better."

"How do you think your man's doing?"

"So far, so good."

And so it goes. The Justices conform almost to the profiles Clifford and Jekyll have mapped out. About halfway through his allotted time, Jekyll winds up his First Amendment argument: "In entering into a sacramental marriage, Petitioner engaged in a form of worship. That is what churchly marriage is about, or any form of religious observance that is consistent with the larger beliefs of society—I'm not speaking of sacramental peyote smoking here, or Mormon polygamy, or the right to celebrate mass in the Alamo, may it please the Court. Today, as we are all well aware, there is a segment of public opinion that holds that religion—like marriage, indeed—is basically a lifestyle option, and no more than that. But to many of us, it is more.

"Does it lie with the constitutional prerogatives of the state to freely abridge the terms of marriage in the sight of God, a relation whose terms are set forth in Bible, Prayer Book, Torah, Koran, or what have you, as long as the terms of that understanding are articles of individual religious conviction that aren't harmful to society in general, or run totally against its grain? By going to no-fault, the state has abrogated a key sacramental expression of Petitioner's faith."

And then Jekyll moves smoothly into the second part of his pleading, the property/money angle. But hardly has he begun when Justice Cleveland breaks in: "I've read your Fifth Amendment argument with great interest, Mr. Jekyll." The Justice has a rich, courtly, musical voice, a voice Clifford has thought since first hearing it on tape should be singing Verdi rather than accompanying cheek pecks and hand kisses. This is a voice capable of higher things than charity banquets and commencement addresses.

"The notion is not mine, Justice Cleveland, but James Madison's. "As a man may be said to have a right to his property,' Madison observed, 'he may equally be said to have a property in his rights.'"

"I respect what Madison said, Mr. Jekyll, but aren't we talking about apples and oranges here? Do you assert, sir, that what you have characterized before this Court today as a, quote, moral claim, unquote, is constitutionally the same as a piece of land? That honor and real estate amount to the same thing under the Fifth Amendment?"

"With respect, Mr. Justice, if we accept the concept of 'intellectual property,' why not 'moral property'? If I may quote my learned brother-in-the-law Richard A. Epstein, James Parker Hall Distinguished Service Professor of Law at the University of Chicago, 'Why not seek the most general moral principle behind the Fifth Amendment? As the guardian of other rights, private property protects both free speech and religious association from government regulation and retaliation.'"

Like a kid in class, Justice Chen has been twitching his hand. Now he breaks in. "As it isn't specified in briefs, Mr. Jekyll," he asks, "perhaps you'd care to enlighten us as to the extent of Petitioner's pecuniary claim?"

In other words, Clifford thinks, *how much are we talking about here?*

Chen's question has lowered the tone of the proceedings; Clifford can feel it around him in the courtroom, see it in the Justices' faces. It shouldn't matter whether the stakes are a billion or a buck.

"With respect, Mr. Justice Chen," Jekyll answers in his best professorial manner, "let us simply say that a good deal of money is involved. As briefs make clear, both Attorney General Hewitt and I feel that to go into further detail would confuse the issue, since the principle we're arguing would apply as equally to ten cents as to ten million dollars. Suffice it to say, may it please the Court, we are speaking of what is called in the business press 'serious money.'"

He looks over at Isobel Hewitt. She nods her agreement.

"In our system, we speak freely of—and enforce aggressively— the monetary worth of 'intellectual property,'" Jekyll continues, very grave and solemn now, obviously very much at home on this particular battlefield, "of copyrights, ideas, original expression, so why should we not speak with equal vigor of 'moral property'? Petitioner has been damaged to the same extent as if Petitioner's spouse was on the brink of making over, say, an undivided interest of several million dollars in real property that the state has suddenly moved to confiscate without compensation through a more or less surreptitious amendment of its divorce code."

"But what you're concerned with is the money effect of the state's conversion to no-fault vis-à-vis Petitioner's bargaining position in a fault divorce settlement. Is that correct?" This from Justice Chen.

Justice Dugdale, who has been silent so far, breaks in. "Now wait a minute!" she exclaims. "'Bargaining position'? 'Bargaining position'? Deriving from what? Petitioner's right to assert fault under the old law?"

Jekyll nods. "Exactly, Madam Justice."

"In other words," Dugdale continues, in a rising tone of indignation, "the change in the law deprived Petitioner of the right to go into open court with evidence of misconduct. Which means, reading between the lines, deprived Petitioner of the opportunity to force the wayward spouse to choose between paying Petitioner off or facing down the stigma of being publicly held up as an adulterer or adulteress under the old fault law. Which means that this Court is being asked to endorse blackmail as a Fifth Amendment right! Isn't that what you're asserting?"

"With respect, Madam Justice Dugdale," Jekyll says, "I don't see how the word blackmail can be applied to any course of action sanctioned under law."

"But what about courses of action no longer sanctioned? No longer sanctioned because no longer appropriate?"

Jekyll holds his ground. "The essence of freedom in this country is the right to proceed under law, if the law permits. The exercise of what were, at the time in question, legal rights by Petitioner protected by the Fifth Amendment cannot be called extortionate. Blackmail—extortion by threat of disclosure—is a surreptitious affair, and is properly illegal. The statutory right to go into open court to state one's grievances, assert one's rights, and to claim the remedies available under law cannot possibly constitute blackmail.

"Actually," he continues, "the 'takings' clause and what we call 'taking the Fifth' are not all that far apart. The protection against self-incrimination—the so-called right to, quote, take the Fifth, unquote—plainly envisions an intangible property right—of conscience, let us say—that is to be as secure from state invasion or seizure—that is to say, forcible public disclosure no matter the cost—as an individual's home and hearth."

Dugdale scowls, but says nothing. The white light on the podium comes on. Five minutes left on Jekyll's game clock. He pauses and looks expectantly to the bench. The Chief Justice looks over at Justice Ramirez, who hasn't yet been heard from. Ramirez seems lost in space, light years away, in another galaxy. The Chief redirects her attention to Jekyll.

"Mr. Jekyll," she says, "there is a bit less then five minutes left in your half hour. If you wish, you may hold these over for rebuttal."

"With respect, Madam Chief Justice, and may it please the Court, I would. At this juncture, therefore, I would wish only to add this thought for the consideration of this Honorable Court: we must not disregard the generally pernicious effect that no-fault divorce law has had on American family life, most notably on women and children. The correlations between divorce rates and family financial and psychological pressures seem unarguable. To the extent that we come before this Court seeking redress for grievances applicable in a general fashion, to persons other than Petitioner, it is with this point uppermost in mind. This concludes our argument for the moment. Thank you."

He sits down. The courtroom buzzes. *You done good, Arthur,* Clifford thinks.

"Goodness," says Connie, "that was really something. I'm totally surprised!"

"I'm not," Clifford says—not altogether truthfully. "I told you that he's not the monster the media paints him. But since you ask: I thought he did very well."

"So did I, amazingly."

"Why amazingly?" Clifford grins at his wife. "He had great coaching." She smiles.

The halftime interval is just long enough for water glasses to be changed at the lectern and the clocks to be reset. Then the Chief Justice looks down at Isobel Hewitt and says, "Attorney General Hewitt, when you are ready."

Hewitt rises and takes her place at the podium. She looks trim, fine and militant in her high-collared, dark, tailored suit. Clifford starts to feel uneasy. Hewitt exudes might and right. When Jekyll finished, it seemed a walkover. Now...

"Chief Justice Smiley, Honorable Justices, may it please the Court," she begins. Her speaking voice is attractive: low and clear, it carries well. "As Justice Holmes memorably observed in his famous dissent in *Northern Securities Company v. United States*, 'Great cases, like hard cases, make bad law.' This case perfectly fits the Justice's definition of a, quote, great case, unquote. 'Great cases are often called great,' said Holmes, 'not by reason of their real importance in shaping the law of the future, but because of some accident of immediate overwhelming interest which appeals to the feelings and distorts the judgment.' I would submit that such is the case with the present action. Indeed, may it please the Court, this case is hung like a Christmas tree with what Justice Holmes characterized as 'accidents of immediate overwhelming interest.' I am speaking of issues and considerations, diversions and sideshows—we are all aware of them, some have even been presented to this Court this morning—which like glittering ornaments distract from the main principles at issue here.

"It is our contention that, of these, two considerations outweigh all the others. First, the constitutional necessity for the elected political power, at any level you may choose, federal, state, or local, to be free to make laws that are in tune with the temper of the times and consistent with the standards and wishes of the majority of its citizens, and that do not unreasonably impinge on the rights and property of any individual citizen. Laws that will—that must—change—be adjusted—to reflect the changing demands of civil society over time. The state—by which I mean elected legislative bodies with powers as limited as local school boards or as far-reaching as Congress—is the only effective instrumentality for those adjustments. The alternative is anarchy. When, for example, we in our state changed our minimum drinking age from eighteen to twenty-one, in an effort to reduce our automobile fatality rate, there were taverns and others having an economic interest that was being sacrificed to the public good, as our legislature saw it, or to social policy, as Mr. Jekyll might put it, and yet no lawsuits were brought by the notionally injured parties. The cardinal principle of federalism is that if the states are to govern, then they must be allowed to do so. In seeking to stuff his First Amendment scarecrow with Constitutional straw, Mr. Jekyll's brief is dismissive of the Court's finding in *Employment Office v. Smith*, but we would remind this honorable Court of its finding that the right of free exercise protects persons only from laws directed *against* their particular religion, not from neutral laws of general applicability that happen to burden their religious practice."

She lets that thought hang in the air for a moment, then goes on: "The second principle that we assert is that marriage and personal sexual conduct are private affairs and are no one's business except the parties involved. Repeatedly in recent years, this Court has held, in decisions arising from cases as diverse as *Roe v. Wade*, *Webster v. Reproductive Health Services,* and *Griswold*, as well as in the Chief

Justice's predecessor's role with respect to the findings relating to the conduct of the Office of Independent Counsel, that privacy is among the most sacred personal rights available to Americans, and that if there is one sphere of private life to which this sacred right applies unquestionably, it is marriage and sexual practices within marriage. Repeatedly, most recently in *Zablocki v. Redhail*, this Court has indicated its animus to legislated infringement of the right to marry, a position that we infer to apply as well to the obverse of the coin, namely, the right to divorce in a timely and equitable manner as painlessly and fairly as the efforts of representative government can make it. To overturn our move to no-fault would repudiate the Court's position that in marital relations, all marital relations, privacy is of the essence."

"Which you define how, Attorney General Hewitt?" interrupts Justice De Vito.

"Define what, Justice De Vito?"

"Marital relations, quote unquote, Mrs. Hewitt. What exactly do you mean by 'marital relations?' Isn't divorce a marital relation, quote unquote?"

"We define—that is, the state understands—the term to include every aspect of the marital condition, from the civil or religious ceremony up to and through the decision of the parties involved—the decision of one or of both parties, let me make that clear—to terminate the marriage."

"From courtship to courtroom, eh?" interjects Justice De Vito.

Hewitt smiles thinly. "It is common to speak of the Nanny State, Mr. Justice De Vito. But what of the Mother-in-Law State, the parent who never leaves, who moves in with the newly married couple and remains there until driven out by death or divorce or threat of physical or financial violence? You wouldn't call such an in-law a good parent. Good parents know when to let their children go, and it is our state's intention to *be* a good parent. Our decision to convert our divorce code to no-fault reflects our desire to take ourselves out of the situation completely. The state's role in these painful situations, if any, is to mediate, not to facilitate one party's ability to inflict public disgrace or discomfort upon the other."

Now Justice Mornington-Kaplan pounces.

"In other words, Attorney General Hewitt, you're saying that what one does with one's body, as far as the state is concerned, is one's own business, period? That what holds for abortion also applies to adultery, regardless of the consequences to others? Regardless of the moral strictures involved? You mentioned *Roe* and *Webster*, so I assume that is your position?"

Now the questions come staccato and rapid, like a burst of machine-gun fire intended to blow away everything in the field of fire. Mornington-Kaplan's face wears an expression of extreme distaste for Hewitt. *The sister-in-law syndrome*, Clifford thinks: the instantaneous, almost wholly incomprehensible and puzzling dislike one woman will conceive for another with hardly as much as a word or a look ever having passed between them.

For the next minute or so, the two women fence, neither scoring a palpable hit. Then Mornington-Kaplan challenges Hewitt on the basis of "polls, conducted by recognized experts and cited by Petitioner in briefs, that show that where no-fault has been adopted, the effect has been almost wholly destabilizing."

Now it's Hewitt's turn to show her tiger's teeth. "With respect, Justice Mornington-Kaplan, statistics are available to prove almost any side of almost any issue. There's an equally vociferous body of informed opinion out there that holds that fault divorce locks people into loveless, often violent situations that are harmful to all concerned, especially children, and that no-fault actually works to relieve these stresses. No referendum to recall a no-fault initiative has passed, though several have been attempted; we need only look at Michigan, most recently. The best the state can do is try to find the most neutral posture it can. We are not social engineers. What we have to be concerned with here are issues of law and freedom of choice."

"That may be," says Mornington-Kaplan testily, "but how can you profess to do that except on the basis of reliable scientific evidence and sampling?"

"As someone engaged in politics, Justice Mornington-Kaplan, I have to say I have grave reservations as to the reliability of that evidence, or any evidence based on what people tell pollsters with respect to social behavior. The difference between how people behave in their own lives, and the lives that they describe themselves as living to pollsters, is mind-boggling. For example, take the adultery statistics already cited by counsel for Petitioner. Add to those the following: *Newsweek* not long ago reported that the percentage of Americans who strongly disapprove of adultery has risen almost as dramatically as the percentage of Americans who admit to having committed adultery. The percentages, moreover, are roughly equal."

This produces a nervous ripple in the courtroom, causing the Marshal to call for order, and bringing a look of absolute hatred to Mornington-Kaplan's narrow face.

Now another voice, almost imperceptibly accented, cuts in: Justice Ramirez.

"When you refer to 'freedom of choice,' Mrs. Hewitt, are you implying that the state simply should get out of the way on these issues, the way it has in economic affairs? Is it the policy of your state—your administration—to work toward the moral equivalent of a free market?"

"We are trying not to interfere, Justice Ramirez. That is all. There is no market ideology at work here. Nor any intent of moral appropriation."

"But is that right?" the question bursts from Justice Chen. "You could set benefit-effective, fault-related formulas with respect to the division of marital property. Make it more or less automatic. Convicted of armed robbery, you get X years in jail. Convicted of adultery, say, or mental cruelty, it costs you Y percent of your assets and income. A kind of moral actuarial table, you might say."

"We could try to do that, Justice Chen," Hewitt says, with a patient smile, "but I can assure you that the divorce bar in our state would see to it that we didn't." With this, she smiles at Jekyll. Jekyll smiles back. It's as if they're flirting.

"I think we can take it as a given that it was never the state's intention to countenance blackmail, right, Mrs. Hewitt?" This from Chief Justice Smiley.

"That's correct, Madam Chief Justice. May it please the Court, but I assume the Justices are at least vaguely familiar with the business not long ago involving the news program *60 Minutes* and the tobacco companies? In that instance, an effort was made to discredit the testimony of a former tobacco company employee, a so-called 'whistleblower,' by digging up dirt on the man's private life. To do this, it was intended to bring forth allegations that were part of the record in a divorce proceeding in the state of Kentucky. Those allegations were not allowed to be made public, because they were sealed in the court record, precisely because Kentucky is a no-fault state. Here, clearly, no-fault was on the side of the angels."

Now Justice Dugdale, nostrils flared like an angry horse, returns to the hunt. "I want to go back to an earlier point, Mrs. Hewitt. You're essentially arguing that adultery, say, is a judicial notion whose time has gone. If that's so, why is adultery still on your state's statute books as a crime?"

"I think we both know the practical answer to that, Justice Dugdale. Politics as usual. It's like the polls: the majority wants it both ways. Yes, it's on the books. No, it's never prosecuted. In fact, the last time it was prosecuted in our state was in 1876."

"Well, it certainly seems to me," says Dugdale, full of intellectual self-congratulation, "that as long as you keep adultery on your books as a crime, you've got a problem."

"Justice Dugdale, I don't disagree. Anyway, look, here's our position as regards adultery within the legal context of marriage. No matter what view of it is taken by an individual, or a government, or even the Bible, infidelity is a matter of choice grounded in the same constitutionally protected autonomy of belief that allows the choice of a faith or the selection of a church in which to be married. That choice, I repeat, is none of the state's business."

Now several Justices all speak up at once: Hartman, Dugdale, De Vito, and Chen. There's a pause while Smiley sorts out the traffic jam. Clifford looks at his watch; Hewitt must be under ten minutes to go. Smiley makes her mind up and signals Hartman to take the lead.

"Respondent has made much of the right to privacy," he observes, "and has depicted the state as a virtual—and virtuous—crusader on behalf of privacy. This is all well and good. It is also true that this and previous courts have in the last decade or so greatly expanded the juridical notion of what constitutes privacy as protected under the Fourth and Fifth Amendments. In the opinion of some, this expansion has been egregious. Now, as to how this might apply in the present instance..."

He continues for almost two more minutes, piling citation on citation before winding up. Clifford nudges his wife. "Hartman could bore for England," he mutters.

"That may be," she whispers in return, "but he could cause Hewitt to lose her thread."

"Fat chance." And, sure enough, when Hartman finishes, Hewitt's response is unruffled and confident: "I can only say what I have said all along, Mr. Justice Hartman. If Petitioner wishes to release the details of spousal fault directly to the public, fine. If Petitioner's spouse should seek in whatever form, in court or out, by any means available, to enjoin or forestall the disclosure of damaging or embarrassing details of private life, fine. But leave us out of a process that some might construe as extortion under law."

"That may be, Ms. Hewitt," observes Justice Chen, "but to revert to a point made earlier, can a course of action that is perfectly legal be considered extortion? What you refer to as extortion seems to me very much like a consensual exchange of intellectual property—information—for money."

"I don't think that's the state's business."

"It certainly has to weigh on the state's thinking, Ms. Hewitt," Chen responds.

"Believe me, it has, Justice Chen. May it please the Court, we know there are problems with no-fault. We think those problems are less onerous than with fault. How one party treats another in a pecuniary settlement depends on a number of things. How much money is available, how high feelings are running, how badly the exiting spouse wants out, how crafty the opposing lawyers are. Ultimately, it may come down to a matter of private, individual conscience. We would hope so, especially if there are children involved. We can set guidelines, we have set guidelines, but we cannot act, at least we don't choose to, as a surrogate conscience for the electorate. We take what they give us and do our best to turn it into workable law."

The white light flashes on: five minutes. Hewitt shifts, vocally, into higher gear. "The fact is, Chief Justice Smiley, to further address your earlier question, a former head of the family law chapel of our state bar association, a subunit of the ABA Chapel headed for a time with distinction by counsel for the Petitioner, has called fault divorce 'barbaric.' And yet, let's face it: lawyers may condemn fault, but they love it. It drags out the process, creates work, yields fat settlements the judicial probity of which is very much open to question. The head of the section on family law of the Bar Association of Michigan, a state whose turmoil on this issue has been much in the news, has been quoted in *The New York Times* to the effect that fault divorce produces more litigation, more expense, and more adversarial behavior, which for children often means being exposed to a psychologically wounding crossfire of character assassination between the parents, perpetrated and egged on by their attorneys.

"The fact is, may it please the Court, that every study indicates that fault is seldom the reason for a divorce. Nationally, less than ten percent of fault divorces invoke adultery as the fault basis. In our state, the percentage has been almost one-third lower. No-fault faces the one big fact: people no longer divorce mainly in order to remarry or to consolidate their emotional and sexual life with someone else's. They divorce in order to be on their own, and if the divorce cannot be easily obtained, the partner wishing to leave the marriage will simply do so. The argument that fault divorce keeps marriages together, that it discourages marital breakups, is not one that the state can be bound by. For a couple—for two individuals—to decide to remain together, or to divorce, even in the face of the admitted infidelity of one or the other party, or both, is those individuals' decision to make, not the state's. And not this honorable Court's."

She pauses here to take a sip of water. Then she picks up her thread. "Divorce is a fact of American life. Does the shift to no-fault exacerbate or change that fact? What can the state do but reflect a trend that clearly embodies the social momentum of the populace? We are aware that this may involve a trade-off of misery. We are aware of the statistics regarding spousal abandonment. We are aware of the statistics regarding defaults with respect to child support. We have read studies, like that put out by the University of Wisconsin, that if the divorce laws were more onerous, far more people would simply live together and procreate outside marriage, which would measurably deepen the financial and social insecurity of partners and children, and which to a great extent already seems to be happening in this country. We know all these things, may it please the Court, and we believe our current posture is the only reasonable way to confront them."

The red light in front of her blinks on, and she sits down. Smiley looks at Jekyll.

"Mr. Jekyll, you have three minutes left on the clock."

Jekyll rises. He smiles down on Hewitt. She returns the smile.

"Madam Chief Justice, Respondent has argued both elegantly and eloquently. She adduces much social evidence in support of her position. But I must say this: sociology, which is intuitive as well as factual, is at best an uncertain guide when it comes to formulating law. If we try to use so-called trends as the springboard for legislation, like as not they will prove slippery underfoot, because trends, as this Court will have noted this morning, can be employed to justify the reasoning of anyone citing them. For every season, there is a trend, you might say. That said, it does appear that personal gratification—of which adultery is surely a prime and prized example—is no longer broadly accepted as the supreme if not the sole objective of existence."

"That's all very well, Mr. Jekyll," interrupts Justice Dugdale. "But what if those trends you disparage are in fact broad-based? Respondent contends that the state is bound to reflect the consensual leanings of the electorate?"

"With respect, Justice Dugdale, I disagree with the state. Take this Court's holding in *Thornburgh*: I may not be letter-perfect, but as I recall, it went something like this: 'No individual should be compelled to surrender the freedom to make a crucial moral decision simply because that individual's value preferences aren't shared by the majority.' Does my recollection accord with Madam Justice's?"

Dugdale nods.

"May it please the several members of this honorable Court, there is something to be said for matching law to 'the action and passion of the times,' if I may also quote Justice Holmes. Professor William Stuntz of the University of Virginia Law School not long ago wrote, 'Today the focus is on divorce's social consequences, especially its consequences for children. Moral consequences are still outside the conventional debate, but the direction is promising...not simply about rights and property, but about morals and virtue and obligation.'"

"May it please the Court, it is to our children's moral inheritance that we must devote our collective wisdom to seek in law what the Preamble to the Constitution describes as 'the blessings of liberty for ourselves and our posterity,' because our children—and their welfare—are our true posterity. In 1888, in *Maynard v. Hill,* the Court found that marriage is, quote unquote, a special relationship and not merely a form of contract, and that marriage therefore requires a different jurisprudential perspective. Ms. Hewitt's brief argues that it is not the state's business to interfere in the most personal choices made by its citizens. My point is that neither is it the state's right to cancel the moral basis of those choices—and that as between the two, it is the latter that is more crucial to our democracy."

He's hurrying now, pushing the words along, trying to get it all in before the red light comes on. He has the Court's whole attention. *This is your Daniel Webster moment, Arthur,* thinks Clifford. *Go for it! Your life's summation, the apex of your art, your moment of transcendence and redemption. Stay cool, and hit 'em with everything you've got!*

"May it further please this Honorable Court," Jekyll says, the words spilling from him clear and distinct, not a hitch in his delivery, letter-perfect, "although our pleading involves certain generic issues of law, and of moral choice, issues that might conceivably affect tens, perhaps hundreds of thousands, of individuals, at bottom it is about this one individual's rights in these particular circumstances, and it is on those circumstances that it must be judged, not—as my learned opponent's brief urges—on grounds of broad social policy or philosophy. At the end of the day, we insist simply on this: we understand, we appreciate, we sympathize with the state's wish to achieve a position of moral neutrality, but in its haste to get out of the way, for the supposed benefit of the many, the state cannot—it must not—be allowed to trample the rights of any single individual."

The last word is barely out of his mouth when the red lamp lights up.

Smiley raps her gavel. "Mr. Jekyll, your time is up. The Court thanks Attorney General Hewitt and yourself. This case is submitted."

As Jekyll sits down, Clifford feels a surge of pride that practically lifts him out of his seat. Pride of authorship, pride in judgment, pride in having the courage and the wit to help this untried, dubious divorce lawyer argue a case that has had the courtroom—hell, had the nation!—enthralled. He's had a lot of successes in his life, but never one as elating as this. His chest feels as if it's filled with helium.

The great courtroom has fallen utterly silent, no one moving, no one speaking. It's as if a stun grenade has been set off. Clifford's seen audiences behave like this before: people hanging on to an extraordinary performance on which the curtain has just fallen, refusing to let go of it.

Except that in this theater there are no curtain calls into which the audience can pour its pent-up energy with applause and huzzahs. Finally, Chief Justice Smiley breaks the spell. She smiles at the courtroom, and says, "Before we hear the next case, we shall take a brief recess to permit visitors having urgent business elsewhere to leave." In other words: celebrities are free to go now. She raps the gavel again and rises, offering Justice Newbegin her arm. The bench empties.

Now, slowly, people here and there get to their feet and begin to leave. Others follow and in short order the entire courtroom is in motion, clogging the aisles. Outside, the sky has cleared, the weather has turned clement, and there's no need to put on the raincoat he's carrying. He goes over to one of the giant columns of the portico and leans against it. All of a sudden, he feels totally, remarkably empty. Drained of all exultation, all energy—because it's over.

The thought is infinitely depressing. Sure, there will be an aftermath. It's likely to take months before there's a decision, during which he'll surely feel a certain steady hum of anxious expectation, but it's over.

He moves away from the column toward the edge of the portico and looks around. The crowd has mostly dispersed. Only fifty or so people remain, grouped in small clumps and clusters: each with a celebrity or "personality" in the center, surrounded, as by petals, by members of the celebrity press eliciting comment. In the center of one, the Warren Beattys, Oprah in another. Jekyll is over by the rail, talking to a scattering of reporters, Hewitt a bit farther along.

So what do I do with myself now? He searches the wide porch for Natalie Sloan—mutual congratulations are in order—but she's nowhere to be seen.

He gently detaches Connie from the reporters and photographers. "Come on, let's go congratulate Arthur." They go over to Jekyll.

"Arthur, I'd like you to meet my wife. Connie, this is Arthur Jekyll."

Jekyll takes Connie's hand and executes a smart little bow. "I've heard so much about you, Mrs. Grange. It's an honor to meet you. May I add, I'm a big fan." He turns to Clifford. "So—how do you think it went?"

"Arthur, you were just great!"

"You certainly were," says Connie. "And so was Isobel Hewitt."

"Ah, you know Ms. Hewitt?" Jekyll asks. He looks questioningly at Clifford.

"I met her when I went to Hartford for the announcement of my friend Annabelle Villers's new plant. The governor gave a lunch afterward."

"I see. Is Ms. Villers here?"

"She was planning to come," Clifford says, "but business intervened."

At that moment, a young woman materializes next to Connie. "Mrs. Grange?"

"Yes?"

"I'm one of Justice De Vito's clerks. He'd be honored if you could join him in chambers for lunch. You—and Mr. Grange, of course." She smiles at Clifford.

"I'd love to," says Connie. She looks at her husband. "I'm not sure about Mr. Grange. Can you stay?"

"I'm afraid you're going to have to count me out," he says. "I'm going to go back to the Jefferson, pick up my stuff, and catch the 2:30 train."

Connie draws him aside. "Don't be so pig-headed! This could be very interesting, and Ronnie's got a plane waiting for me at Reagan. We'll be home by six."

Clifford doesn't reply, simply shakes his head. Connie frowns, says, "I see," and then tells the clerk, "Tell Justice De Vito that I'd be honored, but that Mr. Grange sends his regrets." Then she turns to Jekyll and extends her hand. "Congratulations again, Mr. Jekyll. If they gave out Emmys for oral argument, I'm sure you'd be nominated."

Jekyll makes a little mock bow. "Don't praise me, Mrs. Grange. Praise the chef." He grins at Clifford. "Your husband is a great director. I couldn't have done it without him."

"You're too modest, Mr. Jekyll," Connie says. She turns back to Clifford. "So—I expect I'll see you when I see you?"

"You shall. Don't wait up."

She goes off with De Vito's clerk. Clifford looks at Jekyll and shrugs. The two men study their shoes. Nothing need be said—until, finally, Jekyll looks up. "You know, Clifford, a good half of the country would give its eye teeth for two hours in the company of Justice De Vito, especially after his appearance on *Letterman*. I'm afraid I have to side with your wife. Would yielding just this once be so bad?" He looks at Clifford, and then grins. "Yes, I suppose it would," he says with a tiny sigh in his voice.

"So—what's next? When do we two meet again, as one witch said to the other?"

"We wait until the Court in all its gravity renders a decision, and that won't be until late this year at best. More likely early next year. For me, it'll be back to the old grind. I have a pile of cases. As I think I told you, this credit crunch is proving to be a positive cornucopia."

"Well, you deserve it. I hate to think what this has cost you."

"Clifford, it's only money." Jekyll puts both hands on Clifford's shoulders. "Clifford, I just..."

"You don't have to say anything, Arthur. The pleasure has been all mine."

He starts to moves off when there's a tug at his sleeve and he turns to find Renee Newcastle, the poetry editor, one of the regulars at the Diogenes. "My God, Renee, what are you doing here?"

"I wanted to hear the argument. The poet laureate's one of my authors and a friend of Justice Newbegin. She got me a ticket."

"It was terrific, wasn't it?"

"It was wonderful. Didn't I tell you how good Mr. Jekyll is? Clifford, will you do me a huge favor?"

"Anything."

She looks at Jekyll. "Will you introduce me to Mr. Jekyll? He probably doesn't remember me from that one time at the club."

"Certainly. Arthur, this is Renee Newcastle, God's gift to American poetry. She's a big fan."

Jekyll beams. "A fan? Of mine? I'm not sure I knew I had any of those." He turns to Renee. "And I know all about you—professionally, that is. You preside over one of most distinguished imprints in American publishing, or should I say one of the few remaining distinguished imprints. Well, Ms. Newcastle, I'm flattered, and honored. I don't suppose you'd care to join me for lunch, now that Clifford here has stood me up."

"I'd like that," says Renee, shyly.

Clifford winks at Jekyll. *You old tomcat!* Nobody had said anything about lunch—or standing up. He bids Renee and Jekyll goodbye and trots down the steps of the Court building.

What with the usual delays and screw-ups, it's well after ten when the car service deposits Clifford at Grangeford. He's feeling marvelous, simply marvelous. It's as if his system has rewired itself. The old gears are starting to turn, to click into place. He's full of exhilaration and excitement: maybe this is the new beginning he's been praying for. If he can deliver the goods in the Supreme Court, what won't be possible.

Once upon a time, he would have rushed upstairs and awakened Connie, wanting to share this crackling new positive sense of life, but now he doesn't feel like it. He doesn't want this mood to pass, and he somehow senses that his wife would find a way to kill his joy. Not necessarily intentionally—although how can he ever be sure, now?—but just by being there. She might even want sex, and where would that leave him? It's a lose-lose situation: trying to fake it, or refusing, and thereby becoming the bad guy.

He decides to bed down on the library sofa. Connie has an extra-early call the next day (he still knows her shooting schedule by heart) and he'll say he didn't get in until after midnight. He rummages around in the liquor closet and locates a bottle of very old Armagnac his father brought back from France in 1945, a bottle that he's reserved for a very special occasion—he'd planned to crack it when *Crown Heights* got an Oscar nomination, ha, ha! He uncorks it carefully and pours a couple of fingers into an oversized Baccarat snifter that Connie gave him three birthdays ago, mouths a silent toast to his father's memory, and takes a sip, and then toasts Arthur Jekyll, and takes another sip and toasts himself. Going down, the brandy stings like heartburn, but the aftertaste and the slow, suffusing glow are worth the sting. *If firelight had a flavor*, he thinks, *this is how it would taste*. He takes a final sip that drains the glass. *God bless us all! God save this Honorable Court! And—for God's sakes—let right be done!*

Whatever the hell that turns out to be.

CHAPTER TWELVE

February 16

It's a wild afternoon. Windy and wet, with thick, whirling traceries of what the weather shows call "wintry mix" hooping across the landscape and slapping the windows of Clifford's studio. The snow is starting to stick; the weather reports on radio and TV are dire and since this evening's Diogenes speaker isn't someone he's much interested in, anyway, Clifford decides to skip going into the city. Who needs to hear another of those used-to-be-this, used-to-be-that Beltway-to-Wall-Street multimillionaires who are popping up all over the talkscape these days, offering platitudes and palaver about deficits and Social Security and how the poor don't save enough—which is like complaining that not enough people in wheelchairs sign up for the pole vault. And of course the paradox is that people like the guy speaking tonight are the ones mainly responsible for putting the country in the financial mess it's in; they're the ones who run things, the ones who pay off the politicians and get to borrow money at wholesale prices and view the tax code as a form of bespoke tailoring.

February's never much of a month, to begin with, and this one has been especially lousy around the world. The Middle East remains a mess, ditto sub-Saharan Africa, Pakistan, Afghanistan, parts of Southeast Asia, and, for all Clifford knows, a dozen other places. The economic situation now definitely seems to be easing, and the panic in the stock market has subsided, with the Dow Jones some twenty-odd percent above its crisis lows.

As for *Doe v. Hewitt:* not a word. With the case locked away in the chambered nautilus of Supreme Court deliberation, the American thirst for sensation has moved on in search of fresh quarry. Generally speaking, it's as bad a time for the gossip industry as for Washington lobbyists. *Ad Age* reports a falloff of as much as twenty percent in the weekly newsstand sales of publications devoted to celebrity gossip, and the ratings of so-called reality TV shows have fallen through the bottom of the charts. The old Kool-Aid of personality journalism and partisan political correctness and pork-barrel politics has been recognized for the acid swill it always was. Advertisers are said to be recalibrating their upcoming campaigns to appeal to a grown-up audience forced finally by events and personal circumstances to grasp that life in America has become a hard, serious, expensive, and risky business.

The media, naturally, hardly know how to cope. Audiences seem to demand people who actually have something useful to say and to tune out those who are merely moving their mouths. Shouting is no longer the mandatory tone of voice; opportunism and overstatement no longer automatically pass as analysis and comment. Blogs are seeing a sharp falloff in unique views. People are just plain tired of blahblahblah, they want answers. At Grangeford, too, the commonsensical middle way has taken hold. All told, Connie and Clifford are doing okay. They've gotten used to Jenny's absence, and, besides, she's home so much that Clifford has actually wondered if "boarding school" isn't an oxymoron. And when she's not home, she's in virtually constant communication with her mother via e-mail and cellphone.

Jekyll is fast becoming a memory. Clifford seldom hears from him, and they haven't seen each other since October, when they shook hands in Washington. Clifford's beginning to think that theirs was a shipboard romance. Jekyll's got a life and people with lives move on, and that's what Jekyll has done: moved on.

Clifford meanwhile tries to keep busy, to keep the dull coals of hope and possibility glowing, if only faintly. He fills yellow pad after yellow pad with notes, scenes, projections of projects. He'll read for a while. He'll wander around the Internet. He'll indulge what he calls "my Shakespeare jones"—read a play, listen to audiotapes, watch videos, devour the commentary of everyone from Dr. Johnson to Bradley to Harold Bloom. He goes on culture jags: last month it was Falstaff: both parts of *Henry IV, The Merry Wives of Windsor,* Orson Welles's *Chimes at Midnight,* Verdi's opera, Elgar's symphonic "study," Gordon Getty's song cycle "Plump Jack," an off-Broadway musical that transposed the merry wives to a Texas country town, a parcel a day from Amazon.com containing commentaries and rival editions. Currently it's poetry—and the gloomier and more pessimistic the better: he's discovered Edward Arlington Robinson, whose "Miniver Cheevy"—about a child of "scorn"—and "Richard Cory"—about a suicide—particularly fit his darker moods. Oddly enough, he finds this kind of poetry cheering and an effective way to deal with his blacker moods—an outcome that causes him to wonder whether he may be going crazy. And, for diversion, there are always new gadgets—iPhones, GPhones, a new BlackBerry—which require hours of comparison feature- and plan-shopping. There's screenwriting software, personal finance software, voice-into-text software. He's spent hours talking to tech support on three continents. None of this is the same as working—but it's something to do. And at least, thanks to his wife, he doesn't *need* a job.

And so the days wind by at a gentle amniotic pace, time seems to fill up on its own, with no conscious expenditure of effort or focus on his part, then be gone. It's like being on an endless cruise: pleasant in its way, but not really a life.

Outside, the wind tunes up to a higher note. The snow seems to be falling faster. He picks up a pad and starts to jot down notes for a screenplay idea that came to him in the shower. And then the phone rings, its shrill chirrup barely audible above the banshee wail of the storm outside, and the caller ID displays Jekyll's number, and Clifford's stomach plunges as he realizes what this may be about.

"I fear I have bad news," the lawyer says without preamble.

"You're not telling me we lost?"

"I'm afraid so. The decision has just been read out. The Court upheld the no-fault statute by a vote of five to four."

"Arthur—this is not possible! You were brilliant! How the hell could they come down that way?"

"De Vito, Hartman, Cleveland, and the two lady Justices made the majority. For us, it was Smiley, Chen, Ramirez, and Newbegin— who died last night, if you haven't heard." Jekyll must be horribly disappointed, but his voice is steady. "So there you are. 5-4 against us. A damned near-run thing, as Wellington said of Waterloo."

There's a pause now, as both men process the news. Finally, because someone needs to say *something*, Clifford asks, "So what next?"

"Clifford—I'm afraid that after the Supreme Court there is no 'next.' Not jurisprudentially, at least. But that doesn't mean that all is lost as far as you're concerned. You still possess powerful leverage. You—we—we could…"

"Don't go there, Arthur," Clifford interrupts. "I told you, we lose, I'm out. I'm not going to blackmail anyone."

"As I must have said to you a hundred times by now, Clifford, give it some thought. The pockets on the other side are deep. My own inclination is to fight on. Aside from the prospect of leaving as much as $200 million on the table, it rankles that they're going to get away with their scam. They should at least pay."

"For one thing, they're not that deep any longer. Even though her stock has come back somewhat, so that Belle may not be tapped out, she's definitely down to the shorter hairs, at least that's what she's hinted to Connie. You saw that she bought that big collection. It may be that her eyes were bigger than her wallet."

"A businessperson as resourceful and daring as Ms. Villers will find a way if she has to."

"Maybe so—but not on my account. On top of which, I flatter myself that I was never in this for the money. I suppose that makes me an asshole by most people's standards nowadays, but, frankly, I'm so used to being an asshole by now, it doesn't bother me. Anyway, Arthur, this was really always your play. I was simply a walking set of facts that you and Hewitt could stipulate. It was your case—and your dream. And you got what you wanted: to argue a good-sized case before the Supreme Court—which you argued the shit out of. Which is good enough for me. So now you know what we're gonna do? We're gonna let the son of a bitch die. I have a life no one could complain about—even I'm beginning to see that—and a great kid, and my wife is doing fabulously, and I have sixteen P.G. Wodehouses I haven't read. What more could a man ask?"

"This could be dealt with in a way that would virtually leave you above suspicion."

"Maybe it can—but it's not going to. I know it sounds corny, especially the way we live now, but I gave my word to myself on this subject, and I'm going to keep it. Which also goes for you."

"Well, you know what you think is best for you."

"If I don't, who does?"

He hears Jekyll sigh. Then: "Clifford, you're the client, and I bow to your wishes. So let me just say this: I owe you one. For your trust. For your patience. For your guts. For the generous provision of your theater skills. For your genius as a mimic."

"The pleasure was all mine."

"Well, then, time to get on with the rest of our lives, Clifford. Good luck and Godspeed." Jekyll pauses. "Let's see," he says in an abstracted way. "is there anything else? No, I guess not. So—there we are. All I can say is onward and upward, Clifford. I hope I'll run into you at the club."

"I'm sure you will. And, Arthur, thank you. Maybe it didn't turn out the way we hoped, but maybe that's for the best. And any way you cut it, it's been a hell of a fun trip. A goddamn gas!"

Seconds after Clifford hangs up, he remembers that there was one thing he might have asked Jekyll about, something that just a day or so ago seemed to pop into his mind for no good reason: whether there was any news on the Vargas front, whether anything had come to light that bore on his and Jekyll's speculations as to who might have wanted Connie's paramour dead. He decides it's not worth bothering about. Besides, larger, grimmer thoughts are flooding his mind. Namely, that the way it's turned out, he's the only loser. Everyone else has ended up where they wanted, with what they wanted. Connie has gotten away with it; the Supreme Court says so. Annabelle, too: she has her institute, her billion-dollar art collection, and her prize asset is unimpaired. Jekyll got to play Daniel Webster—and even if the decision went against him in the end, he pitched a hell of a game and he knows it and always will. So who's left with the empty stocking? Whose is the lump of coal under the tree? Clifford Grange's, naturally. It's enough to make a guy cry. Or make himself a cappuccino. He shrugs into a down jacket, pulls a watch cap down over his ears, and crunches his way back up to the main house.

In the little study off their bedroom, it being her Wednesday off, Connie's stretched out on the chaise longue, studying a script. Hollywood is always sending her stuff, trying to get her brand power "attached," as they say, to a film and thereby rendering it bankable, and if she knows the agent or the producer, she'll look it over as a courtesy, but that's as far as she'll go. TV stardom is one thing, and movie stardom quite another: chalk and cheese, they don't translate. It's a different kind of acting, a wholly distinct audience vector.

"Sorry to barge in," he says. "I've got some news you may be interested in. Jekyll just called. We lost in the Supreme Court." It's all he can do not to say: *And you won!*

"No!" Her surprise sounds genuine. From the beginning, he's been pretty certain she's been left out of the Belle-Santiago loop, that she knows nothing of the backstage fun and games.

"Yeah, five to four. My guess is, the Court doesn't want to rock the boat."

"Is that what Jekyll thinks?"

"Actually, we didn't get into the philosophy behind the verdict. I think this hit him pretty hard. Damn few lawyers get a shot like this, especially lawyers like Jekyll. He probably figures it's game, set, match. Anyway, he thanked me for my help and that was that. He's like you, I guess. Doesn't care for the taste of spilt milk. Moves on. So there it is. A lot of work for nothing."

She looks up at him. "Not really 'nothing,' darling. You worked hard and it was a great show."

"If you say so."

She doesn't respond, just goes back to her script. He shrugs and goes back down to the kitchen. He no longer feels like coffee—he's jazzed enough as it is—so he zaps some frozen soup in the microwave, pours it into a Thermos, and returns to the studio.

He sets the thermos down and gathers tapes, notes, transcripts—all the stuff he got from Jekyll—and stuffs them into an empty Amazon.com carton. He looks around to see if he's forgotten anything, and snaps his fingers in sudden realization. From its hiding place behind his old bound scripts he retrieves the evidence of Connie's misconduct, evidence no one but Clifford has ever seen. He places it on his desk and studies it. The images preserved in the small rectangle of plastic, silicon, and metal spark up in his mind, which becomes an internal screening room. For perhaps thirty seconds, he watches the show. It no longer makes him wince, which is something. Then he picks up the memory device and goes to the pot-bellied stove, pries up the lid, and before he can change his mind, tosses the device on the simmering coals, watches while the flames curl and blacken it, and then slides the lid shut and pours himself a drink. The soup can wait.

At almost that exact instant, in a Range Rover parked some seven hundred miles to the southwest, Annabelle Villers puts her cellphone down and shivers with relief. Even her caller sounded relieved, and Santiago is a man not easily moved. His news is good: the Supreme Court has ruled against Doe. The nightmare is over.

She's parked at a high point overlooking the site where the Villers Institute for the Study of Italian Art and Culture will someday stand. Right now all it is, is a bunch of stakes with little cloth flags on them and a couple of bulldozer cuts. Construction won't start for another few months yet, once the ground softens and the rains of spring have finished.

She gets out of the car and walks along the edge of the site. It really is very Tuscan, this piece of earth. Her mind turns to the call she had from First Gotham yesterday. Cecile was very excited. The investment bank has had a feeler from a big international packaged-goods conglomerate about the possibility of acquiring Summerhill. Cecile guesstimates the offer could be worked up to as much as $6 billion, a huge premium over the company's present depressed market value. Apparently the Constance Grange brand is all that matters.

After hanging up with Cecile, Annabelle's done her own personal arithmetic. It's positively seductive. This could put over $2.3 billion in her pocket. All she'll ever need. The Supreme Court has removed the only shadow hanging over the company. She's free to sell with an unencumbered conscience, at a price that will enable her to see that Summerhill's people are taken care of. Well taken care of.

She decides to sleep on the merger possibility before talking again with Cecile. It's starting to drizzle so she heads back to the car and drives to the office.

"Honey," her secretary tells Annabelle when she walks in. "You just had kind of a funny call. Some New York fellow, said he was callin' from his plane, said he didn't need to speak to you directly now, but to tell you he'll be here about five. And will see you then."

"Who is this person?"

"He didn't give his name. Just said that he's a substantial share-holder in our company and that he needs to get with you about a really urgent matter of stockholder business."

"Did you tell him I'm out of the office? I don't see any Tom, Dick, or Harry who walks in, big shareholder or not!"

"I told him you were out of pocket. He says he'll hang out until Christmas if he has to, says it's that urgent. Says he'll camp out on the doorstep."

"He says what? Who is this man?"

"Says his name is Mr. Hyde. Says you'll know who he is if you know Robert Louis Stevenson. I haven't got the slightest idea what he means by that. Do you?"

Hyde? Robert Louis Stevenson? Annabelle wasn't educated for nothing. It takes her about twenty seconds to get it. This can only mean trouble.

FINALE

•

All's Well That Ends

October 14

On a fine Friday in early autumn, with the weather several degrees warmer than usual for this time of year, a splendid company converges on Asheville for a weekend-long celebration. The occasion is the groundbreaking of the The Villers-Summerhill Institute for the Study of Italian Art (known hereabouts simply as the Villers).

Already the press is declaring that the Villers, when it finally opens, will be the only true North American peer of Harvard's I Tatti and NYU's La Pietra in Florence. Comparisons with the Getty Center in Los Angeles have also been ventured. The 152 acre, $1 billion institute "campus" will include a gallery, library and study center, housing for resident staff, including a separate villa for the as-yet-undesignated first director, and a ten-suite guesthouse for visiting scholars and dignitaries. In a nation and state still ravenous for upbeat, positive news, a combination of time, taxes, political expediency, and actuarial realism have argued for an early celebration, no expense spared, no particle of potential glamour overlooked.

As limousines and helicopters discharge their glittering human cargo, final touches are being put on splendid floral centerpieces and elaborate place settings, squadrons of cooks are assembling their ingredients under the stern eye of the Italian prime minister's personal chef, and Peter Duchin and his band begin to tune up for the evening's formal dinner dance, the kick-off for the weekend. The next morning, a few miles away, there will be sonorous words of blessing and thanksgiving and official gratitude and a few ceremonial spadefuls of earth will be turned by various dignitaries. Afterward, there will be a daylong program of seminars and lectures and concerts, with golf, tennis, hiking, and horseback riding for the not so culturally inclined, then a cocktail party, and a round of smaller dinner parties, for which the pecking order has been refined down to the last atom of social and cultural pedigree.

On Sunday morning, Joseph Cardinal Santiago, Archbishop of Southern New England, will offer a Mass of Celebration in Asheville's imposing Basilica of Saint Lawrence. Santiago is recognized as a key figure in the establishment of the Villers. Not only has His Eminence secured assurances of important loans from the Vatican to the institute's inaugural exhibition, scheduled for two years hence, but he has also godfathered a $100 million gift to the institute's endowment from the Forest Fields Charitable Trust, of which he is a trustee.

The *crème* of Asheville has thrown open its doors, brought out its best china and linens and silks and satins, and scheduled a dazzling social and cultural round. Annabelle Villers has taken over the entire Biltmore estate, the one-time Vanderbilt family vacation compound, for tonight's opening gala. Biltmore is the largest private residence ever built in the United States, designed in the 1890s by the eminent architect Richard Morris Hunt, with its splendid gardens laid out by Frederick Olmsted, architect of New York City's Central and Prospect Parks, its two-hundred-fifty-room hotel (where Ms. Villers's most important guests will be housed) and its complex of stables, sporting facilities, and world-renowned gardens. Rumor has it that the weekend is going to cost the hostess and BME and

Alimentaria, who are jointly underwriting this evening, a cool $15 million—not including insurance.

Well, Annabelle Villers can certainly handle her end. Just a week ago in New York City, final papers were signed for the acquisition of Annabelle's company, Summerhill Farms, by Alimentaria Generale of Lugano, Switzerland, for a total consideration in cash and stock of $7.2 billion. The financial press estimates Annabelle's share of the proceeds—including the holdings of the institute's endowment—at $3.4 billion, roughly twice the endowment of the Metropolitan Museum in New York. As *The Wall Street Journal* has pointed out, this means she will have taken nearly $3 billion (including nearly $500 million of stock previously sold by her) out of a company worth perhaps $40 million when she took over its management twenty-three years ago, a performance worthy of Warren Buffett—who is expected for the weekend.

To share in this great occasion, one-thousand-odd guests have streamed into the Asheville area. People are saying it's the most star-studded arts event since the Metropolitan Museum's farewell dinner for Philippe de Montebello. The list is headed by the First Lady and her daughters; the vice-president of the United States is also attending; on hand will be North Carolina's governor and the state's entire congressional delegation; the governor of Connecticut, as well as Attorney General Isobel Hewitt and the speaker of the state assembly; three Supreme Court justices—Cleveland, De Vito, and Mornington-Kaplan—will be in attendance, along with pillars of the North Carolina bar and bench; important officials of jurisdictions—both here and abroad—which represent significant domestic and overseas markets or bases of operation for Summerhill and its new parent; a small regiment of Barrow Media's top executives and aides; the CEOs of the sixteen North Carolina-domiciled Fortune 500 companies. First Gotham, formerly lead investment banker to Summerhill and now co-lead U.S. investment banker designate to Alimentaria, is sending a delegation led by Cecile Frost, its newly anointed vice chair. Also expected are top officials of a half-dozen major money-center banks, of the top management-consulting and accountancy firms, and of other regional and state financial powerhouses.

And that's just the business side. The cream of the cream of the art world is on the list: the most important dealers, respected art historians, illustrious museum directors and their chief curators, the directors of I Tatti and La Pietra, the *sovrintendenti* of a good dozen art districts and museums in Italy, and the counterparts of these worthies in the field of Italian Renaissance letters, music, and history. There will be a number of important living artists present, since it is a stated goal of the institute "to encourage creative interaction between artists of our time and the great masters of the Renaissance."

The presidents, chancellors, and head basketball coaches of the major North Carolina universities will also be in attendance tonight, along with emissaries from a good two dozen other seats of learning here and abroad. The cream of North Carolina society will be here: *le tout* Asheville, of course, and *le tout* Raleigh-Durham, *le tout* Winston-Salem, *le tout* Wilmington, *le tout* Charlotte, *le tout* Chapel Hill. Finally, there'll be a mixed bag of so-called bold-face types of greater or lesser, older and newer, candlepower, drawn from Hollywood, TV, and the New York-Los Angeles media axis; every important PR firm in the world has besieged the Villers's party planners with attempts ranging from wheedling to bribery to get their important clients added to the guest list.

It promises to be, by a long way, the most grand and glamorous social occasion in this state in perhaps a century; nothing like it has happened in and around Asheville since the Gilded Age, when tycoon-filled private railway carriages streamed south and west to the Great Smokies to enjoy the majesty of the landscape, the purity of the mountain air, and the refinement of the Vanderbilt family court— possibly the closest America has ever come to Versailles.

The VVIPs, the bluest of the blue chip guests, have been put up at the four-star Inn on Biltmore Estate. The First Lady is ensconced in the William A.V. Cecil suite, the choicest accommodation. Other overseas and U.S. notables—Annabelle's A-list of connections in church, state, art, and business—have been assigned suitable lodging. Appropriately, the Adele Sloan Burden Suite, named after Biltmore founder George Vanderbilt's niece Adele Sloane Burden, has been allocated to Constance Grange and her husband. After all, as Annabelle would be the first to admit, none of this would be possible without Connie.

The Granges' lodgings command a splendid panorama of the surrounding mountains, with, in the nearer distance, the great elegant bulk of Biltmore House shouldering its way above the great carpet of forest. The vista reminds Clifford, standing on the balcony, of the landscape in Annabelle's latest prize acquisition: the *St. Jerome in the Wilderness* on view downstairs, painted around 1500 by the Venetian master Giovanni Bellini, and thought by experts to be a previously unknown pendant to the famous painting of St. Francis in New York's Frick Collection. The picture is said to have cost $125 million, cheap by comparison with what other collectors have paid for Klimts and Lucian Freuds. Annabelle has confessed to an art reporter from *The New York Times* that "my newest baby" is the favorite of all her collection; that it captures the qualities of the Italian landscape that first won her heart and eye.

Behind him he can hear his wife unpacking. This weekend should provide Connie with a nice measure of distraction and star worship, which perhaps will relieve some of the pressure that seems to be building within his marriage, pressure that, should it keep building, may expand to the point where it blows things apart. A year ago, even up to a month ago, things seemed at least stable. Now they're not, but how could they not be with everything different, with the internal dynamic perhaps not reversed but certainly retriangulated. Still, he would have hoped that his wife would accept his good fortune, or at least keep her resentments to herself. But she hasn't—and it's starting to show—and it's definitely starting to grate.

Connie's by turns short-tempered, impatient, sarcastic, and withdrawn. Only occasionally does what her husband now thinks of as "the old Connie" shine through. Her moods pretty much slide right off him, because his frame of mind is so good and strong and positive.

He wishes he could help; that is, he *still* wishes he could help, but not so much. It simply takes up too much of the time, energy, and ingenuity that he really must devote to other business. What has brought on this short-fused emotional state? Clifford has worked hard to convince himself that Connie's touchy state of mind can be ascribed to factors other than his own sweet, sudden, and astonishing change of circumstances. He's made a little list. One possibility he's dismissed from the get-go. His wife's tetchy mood doesn't bespeak another man. That's something he'd lay ten thousand to one against. So what is it, then? Age? Is she pre-menopausal? Is it the show? They've been having cast and writer problems, and next fall—the episodes are being shot now—*Here's Constance!* will enter its ninth season. Is it stale? Is Connie? Comparable huge hits began to run out of gas at just this point. Could it have to do with Grangeford as an "empty nest"? In mid-September, he and Connie drove Jenny up to Andover to begin her sophomore year. When they bade their daughter goodbye, it was as if Connie was losing Jenny forever; she practically had to be dragged into the car, and on the trip home, she had just sat silently, oblivious to her husband's attempts to cheer her up, to shower her with his own hale good feeling. And it would seem her parting intuition was justified. Her first year at boarding school, Jenny had been on the phone, home for weekends, constantly in touch. Now it's different. If their daughter phones twice a week, that's a lot, and she isn't planning to come home until Thanksgiving. Well, it's what happens: Jenny's simply moving into her own life and her parents will simply have to adjust.

Plausible though they may sound, none of these explanations feels right. What does is the single big change between the status quo at Grangeford as recently as Labor Day, and this status quo now, which seems to have triggered what Jekyll once mentioned to Clifford as "the Newton's Third Law of Marriage: to every action there is an equal and opposite, and usually angry, reaction." Try as he may to fight off the notion, Clifford can't help concluding, ultimately, that what's eating Connie is the fact that he's back at work.

It began with a phone call just after the Granges got back from Sleeping Bear.

The caller was a Marcia Johnson, a former top producer at New Line and newly appointed CEO of Forest Fields Films, a film division being set up by the big Native American casino company as a joint venture with Barrow Films. The venture's strategy would be to concentrate on multi-installment spectaculars with strong, connective storylines to complement ongoing central characters, patterned on *Harry Potter* and *Lord of the Rings,* as opposed to pure character-based franchises like Spiderman and Batman. Films with a large CGI component and a lot of symbolism and myth to catch the fancy of the *Da Vinci Code/Lord of the Rings* audience. The way Johnson laid it out, it made sense.

The reason for her call, she told Clifford, was that she'd gotten wind somewhere—she couldn't quite recall where, exactly—of his "Valhalla Project," a twenty-first-century updating of Wagner's *Ring* set in Las Vegas and Dubai. It sounded like the sort of project Forest Fields Films should be looking at. Would Clifford be free to meet and discuss it?

Would he ever! He was in her office the next morning, pitching the epic that he'd been refining and re-refining for four years. Marcia Johnson seemed enthusiastic about it; she seemed to "get" it—asked smart questions, made shrewd suggestions. She'd treated Clifford like the serious artist he is.

When he left her office, he expected it would be a month or so before he heard from her, if ever. But she called back three days later and said she'd like to take it to the next step and have him do a treatment of the complete four-picture cycle. How would $2 million sound? Could his agent get together with her people to hammer something out?

Of course he didn't have an agent. He no longer even had a regular lawyer. The only lawyer he felt he could talk to was Jekyll. He called him and asked him to represent him in the Forest Fields negotiations. Jekyll said sure—although he wasn't an entertainment lawyer, and wouldn't Clifford be better off using someone like Jeremy Nussbaum, or the Janklow office? But Clifford insisted—he owed Jekyll big time—so Jekyll got together with the film people and a deal was negotiated in less than a week– the first $1 million advance was paid into Clifford's bank just last Wednesday—and the bean counters are working up a $150 million budget for "Film #1"—as it's called in the contract.

Hollywood is a herd place, and deal gossip snowballs. Days after the contract was signed a squib—"Veteran Helmer-Writer Clifford Grange Set Up at FFF on 4-Pix Wagner Deal, Clooney Rumored Attached"—appeared in *Variety,* and the "expressions of interest" have started to come in: Nicole Kidman's people want to talk about the Brunnhilde part, and Anthony Hopkins's about Wotan/"Warden," and what about Chris Rock for the Loge character, and who should Denzel be cast as, or Antonio Banderas, or Javier Bardem? And, of course, Clifford's own phone has started ringing, people who haven't called in years, who've turned away in restaurants when they've seen him come in. All of a sudden it's, "Hey, buddy, how ya doing, what's new? We should take lunch. How about Michael's next Tuesday? The Four Seasons? Da Pietro?" No more "Are you who I think you used to be?"

And it isn't just Hollywood. The minute Belle heard about the project, she was on the phone, full of congratulations and enthusiasm—and a request to take $15 million of her own money. Thanks to her, First Gotham is also in the game, talking about raising a $50 million limited partnership from places like Harvard and Yale. And the final irony: In the *Wall Street Journal* Ronald Barrow has been quoted to the effect that Valhalla will be a first step in a series of entertainment "strategic alliances" with Forest Fields. The template has thus been recut, and then recut again, and today, as it now stands, Marcia Johnson can call on up to $800 million of financing from all sources.

It's barely occurred to Clifford to ask where Marcia Johnson heard about Valhalla. After all, it wasn't exactly a state secret. Connie knew, of course—and she might have said something to any of the numerous show-business mouths with which she was likely to come into contact. Clifford can't recall saying anything about it to anyone at the Diogenes, or any of the few former comrades he'd been in touch with, but he may well have. Jekyll knew, and Belle, and he wonders whether either of them may have taken a hand behind the arras, but one thing he's not going to do: question his luck. This one chance may well be all he'll get, and big as Valhalla—which Peter Jackson will direct—may be, it's still only the first film of four, and needs to be a success if Clifford's deal to direct the third and fourth installments is ever to kick in. For the moment, then, he will tell himself, with a half smile and fingers crossed, that his is just a case of patient, suffering virtue and talent finally rewarded. And luck—never leave out sheer idiotic blind luck.

Be that as it may, he can't get around the perception that his good news has turned into—maybe always was going to be—a source of aggravation for his wife. Call it Star Is Born Syndrome. Call it whatever you want, but it seems that in Connie's view, their marriage simply isn't ample and elastic enough to accommodate two stars under one roof. Gable and Lombard, Martin and Charisse, Brangelina: those are exceptions to the theory. Well, she's just going to have to get used to it, come to terms, or this marriage is going to be in trouble, because Clifford's going to go forward while he still has a chance, he's not going to apologize. It wasn't just a contract to write a couple of films and possibly write and direct two more, it was a whole new lease on life. Connie got her big break; now it's his turn. He deserves this.

"What time do you think we ought to go down?" Connie calls from the bedroom.

"I don't know. The invitation says six o'clock cocktails and viewing, dinner at seven thirty, but I'm sure they're running late."

He returns to the bedroom. His wife is standing before a full-length mirror in panties and a half-bra, turning slightly this way and that, studying herself. Clifford is already dressed, black tie neatly knotted, needing only to put on his tuxedo jacket.

"You look good," he says. "Real good for an old dame."

"Thanks for nothing," she replies. Once upon a time, her tone would have been different.

"I'll be in the living room," he says. "Whenever you're ready."

Entirely caught up in her image, she doesn't seem to hear him. Her expression as she studies her face in the mirror isn't happy, and he can guess why, because you can't fight age, and when he looks at her now he sees stuff that wasn't there as recently as last year: barely noticeable irregularities and coarsenings of plane and curve and surface texture and tint, a certain loss of overall tone, the line not as plumb right as it once was. Still, this isn't about a few crow's feet. That he's certain.

When at last they go downstairs, they find Annabelle just inside the entrance. A few people stare openly at Connie; others, trying to pretend disinterest, equally pointedly look away. The effect a star's presence has on the laity always amuses Clifford. Annabelle has promised Connie that publicity intrusions will be kept to the minimum possible, but a star is a star, and the two women barely have time to air kiss before Connie is snatched away by a Summerhill/ Alimentaria flack and led to a side room for a bit of "red carpet" time with a select press pool.

Clifford turns back to Annabelle and finds her talking to a woman he recognizes immediately: Isobel Hewitt.

"Nice to see you, Ms. Hewitt," he says. "Congratulations on *Doe*."

"I feel fortunate that the Court saw matters our way."

She turns away and heads off just as a large man lumbers up and swamps Annabelle with a theatrical embrace.

"Clifford, may I present our governor. Ah, here's Connie." Introductions are made, then someone else arrives, requiring a fresh round of introductions, then someone else equally important, and before Clifford knows it, Connie's been engulfed by the process and is in the receiving line, and he's become utterly superfluous to the moment.

He mutters his excuses to the world at large and melts away, eyes peeled for a waiter with a drink tray. He makes his way down the vast main hall to the stately public rooms in which the displays have been placed: the Bellini and a few other choice objects from the institute collections, along with a detailed model of the institute campus surrounded by a great variety of plans and renderings. The Bellini is surrounded by worshippers, so he examines some of the other objects on exhibition: a handsome gold-ground *Calvary* dated 1412 by Lorenzo Monaco, a pristine state of Pollaiuolo's engraved *Battle of the Sea Monsters,* a marble bust attributed to Ghiberti, a jewel-like little hunting scene by Uccello.

He's looking closely at the latter when a voice he knows says, "Beautiful, isn't it?"

He turns around to find Arthur Jekyll, resplendent in a very elegantly cut double-breasted dinner jacket, with a woman on his arm. It's Renee Newcastle.

Clifford can't help himself. "What the hell are you doing here, Arthur?"

"Be polite. Say hello to Renee."

"Hello, Renee. How come you didn't tell me you were coming when I saw you at the club last week?"

"Arthur wanted to surprise you." She squeezes Jekyll's arm.

"Well, he has. Both of you. When did this get started?"

"After you introduced us in Washington," says Renee.

Clifford raises his glass. "Well, here's to you."

Glasses are clinked, then Renee excuses herself and wanders off into the adjacent gallery.

Clifford looks at Jekyll. "What the hell are you doing here? Isn't this kind of out of your bailiwick?"

"You might say so. Actually, it's thanks to you—indirectly—that I was invited. When you asked me to negotiate on your behalf with Forest Fields Films, I became reacquainted with Cardinal Santiago, whom I had met earlier in connection with *Doe.* He thought it might make sense for me to meet Ms. Villers."

"Why? What can you possibly have in common with Belle?"

"That was exactly my first reaction, but His Eminence persisted, and a lunch was arranged. We found we had a number of interests in common—including a deep mutual fondness for you."

"How come you didn't tell me?"

"It just slipped my mind. I rather imagine I expected Annabelle to tell your wife and your wife to tell you."

And maybe she did tell Connie, Clifford thinks. Which would really have fried Connie's ass. No wonder she didn't pass it on.

"Anyway," Jekyll continues, "one thing has led to another. She's gotten me involved in her institute as a kind of unpaid sounding board on certain matters, and she put me on her visiting committee. Renee and I are meeting her in a fortnight in Florence for a private tour of the Uffizi."

"Jesus, Arthur"—-Clifford shakes his head—"you never cease to surprise me. What a turn of events. How funny and weird life is."

"Provided one works at it," says Jekyll. "And provided one has friends like you to put one in Fortune's way. Since *Doe,* my life has changed, too. I remain the scourge of Palm Beach, thanks to a very helpful nudge from Wall Street—and I suppose you can throw in Greenwich as well, there being no fury on earth as wrathful as a hedge-fund wife who's been put on a tight Manolo Blahnik ration— but a certain element of respectability has crept in. Invitations to speak, to participate on—even to chair—bar association panel discussions and seminars; I've been on *Charlie Rose,* been offered a visiting professorship at the New School, invited to join the Council on Foreign Relations..."

"You don't watch it, Arthur, you'll turn into a total asshole."

Jekyll chuckles. "I'll try to keep that in mind. Do you recall how, somewhere along the way in this great adventure of ours, you remarked how topsy-turvy it all seemed: doing good by doing bad, the irony of it all?"

"Did I? Well, look, let's not fight it. All's well that ends well. And speaking of happy endings, what about you and Renee?"

"As you recall, she and I then had lunch in Washington, which was very pleasant. Then, back in New York, I got a letter from her. A fan letter. I'd never gotten a fan letter before. Cuff-links I've been given by grateful clients, and God knows how many Patek Philippe and Rolex wristwatches, and once or twice a Mercedes-Benz—stuff I've given straightaway to deserving charities—but never a fan letter, never anything that measured my worth in words instead of carats, horsepower, or ounces of gold. So I wrote back, and after that, one thing led to another and here we are. The role of matchmaker suits you, Clifford."

"The credit is all yours. It just goes to show what a few good licks on 'the harps of the blessed'—isn't that how someone described Daniel Webster's eloquence?—can do for a chap."

"I blush. And how's your life, Clifford? You look to be a new man as well. This new venture must be revivifying. How's it coming?"

"There are times I can't get the words down fast enough, not to mention the pictures in my head."

"Excellent. And your daughter? Doing well at Andover?"

"Loves it!"

"And your wife? She's here, isn't she?"

"She is. I'm afraid that's a more complicated story."

"I'm sorry to hear that."

"Don't be. So far, it's just a series of minor upsets and irritations. Funny, isn't it? You remember how Freud said that love and work were the two main constituents of happiness? How come they never seem to come at the same time?"

"Perhaps Freud should have spoken of 'love and money.' In my business, at least, the former seems generally to be a function of the latter."

Clifford shrugs. "That's certainly worth a thought." Then his face brightens as he asks, "Hey—I almost forgot? Any news of Natalie? How's she doing?"

"The last time we spoke—about three weeks ago—she seemed despondent."

"Professionally or personally?"

"It's hard to say. A bit of both, probably. As a matter of fact, she's taken a leave of absence from Cardozo this semester and gone off to, of all places, Lisbon."

"Lisbon?"

"That was my reaction. I could see going to Paris or London or Barcelona or Florence, but Lisbon...anyway, when I asked her about it, she said she was finally in the right mood to go there, whatever that means. When I told her I was coming down here, she said to say hello and congratulate you on the film project. I think she'll be back in April. You should give her a call some time. Let me give you her cellphone number."

As Jekyll writes the number on a business card, music starts up inside, "In That Mountain Greenery," a good old tune, very danceable. Clifford checks his watch. "Dancing already—and they haven't even rung the dinner gong. Man, this is going to be a killer evening. Maybe I better look in on Connie."

Just as they separate, Jekyll remarks, "You know, it was odd, being introduced to your wife after...well, after all that's happened. I feel the way I expected a visitor to King Menelaus's court must have felt on meeting Helen, long after Troy was ashes: wondering whether this poised, calm, still-young woman could really have been the cause of all that commotion and carnage. How's your Dante?"

"Okay, I guess."

"Do you remember the lovely last line of the *Inferno*? *'E uscimmo reveder le stelle.'* It means 'And so we escaped to see the stars.' That's how I feel."

Clifford laughs out loud. "Arthur, you read too many books. Connie isn't Helen of Troy; you and I aren't Virgil and Dante. The landscape isn't littered with the corpses of great warriors, and nothing's burning, and we've hardly passed through the circles of hell, even though there were times when it felt like it. Still, I know what you mean." And with that, they go back inside and make for their separate tables.

Clifford gets through dinner somehow, but at the first decent moment, after the toasts, when the band begins to play and people get up and circulate, he decides to slip away and return to the suite. Just as he exits the ballroom, he sees Jekyll go across to Annabelle's table, sees Annabelle and the governor rise, the governor bow and hand her off, and then she and Jekyll move out onto the dance floor.

As they await the downbeat, they turn their heads to watch Clifford leave the room. "Do you think he'll ever be happy?" Annabelle asks.

"I think he's further along the road than he lets on. He's a genuinely creative type. Such men need their books read, their movies seen, their plays put on."

"I hope you're right. My goodness, Arthur, you dance awfully well for a jackal."

"I thought we agreed to clean up our language."

"Speaking of which, I just have to ask you. When you came down here after the Supreme Court decision, did you really mean what you threatened? That if I didn't agree to speak to Cardinal Santiago about Clifford and his movie project, you'd report me to the SEC for withholding material information? That was very wicked of you."

"Well, I still had a client whose interests I felt bound to serve, even after the Court handed down its decision. At that point, I was no longer obliged to play by my client's rules and was free to play by my own. And don't forget that I was a stockholder of yours. I would have been well within my rights to go to the SEC with my suspicions. At the time you collateralized that stock to First Gotham, not to mention the shares you sold to the public, *Doe v. Hewitt* was still pending argument, and you were—on the basis of firsthand testimony, I won't say whose—in possession of information that was, by any standards, material and adverse concerning the vulnerability of your Constance Grange brand. Information the public disclosure of which could have seriously affected the value of Summerhill stock— and most particularly your ability, as an insider, to sell. People—need

I name names?—have been sentenced to Camp Cupcake for less. Even though your offense may have been identical to Martha Stewart's from a legal standpoint, in your case the sum involved was many, many times greater, and we live in an age that tends to equate 'how bad' with 'how much.' If Martha got five months in prison for a mere $42,000 in hot profits, think what a billion and a half could mean, especially to an ambitious New York prosecutor with statehouse visions dancing in his head. In both instances, all it would have taken would have been to cast a few crumbs on the waters of the Internet. When I came to see you, I had no doubt that you'd quickly appreciate the gravity of your position, and to your credit you did."

"But you really wouldn't have turned me in, would you?"

Jekyll smiles. "I think I'll just take the Fifth on that one. Actually, the SEC was only one of two aces in the hole I was prepared to play."

"Really? And what, may I ask, was the other?"

"Tell me: does the name Alejandro Vargas mean anything to you?"

Annabelle frowns, then imperceptibly nods and murmurs, "You know that it does."

"Are you aware that the gentleman in question was murdered in Miami two years ago come November?"

Annabelle draws back; in her face and eyes, Jekyll reads total surprise. "He was *what*?" she asks.

"Murdered. But you see, here's the thing. People like to say that what's needed to solve a murder are means and motive. In this sad instance, both might have been plausibly laid at your door."

Annabelle responds with a snort of derision. "Arthur, are you crazy? I never—"

"Of course you didn't. But a very enticing circumstantial connection could have been made, knowing what we both know you knew of certain of the decedent's randier activities. And you know how the press, and even juries, prefer noisy circumstantialities to quiet certainties. However, I'm pleased to report that the matter is closed. I've learned through a friend in the Dade County Homicide Bureau that the killing in question resulted from a dispute over a narcotics share-out, a misunderstanding that simply got out of control. Which makes the verdict in your case: not guilty."

Annabelle stares at him. "Arthur—I don't know what to say. You wouldn't have..." Her voice drops off; she looks closely at Jekyll—and then breaks out in a grimace of disbelief. "Yes, you would have, wouldn't you?!"

"Whether I would have or wouldn't, my dear Annabelle, is now moot," Jekyll replies genially. "It's over, finito: *tutto è disposto,* as they sing in *Figaro,* and so I say, on with the dance!"

"Arthur, you are such a rogue. A terrifying, brilliant, merciless rogue!"

He gives her a twirl. "A graceful compliment gracefully accepted," he says, and hums a few bars of the tune the band's now playing: "If I could be with you..."

"I even have some news for you," she says. "As regards dear Clifford, our friend in the scarlet vestments was an even easier pushover than you predicted. But the real surprise was Ronnie. You know, when I went to see him, he had no idea about Clifford being on any blacklist."

Jekyll chuckles at this, moves his partner into an easy dip, and murmurs as they come out of it, "I'm not surprised. But failure can beget paranoia, and we all know the rest. Still, I don't think we'll tell Clifford that, do you? It would be terrible for his ego—and an artist needs his ego."

"And for gracious sakes, Connie must never find out that it was I who went to bat for her husband."

"I think that secret is safe with everyone. The important thing is, it's done. The bottom line is, either my client deserved a better ending, or everyone else involved deserved a worse. That's sort of my operating mantra. Some for all or none for all, you might say."

"That's very amoral of you, Arthur."

"You may not have noticed, but I happen to be a very amoral person. My goodness, look at that!"

"Look at what?"

"At the way Mrs. Grange is dancing the tango with your friend the Italian arts minister. They say he's a regular goat. Makes Sarkozy look like a choir boy."

"Well, if he is, it's no longer my problem." They both laugh. Then Jekyll says, "Oh dear, here comes the senator, and he has that relentless look about him. I think I'll just go and have another look at that Bellini. What a coup for you to have it. Ah, Senator, she's all yours."

Upstairs, Clifford has settled himself with Wodehouse's *Uncle Fred in the Springtime*, and barely notices the time pass until, when Connie returns to the suite, he looks at his watch and sees that it's just after midnight.

"Where'd you go?" she asks. "Unhook me, will you?"

He does. "I was bored," he says. "I take it you enjoyed it?"

"I thought it was terrific. Belle has done herself proud. I sat next to that charming Italian minister of the arts. He's very interested in American popular culture, so I invited him to come to the studio and watch us shoot." She flops on the bed, spread-eagled on her stomach. "He's the most terrible flirt. And I do wish you'd make more of an effort. Just because—"

"Just because what?"

She raises herself on one elbow, looks at him. When she speaks, she pronounces each syllable of each word deliberately. The intent to pierce is palpable. "I was going to say that you needn't behave like a jerk just because you've gotten lucky all of a sudden."

He grins in a way that he knows will irritate her. "They say luck is the residue of design."

"Whatever the hell that means." Her articulation is messy; she's more than a little tipsy.

In for a penny, in for a pound, he thinks. *Why not?* "What's the problem? Jealous of my success?"

"Oh, shut up!" She flops back on the bed. "Asshole!" Then thinks about it and adds, "Well, even Norman Maine had his good days, I suppose."

What Clifford says next comes out completely without thinking. "Yeah, well, you won't have to put up with poor old Norman for a bit. I'm thinking about going to Europe to look at some locations, Spain and Portugal, mostly." Where this is coming from, he has no idea, but he can't stop himself. "Three weeks tops, but not to worry, I'll be back in plenty of time for the Andover parents weekend. Hopefully by then you'll have recovered your patented and highly compensated sunny disposition."

She doesn't answer. She's out cold.

He walks out on the balcony and gazes at the dim gardens and the great soughing forest; in the distance, the lights of vehicles negotiating the spiraling switchbacks of a mountain highway flicker like fireflies. *If this was a '40s movie,* he thinks, *I'd be smoking a reflective cigarette. And then I'd become aware of the music and the party sounds, and I'd flick the butt over the balustrade, smooth my hair back, smarten my tie, square my shoulders, and go off and win the girl.*

But this is the twenty-first century, where nobody smokes, not even in North Carolina, and it isn't a movie, and—most important—the girl's not here. The girl—if she can be called that—is three thousand miles away in Lisbon.

He reaches into his pocket, takes out his phone and the slip with Natalie Sloan's cell number. He thinks for a second or two, then checks his watch and calculates what time it is in Lisbon. Closing in on 6 a.m. *A little early to call, but as the man says, if not now, when?* He punches a number into his cellphone.

From the balcony directly above, Arthur Jekyll watches Clifford come outside, watches him reflect, then watches him dial his cellphone. *If I'm not mistaken,* Jekyll thinks, *in another second, a cell-*

phone will start ringing on the banks of the Tagus. He wonders what kind of a day it will be in Lisbon. A happy one, he hopes. The thought is warming.

It's a spectacular night, as if the galaxies had been instructed to do their part for the evening's splendor. Staring up, he feels himself entangled in huge thoughts, aloft in the great, sighing drift of the cosmos, brushing against truths vast and unknowable. His bosom feels like it contains the entire universe. He finds himself thinking of Matthew Arnold's "Dover Beach," the famous poem that begins "The sea is calm tonight..." and goes on to end with the lines about ignorant armies clashing by night on a darkling plain.

"'Ignorant armies,'" he thinks. That's us, all right. How little we understand each other and the force of our fantasies and our ambition and our longings and what they will lead us into doing—to ourselves, to others.

And yet, somehow, it seems to have worked out. That's the paradox in all this. It's just as Clifford said: it has all come right thanks to getting it all wrong. Upside down—inside out—topsy-turvy. What they think we think they know and so on and so on and so on. A mixture of lies and pretense and half-truths and misunderstandings and conflicts of interest can sometimes and somehow yield truth and virtue and personal redemption. It doesn't make sense—but then, what about life does? As they say in Washington, if everyone's lying, no one is.

But that's a sour note on which to conclude this story, he reflects.

A better one would be: right can be done. Somehow, some way—and always worth striving for, no matter what.

Not all the right in the world, surely, and possibly not perfect justice perfectly executed, if that's what is wanted, but probably as much as can ever be achieved by a bunch of fallible, selfish human beings falling all over each other in pursuit of what they want, or think they do. Bumping and scraping and bawling like children in a darkened funhouse, fumbling their flawed and anxious way through hall after hall of mirrors and trap-doors in the puzzle palace of existence toward a distant exit they can only intuit, which they may never reach.

"Arthur, come to bed," he hears Renee call. "Tomorrow's going to be a big day."

Yes, he thinks happily. *Yes, it will*. And the day after that. And the day after that. And with this thought, he casts one long last fond glance at the sky and goes inside.

The End